SWEEP OF THE HEART

Sweep of the Heart
Copyright © 2022 by Ilona Andrews
Ebook ISBN: 9781641972390
KDP POD ISBN: 9798364351043
IS POD ISBN: 9781641972499
Cover by Doris Mantair
Interior art by Isabeau Backhaus

NYLA Publishing
121 W. 27th St, Suite 1201, NY 10001, New York.
http://www.nyliterary.com

SWEEP OF THE HEART

ILONA ANDREWS

In memory of Gerean Ejosa (Geri Reads)

ACKNOWLEDGMENTS

We are grateful to many people who have helped this manuscript on its journey to become a book. We would like to thank our agent Nancy Yost and the wonderful team at NYLA, our developmental editor Rossana Sasso, our copyeditor, Stefanie Chin, and our installment copy editor, Stephanie Mowery. We're grateful to Doris Mantair for the beautiful cover and Isabeau Backhaus for the striking interior illustrations. Our world never looked so good.

We would like to extend our thanks to Kimberly Maciejczyk, DVM, for Gorvar's veterinary care, and Rosie McGraffin and Kerris Humphreys for all things Scottish.

Thank you to the beta readers who generously donated their time and suffered through the early drafts: Harriet Chow, Francesca Virgili, Loredana Carini, and Fern DeYoung.

Most of all we would like to thank you, our readers, for your dedication to the Innkeeper Chronicles. You keep us going.

LETTER TO THE READER

This was a long fun book to write. We wanted to bring the vibrance of the Innkeeper galaxy to you, and this book has many characters, so we are providing you with a quick reference for the candidates as well as the Dominion players and most important observers. You will find it under Character List.

Those of you who followed this story on our website, when it was posted every Friday, really enjoyed the "Story So Far" summaries before each new chapter, so we kept them in.

We also included Dina's delicious apple cake recipe from Chapter 1 and some of the funnies that helped the Book Devouring Horde vote for their favorite candidate on the blog.

[1]

A new adventure begins. But first, cake.

There was great wisdom in striking the iron while it was hot. I took a sip of my iced tea and brushed a little bug off the skirt of my yellow sundress. I was sitting on the back porch of Gertrude Hunt Bed and Breakfast in a comfortable wooden recliner. In front of me our backyard spread, flooded with golden sunshine. The lawn was still green – we'd had a lot of rain this year – but the heat of Texas summer poured from the sky, bringing everything to a standstill. The squirrels napped in their nests deep within the oaks. The mice and bunnies hid in their burrows. Even the bugs fell quiet, too hot to trill. Beast, my tiny black-and-white Shih Tzu, lay on her back by my feet and snored softly. The fan in the porch roof above me was going full force, but my forehead was still sweating.

Such a lovely hot day. Perfect day to take a nap.

I drank another swallow of my tea and closed my eyes. Behind me, Gertrude Hunt unfolded, a complex collection of rooms and passageways many times larger than its physical footprint visible from the street and the subdivision on the other side of it. I focused on the kitchen. A seven-foot-tall shape moved within it, big, with foot-long quills thrusting from its back. The shape wiped down the counter, holding the rag with large, clawed hands.

Nap. Nap, nap, nap, you want to nap... If only I had powers of suggestion, my life would be so much easier.

I opened my eyes.

Next to me Caldenia fanned herself with a glittering fan and took a sip of her Mello Yello. "Still no luck?"

I shook my head.

"Then I will have to help you, my dear."

She rose, put her straw hat on, and strolled into the kitchen. At first glance, our permanent guest looked just like an older Southern woman with a gentle tan, long platinum-gray hair pulled into an elegant updo, and a beautiful face with what people called "good bones." She chatted with neighbors, grew tomatoes with resounding success – I made sure that the inn watered them and added fertilizer at appropriate times – and mastered the art of smiling without showing her teeth. They were pointed and sharp, like those of a shark.

I concentrated on the kitchen.

"This heat is stifling," Caldenia announced. "I'm going to retire for the afternoon. You could use some rest as well, Orro. If I were you, I'd take this opportunity to nap before dinner begins."

Orro rumbled something.

I felt Caldenia move through the kitchen and up the stairs toward her suite.

In the kitchen, Orro stopped, stared out the window...

Come on...

He carefully folded the towel, hung it on the towel rack by the sink, and ambled out of the kitchen, heading toward the narrow winding stairs leading down.

I held my breath, tracking him with my magic. Down the stairs, down, down, and to the cozy den where he made his lair. He stepped inside and shut the door.

Now!

I jumped out of my recliner. Beast leaped three feet into the air, landed on her feet, and barked once, looking from side to side.

"Shh!"

I swung the back door open and dashed inside the kitchen. Beast chased me.

I sprinted to the oven, turned it on to bake at 350°, and spun around. The door of the pantry flew open, displaying 3,000 square feet of space filled with shelves and refrigerators. Tendrils of striated wood burst from the ceiling, shot into the pantry, and dragged ingredients onto the island: sugar, flour, baking powder... I grabbed eggs, butter, and a bag of Granny Smith apples from the only refrigerator visible in the kitchen. The inn hauled a heavy KitchenAid mixer out.

"Not that one, the small one," I hissed. "That one is too loud."

The KitchenAid vanished back into the pantry and another tendril delivered the handheld mixer into my hands. I put two large bowls onto the island and reached out with my magic.

The creature who ruled our kitchen with an iron claw was settling into his nest bed. Operation Apple Cake was a go.

I creamed the butter in the bowl and added a ¾ cup of sugar to it. Baking a cake for the man you love was stressful enough. Baking a cake in a kitchen run by a Red Cleaver chef was an impossible feat. Orro viewed both the kitchen and the pantry as his sole domain. Trying to cook anything meant being observed over your shoulder, treated to a detailed critique, followed by multiple offers to help, followed by hurt feelings when said offers were politely and repeatedly declined, culminating in pouting and declarations of woe. If he was really in the moment, he would throw an existential crisis into it.

3

Orro typically slept for at least an hour and a half. My cake only took 50 minutes to bake. If I played my cards right, it would be cooked before he ever caught on. He would not mess with it once it was cooked.

I folded my dry ingredients into my wet ones, mixed everything, poured it into a greased springform pan, and focused on peeling the apples.

Sean had gone out this morning to get more firewood. The inn required wood in the worst way, and we'd been going through a cord, sometimes two, every few days. It wouldn't have been a problem if we were a BBQ joint, but we were masquerading as a quaint bed and breakfast that did very limited business. Sooner or later, someone would start wondering what we were doing with all that wood. Sean staggered our firewood orders between different suppliers and bought waste wood whenever he could find it. Usually we ordered firewood online, but he had found a supplier a couple of hours away who would deliver a full tri-axle load, seven and a half cords. The only catch was, they wanted payment up front in cash.

Sean didn't like to leave the inn.

He didn't mind it as much when he had to go to places other than our planet. Earth was home, the place where he was born and grew up, and Sean had learned how to pass for a human. But then he walked out into the Great Beyond. The universe bathed him in its breath. He saw the countless stars and other planets, fought enemies he couldn't have imagined, and learned the true nature of his people.

Out there, he could be himself, an alpha strain werewolf. Here, on Earth, he had to pass for an ordinary man and, after years in space, it no longer came easily to him.

I mixed cinnamon, sugar, and lemon juice into my peeled, sliced apples, added a bit of flour, layered them on top of the dough, popped the pan into the oven, and exhaled. Halfway there.

"Thirty minutes," I told the inn.

The inn creaked in acknowledgment.

Sean wanted to get the firewood. I offered to go with him, but he declined. I couldn't make it easier for him while he was out, but I could greet him with his favorite cake when he came back.

A gentle chime rolled through my mind. A familiar presence entered the boundary of the inn. I motioned with my fingers and the wall sprouted a screen. On it, Officer Hector Marais carefully maneuvered his Red Deer PD cruiser up my driveway. Usually, he parked on the street. Driving up like that meant he had a special delivery.

I wiped my hands with a kitchen towel and headed to the garage. No rest for the wicked.

––––––

OFFICER MARAIS OPENED THE TRUNK OF HIS CRUISER AND BENT down to give Beast a pet. In his mid-thirties, bronze-skinned, athletic, with blue-black hair cut short and a clean-shaven jaw, he was the very definition of the modern police officer. Everything from the collar of his uniform to the soles of his boots was "squared away" as Sean said. If the police department ever needed a model for a recruitment poster, there was nobody better.

He truly was a model police officer, completely committed to protecting residents in his jurisdiction. Which was why once he found out that aliens existed, and that Earth enjoyed the special protected status, he took it upon himself to add extraterrestrial policing to his regular duties. If any normal Earth mechanic ever popped the hood of his cruiser, they would faint on the spot. We were very fortunate that Red Deer made its officers buy their vehicles through a subsidized program.

I looked into the trunk. A woman lay inside it wrapped in a stun net. She was a little older than me and wore a gray combat suit. In good shape, lean, with attractive, bold features. On Earth someone would think she was a star athlete, track, or tennis maybe. Her tan skin had a slight cinnamon tint, her hair was dark red and braided away from her face, and her green eyes regarded me with open hostility.

The stun net, one of the fun modifications Sean and Marais had added to the police cruiser, was self-guiding and acted like a taser on contact, short circuiting the neural pathways. Marais had practiced firing it on Sean in an abandoned warehouse parking lot. He'd chase him with the cruiser and Sean would do his best to evade, while I served as a lookout and tried not to have a heart attack every time I heard a car coming. Marais hadn't had a chance to use his new gadget until now.

The net should have stunned the woman into a mild coma. Instead, it seemed to just piss her off. She glared at me like I was everything that was wrong with her life. I leaned closer. A faint golden sheen rolled over her irises.

A werewolf. Made sense.

"Where did you find her?"

Marais nodded at the car. "I'll show you."

I nudged the inn. A thin wooden tendril slipped from the floor and brushed against the hood of the vehicle, accepting the transmission from the cruiser. Gertrude Hunt produced another screen showing the view from Marais' dashcam camera. He had two sets in his car, one the standard issue from Red Deer PD and the other bootleg from us.

The street looked familiar. He was on Rattlesnake Trail, by the high school, heading east, with the walled subdivision on one side and the school's baseball diamond on the other. Bright summer sunshine flooded the mostly empty road. The record temperatures chased the kids inside or to the pools, and their parents were still at work.

A dark humanoid shape shot past the car. Marais was going at least 35. Top human speed was 28 miles per hour and whatever that was blew by his vehicle like it was standing still.

"Someone was running at superhuman speeds in broad daylight for all the honest world to see," Marais said. "Apparently, she thinks the Earth Treaty doesn't apply to her."

The Treaty applied to everyone.

I motioned to Gertrude Hunt. A much thicker tendril emerged from the ceiling and plucked the woman out of the trunk. The stun net dropped to the floor. The inn's tendril split into smaller branches, wrapping around the woman, and spun her in the air, rifling through her clothes. Weapons rained to the floor of the garage: a short-range energy sidearm, two knives, a monomolecular cleaver short sword, and three small sticky bombs, each the size of a large grape. When attached to a door and detonated, they could blow a hole through the strongest terrestrial safe.

Nice.

The tendrils twisted my captive upright and lowered her to the floor, anchoring themselves through the floorboards. She glowered at me and snarled.

Beast snarled back by my feet.

The werewolf woman didn't seem impressed. In her place, I wouldn't have taken the seven-pound shih tzu seriously either. It was a potentially deadly mistake.

"You are in violation of the Earth Treaty," I told her. "Do you know what that means?"

She didn't answer.

"The Treaty expressly forbids exposing the human population to the existence of extraterrestrial life. Any traveler wishing to visit Earth must make arrangements with an inn like this one. Have you made such arrangements?"

No answer.

"She knows," Marais said. "I read her the rights on the way. She was heading this way when I apprehended her. Probably to see you."

"Not you." The woman sneered.

Oh. Another one.

"Thank you, Officer," I told Marais. "I'll take it from here."

"Never a dull moment." He opened the front door of his cruiser, reached for a hidden button in the dashboard, pressed it, and the net slid back into the trunk, primed and ready to be reused.

"Oh! I have something for you."

I held out my hand. The ceiling parted and a vacuum-sealed parcel landed in my hand, two skeins of wool yarn, shimmering with blue and green. "For your wife."

"Thanks. She'll love it. What kind of wool is it?"

"Tell her it's muskox." It was close enough unless someone did a microscopic analysis. It was a gift from a guest, and Officer Marais' wife ran a knitting blog. She would enjoy it much more than I would.

"Thanks again."

I watched Officer Marais get into his vehicle and drive off. A moment later I felt him cross the boundary of the inn.

It was just me, the female werewolf, and her undying hatred for me. I didn't take it personally.

The werewolves of Auul were poets, and storytelling was in their blood. Sadly, the saga of their planet had turned out tragic, the way sagas often do. They were invaded by an overwhelming force, so they bioengineered werewolfism to repel it. Then decades later, the enemy made their own version of supersoldiers and invaded again. The people of Auul built teleportation gates, knowing they would destabilize their planet, and created even better werewolves, the alpha strain, more dangerous and deadly, to guard them as they evacuated.

The alpha strain werewolves protected the gates to the bitter end, until the cosmic forces that powered them tore Auul apart. Almost all of them died in that last stand.

Sean was the son of two alpha strain werewolves who somehow made it out just before the cataclysm. He was born against all odds, he was freakishly powerful, and after serving in the military, he met me, learned where he came from, and caught a glimpse of the galaxy. It had beckoned, and Sean had followed its starlight. Everything he had done since had become the stuff of legend.

He had fought a devastating war on Nexus, bringing both the Hope Crushing Horde's and the Holy Anocracy's offensives to a halt. He was a superb strategist, an excellent tactician, and he had no equal in close-quarters combat. He could lead an army or stand alone against overwhelming odds.

It was simply too much for the werewolves. Here was the son of their heroes who came out of nowhere and became the best werewolf ever. They were a people without a planet, refugees scattered across dozens of worlds. They needed a folk hero in the worst way, and Sean proved to be irresistible. Everything about him was legendary and mythical. The fact that he shunned fame and glory only made it worse.

Werewolves favored a direct kind of courtship. In the past few months, we'd had several female and male visitors who'd arrived at Gertrude Hunt to declare their admiration and interest. Luckily for me, the man was very different from the legend he had inspired.

The image on the screen changed into a big timer counting down. 30... 29... 28...

My cake!

"I have to go," I told her.

"I want to talk to him!" the werewolf woman snarled.

"He should be back soon."

"When?"

"Hopefully not for another twenty minutes. It will give you a chance to rehearse your speech."

She blinked but recovered. "I don't have a speech!"

"You say it like it's my first time. There is always a speech."

The timer reached zero and went off.

"Got to go."

I took off down the hallway, escorted by Beast, while the woman's curses slowly grew fainter behind me.

[2]

Are we about to witness werewolf courtship? Will Orro discover the illicit baking happening in his very own kitchen, right under his quills? Or is something even more dangerous afoot?

The story continues...

The cake rested in the springform. The meringue topping was blush and slightly crispy. It cracked a little, which would get a side eye from Orro, but I didn't care.

I reached out and poked the springform. Barely warm. Okay.

A familiar presence crossed the inn's boundary. The magic of the inn shifted in response. If Gertrude Hunt was a dog, it would've raised its head and wagged its tail.

Sean was home.

Another presence followed, creeping up our driveway. I motioned to the inn, and it produced a screen for me and tossed the feed from the side cameras onto it. Sean's truck had driven up and parked in front of the garage. Behind it, a massive white tri-axle with a black dump bed filled with firewood slowly backed its way up the gentle slope of the driveway and around the house.

I took a long knife and carefully worked it around the perimeter of the springform, slicing through the meringue. If you tried to open the pan without it, half of the meringue would come off.

Sean got out of his truck. He was tall and corded with hard, lean muscle. You could tell just by looking at him that he was both strong and fast, but there was more to it. Sean looked ready. He projected a kind of calm but alert assurance, and you knew with a deep, instinctual understanding that if a threat appeared, he would respond instantly and with overwhelming force.

People sensed it and felt the need to label it. Since we lived in Texas, most of the time they ended up asking him if he played football, because somehow saying "that guy played football" provided a reasonable explanation for Sean's combat readiness.

Beast took off, out through the doggie door, and straight to Sean, dancing around his feet and wagging her tail. He bent down to pet her.

I unlocked the latch on the pan and gently eased it up and over the cake. Perfect.

I dropped the springform into the sink, set the coffee pot to brew some decaf, and went outside, just in time to watch the dump truck unload a huge pile of firewood onto our grass. I went to stand next to Sean. He smiled at me and wrapped his arm around my shoulders. I leaned against him and felt him relax.

You made it home, honey. It's all good.

The driver, a middle-aged heavyset man with a ruddy face and short salt-and-pepper hair, got out and eyeballed it.

"Seven cords," he told me proudly.

"Looks great," I told him.

"Your husband didn't pay for stacking," the driver reported. "He said he needs the exercise."

I smiled at Sean. He wasn't my husband, but there was no reason to point that out. "We'll take care of it."

The driver winked at us. "You two are a cute couple. Say, were you a linebacker in high school?"

"Yeah," Sean lied with a straight face.

He had done all sorts of sports in his childhood, but none through his schools. He was too good and too physically gifted, and his parents wanted to avoid attention. Most of his high school extracurricular activities had been split between several martial arts schools with carefully vetted teachers. He'd had an easier time blending in while in the Army. High school sports prioritized individual achievement and stardom, while the Army emphasized teamwork.

"Thought so," the driver said. "Well, you folks have a good one."

"Take care." Sean raised his hand.

The driver got back into his truck and started down the driveway. The grass around the wood pile shivered.

"Not yet," Sean said.

The lawn became still.

The dump truck rolled to the end of the driveway, sat there, letting the traffic pass, turned left, and sped down the road.

"Okay," Sean said. "Take it."

The lawn split, opening a black pit under the firewood. Gertrude Hunt gulped the whole seven cords in a single swallow, and I felt the impact roll through it. The lawn knitted together, as if zippered. No sign of the wood pile remained.

Sean raised his head, and his lips stretched into a slow, lazy smile. "Mmmm, apple cake."

Surprising a werewolf with food was a lost cause. "We have a visitor."

"I know. I smelled her by the garage. What does she want?"

"To talk to you."

He sighed. "Fine. Let's get it over with."

We walked over to the garage. The door slid open. The werewolf woman blinked against the sudden sunlight and saw Sean.

13

Her shoulders straightened. She tossed her hair back with a strategically impatient jerk of her head.

Here comes the speech.

"So that's what you look like." She'd pitched her voice lower, going for husky sexiness. "Not bad."

No reaction.

"A man like you stuck in a place like this. What a waste."

Sean said nothing.

"Wilmos is missing," she said.

Wilmos was a first-strain werewolf, a veteran, one of the oldest survivors of Auul. The werewolfism kept him spry, but he was an adult when Sean's parents were born, and he was instrumental in creating their alpha strain. After Auul was destroyed, Wilmos made his name as a mercenary. Now he ran a weapons shop at Baha-char and served as a go-between for mercenaries and the people who needed them.

Wilmos thought Sean walked on water. We'd met by chance, and when Sean decided he wanted to see the universe for himself, Wilmos showed him the ropes. He was the one who'd gotten Sean into that Nexus mess, and I would never forgive him for that. Ever.

Wilmos was also responsible for our current enthusiastic suitor problem. During the war on Nexus, Sean had assumed the identity of Turan Adin, an unkillable general who led the Merchant forces of Clan Nuan. In reality, Turan Adins dropped like flies, but their armor covered them completely, hiding their faces, so when one of them died, the Merchants simply hired a new one, put the armor on them, and sent them back into the slaughter. Some only lasted a few days, others a few weeks. Sean was the last Turan Adin. He had survived for 18 months.

When that war finally ended, Sean gave the armor back to the Merchants and stayed with me because he loved me. Nobody was supposed to find out that he used to be Turan Adin. However, Wilmos couldn't keep his mouth shut. He was bursting at the seams with pride and little by little he let that cat out of the bag, one secret conversation at a time. The werewolves knew.

The werewolf woman narrowed her eyes at Sean. "Word is, Wilmos asked you for help and you turned him down because you were too busy playing house with a human girl. People say you're a coward. That you've gone soft. The wolf who subdued otrokars and vampire knights, reduced to a mere shadow of himself. So, I came to see for myself what happened to the hero of Nexus. You used to be somebody. What's that like? To just give up and turn your back on a friend?"

She leaned forward as much as the restraints would allow, focused on him. She'd challenged him in his territory, and now she expected him to react. She would've liked it if he'd hauled her upright, slammed her against the wall, and growled in her face. It would be a display of dominance she could understand. She would submit, and then they would go to search for Wilmos together, without me, so she could prove to him how much more awesome she was as a potential mate.

Sean opened his mouth. "I don't know you."

The werewolf woman blinked.

He held his hand out. His broom landed into his fingers, except for him it was always a spear, a sturdy shaft tipped with a razor-sharp blade.

"Your welcome is withdrawn." He tapped the butt of his spear on the floor.

The inn opened, walls and rooms flying out of the way, revealing a hallway leading to a distant door. It snapped open, and the bright sunshine of Baha-char flooded through it.

The tendril binding the werewolf woman jerked her off the floor.

"Wait!" she screamed.

The tendril shot toward the door and tossed her out, into the light. The door slammed shut. The normal architecture of the inn reasserted itself. Beast let out a satisfied bark.

"A little rough," I said.

"She'll land on her feet. This is getting tiresome. They need to get the message."

We started toward the kitchen.

"What was that about Wilmos?" I asked.

Sean shrugged. "No idea."

"Liar. You big fat liar. Did he ask you for help?"

"He always asks me for help."

That was true. From Wilmos' point of view, every job could benefit from Sean's presence. He visited the inn at least once a month, and Sean always stopped by his store when we went shopping at Baha-char. I couldn't recall a single time the conversation didn't end with, "I've got this little project I'm working on."

Wilmos genuinely liked Sean, and not just because Sean was the pinnacle of everything the people of Auul had tried to achieve. Sean also cared about me, and that made me important to Wilmos as well. If anything happened to us, the old werewolf would come running with a truckload of weapons and would sacrifice himself to save us without a second thought.

Sean saw Wilmos as the closest thing to a grandfather. Logically he knew that his parents were superb fighters, but they were his parents, who had settled into a mundane life on Earth. Wilmos wasn't just an old, grizzled veteran who told war stories and went on adventures. He was bigger than that. To Sean, he was an elder, a link to the planet that was forever lost. A part of Sean knew that he never quite fit into the "normal" life on Earth. I had introduced him to Baha-char and aliens, but Wilmos was the one who had opened the door to the galaxy for him.

"You think he might be in trouble?" I asked.

"Last I checked, Wilmos was fully grown. He is well-armed, well-connected, and able to take care of himself. Just like he did for fifty years before he met me."

We walked into the kitchen. Sean sighted the cake and went straight for it.

16

I took a plate out of the cabinet, added a fork, and handed it to him. He took a knife from the butcher block, cut a quarter of the cake, slid it onto the plate, and looked at me, his eyes hopeful. "Coffee?"

"Freshly brewed."

I poured him a mug of decaf, added some creamer, and brought it over to him. Sean took a sip of his coffee, then a bite of his cake, and sighed happily.

"The cake is delicious," he said. "Thank you."

"I'm glad you like it."

I cut my own slice and sat down across from him. He reached out. I took his hand. He squeezed my fingers, smiled, and ate another bite of cake.

[3]

Mysterious things are happening in Baha-char, the intergalactic bazaar we know, love and yearn to shop at. Will Sean and Dina really not investigate Wilmos' disappearance?

Sean frowned at the communication unit. We stood in the narrow alley just outside the door leading to Baha-char, dressed in our travel innkeeper robes. His resolve to not look for Wilmos lasted about as long as his piece of cake.

"Nothing?" I guessed.

"It isn't picking him up."

He pulled his hood on, hiding his face. I did the same, and we started down the alley toward the wide street, where the myriad of galactic shoppers of all shapes, colors, and species flowed like a river through the canyon of tall, terraced buildings.

Wilmos' shop lay off the beaten path, just inside an alley branching off from the main street, its door sheltered by an archway. Sean turned into the alley and stopped. I stopped too.

He inhaled. A second passed. Another.

"What is it?" I asked him softly.

"It smells like Michael."

Dread washed over me. My fingers went ice cold. Michael Braswell had been my older brother's best friend. He'd become an ad-hal, an innkeeper enforcer, one of many responsible for neutralizing threats the innkeepers couldn't handle, then he'd disappeared. Nobody had seen him for over a year until he blocked our way on the street at Baha-char and tried to kill us. He was no longer the Michael I knew. He was decay and rot, a living corruption oozing foul magic. He'd almost killed me, and then his corpse had infected Gertrude Hunt and tried to kill another ad-hal.

"The scent is old," Sean said. "Stay behind me."

I followed him to the door. Sean keyed a long code into the electronic lock. It clicked, and the thick, reinforced door swung open. He stepped into the gloom. The automated lights came on, bathing the store in a sharp artificial glow.

The shop was in shambles. Wilmos had a place for everything, and his wares were arranged with military precision. Now the place looked like a bomb had gone off inside it. Weapons littered the floor among shards of glass. Store shelves hung half torn from the walls. Ahead, a counter had been split in two and by it, on a pile of glass, sprawled a large lupine body covered with blue-green fur. Gorvar, Wilmos' pet and guard, one of the last Auul wolves.

Dear universe, what the hell happened here?

"Clear," Sean said.

I rushed to Gorvar. His fur was matted with congealing blood, still viscous but old. I put my hand on his neck, searching for a pulse. His eyelids trembled. He raised his head, trying to snap, but he had nothing left.

"It's me," I told him.

Recognition sparked in his green eyes. Gorvar whined softly.

"Hold on, big guy." I spun to Sean. "We have to get him to the inn."

Sean scooped the massive beast into his arms and carried him out like a puppy. I followed, pushing the door shut behind me. The lock clicked.

We hurried through the streets, dodging traffic. The shoppers of Baha-char had seen everything, and nobody paid us any mind. In fifteen minutes, we reached the inn's entrance. Sean handed Gorvar to the inn.

"I have to go back."

I brushed a kiss against his lips. "Be careful."

He nodded and took off at superhuman speed.

I entered Gertrude Hunt. "Medward. Quickly."

The inn gulped Gorvar's body and opened the stairs. I took them two at a time. I had no idea how, but I had to save Wilmos' wolf.

———

THE MEDWARD WAS HIDDEN IN THE LOWER LEVELS OF THE INN, JUST under the main floor. A sterile room that could be hermetically sealed off in an emergency, it housed a decontamination shower, a storage with six different stasis pods, and until recently, a single ancient med unit that was barely up to the task. Fortunately, we had junked it three months ago and replaced it with three brand new, state-of-the-art robotic stations, upgrading our medbay to the full medward.

The new med units were a gift from Maud. My sister was now the Maven of House Krahr, which meant she was in charge of all of their diplomatic efforts, and her position came with a significant salary. She bought the units for us with her new Maven money and had them sent over on one of Arland's scout ships. According to Maud, Gertrude Hunt was seeing more action than an average vampire stronghold on a hostile planet, and thinking of us trying to cope with our outdated med unit kept her from sleeping at night.

When I was a kid, Maud would buy me cute clothes at

discount sites online. Now she bought me advanced medical equipment. Nothing really changed. My big sister was still trying to take care of me.

I looked at Gorvar sprawled in a complex medunit. He had four deep lacerations that carved him from his belly halfway up his side. Something had dug into his stomach with its claws and dragged them up, ripping gashes in his flesh. The edges of the wounds were trying their best to turn necrotic, but Auul wolves had insane immune systems. It was part of the reason their DNA had been used to bioengineer werewolfism. Whatever contamination had invaded his body had to be very potent, because normally the wounds would've closed by now.

Gorvar had lost a lot of blood. Our old medunit wouldn't have known what to do with him, but the new one analyzed his injuries in seconds. It had pumped him full of antibiotics and fluids, and its robotic surgery arms repaired the cut in his liver, cleaned his wounds, cut off a very thin sliver of the injured tissue to combat the worst of the necrosis, and sealed the lacerations. His pulse was weak but steady, and the medical unit's read outs assured me that in its opinion, he was stable.

Now I just had to wait for Sean to come back.

He had smelled corruption by Wilmos' store. Wilmos wasn't at the store, so Sean would follow that corrupted trail. He told me before that the stench of corruption lingered much longer than normal scents. It stained everything it touched.

Corrupted Michael had thick yellowed claws. Sometimes I had nightmares of him chasing me through Red Deer dripping decay and reaching for me with those claws while I desperately tried to find my way back to the inn. My distorted memory made them much bigger in my mind, but objectively speaking, the wounds on Gorvar could have been made by claws just like those.

After I brought Michael's corpse to the inn to analyze it, the corruption that inhabited his body acted almost like a living thing, a pathogen that actively tried to contaminate the inn. I had purged that infection from Gertrude Hunt, but I had done it in my inn, where I was strongest. When Sean and I fought Michael on the streets of Baha-char, we almost lost. We might have died, if Wilmos hadn't jumped in with a high-impact version of an alien Gatling gun.

Was the damage at Wilmos' shop a retaliation for that fight? If so, why now? That happened months ago. Or was it something else? It couldn't be a coincidence.

I had hoped Michael was the only one. I had alerted the Innkeeper Assembly to what happened, but they hadn't said anything about it.

Sean would be fine. He was strong and fast, and this wouldn't be his first encounter with a corrupted creature.

Of course, he would be fine.

There was no reason to worry.

There was definitely no reason to rush to Baha-char. If another corrupted ad-hal like Michael attacked him, Sean would draw him here, to the inn, and I needed to be ready for it.

Gertrude Hunt groaned. It was an odd sound of wood stretching.

The inn was branching. Shortly after Maud and Helen left the inn, Gertrude Hunt began to grow. Right now, in the far corner of Gertrude Hunt, a simple hallway led to a barrier glowing with pale silver. Eventually that barrier would vanish, and a door would form, opening to another world or possibly a different dimension. That's why the inn had been gobbling up firewood by the cord. When that door opened, which could be any minute, one of us needed to be there because we had no idea what lay on the other side. Another reason to sit tight.

How long did it take to inspect the store anyway? He should have been back by now.

Magic chimed in my mind. The Baha-char door opened, and Sean entered the inn. Finally.

I jumped up. The inn dropped a staircase in front of me and I climbed it into the kitchen.

By the island, Orro drew himself up to his full seven feet. His dark quills rose slightly.

"You have made a cake," he started.

"Not now," I told him and hurried into the hallway.

Sean was waiting by the Baha-char door. It was still open. His eyes had that focused, clear look they got just before he expected to jump into a fight. My pulse sped up.

"I need your help."

My robe was still on. The inn dropped my broom into my hand. I jogged out the door back into the Baha-char sunshine, and we rushed through the streets, dodging passersby.

"Gorvar?" he asked.

"Stable. Where are we going?"

"One of those corrupted assholes took Wilmos out of his store and went through a temporary portal gate. There was a witness. He says he knows where the portal leads, but he refuses to tell me."

———

THE GATE LAY FAR FROM THE CENTER OF THE BAZAAR. WE'D BEEN walking and jogging for over twenty minutes, and we had left the brightly decorated streets behind a while ago. Here the air was ominous, the canvas roofs of the stalls faded and tattered, and trash littered the cobblestones. This wasn't the fun-shopping part of Baha-char. You didn't come to this place unless you wanted something specific you could only get here, and the grim-faced vendors gave us dark looks as we passed.

A merchant on our left, a strange creature with the shaggy body of a sloth, a massive beak, and furry tentacles instead of limbs, screeched at our approach. It was hanging upside down from the top frame of its shop, anchored by its hind tentacles, and

I had no idea what species it was, which almost never happened. When we got home, I would have to look it up.

A large stone arch loomed ahead, its brown stone worn and scarred. Remnants of red banners hung from it, bleached by the sun to a dirty pink and torn to shreds by the desert wind. Tall buildings with barred windows crowded the arch on both sides, creating a long gloomy tunnel.

We strode through it. A draft fanned us, bringing a thick, potent scent, an off-putting musk. Some large animal had marked its territory here.

The musk grew stronger. I fought the urge to clear my throat. I could taste it on the back of my tongue. Next to me, Sean grimaced and kept going.

The tunnel ended, and we emerged into a round plaza formed by a single circular building. Three oversized stories high, the building stretched to the sky, offering rows and rows of balconies and stone benches. Strange creatures and elaborate glyphs had been carved into its sandy stone façade, once sharp, but now smoothed and blurred by elements and time.

The plaza itself was perfectly round, formed with remarkable precision and paved with giant triangular slabs of stone that radiated from its center. In the middle of it two stone towers rose, each shaped like a fifty-foot-tall, three-dimensional crescent. The two crescents faced each other, crowned with green flames burning in metal braziers at their apexes.

"This is the Old Arena," I whispered.

Sean glanced at me.

"They used to have gladiator fights here thousands of years ago, before they built the other two arenas. See that gate across from us? The gladiators entered there and then fought to the death. When a fighter died, their flame would go out."

Something shiny caught the light at the base of the closest crescent. I squinted. A metal bug as big as my fist. There was another one on top of this crescent, and two more at the opposite tower. Soot marked the stone around the bugs. Sean was right. Someone had set up a short-term portal. The beetles packed enough power for a couple of hours and then burned themselves out.

Directly opposite us, something stirred in the gloom of the gate. Something large.

A massive leonine paw moved into the light, easily five feet across. Claws shot out and struck the stone.

Oh no.

A colossal shoulder followed, then the other, then the broad muscular chest sheathed in sandy fur, a thick neck crowned with a dark rust mane, and finally the giant head, a strange, disturbing mix of lion and human, anthropomorphic, horrifying, yet cohesive. This wasn't a mishmash of two species. This was a naturally evolved being, who just happened to resemble a huge predatory cat with human eyes on its face.

Sean's upper lip wrinkled in a precursor to a snarl. If there ever was a monster designed to terrify his people, an Auul kaiju guaranteed to evoke instant revulsion among the werewolves, the creature in front of us would be it.

"Is that the witness?" I asked.

"Yep."

A sphinx. Crap.

[4]

When we last left our intrepid heroes, they found clues that Wilmos' disappearance was linked to the corrupted ad-hal threat encountered in previous adventures. A most mythical guardian now stands in the way to more answers.

Settle in for a guessing game.

The sphinx approached, his movements unhurried, almost lazy, circled the two towers, and lowered himself to the ground. His head was by the left tower, his tail by the right. He curled around the two spires like a cat clutching a toy to his belly. The huge gold hoops in his ears tinkled.

Sean watched him. He wasn't focusing on him the way he sometimes zeroed in on his opponent. Rather he was watching him with the detachment of a satiated wolf seeing a bunny hop around in a distant field, curious, but not enough to get up. It was a ruse. Sean was all in. The sphinx had put himself between Sean and Wilmos, and Sean wouldn't tolerate that.

The sphinx stretched. The sun slid over his isabelline fur, highlighting the paler belly and chest and drawing the eye to the rust-brown bands on his limbs and tail. A thick line of darker fur ran from the inner corners of his brilliant violet-blue eyes over his upper lids to the outer corners and across his cheeks, a feature that once inspired centuries of kohl eyeliner.

"No wings?" Sean murmured.

"We don't want to see the wings."

"You came back," the sphinx purred. His deep voice reverberated through me. "And you brought a friend."

This was bad.

"Did he ask you any questions?" I whispered.

"I offered to answer his question if he solves my riddle." The sphinx studied the claws of his right forepaw. "He declined."

I exhaled.

"Would you like to solve my riddle?"

"No. Why are you here? Your kind is not permitted at Bahachar."

The creature's tanzanite eyes flashed with an angry fire. "Permitted? I go where I please."

Only four dark rings on his tail, and the gold hoops in his ears were simple. This was a very young sphinx, an adolescent. Fully grown adults had seven rings and their jewelry was ornate and elaborate. This one couldn't be more than 300 years old.

"It's a simple bargain," the sphinx said. "Solve my riddle, and I will tell you where the thing took the old werewolf. Is it your father, your grandfather, male human? Is he family? I would do anything for the sake of my family."

"Don't," I warned Sean.

The sphinx inhaled, sucking the air in. A slight draft pulled on my hair and robe.

His eyes flashed again. "I smell fear. Scared little werewolf. Don't be afraid. There is nothing to worry about. I promise to make your riddle very simple. Just hard enough for your little brain."

"Don't answer that," I told Sean.

There had to be a way around it.

"I'll do it!"

I turned. The female werewolf from earlier strode into the arena, her head held high. Oh no.

"You don't know what you're doing," I started.

"Be quiet, human." She marched forward, giving Sean a look of withering scorn. "Ask your riddle. I'll answer."

The sphinx pivoted toward her.

"You're in danger. This is a terrible idea," I told her. "He—"

"Unlike some people, I'm not a coward." She faced the sphinx.

"Stop!" Sean snapped.

She ignored him. "Ask your riddle."

Magic swirled around the sphinx. Two massive golden wings thrust from its back, unfolding, each synthetic feather sharp like a glossy metal blade. A shadow fell upon the arena as they blocked the sunlight.

"The pact has been made," the sphinx announced.

Thin tendrils of gold light wound about the werewolf woman, binding her in place.

"Say my name, and I will disappear. What am I?"

The werewolf woman opened her mouth. Uncertainty flared in her eyes.

"Not another word," I said. "If you answer wrong, he will devour your mind."

The sphinx's feline lips stretched, revealing a row of four-foot fangs, white and sharp like swords.

The werewolf woman paled.

"This is why they're banned from Baha-char," I told her. "They trap beings with their riddles and when they don't get the right answer, they absorb their minds. Your body will live on, but you will not. Don't say anything. Don't even cough. He can't touch you until you make a sound."

She clamped her lips shut.

I had to save her. I had to do something.

Sean had a familiar contemplative look on his face. There were many species Sean could kill with a knife, but a battle with the sphinx would be incredibly difficult. No, we needed to beat him on his own terms. We needed...

Wait.

"I'll be right back. Sean, don't do anything until I come back."

I took off at a run. Behind me the low rumble of sphinx's chuckle rolled through the Old Arena.

I dashed through the streets, veering left and right. Here's hoping he hadn't left yet.

The side street spat me out onto one of the main thruways. I crossed it and climbed the stone stairs on the side of a building leading up to a terrace above. The Tooth of Shver, a massive ivory fang twelve stories tall and carved into a terraced palace, rose to my left, and the sapphire glass tower was straight across. Okay, I knew where I was.

I jogged along the terraces, crisscrossing the streets on narrow bridges, turned right, jogged for another four blocks, turned right again, and finally emerged onto a wide street.

A towering tree rose in front of me to a hundred and fifty feet, its bark hard and smooth, more stone than wood and swirling with deep red, gold, black, and creamy white as if it were made of brecciated jasper. Its thicker limbs were a full twenty feet in diameter, its thinner branches were about five feet across, and most of them were hollowed, punctured with windows and ornate doors. Balconies curved around the entrances, cushioned in the tree's foliage.

I headed to the entrance, a ten-foot-tall door in the thick trunk, and knocked.

Twin cameras swiveled toward me from above, looking like two dandelions on thin stalks. A high-pitched voice emanated from a hidden speaker.

"What do you want?"

"I'm here to see the First Scholar."

"The supplicant hours are not now. Come back tomorrow."

"I must see him. It's an emergency."

"The First Scholar is busy. He has no time for you now. Come back tomorrow."

Oy. "The First Scholar knows me."

The voice let out an exasperated chirp. "Human! The First Scholar is very important. Very busy. You are a not-important stupid human. Go away!"

If making a good impression wasn't crucial, I'd have been hopping up and down from sheer frustration. "Tell him Dina of Earth is here to see him."

"Dina?" A voice asked from above.

I backed away from the door. Far above me, the First Scholar emerged onto the balcony of one of the higher branches. He was about three feet tall, plump, and old, with feathers that had gone completely white except for the touch of scarlet on his bushy tail and the tips of his wings. Two dinosaurian arms thrust out from under his wings and gripped the balcony rail with clawed hands. His beak was yellow, and his eyes were round and bright like two brilliant zircon jewels.

The official name of the species was koo-ko. Sean called them space chickens and refused to keep to the proper name. They had held a philosophical debate at Gertrude Hunt during last Treaty Stay, an innkeeper holiday, and since nobody died, it was considered a resounding success.

The First Scholar spread his wings. "Dina!"

"First Scholar!"

"We meet again!"

A smaller, younger male koo-ko with turquoise tips on his wings emerged from the doorway behind the First Scholar and plopped an elaborate headdress of golden wire and jewels onto his head.

"Your tree has many branches," I told them. Flattery never hurt.

30

The First Scholar preened. "Yes, it is splendid, isn't it? It can house all our students, faculty, and staff. What brings you here?"

"I need your wisdom, Great Scholar."

The First Scholar's eyes sparkled. "What may I do for you?"

"Someone I know has been trapped by a sphinx."

The First Scholar's feathers stood on end. "Here? At Bahachar? They are banned from the Great Bazaar!"

"It's a juvenile male. The riddle has been asked, and by the time the authorities catch on, it might be too late. Please help me, First Scholar. I will be in your debt."

The First Scholar drew himself to his full height. His headdress listed to the left, threatening to fall off his head. "Not another word. I will take care of this."

The koo-ko assistant pointed at the doorway and murmured something.

"It will be a teachable moment," the First Scholar declared and waved his wing at the doorway. "Come!"

A flood of koo-ko of all sizes and colors erupted onto the balcony. They spilled over the rail, spread their wings, and glided to the ground around me. One, two, five...ten...I lost count. Their belts and harnesses differed but every single one came with a holder containing a fat scroll. It looked like they were carrying a personal roll of toilet paper with them. Normally it made me giggle in my head, because somewhere deep inside I was seven years old and potty humor was still funny, but right now any humor was in short supply.

The First Scholar pushed his headdress back onto his head. "Pay attention, young ones. This will be an experience you must commit to memory. Form a flock and bring me my teaching stick!"

———

I RUSHED THROUGH THE STREETS. THE KOO-KO HAD NO TROUBLE keeping up with me despite being about half my height. If needed, all of them could outrun me and then some. Including the First Scholar and two of his helpers, one carrying his hat and the other dragging a long stick of polished blue wood with a bright red tassel attached to its tip.

"Tell me the riddle," the First Scholar asked.

" 'Say my name, and I will disappear. What am I?' " I was pretty sure I knew the answer but "pretty sure" didn't count when a life hung in the balance.

"You're right. The sphinx is very young. No matter. Youth isn't an excuse for willful flouting of the rules, although it is certainly the right time for it."

We turned into the dark alleys. The shaggy sloth creature saw us and waved a little piece of bright red cloth like a flag as we passed. The other vendors stared. They had now seen Sean run into the Old Arena, then run out, then come back with me, then I ran out, and now I was back leading a flock of koo-ko. It was more excitement than they probably had seen the entire month.

We spilled into the Old Arena. Everything was as I had left it: the sphinx, Sean, and the female werewolf, still locked in the glowing golden helix of the sphinx's power.

"Why don't you answer?" the sphinx purred, power vibrating in every vowel. *"Go on. Take a chance. You cannot wait forever. Soon you will soil yourself. Then will come thirst, then hunger. You are a brave warrior. Is that how you want to die? Alone, wasting away in your filth because you are too scared to answer a simple riddle?"*

"Keep quiet," Sean told her.

"She has answered you," the First Scholar declared.

The sphinx turned its massive head and looked at us.

The First Scholar's assistant on his left deposited the head-dress onto the elder's head. The assistant on his right thrust the stick into his clawed hand. The three dozen koo-ko arranged themselves into a crescent behind the First Scholar.

A violet sheen rolled over sphinx's eyes. "And who are you, small bird?"

His voice was back to normal. The power-saturated sound only occurred when he spoke to the one bound by his riddle.

The First Scholar raised his stick, sending the tassel flying. "Do not change the subject. By the very act of remaining quiet, she has answered your riddle, for the answer to your question is silence."

The sphinx frowned.

"The right answer has been given. Release this creature as per your bargain," the First Scholar demanded.

The sphinx pondered it, clearly stumped.

"That is not a proper answer," he finally said.

"Then ask me another question, and I will answer for her," The First Scholar declared. "She is but a humble warrior, while my mind holds decades of academic knowledge. She is a snack, but I am a delicious feast."

The sphinx smiled, and the nightmarish forest of fangs in his mouth glinted in the sun. The golden glow around the female werewolf died and she tumbled to the ground.

The sphinx opened its metallic wings, the golden feathers reflecting sunlight in a blinding glow. Golden light spiraled around the First Scholar. He was barely three and a half feet tall, counting the headdress, and the sphinx was forty feet at the shoulder.

The koo-ko scholars cooed in unison, the sound of collective anxiety.

The First Scholar raised his head. "Ask your question."

"The more there is, the less you see. What am I?

"Darkness."

The Sphinx opened his mouth. Nothing came out.

"That is an embarrassingly easy question. Ask another," the First Scholar said. "Go ahead."

"Once offered one, you shall have two or none at all—"

"A choice. Let us try again. Reach deeper."

"I have one color but many sizes. I touch you yet you never feel me. Light gives me existence, darkness--"

"A shadow." The First Scholar sighed. "Let me save you the trouble. Wind, time, self, light, youth, fire. Shall I continue?"

The sphinx stared at him, mute.

A few seconds passed.

"How?" the sphinx managed finally.

"You're obviously going through Bartran's *Guide to the Questions of an Inquisitive Mind and the Nature of Existence*." The First Scholar turned to his students and waved the stick. "Note this moment."

The koo-ko pulled scrolls from the holders on their belts and produced styluses.

"Those of you who idly wonder why you should read the classics and when you would ever have the opportunity to use the fundamental knowledge contained within, take heed, for you never know when you may encounter a sphinx on the crossroads of life. This sphinx," the Scholar pointed at the towering creature with his stick, "is but an allegory. He and his kind are forbidden here, so you would be forgiven for thinking your mind is safe, yet here he is, ready to devour the unprepared. Such is the existence of a scholar, forever seeking knowledge and defending one's right to obtain and share it while perils await at every turn. It is a noble pursuit."

The First Scholar's voice quivered with emotion. The koo-ko students dutifully recorded every word.

"Always remember, knowledge is a product of labor. It is to be shared but never taken. For if you set out to rip knowledge away from others and hoard it like a jealous merchant hoards their wealth, you too will be shunned like this sphinx and banished from the circle of your peers."

No doubt, this would become one of the koo-ko philosopher legends.

The First Scholar turned to the sphinx and waved his stick at

34

him. "And you, you are not supposed to be here. More, you have come here unprepared. Bartran provides the first building block to one's understanding of existence, but he, by design, shows you the mere tip of the iceberg, just enough to demonstrate that the enormous underwater mountain is there and to prompt you to dive into the frigid waters to seek your own understanding. You have decades of study ahead of you before venturing forth again. Answer the question of my dear human friend and then return humbly to your teacher, who is, without a doubt, deeply disappointed in your conduct."

Sometimes when Olasard persisted in his feline entitlement, I gently booped him on the nose with my finger. The gray Maine Coon always looked stunned, as if I had committed an outrage so great, he simply couldn't come to terms with it. The sphinx looked just like that.

The First Scholar banged the butt of his stick on the ground. The tassel danced. "Answer!"

"Where did the portal lead?" Sean asked.

"To Karron," the sphinx said.

Wilmos was doomed.

[5]

Foolish sphinx. He was no match for First Scholar Thek, Recipient of the Starlight Quill, Sage of the Great Tree, the most erudite of philosopher space chickens!

But what is it about Karron that dooms Wilmos so? Read on to find out.

We were in the War Room, a round chamber where a root of the inn emerged in a round platform, allowing for a tighter connection to Gertrude Hunt. Innkeepers and our inns existed in symbiosis, always aware of each other but distinct and separate. Linking with the root merged us into one.

Screens lined the walls, some physical, some holographic projections. The one to my left was wrapped in thin tendrils of wood. They pulsed with pale light at regular intervals as the inn untangled the feed from Wilmos' shop, crunching through the encryption. I asked Sean if Wilmos usually encrypted his surveillance footage, and he said yes. Apparently, the old werewolf was touchy about random people knowing his business. It was taking so long that I formed a couple of chairs for us. I sat in mine, but Sean stalked around the room, his steps measured, his face unreadable.

In front of us, on a huge screen, Karron hung like the ominous orb of some cosmic magician.

A large planet, almost twice the size of Earth, Karron floated in an envelope of green atmosphere. It wasn't a cheerful grass green that hinted at plant growth or the blueish green of shallow oceans and life-giving water. No, it was a deep, sickly shade of green, the kind of color one could find associated with undeath in a video game. Beneath the green, the outlines of rust-colored continents curved around the planet interrupted at the poles by vast placid seas.

"Tell me again," Sean asked.

"It's a cold hell made of methane and dust. Methane liquifies at -260 F. Those polar seas are -300 F. There is no oxygen or phosphorus. The atmosphere is soup, dense and nitrogen-rich. The snow is made up of hydrocarbon particles."

I zoomed in on one of the continents near the equator and the uniform rust broke into individual swirls and ridges as if some enormous being had left a fingerprint on the planet's surface.

"The dunes of Karron are born of electrified sand and methane winds. The wind blows east, but the dunes point to the west. That's because the electricity makes the hydrocarbon particles of the sand stick together. At the equator the dunes are over 100 yards deep. A craft attempting to land there will be swallowed whole. The static charge of the sand will fry circuitry and wiring, and most of the typical ship drives will stop functioning."

"Buried alive, blind, deaf, and unable to move," he said.

"Yes. Even if the craft hovers in the atmosphere without landing, it would be like flying through a sandstorm except that the sand is sticky and would immediately clump to the hull. Within minutes, the craft would become a ball of sand with a hefty charge. If the weight didn't bring it down, the havoc that the dust would play with all the systems would."

"What about the oceans?"

"The file on Karron," I told the inn.

The screen blinked. A dark ocean spread in front of us, a deep olive green. Something rippled under the surface. The liquid bulged, and a mass of flesh emerged, formless but solid, like a microscopic organism somehow enlarged to a gargantuan size. The pallid flesh slid and slithered, pulsating, twisting, a Lovecraftian nightmare, and vanished into the frigid depths.

"I thought you said no oxygen or phosphorus," Sean said, his face grim.

"It's cyanide-based life. Vinyl cyanide membranes instead of lipid ones. That's about all we know about the Karr. They live in the oceans, they destroy anything that tries to intrude into their domain, they do not trade, and they do not communicate. They never leave the planet."

"What do they eat?" Sean wondered.

I spread my arms. "Your guess is as good as mine."

Sean's eyes were dark. I knew exactly what he was thinking. There was no way in. We would never make it to the surface, let alone land safely.

A tendril brushed my arm. Gertrude Hunt had sensed my anxiety. I patted the tendril gently.

A soft pulse of magic told us the recording was ready. Sean waved it onto the central screen.

The shop lay empty except for Gorvar dozing on a padded pillow on the floor. I fast forwarded. Hours flashed by in minutes. Occasionally Gorvar rose to stretch or drink some water.

More footage.

Finally, the door slid open and Wilmos strode into the shop, carrying a huge bag with odd bulges that looked suspiciously like weapon barrels stretching the fabric from the inside. Gorvar jumped up and bounded over like an overgrown puppy. Every time I saw Gorvar, he was either menacing or aloof and indifferent. Now he was spinning around in circles at Wilmos' feet. If I wasn't watching it, I wouldn't have believed it in a million years.

Wilmos put the bag down and crouched. Gorvar licked his face. The grizzled werewolf hugged his pet. "This was a long one, wasn't it? I'm getting too old for this shit. Hang on, I brought you something."

He reached into his bag.

The doors behind him snapped open. A creature surged into the shop. It was eight feet tall and clad in a tattered dark robe with a deep hood and wide sleeves.

Wilmos yanked a weapon from inside the bag, spun around, planted one knee on the floor, leveled an energy hand cannon at the intruder, and fired. A glowing packet of energy left the barrel with a telltale zing like loose change shaken in a Coke can sizzling with electricity.

The robed figure dashed sideways. Wilmos' burst missed, hitting the shelves instead. Weapons went flying.

The creature zigzagged, as if weightless. Wilmos kept firing, each burst chewing through the carefully arranged merchandise on the walls.

The intruder jerked its arms up, and for a second, I saw its hands, pallid, bony, with too-long fingers tipped with yellow claws. Wilmos sighted and fired. The energy spark hit the creature dead on. The air in front of it rippled, and the burst died, absorbed. Wilmos tossed the cannon on the ground and yanked another firearm from the bag.

A ball of orange lightning tore out of the intruder's claws and streaked toward Wilmos. He lunged to the side, but the lightning chased him and splashed over his body. Wilmos convulsed, drumming the ground with his heels.

Gorvar shot forward at the intruder. The robed figure caught the huge wolf by his throat and clawed him, once, twice, almost impatient. Gorvar flailed, his eyes full of rage. The creature stabbed his stomach with his claws and ripped them upward, tearing through fur and muscle. The light dimmed in Gorvar's eyes. It tossed the wolf aside, almost contemptuously, as if he were a discarded wrapper, and moved over to Wilmos.

The big werewolf wasn't moving.

The robed figure picked him up by his belt. A shimmering gray bubble streaked with red veins formed around the two of them, lifting the intruder above the ground. The bubble and the two beings inside of it flew toward the door and out into Baha-char. The doors of the shop slid closed.

I motioned to the inn, rewinding the recording to the spot where the creature raised its arms, and paused it at the precise moment the ball of orange lightning broke free of its fingertips. The tattered robe, the bony hands that could have belonged to a corpse, the yellow claws, and finally the lightning. There was no doubt. It was just like Michael. I looked at Sean and saw the confirmation in his eyes. He remembered the fight as well as I did.

We were looking at another corrupted ad-hal.

"He was targeted because of us," I said.

"It's too early to tell," Sean said. "Wilmos has his fingers in a lot of pies."

I pointed at the screen. "A corrupted ad-hal, Sean?"

He didn't say anything.

"If Wilmos even suspected a corrupted ad-hal was around, he would've come to us immediately. He fought Michael with us. He knows what they're capable of. And it didn't kill him. It took him."

Wilmos was bait. We both knew it.

"If Wilmos is bait, and this is a trap," Sean said, "then we're meant to follow. The trap only works if we walk into it." He looked at Karron still looming above us. "How are we supposed to follow it there?"

"I don't know. Maybe it expects us to die trying."

"Why?" Sean frowned. "Seems too elaborate. Why is it even targeting us in the first place? Does it want revenge for Michael?"

"I don't know."

"It's chancy. If it were me, I would just wait and ambush us at the shop. We fought one of these assholes, and it almost kicked our asses. Two or three could finish us. Why not take Wilmos out of the equation, wait for us to show up, and then..." He hit his left palm with his right fist.

"I don't know." I got up. I was tired of not knowing. "A communication screen, please."

The inn helpfully sprouted one for me on the wall.

"Who are you calling?"

"Someone who knows more about Karron than I do."

"Another innkeeper?" Sean frowned.

"No." Innkeepers didn't care about Karron. There was absolutely no chance that one of its residents would ever make a stop at an inn. No, I needed someone with an in-depth understanding of the galaxy. I knew just the person.

Now we just had to figure out what it would cost us.

———

THE GALAXY WAS FULL OF NATIONS. SOME WERE REPUBLICS, SOME were empires, others were democracies, anocracies, autocracies and other forms of government not found in human dictionaries. At any given time, many of them were in conflict with each other. Interstellar battles were expensive and required a prohibitive amount of resources, and most nations recognized the need for peaceful adjudication, which was where the Arbitrators came in. They tried to resolve disputes between cosmic powers before they flared into devastating wars.

The Office of Arbitration was an ancient and mysterious entity, and the Arbitrators themselves were beings of unprecedented power, carefully chosen from a variety of species. They possessed encyclopedic knowledge of the galaxy and commanded great respect, and they were to be treated with the utmost courtesy at all times.

"You look like one of your corpses," I said.

On the huge screen George dragged his hand over his face. Normally he resembled one of Tolkien's elven princes, tall, lean, golden-haired, and elegant in an ethereal way. He liked when people underestimated him, so he often pretended to have a limp and walked with a cane. I had it on very good authority that he was a superb swordsman. He was an even better necromancer. That, I had witnessed personally. Seeing thousands of undead claw their way out of the barren soil of Nexus was something I would never forget.

The George I saw today was entirely different. His long blond hair had broken free of his ponytail and hung around his face in greasy strands. Dark bags clutched at his eyes. He looked haggard, and his silk doublet, which must have been as white as fresh snow at some point, now resembled snow after a week had passed and most of it melted into mud.

He stared at me, his blue eyes distracted. "Hello."

"When was the last time you slept?"

The Arbitrator pondered the question. "Some time ago."

He didn't seem like he was altogether there. He must've been extremely sleep deprived. Judging by the blue tint in the white of his eyes, he had taken a lot of boosters to keep himself awake, probably one after another. Whatever the problem he was facing, he'd smashed his computer-like brain against it, and it left him stumped.

"You should shower, George. And then sleep."

He raised his finger. "Not yet."

"Why?"

He thought about it. It was almost as if his brain was on a five-second delay. "Valkkinians."

Ah. Valkkinians were exceptionally difficult.

"Light or dark?"

"Dark."

That man had the best luck. "They refuse to see you?"

"Yes."

"You offered fire?"

"Yes."

"And rubies?"

"Yes."

"Record what I'm about to say so you will remember."

He obediently waved his fingers at the display.

"You're going to take a shower. You must be clean. Don't use anything with perfume in it. Don't tie your hair, don't shave. Then you are going to land near Oharak Mountain, by a stone stele. It's 900 feet tall, you can't miss it. You are going to take your shoes off and walk barefoot up the mountain path. Every 67 steps you will stop and kneel. Do this five times, then wait. An elderly Valkkinian will come to see you. Tell him you are my friend. He will help you."

George struggled with it for a few seconds. "How do you know him?"

"He stayed at the inn."

"Valkkinians have never stayed at Gertrude Hunt. I checked."

"Not my inn. My parents' inn."

George frowned. "That can't be right."

"Why not?"

"Because I asked your brother, and he said your parents never hosted them."

My heart made a valiant effort to leap out of my chest. Klaus was alive.

I kept my expression calm. "Klaus didn't encounter them. It was right after he and Michael turned twenty-one. They went on a month-long trip to Japan. Michael was a Toyotomi Hideyoshi fan, and he really wanted to see Osaka Castle."

George stared at me.

"George! Shower. Stone stele. Lots of walking. Call me when you're done. I need your help with Karron."

I would tell him to sleep first but it would be pointless.

George scrambled to his feet and stumbled away, pulling his shirt off his back. I aborted the connection.

Sean tilted his head at me. "Your brother is alive."

"And he is an Arbitrator."

That explained everything. Whatever George was working on had to be vital and secret. Arbitrators were extremely close-mouthed. They wouldn't go to just anyone for information, but George and I had a prior professional relationship. I was trustworthy.

There was no reason George would seek Klaus out when he knew where to find me. There was only one reason he would prefer Klaus over me: Klaus was in. He was an Arbitrator and therefore cleared for all classified information. And it also meant that Klaus was either on equal footing with George or his senior.

That's why Klaus went off the grid. I was afraid he'd died.

I leaned back in my chair. When I got a hold of my brother, I would pitch a fit. He had no idea what was coming to him.

No idea.

"Do you think George will get back to us?" Sean asked.

"He will. As soon as he can."

George had many flaws, but he always paid his debts.

[6]

Things are never simple when George gets involved. When we last left the inn, Dina had a surprising reveal about her brother Klaus and a plan to save Wilmos was beginning to take shape.

Let's see what our favorite Arbitrator has down his elegant shirtsleeves.

Twenty-six hours later, Sean and I sat in front of the communication screen again. The elven prince was back. He was still a bit too pale, and there were lingering traces of fatigue in the lines of his face, but he was alert, clean, and well dressed. George's fashion sense fell somewhere between a musketeer and a gentleman privateer. He was fond of shirts with wide sleeves, beautifully tailored vests, and tall leather boots. The embroidery on his dark blue vest was swoon worthy.

Sean would look great in that vest. Well, not that vest exactly, Sean would need a larger size. Maybe for Halloween...

I stopped myself. I had spent the entire day checking on Gorvar, worrying about Wilmos, and trying to research some way to Karron. I was so worn out, my brain had resorted to nonsense in self-defense.

"Thank you for your assistance," George said. "It was most helpful."

"I take it, your issue with the Valkkinians is resolved?" I asked.

"Yes."

If one of us didn't step into the breach, we would be dancing around the Klaus issue all night.

I raised my head. "How is my brother?"

"He is well," George replied. "A rather unfortunate slip up on my part. I would appreciate it if you would attribute it to fatigue rather than indiscretion. Apparently, one-hundred and fifty hours without sleep significantly impaired my cognitive functions."

Sean whistled quietly. "Six days is pushing it."

George grimaced. "So it would seem. Lesson learned. Klaus has his reasons for his current course of action. You and your sister are very dear to him."

"You don't have to cover for him," I told him. "He can explain himself when we meet."

"You mentioned Karron," George said. "I understand there was an incident at Baha-char?"

And he knew every detail of it. There was a whole flock of koo-ko present at the scene. By now the furthest reaches of known space were aware that Wilmos had been taken from his shop and only the shocking heroism and tremendous wisdom of the First Scholar had uncovered the kidnapper's destination. I didn't envy the juvenile sphinx. He was likely gone from Baha-char and back with his own people, where he would have to explain how exactly he managed to spectacularly embarrass his entire species in front of the known galaxy.

"A being resembling a corrupted ad-hal took Wilmos to Karron," Sean said. "I need to get to that planet."

"Quite impossible, I'm afraid," George said. "Even our office doesn't possess a craft able to survive a landing on and take off from that world."

All of the hope went out of me at once.

"Not impossible," Sean said. "Wilmos was taken there. Someone has the means to take him there and keep him alive, otherwise why not just kill him?"

"Clearly, they would like you to die in the attempt to rescue him." George tilted his head to the side. "There is, however, a galactic power that maintains a portal gate to Karron."

I sat up straighter.

"Why would they have a gate on Karron?" Sean asked.

"They have an outpost there."

"What a coincidence," Sean said.

George arched his brows. "Not at all. It's not a coincidence, it is by design. Civilizations bring me their problems, and I find solutions. He has a problem, you are the solution to it, if you choose to be, and vice versa. That's how the galaxy works."

"And then both parties owe you a favor," I said.

"Naturally."

"Who is it and what does he want?" I asked.

He told us.

Wow.

"If you do this and it goes well, you could ask him for almost anything. He will be publicly indebted to you. I have raised the possibility of access to Karron with his chancellor. If you honor their request, they are happy to let you use their portal as many times as necessary. Their facility has been mothballed for a decade, but all the life support systems within it are still operational."

Wilmos' kidnapper had to be keeping him alive, otherwise why take him in the first place. That facility was the only habitable place on Karron. Wilmos had to be inside it.

George gave us a grave look.

"The universe is full of possibilities, so mathematically another way to travel to Karron exists, but I don't know what it is. In my expert opinion, this is your best chance to rescue your friend. This entire affair is wrought with risk. The scale of the event they want you to host is unprecedented for an Earth inn. Even if everything goes well, which we all know it won't, you still must physically travel to Karron and enact the rescue on your own. Please give this matter serious consideration. I have grown fond of both of you, and I would hate for you to throw away your lives. I will need an answer in twenty-four hours."

He terminated the connection.

"I can't ask you to do this," Sean said. His face was completely neutral.

"Wilmos would do it for either of us," I said.

Sean's stone face didn't fool me for a second. My parents were missing. Their entire inn had vanished in an instant with them inside it. The house, the guests, the garden, everything was gone, and only an empty lot had been left behind. Nobody had any answers. Nobody could even hazard a guess as to what happened. The uncertainty of not knowing was awful.

I'd been looking for them for years, and I would never give up. They were out there, somewhere, waiting to be rescued. I knew exactly how Sean felt, and I would do almost anything to spare Sean what I had gone through.

We had a location. We had to try.

"Will Caldenia be a problem?" Sean asked.

"Absolutely." And I had no idea how I would even broach the subject with her.

We thought about it some more.

"I'm going to get him out," he said.

I shook my head. "No, Sean. Not you. Us."

"One of us will need to stay at the inn."

"If they just wanted just you, they could have grabbed you during any of the outings you and Wilmos went on. They want me, or possibly both of us. We will go together. But first, we'll have to pull off this nightmare event."

"Nothing can ever be easy," he said.

"No. We can't even just walk into a trap like normal people. We have to work really hard first."

He laughed, a quiet wolf chuckle.

I raised my hand. "One vote for yes. Any opposing?"

"We haven't done anything dumb or dangerous for almost six months." Sean pushed away from the wall on which he was leaning, walked over, and kissed me. "Let's do this."

––––––

"It's a spouse selection," I explained.

We sat in the kitchen, Sean and I on one side of the table, Caldenia and Marais on the other, with Orro on the end, on Sean's right.

"It involves a powerful head of state," I continued. "The spouse selection is very complex. The choice of the candidate depends on the genetic traits the spouse can offer, on what faction they represent, and on the political benefits that match will bring."

Marais frowned. "But they are all the same species, right?"

"Not necessarily," Sean said.

"It's an old, established practice." Caldenia waved her hand. "With the genetic science available to those with enough resources, gender and species don't matter. As long as there is enough compatibility, you could marry a whale, Officer Marais. They would splice the DNA together into an offspring with the desired genetic traits and let the child mature to term in an artificial womb."

Marais shook his head. "I'm not sure I'm comfortable with that."

"It's not about comfort but survival." Caldenia bared her sharp teeth. "I carry the genetic roots of seven species in my body thanks to some long-term planning by my ancestors. They have served me very well."

"The selection has been narrowed down to twelve candidates from one hundred and five," I continued.

Caldenia's eyes sparkled.

"Twelve is a lot," Marais said.

"You have your two or three favorites but keep the others in the running for political considerations," Caldenia explained. "And for the spectacle. There must be pageantry, after all. Spouse selections are greatly entertaining. A well-timed spouse selection followed by a lavish wedding can often quell civil unrest before it has a chance to explode in your face."

"The ruler has an issue," I said. "The prospective spouses-to-be keep killing each other."

Caldenia leaned back and cackled. "This is absolutely delightful."

"Apparently, it wouldn't be problem under normal circumstances," Sean said. "However, their religious leader is at the end of his life. He must find a suitable candidate to whom he can transfer his holy gift before he expires. Random murder interferes with that on a psychic level, and by law, he is required to be present for the entirety of the spouse selection."

"I love it." Caldenia grinned.

She would be a lot less happy in a minute.

Sean kept going. "They've tried everything to secure their premises, but each candidate has twenty retinue members, and they keep nuking each other in elaborate ways. They need a safe ground."

Orro raised his hand and counted on his claws.

"We're it," I said. "If we can help him get to the altar, he will give us access to the special portal and their abandoned mining outpost on Karron, so we can go look for Wilmos."

"What were they mining?" Caldenia asked.

"Fuel for a weapon," Sean told her. We had done some research. "They mined a bunch of it and then decided the weapon was too inhumane to be used."

Caldenia raised her eyebrows. "It broke."

"Probably," I said. "The point is, we have no other way of entering that planet."

"How many?" Orro asked. "How many beings total?"

I tried to sound upbeat. "Three hundred. The ruler's retinue, the candidates and their escorts, and the observers. A lot of powers in that region of space are sending diplomats to see what will happen, since the marriage will affect the balance of power."

Orro blinked. "How many species?"

"At least fourteen. Probably more."

He blinked again.

"Screen please," I told the inn.

Gertrude Hunt sprouted a small screen on a tendril and held it up to Orro. He scrolled through the guest list.

"They are due to arrive in two days if we say yes," I said.

"Of course, you must say yes." Caldenia clapped her hands. "This will be marvelous."

I had to do it now. "Your Grace, there is one tiny issue. The ruler is..."

"Don't tell me!" She jumped up. "I want to be surprised."

"*Letere Olivione...*" Sean started.

"Not another word! You will not ruin this for me."

She swept out of the kitchen, the sleeves of her long green gown flaring from the wind of her passage.

"Well, shit," Sean said.

I slumped onto the back of my chair.

"I take it there is a problem," Marais said.

"Not yet," Sean said. "But there will be one."

I groaned. This was exactly what I was afraid of.

"I can get her. We can have the inn hold her and tell her," Sean offered.

"She would be mortally offended." I sighed. "Do you want to deal with her carrying a grudge for the next six months? Because I don't."

Orro had stopped scrolling and was staring at the screen, his eyes distant.

"Orro?" I asked gently. "Are three hundred guests too many?"

He raised his head. His eyes focused. "What are you implying? Are you implying my skills are not sufficient?"

Oh no, no, no, we're not taking that scary road into Orro's Offended Woods.

"She is asking if you need some assistance," Sean said.

The chef frowned, pondered it for a second, and his eyes brightened. "Two!"

"What?" I asked.

"I will need two assistants! Maybe three. I need the species list. I need to go shopping. I need to go to Baha-char! I need things and money!"

He jumped up and ran at the pantry door. The inn helpfully slid it out of the way before Orro could collide with it head-on, and the chef vanished into the storage room.

Sean turned to Marais. "We would like to hire you for security to watch the place from the street. Just in case."

"You don't need to do that. I'll help you anyway."

"We absolutely have to pay you," I told him. "It would be time away from your family."

Marais thought about it. "I have to check regulations. There might be something in there that prevents me from taking a part-time job. Let me figure this out."

"Thank you," I told him.

He got up and left. It was just me and Sean now.

"Do you have any contacts who deal in bioweapons?" I asked.

"Wilmos has some nasty stuff in his shop. I can take it, I'm sure he won't mind. Why?"

"One of the candidates is backed by the Dushegubs."

Sean frowned. "I've read about those. They are sentient trees. Are they problematic?"

"They are not sentient. They are sapient, but unable to feel

52

emotions. Dushegubs are calculating, homicidal, moving trees that feed on animal life. They know that other creatures have emotions and what those emotions are, and they don't care. Their first option is murder, their second option is murder, and if that fails, they go straight to murder."

"Well, at least they have their priorities straight."

"They are banned as a species from the inns. I will have to apply for special permission to host them, and if we get it, we might have to kill one as an example."

Sean stared at me.

"Trust me on this," I told him. "Every time Dushegubs stay at the inn, someone dies. If we are lucky, it's one of them."

"Won't it cause an issue with our bachelor?"

"I told them up front about it. They don't care if we burn the entire Dushegub delegation to the ground. Apparently, their presence is so oppressively bloodthirsty, they give the Holy Ecclesiarch migraines."

"This is going to be fun," Sean said.

That was one way to put it.

[7]

George knows a way to the inhospitable planet Wilmos is trapped in, and he knows how to trade a favor to get access to it. Color none of us surprised.

Will the latest caper he gets Gertrude Hunt involved in be too dangerous for even our beloved innkeepers to host?

Cue the Intergalactic Bachelor show!

The inn chimed, announcing visitors. I groaned softly and opened my eyes, abandoning the Dushegub containment unit in mid-renovation. The tangle of Gertrude Hunt's branches cradling my body hummed with energy. I had cocooned myself to speed things up.

We had managed to convince the Seven Star Dominion that 48 hours was an unrealistic timeline. I used the Assembly as a shield and told them that we needed to file for the necessary permits, which was only a half-lie. Being a Republican Monarchy with a developed bureaucracy, the Dominion agreed that the need for proper procedure had to be followed. It bought us five days to

54

prepare. Today was day three. Tomorrow the Sovereign's chancellor would be stopping by to inspect the premises so we could make adjustments.

I had spent the last three days working from the moment I opened my eyes to the moment I passed out in our bed. I ate little, slept less, and this evening I had reached a kind of weird, depersonalized state, where I was still sort of me, but mostly I was Gertrude Hunt, frantically shaping rooms out of nothing.

The effort of calling up a vid screen to see who was outside was beyond me. I needed a few seconds.

A wall parted, and Sean emerged, looking haggard. The lines of his scars were more pronounced, and his eyes were red. Even the werewolf genes couldn't compensate for the sheer amount of work we had done in the last 72 hours.

"It's Brian," he said.

Brian Rodriguez ran the largest regional inn located in Dallas. He knew my parents before they and their inn disappeared without a trace, and we had helped each other in the past. Like my parents, he also sat on the Innkeeper Assembly. Innkeepers were notoriously reluctant to leave their inns unless it was absolutely necessary. Why was he here in person?

Sean waved a screen into existence. On it, Mr. Rodriguez got out of a blue Toyota 4Runner. He was in his fifties, a man of average height with bronze skin, dark hair sprinkled with gray, and a short beard.

My brain very slowly made the connection. Mr. Rodriguez <- Assembly <- Requests.

"They are denying us the Dushegub permit." I pushed the branches wrapping me. They parted, lowering me to the floor. "He's come to tell us in person."

The passenger door popped open, and Tony stepped out. Tony was Mr. Rodriguez 2.0, but about twenty-some years younger, three inches taller and without the beard. He was the nicest guy. He was also an ad-hal.

In his everyday human shape, Tony looked perfectly harmless. He had an easy smile and an even temper, and if you walked into a room full of people and tried to pick out the one capable of paralyzing his targets and taking them to a planet with a dying sun where they would suffer a century of solitary torment, he would be the absolute last pick.

Innkeepers wielded near absolute power within our inns, but outside of them, our capacity was very limited. The ad-hal had no such problems. Their power came from within them. They weren't tethered to any inn, and they only showed up when a problem went from a disaster to a full-blown catastrophe. Some innkeepers went decades without encountering an ad-hal. We knew our regional ad-hal by name and fed him dinner on a regular basis. Except this time, he wasn't coming over to fanboy over Orro's cooking.

"If the Assembly refused to grant us the permit, I'm going to appeal," I said. And I would be very insistent. They would give me that damn permit.

Sean growled under his breath. His opinion of the Assembly wasn't high.

Each innkeeper was an island unto themselves. We had great autonomy, and since all the members of the Assembly were prominent innkeepers themselves, they jealously guarded that independence. That also meant that assistance was in short supply. We were expected to solve our own issues. However, the Assembly did have the power to block certain guests and entire species from visiting Earth. Technically, they could veto our entire event and there wasn't much we could do about it.

We met our visitors at the front door.

Mr. Rodriguez gave me a hug and shook Sean's hand. "Sorry to drop in on you unannounced."

"You're always welcome," Sean told him.

Tony grinned at us. "Hello!"

Neither of the Rodriguezes looked tense. Maybe this wasn't

the permit-denying kind of visit. Or maybe they were just absolutely sure that we would go along with what the Assembly decided.

"Please follow me," I said. "Sorry about the renovations."

I led them through the front room past the silent, empty kitchen, into the hallway just under the portrait of my parents. The hallway's door slid open, and we stepped into another world.

A cavernous chamber lay in front of us, 100 yards long and 60 yards wide. I had expanded the main ballroom until my bones hurt. It was somewhat bare now since we hadn't settled on the appropriate finishes.

Mr. Rodriguez raised his eyebrows.

We kept walking. On our right, a wide arched entrance led to the new kitchen. Statistics said that an average restaurant kitchen in the US ran around 1,000 sq. ft., but those restaurants didn't have to accommodate the dietary needs of over a dozen species. Orro's new kitchen was a 4,000 sq. ft. monster. Half of it was taken up by the culinary equipment, ovens, ranges, and stainless-steel prep tables, and the other half held another 8 long tables specifically for plating. Each of those tables came equipped with a custom-build storage unit sprouting from the ceiling, which contained dinnerware, sauces, syringes, and a variety of mysterious culinary tools.

Orro's new assistants flittered between the prep tables, furiously chopping and blending something. Orro was trying to finalize the menu.

"An upgrade." Tony whistled.

"We had to," I said.

The two sous chefs ignored us. One was a juvenile Quillonian, who looked like a smaller version of Orro, and the other was an auroch, a five-foot tall, russet-furred being with delicate appendages, a vaguely antelope face, and four horns crowning her head. Like Quillonians, aurochs had a ridiculous number of tastebuds. They had evolved as herbivores and had to distinguish between toxic and non-toxic plants by taste.

"Where did you get them?" Tony asked.

"Orro went to see his mentor," Sean said. "Apparently, Chef Adri called for reinforcements from some fancy culinary academy, which promptly fell over itself to participate."

"I bet," Mr. Rodriguez said. "That is one hell of a guest list. Any new chef would want that on their resume. I'm surprised they didn't have a fight."

"Oh, they did," Sean said. "Once they realized there were only two open spots, there was a spectacular brawl. Those two are the winners."

The auroch looked like she couldn't hurt a fly. Looks could be very deceiving.

Chef Adri also sent a plating specialist from his personal restaurant, a Vaskebiorn, who, contrary to the innkeeper nickname for their species, didn't look like a raccoon except for her hands. She looked like an odd, yet devastatingly adorable hybrid of a fox, squirrel, and monkey with short golden fur, and her dexterity was off the charts. Her name was Droplet, and she and Orro had already clashed twice. He tried to bully her by raising his quills, and she smacked him on the nose with a pastry bag.

We passed the kitchen and came to one of the dining areas. Sean and I had built three in total, and this one was called the Ocean Dining Hall. It was a large rectangular room. Three of its walls were pale cream stone, tastefully decorated with a carved relief along the ceiling. The fourth wall opened onto a terrace that overlooked an alien sea, an endless shallow ocean with water the color of deep orange honey under a purple sky.

"Kolinda?" Mr. Rodriguez said, studying the jagged dark mountains in the distance that thrust from the water like the fins of some massive beast. "An interesting choice."

"It's a reminder," Sean said. "We can throw them into that sea at any time."

Tony smiled.

I picked the nearest table, and we took our seats. The chair molded to my body as it accepted the weight. Taking a nap would be so nice right now.

The nearest wall split, and the inn deposited a platter of small colorful snacks and four glasses and a pitcher of iced tea onto the table. Orro would never let a visitor go hungry.

Tony helped himself to a tiny emerald-green doughnut and chewed with obvious enjoyment.

"Are you here to deliver a cease and desist?" I asked.

Mr. Rodriguez heaved a deep parental sigh. "No."

Oh good.

"If Wilmos wasn't a factor, would you still hold this event?" Mr. Rodriguez asked.

"No," Sean and I said at the same time.

"Good," Mr. Rodriguez said.

We had told them about Wilmos and the corrupted ad-hal. I showed Mr. Rodriguez the security footage when I filed for the permits.

"We're not trying to make a name for ourselves," I said. "No sane innkeeper would want to host this."

"You don't know how right you are," Mr. Rodriguez said. "The Assembly is very uncomfortable with this entire thing."

"It's not ambition," Sean said. "It's necessity." He looked at Tony. "Can you survive on Karron?"

Tony paused his chewing and thought about it. "Possibly."

"There is your answer," Sean said. "If they are so uncomfortable, they can send some ad-hal to Karron to figure out why corrupted versions of them are running around kidnapping people."

"You know we can't do that," Mr. Rodriguez said. "Our sphere of influence is limited to Earth."

The Treaty that guaranteed Earth's special status was very specific. The ad-hal jurisdiction stopped just outside the solar system. In very rare cases, they would hunt an offender down, but most of the time, even if you went on a killing spree inside an inn, as long as you fled into the greater galaxy, they wouldn't chase you. If you dared to return, however, there would be no escape.

"This entire thing has the Arbitrators' fingerprints all over it," Mr. Rodriguez said. "Is an Arbitrator involved?"

"Yes," I said.

"Is it George Camarine?"

"Yes," I said again.

"That man is a menace." Mr. Rodriguez shook his head. "No other inn on Earth is willing to host this mess. Are you two sure you have to do this? Especially considering your permanent guest."

"We are sure," Sean said.

"The Dominion knows about Caldenia," I told them. "They don't see an issue."

"Your permits are approved in their entirety," Mr. Rodriguez said.

"Nobody wants to offend the Dominion," Sean said.

Tony nodded. "You got it."

"We are raising your rating to 3.5 stars," Mr. Rodriguez continued.

I laughed. I couldn't help myself. It had to be nerves.

Sean glanced at me.

"They are too embarrassed to let the Sovereign stay at a 2.5 star inn," Tony told him.

"We hosted a Drifan Liege during a Treaty stay and they did not raise our rating," I managed between the giggles.

"Yes, but the two of you also allowed a guest and a staff member to make a giant scene at a taping of a TV show and nearly exposed the fact that your chef is a seven-foot-tall alien covered in quills," Mr. Rodriguez said. "The Assembly takes everything into account."

I laughed harder.

"The Assembly has two conditions," Mr. Rodriguez said. "If you stop giggling for a moment, I will explain them to you. First, Tony will stay here in his official capacity to back you up."

Tony grinned, raised his arm, and flexed.

"And second, if the Sovereign comes to any harm during this event, your inn is forfeit."

All the laughter went out of me at once.

Mr. Rodriguez leaned forward. "Think about this very carefully. There is no room for negotiation. Every innkeeper loses a guest once in a while, no matter how good they are or how many precautions they take. You cannot lose this one. The two of you don't even know if Wilmos is still alive."

I straightened in my chair. Around me the inn creaked, reacting to the change in my mood. The room leaned in slightly, as the entirety of Gertrude Hunt waited like a dog sighting an intruder and waiting for a command.

Tony stopped chewing.

"This isn't about Wilmos," I said, each word resonating with magic. "The inn is our domain. If we cannot keep our guests safe, we do not deserve it."

Mr. Rodriguez smiled. "And that's exactly the answer I expected."

[8]

When we last left the inn, extensive renovations were afoot, permits for banned species obtained, the Assembly (finally!) deigned to increase Gertrude Hunt's rating and our gracious hosts were preparing for an inspection.

Let's take a peek inside.

The Seven Star Dominion spread across nine star systems, five of which had more than one habitable planet. The Dominion was a powerful force. Their economy was robust, their scientific research and development was well-funded, and their military was disciplined, trained, and equipped with the latest weaponry. If they ever took over our solar system, within three hundred years Mars would be terraformed, Mercury and Venus would be on the way, and the Moon would sport a massive colony.

The Dominion incorporated four main species, with the human-like sislaf holding a 67% majority. The sislaf ran taller than humans and leaner, with square faces that had wide cheekbones, hollow cheeks, and defined jawlines. Human skin started losing elasticity after we reached our 20s, but that loss was slight. We developed wrinkles and discoloration due to other factors – sun exposure, pollution, tobacco use. The sislaf had long ago conquered that extrinsic damage. They aged more slowly, and they didn't look anywhere as worn as we did.

The man who strode out of the portal was likely in his eighties, middle aged for a sislaf, but he could've passed for a forty-year-old human who had been taking good care of himself. His hooded eyes were too green, the line of his jaw was too sharp, and his features were too symmetrical, but overall, the differences between our two species were minute. If you met him in passing, you'd think he was a celebrity who'd gone a bit overboard with plastic surgery. Except for his skin, which was an even taupe with too much gray undertone to allow him to pass for a local.

He stepped onto the polished floor of the arrival chamber and paused. He was seven feet tall and made even taller by an asymmetric gray headdress that jutted half a foot above his left ear. A gray and white robe hugged his lean frame, cinched at the waist with a wide black belt. His hair was black and cut short.

Chancellor Resven, the Sovereign's right-hand man for "all affairs involving domicile and family."

The portal swirled with pale green, and the second person came through. Also seven feet tall, she was broader at the shoulder, with a powerful build and a particularly even skin tone the color Behr Paint Company called campfire gray. I had just tinted the columns in the Sovereign pavilion that exact shade last night. Her platinum-white hair was short and thick, and her cobalt-blue high-tech armor fit her like a glove. No weapons, tall boots, and a layered navy and white cloak, clearly ceremonial rather than functional, that spilled from her left shoulder in tasteful pleats.

That was an excellent fold for curtains. I would have to remember to tag the footage the inn recorded later.

The two visitors started toward me. Resven walked with the trademark sislaf fluidity, but the soldier strode forward. There was something else in her genes besides the sislaf, and I placed my bet on the Holy Anocracy. The sislaf had been treating their own genotype as a template to be redesigned and modified for generations.

Sean rose out of the floor next to me. He wore a dark blue robe and his "business" face. Nothing about his expression looked specifically threatening. You just knew by some sixth sense that aggravating him was a terrible and potentially painful idea.

Resven blinked. The soldier didn't seem fazed. She must've stayed at an inn before.

"Greetings," I told them.

"Greetings, innkeepers. I'm Capital Prefect Miralitt," the soldier introduced herself. "This is Chancellor Resven."

The Sovereign had sent both his chancellor and the head of his personal guard.

"We've met," Resven said dryly.

Technically, we interacted via a communication screen, so we hadn't actually met, but I didn't correct him.

"Welcome to Gertrude Hunt," Sean said.

Resven looked around the arrival chamber. A large domed room inlaid with weathered brown stone, it housed a portal ring grown by Gertrude Hunt from its striated wood and nothing else. Eight arched doorways led to separate hallways branching off into the depths of the inn.

Normally, placing the portal inside the inn wasn't an option due to security concerns. No innkeeper worth their salt would allow random guests to teleport into the inn. But in this case, we had to make an exception. Having three hundred beings, some of them clearly inhuman, troop across our back yard was out of the question. It would take too long, draw too much attention, and neither Sean nor I wanted to add to our list of many problems. We would get everyone into the inn in a single massive procession and shut the portal off.

"It looks... basic," Resven said.

Miralitt raised her eyes for a fraction of a second. "It looks strategically sound. No place to hide. One group at a time?"

Sean nodded. It was a simple plan – we would welcome each delegation and channel them down the appropriate hallway into their chambers, sealing it behind them.

"How long do you need between the groups?" she asked.

"Fifteen minutes would be ideal," I told her.

"We can do better than that," she said. "I can give you an hour between each party."

"That would be greatly appreciated. Please follow me," I told them.

We started across the chamber toward the main door.

"Why stone?" Resven asked. "Why this particular shade?"

"Because it's radically different from anything found in the Dominion's capital," I explained. "It will immediately reassure the guests that the transition has occurred, while its perceived age will command a certain respect."

"How old is it?" Resven asked.

"I made it yesterday," Sean told him.

We entered a stone hallway. Tiny constellations of lights flared as we approached, illuminating the way.

"The Sovereign is very particular when it comes to his accommodations," Resven said. "Sophistication. Refinement. Dignity. Those are the key concepts of the Capital design. Have you familiarized yourself with Lady Wexyn Dion-Dian?"

"Yes," I said. Lady Wexyn was one of the spouse candidates.

Resven turned to me and paused, so I would understand the full gravity of what he was about to say. "The opposite of that!"

"Lady Wexyn is a free spirit," Miralitt said.

"She is an agent of chaos and entropy," Resven said. "The woman has no decorum, tact, or restraint."

"It is my understanding that Lady Wexyn is sponsored by one of the White Rose Cluster Temples," Sean said. "Which one?"

"Was that not in the summary?" Resven asked.

"No."

"She's sponsored by the Temple of Desire," Miralitt said.

Nothing changed in Sean's face, but I knew him better than they did. The name of temple was important, and it clearly meant something to him.

"The theme must be one of elegant opulence," Resven said. "Graceful, restrained, tasteful, never ostentatious, yet also not cheap. Nothing vivid like the otrokar's barbaric decorations. Nothing drab or blood-soaked like those favored by the Holy Anocracy…"

I chanced a quick glance at Miralitt. Her upper lip rose a fraction betraying a glimpse of a fang. Yep, vampire blood.

"Nothing garish. Nothing vulgar. Nothing…"

We stepped into the main ballroom. The floor was a soft cream with just a touch of sheen. The same shade tinted the walls and against that backdrop silver geometric patterns climbed and twisted in a trademark Dominion mosaic, accented with drops of gold and aquamarines in the corners, as if a ghost of luxury had floated by and brushed them with her phantom hand.

Tall windows interrupted the walls, their angles crisp, spilling sunlight into the space. Between them, at a height of ten-feet, square planters dripped vines with leaves carved from pale green chrysoberyl. The vines bore clusters of delicate golden flowers Gertrude Hunt had shaped from pale amber and berries of golden pearls.

At the far end of the chamber a raised rectangular platform rose, accessible by five steps. On the platform stood the spire throne, an asymmetric, ergonomic chair, formed from the same material as the floor and the walls. Strands of gold slipped through it, with flecks of aquamarines winking here and there. The throne looked like it had grown from the chamber itself, an unmovable part of it.

Resven clicked his mouth shut.

"It's almost as if they know what they are doing," Miralitt said.

"Domicile of the Sun," I said.

Sean moved his hand. The floor and walls darkened to a deeper purple blue, bringing the geometric pattern into focus. Astronomical symbols of the Dominion ignited above the throne in pale turquoise. A glowing constellation of nine stars – the replica of the Dominion itself – descended from the ceiling, illuminating the chamber in soft white glow. The massive purple moon of the Capital slipped onto the darkened sky on the left side.

"Domicile of the Moon," Sean said.

Miralitt clapped quietly. "Respect."

"You are too kind," I said and turned to Resven.

The chancellor looked about for a few seconds. His gaze met mine.

"I suppose this will do," he said.

———

SEAN SETTLED DEEPER INTO THE COUCH AND STRETCHED HIS LEGS, and the inn thoughtfully grew an ottoman under his feet before they had a chance to hit the floor. "Resven is going to be a pain in the ass."

I slumped on the soft cushions. We were in the small break room we had made off the grand ballroom so we wouldn't have to walk too far. It was furnished with couches that felt like clouds and I loved them to pieces.

"He manages the entirety of the Capital palace, all 20 million square feet of it. Being a pain in the ass is in his job description."

My feet hummed. It wasn't even an ache, it was this odd throbbing vibration. I was so tired.

"I thought the half vampire would stab him," Sean said and smiled. "That would have been fun to watch."

"It didn't even occur to him that she would take offence." I leaned my head on the back of the couch. "The sislafs are convinced that their genetic material is inherently superior. Not in a bigoted way, but in 'it will express itself no matter the odds' way. As long as you have at least 12.5 % sislaf blood, they consider you to be sislaf. The insult half-breed is literally absent from their language. To Resven, Miralitt is a sislaf. Her vampire blood is an asset, but in terms of her loyalties and her place in society, it's irrelevant. If you tried to argue that she was as much vampire as sislaf, you simply couldn't make him understand or accept that."

"The blood runs true sort of thing?"

"More like blood is thicker than water, and to them the blood of all other species is water. You're right, Resven will be difficult. He's professionally pedantic, and he hates surprises. As long as we can keep him from being shocked, we will be fine."

"He'd be a great 1st Sergeant."

"I'll take your word for it. What's the significance of the Temple of Desire?" I gave him some side eye. "How do you know about it? Have you visited the Temple of Desire? Was it everything you hoped, and more?"

He raised his hand, palm toward me.

"I'm sorry, are you telling me to talk to the hand?"

"I'm buying time while my exhausted brain figures out how to explain."

"I'll wait."

The White Rose cluster in Cassiopeia, otherwise known as NGC 7789, adorned the Northern Milky Way. A beautiful open cluster of about three hundred suns, it resembled a rose when viewed from Earth, a white blossom with a yellow border on its petals. It glittered with diverse civilizations, and it was famous for its Temples, with entire moons devoted to the worship of universal aspects. The Temple of Kindness, the Temple of Rage, the Temple of Grief... The Temple of Desire explored exactly that, the urge to obtain something beyond your reach at any cost. Within its walls and gardens, the priests and supplicants pondered the exact nature of desire, whether it was inherently selfish, whether it was just, if it could ever be pure and selfless.

Of all desires, the need for the love of another being was considered the highest and most unobtainable. The quest for power, wealth, and enlightenment hinged primarily on those who embarked on it. Their success or failure was almost entirely up to them. But no force could compel another creature to love you of their own free will.

"It's not a brothel," Sean said.

I lost it and laughed.

He sighed. "That didn't come out the way I meant it."

"I've visited."

Sean sat up straighter and pivoted to me. "When?"

"Before we met, when Klaus and I were looking for our parents. I had questions. I was exhausted and desperate. I spent two weeks there, while Klaus was checking other neighboring Temples."

A little evil light shone in Sean's eyes. "Was it everything you thought it would be?"

"It was memorable."

"Care to elaborate?"

I shook my head. "You still haven't told me why it's important to you."

"The Merchants are some of the Temple's most generous contributors," he said.

It made sense. The Merchant clans of the lees, who ran vast financial syndicates, desired things themselves and made their money by catering to the desires of others.

"Clan Nuan?" I asked.

"The second biggest contributor."

He would know. During his time on Nexus, Sean was part of Nuan Cee's inner circle. The shrewd little merchant never planned on letting Sean go. I had wrenched Sean free against all odds. He knew the kind of secrets Clan Nuan would kill to keep.

"Do you think Lady Wexyn is backed by Clan Nuan?"

"Let's say I strongly suspect. I'll know more when I put eyes on her. If Nuan Cee is involved in this, we need to know what he's playing for."

"Does Clan Nuan have business interests in the Dominion?"

"No. It's Clan Sai territory." Sean grimaced. "This worries me."

The trade wars between the Merchant Clans were fought in secret with shocking ferocity. If a war between Clan Nuan and Clan Sai was brewing, we didn't want any part of it, and we could not let it happen here, on our watch.

"How did it go with Caldenia?" he asked.

I put my fingers into my ears and said in my best imitation of Her Grace's voice, "I am not listening, I am not listening!"

"What has gotten into her?"

"Somehow this became less about me warning her than about her independence. No matter how comfortable we try to make her, she never forgets that the inn is a prison where she put herself."

"It keeps her from dying. Well, from being killed."

"True. But a prison is still a prison. I gave up. It will blow up in our faces or it won't."

"Maybe. It all," he waved his hand to indicate everything around us, "could blow up in our faces. This whole thing could end up being a giant shit show."

"Regrets?"

He shook his head. "I know why I'm doing it. I just want to tell you how much it means to me that you know all this and you're still doing it."

I got up and sat next to him. "I know."

He put his arm around me, and I rested my head on his shoulder. Of all the places in the galaxy, this was the best one for me.

The inn chimed, announcing an incoming communication. The two of us groaned in unison.

Sean waved a screen into existence. A man stood bathed in the sunshine of Baha-char. He was short, with almost impossibly broad shoulders and the kind of build that promised overwhelming strength. He wore a white shirt with wide sleeves, dark pants, tall boots, and a short cloak hanging at an angle off his broad back. He'd left the collar of the shirt unbuttoned, revealing the segmented white space marine armor underneath. It clung to him like a second skin, climbing up his thick neck. A dark musketeer hat with a huge feather, white at the base and transitioning into yellow, then red, then green, completed the ensemble. He was carrying a huge gun that rested on his shoulder as if it were a toothpick.

The man raised the brim of his hat with his fingers. Silver eyes stared at us from a tan face with the kind of heavy jaw one usually saw on grizzled male vampires. He wagged his jet-black eyebrows and grinned, showing serrated teeth. The effect was slightly terrifying.

"Gaston!"

"In the flesh," he assured me.

George had two people who watched his back. His brother, Jack, was one, and Gaston was the other. The three of them had been recruited by the Arbitrators from a pocket dimension where an alternative Earth existed with its own magical rules. I had visited it once. George and I snuck back to his homeworld to invite the fourth member of their strike team, Sophie, to join them.

Gaston wasn't altogether human. I never quite figured out what exactly he was, but he was smart and deadly in a fight. He was also a self-proclaimed expert in "skullduggery."

"I've come to assist in any way I can," Gaston said.

"Where is George?" Sean asked.

We had both assumed that George would at least be present to observe. If you cut George, he would bleed pure intrigue. This whole affair with high political stakes would be irresistible to him.

"George can't come. He sends his regrets, however. And me." Gaston winked.

"I thought he settled things with the Valkkinians," I said. I had given him a sure path to victory.

"Oh, he has. It's not the Valkkinians. It's his wife."

"His what?" Sean and I said at the same time.

"His spouse. His much better half. Perhaps I could come in and explain in detail? Over a beer and a bite to eat. I have rushed here from across the galaxy without much to sustain me on the way. Still, as eager as I am to get inside, I must warn you that there is a female werewolf watching me from the roof of the building directly behind me. I'm reasonably sure she will pounce the moment you open the door. Forewarned is forearmed. Please come and fetch me at your earliest convenience."

[9]

When we last left the inn, its new splendid décor had passed the Dominion's critical inspection. Helpful assistants are gathering around our heroes in their moment of need.

And someone made an honest man out of George! Large is the Universe, and the wonders within it.

W atching Gaston eat was like witnessing someone have a religious experience.

He cut a small piece off the duck leg, wielding his fork and knife with the elegance of a concert pianist, slipped it into his mouth, and chewed, closing his eyes. Behind Sean, who sat on the left, the entire kitchen staff waited with bated breath, including Orro.

"Divine," Gaston said finally. "It is a multilayered symphony. The meat melts in your mouth, tender yet with a delightful texture, the skin is crisp yet delicate, an ode to all that is savory. The hint of thyme is sublime, the trace of garlic is almost buttery in its smoothness, and I detect something else, something non-

Terrestrial. A touch of storran herb perhaps? Spring harvest, not fall."

Orro's quills trembled just a fraction. If he had been a cat, he would've purred. "Indeed."

"This is much more than a dish. It is a memory." Gaston smiled, displaying serrated teeth. "I shall treasure it, my friend."

Orro gave a brisk nod and the chefs dispersed.

Some beings viewed food as fuel, some enjoyed it, and yet others were like Gaston. Not simply fans but connoisseurs. Somehow the chefs could identify them by some hidden sixth sense and gave them special treatment. Gaston had been part of George's retinue during the peace summit that ended the Nexus war and Sean's contract with the Nuan Clan. He and Orro had formed a symbiotic bond. The moment I told Orro that Sean went to get him, the entire kitchen snapped into the "VIP Imminent" mode. It was just Gaston's luck that Orro's prized duck, which he had worked on for three days, had finished cooking.

Gaston cut off another piece, speared a sliver of potato dusted with herbs, and chewed with obvious pleasure.

"Should we leave you two alone?" Sean asked.

"No need. It's just so difficult to find good duck confit outside of the solar system. I have had several variations on the theme, but none can compare."

Gaston reached for his wine glass and took a sip. "And of course, the Malbec pairing is perfect. You are so fortunate."

We were sitting in the Ocean Dining Hall with the amber waves splashing past the terrace. After we terminated the call, Sean had gone to fetch Gaston, while I went to tell Orro that his favorite guest was coming. It took Sean over fifteen minutes to come back, which gave Orro enough time to plate and serve his masterpiece. Fetching Gaston should've taken two minutes at most, so clearly an altercation with the female werewolf must've occurred. Neither Sean nor Gaston had elaborated on it.

"I suppose I should begin," Gaston said, dabbing his lips with a napkin. "It all started in childhood, you see..."

The inn chimed. Another return visitor from Baha-char.

"Hold that thought." I got up and stepped away.

I walked outside the dining room, folded space to save time, and reached for the door leading to the galactic bazaar. It swung open revealing a terminally cute creature. He was just under four feet tall, with sandy fur, a fluffy tail, and the jeweled apron of a Merchant. He stood on his hind legs, holding his paw hands in front of him. He twitched his lynx ears, making the two golden hoops in his left ear clink, opened his blue eyes wide, and held out his arms.

"Dina!"

"Nuan Couki!" I bent down and hugged him. It was like squishing the world's fluffiest fox.

"So formal," he said.

"Well, I can't call you Cookie now. You have two hoops in your ear."

Cookie's rise through the ranks of the Nuan Clan was nothing short of meteoric.

"You can always call me Cookie," he said. "I like it."

"What can I do for you?"

Cookie narrowed his eyes into sly slits. "I have not seen you for so long. I miss my dear friends. I have come to spend time with you."

"So Clan Nuan wants to expand its business to the Seven Star Dominion."

Cookie's eyes widened in shock. He clasped his hands to his furry chest. "How could we possibly, even if we wanted to? That's Clan Sai territory. I am simply here on vacation. I work too hard. So hard."

I leaned toward him and kept my voice low. "You're turning into your uncle."

He tapped his nose with one clawed finger. "You flatter me so. It's no wonder I want to come and stay with you."

I almost died of cuteness. That's why other species underestimated the lees. They knew they were adorable, and they made the most of it. But no matter how cuddly Cookie looked, inside his furry chest beat a ruthless heart. Their species were assassins and poisoners, and when it suited their interests, they killed with unparalleled viciousness.

"No harm can come to the Sovereign. If any unfortunate incident occurs, not even the bonds of friendship would save the guilty party. I mean it. If the Sovereign comes to any harm, I will lose my inn."

Cookie's face turned solemn. "I swear to you on my Grandmother's heart that Clan Nuan will not harm the Sovereign."

It was the strongest oath a Merchant could make. They revered their elderly and prayed to their ancestors.

The rules of hospitality dictated that I accept any guest that had not been banned. Furthermore, Clan Nuan and our family were bound by more than business. My sister was engaged to

Arland, the Marshall of House Krahr. She and Helen, my niece, were now on the planet belonging to House Krahr, and a few months ago, during an attempted invasion, Helen had been poisoned. She lived because Nuan Cee gave her the antidote. Our family owed Clan Nuan a debt we could never hope to repay. Although I was sure that sooner or later Clan Nuan would put a price tag on it.

"Gertrude Hunt welcomes you, Honored Merchant."

I bowed my head and invited him in with a sweep of my hand.

"We have been invited!" Cookie called out.

A pack of lees came running around the corner. They came in all shapes and sizes, decorated with veils, carrying things, and pushing a massive antigravity cart loaded to the brim with chests and bundles. One, two, three...seven, not including Cookie.

The lees danced about me, waving their paws.

"Greeting, Honored Innkeeper!"

"You smell like delicious duck, Honored Innkeeper!"

"Thank you for having us!"

Cookie grinned at me.

Well, I suppose that was to be expected. Cookie had moved up in the world, and in Merchant Clans promotions came with bigger budgets and larger staff.

I widened the entrance and pulled the Merchant Rooms I had made for the summit out of storage.

———

"It all started in childhood, you see." Gaston sipped his wine.

We were back in the Ocean Dining Room at the same table in the same seats, with the addition of Cookie, who was treated to his own serving of the "delicious duck." His posse was settling in their rooms and would come to dine later. Like all Merchants, Cookie loved gossip, and Arbitrator gossip was simply too delicious to ignore.

"All of us come from the world where the division between nobility and commoners is very stark. George and Jack are brothers born into a commoner family. They lost their parents when they were young, and they were raised by their older sister, Rose. The three of them tasted true poverty, the kind when you know the exact balance in your bank account down to a dollar and can tell exactly how much change is in your pocket without checking."

That was not something I had ever experienced. My parents' inn was prosperous, and while Gertrude Hunt and I had seen some lean times, we were never truly poor.

"Rose eventually married a man from a noble family, handsome, rich, and very stable, and the two brothers acquired a new and illustrious last name, Camarine. George and Jack received an education appropriate to someone of their new status. Their personalities are very different, but as brothers they share certain traits and being a chameleon is one of them. They adjusted to their new roles perfectly. Unless you knew their history, you would never suspect that those two are anything but noble princes, one elegant and beautiful, and the other fashionably jaded and rebellious. This is important."

Cookie blinked. "Fascinating."

He was clearly committing every drop of information to memory.

"Sophie was born into an aristocratic family. Her grandfather was a noble of a rival country who was exiled to the Mire, this horrible swamp, which I love."

Sean frowned. "You love the swamp?"

"It's home. You should see it when the moon slips from the clouds on a quiet night. The night flowers glow, the poisonous worms fluoresce in every color, and the giant alligator-like reptiles sing to the sky. It is peaceful."

"You are a strange man," Sean told him.

"I'm only ¾ man," Gaston corrected. "But I digress. Sophie is actually my cousin, once removed. Her aunt is my grandmother, which doesn't seem right since I'm older than Sophie, but it is true."

"That's nothing," Cookie said. "I'm my uncle's thrice-removed cousin's seventh son."

Gaston nodded in appreciation. "Family ties are important. We come from a very large family, land-rich, money-poor. The Mire is not a nice place. There was an incident when Sophie was young. She was kidnapped by slavers and put in a hole for a week. In Sophie's head, a little girl went into the hole and a monster came out."

I had no idea. When we met, I could sense there was something there, something dark and painful, but I didn't imagine that.

"The thing is, Sophie's grandfather did his best to raise her and her sister as nobles. They had the education, and they knew the legacy of their family, yet they also understood that they would be stuck rotting in the Mire forever. It had all the makings of one of those potent tragedies. But!"

Gaston waved his glass with a flourish.

"There was a matter of international intrigue. People were murdered, disasters occurred, righteous punishments were delivered through feats of personal heroism. The end result of all this complicated mess was our entire family relocating out of the Mire. Sophie's sister married Declan Camarine's best friend, and Sophie and George were introduced."

"The swamp monstress and the elegant prince," Cookie said.

Gaston grinned. "Indeed. Not falling in love would've violated a fundamental law of existence. Cue decades of angst."

He raised his hand to his forehead in an obviously feminine gesture. "Oh no, I am a damaged killer with trust issues. I do not deserve happiness."

He slapped his hand over his left eye, his expression dark and tortured. "Oh no, I am a necromancer who must manipulate everyone to keep them safe due to childhood trauma, and the woman I love, whom I most want to keep safe, will not permit me to take care of her."

Cookie snickered.

"Incredibly frustrating for everyone involved," Gaston said. "George refused to make the first move in consideration of Sophie's feelings. He wanted it to be her decision. And she, in turn, wanted him to throw himself at her feet and walk away from his professional obligations of playing chess with real rulers and empires as his pawns. They got nowhere."

This was like some cheesy romance novel, except I knew the people involved.

"I had given up on them," Gaston confessed. "And then George became an Arbitrator and dragged the lot of us with him. I have read this wonderful book, called *The Three Musketeers*. It was just like that, except we were missing our D'Artagnan. I believe you were there when George enticed her to return to the pack."

"I was," I confirmed. "It was something. He gave a very passionate speech."

Gaston smiled. "He's excellent at that. I don't know what he said but it worked. However, once Sophie joined us, she realized that nothing had changed. George was still assuming responsibility for everyone and everything, still working himself to the bone, and still manipulating people and beings, except now, he was doing it on a galactic scale. Our little band of misfits had graduated to the big leagues. Sophie left us. Again."

"She did?" I had no idea.

Gaston nodded. "Crushed George's heart. I didn't think he would recover but somehow, he did and threw himself into his work, the way he always does. The story would have ended right there if it wasn't for Ruk Minoody."

"I thought somebody killed him," Sean said.

"Don't ruin the story." Gaston refilled his glass. "Ruk Minoody ruled over a prosperous planet in the central bulge of the galaxy.

The planet's citizens place great value on martial prowess, especially when it comes to settling personal conflicts."

"The planet of swordsmen!" Cookie exclaimed. "I know about them. Uncle once did business with them."

I knew about them too. Their planet was called Harriblex, and they were not all swordsmen, although all of them were martial artists of some discipline. They were excruciatingly polite when they stayed at the inns until someone mortally offended them by stepping on their shadow or some such nonsense and then nothing would stop them from demanding satisfaction.

"The Office of Arbitrators had offended Ruk Minoody," Gaston said.

"Let me guess, he demanded satisfaction?" I asked.

"Exactly. They tried to reason with him. They failed. He sent hit squads to hunt down individual Arbitrators and managed to kill a couple. The Office declared that whoever satisfied Ruk Minoody would be entitled to a single boon."

"Oooh." Cookie opened his eyes wide and put his ears back.

"Exactly," Gaston said. "The line to satisfy Ruk Minoody was long enough to wrap around a planet, figuratively speaking, of course. He loved it. While he kept killing them one by one, Sophie infiltrated his knights, got herself promoted to his personal guard, and challenged him for the throne in front of his entire court."

Gaston paused and sipped his wine slowly, milking the moment for all its drama.

Cookie bounced up and down in his seat. "And then what?"

"She won. They made her their queen."

I had a feeling I knew where this was going and, judging by the grin on Sean's face, he did too.

"The Office owed her a favor, and she claimed it. They asked her what she wanted, and she said she wanted George."

Sean laughed.

Gaston's eyes sparkled. "Sophie finally decided to stop trying to live up to other people's expectations. She knew where her happiness lay so she reached out and grabbed it. She had asked George's consent before demanding this arrangement."

"And he consented?" Sean asked.

"Enthusiastically. The Office didn't want to give George up. He is brilliant and he's a born workaholic. They bargained back and forth for a month. Threats were made. Things such as 'You offended Ruk Minoody, here's his head, honor the bargain, or I will get offended' were said. Finally, they came to an agreement. George is allowed to work four months out of the year."

"Consecutive months?" Cookie asked.

"Not necessarily. He can do it in chunks, but the total duration cannot exceed four months. The rest of the time he has to attend to his duties as the royal consort. Sophie must approve every job he takes as an Arbitrator or he can't take it."

"Oh, sweet cosmos," I murmured. "And he's okay with it?"

"He loves it," Gaston said. "She conquered a planet to marry him. It was the proof he always hoped for, and now he can be with her all the time. George is his own worst enemy. The man doesn't know the meaning of work/life balance. Now he is devoting all his energy to the person he loves most, and he is taking his consort duties seriously, the way he takes everything. Before I left, Sophie was presiding over a court case. George was reading a book on child rearing next to her. The defendant, one of their better fighters, challenged him. George put down the book, killed this veteran in two seconds, and went right back to reading. He is an excellent duelist, you know."

Sean shook his head. I knew what he was thinking. That kind of arrangement would never work for us.

"They were married in a ridiculously lavish ceremony about six months ago," Gaston continued. "They've dealt with the initial unrest, and now they're trying to nudge the planet toward democracy, which the planet is fiercely resisting. It will have to be a slow, gradual change, and they will be busy for years. Most importantly, they are happy. They love each other, but for them love alone is not enough. There must be clearly defined boundaries and mutual respect for them. George is a smart man. He knows this is his only chance at happiness, and he will do nothing to jeopardize it. And now you understand why George cannot be here. The last job he did ended a few days ago, and he barely squeaked in under Sophie's deadline."

Now the booster made perfect sense. George had been trying to finish things before his time ran out and he had to go back to his wife.

"Where does that put you and Jack?" Sean asked.

"Jack is on Harriblex somewhere," Gaston answered. "He told me that for the first time in years he doesn't have to worry about George or Sophie. I asked him what he wanted to do with his downtime, and he told me he would get a house in the woods and not see anyone for a couple of years. He claimed it would be the best vacation he could get and that he more than earned it."

"And you?" I asked.

"As they say, somebody must make the doughnuts. I've been a spy, a gentleman of adventure, and an occasional assassin, and now I am a free agent. George is paying me a hefty sum to help you with this affair. Once that's done with, who knows? Perhaps I'll open a shop at Baha-char next to that old werewolf we all are trying to save."

"So you're not here in an official capacity?" I asked.

Gaston put his palm on the table. "Dina, I'm here to assist in any way I can. Your goals are my goals. Your enemies are my enemies. Tell me how I can help, and I will do my best."

He rose and bowed with an elegant flair, his hand sweeping the air. "My dear friends, I am at your service."

[10]

Our last inn-stalment delivered a long awaited Happy Ever After, the criminally fluffy Nuan Cookie and an inkling at the delights Orro is preparing in his new kitchen.

But it's arrival day for our royal bachelor, his retinue, the candidates vying to be his spouse and observers from all the corners of the Universe.

Gertrude Hunt is the place to be, let's head inside once more.

The portal's rim flashed with green lights.

"Here we go," I murmured.

The four of us waited, positioned around the portal, Sean and I directly in front, Gaston on the left, and Tony on the right. Sean and I wore our robes, Tony opted for a plain brown robe as well, and Gaston decided on black boots, black pants, and a black pirate shirt with a black high-tech ballistic vest over it. The vest, which must've been custom made to accommodate his powerful frame, fit him like a glove and did a good job of masquerading as fashionable accessory rather than impact-resistant armor. Tony asked him what his outfit was called, and Gaston told him that if he had to be menacing, there was no reason he couldn't be dashing as well.

A giant snow globe emerged from the portal. Oomboles, as expected according to Miralitt's manifest.

The eight-foot-wide bubble slid forward. It sat on a two-foot-tall ornate base fitted with a communication screen. The base concealed the moving mechanism and the filtration system, while the globe was a flexible hyper-durable membrane containing the precisely calibrated water particular to oombole oceans.

More globes followed the first, each holding a motionless four-foot-long fish. The globes were dark and translucent and the beings within were mere outlines.

We waited.

Oomboles didn't deal well with portals. They always went into short-term sedation during transit, and their globes would attack anyone who approached.

All twenty-one globes completed the transit.

A minute crawled by.

The lights clicked on in all globes simultaneously, turning the membranes transparent and illuminating their passengers. The oomboles came in every color of the rainbow. They were covered with glistening scales, and their round heads with a slight over-bite, big eyes and brightly colored snail-like antennae gave them hilariously comical expressions. The fringe of tentacles that sprouted under their chin and enabled them to wield specialized tools had been withdrawn into their bodies. Their incredible dorsal fins, disproportionally large with pronounced spines, lay flat.

The oomboles opened their eyes. Our gazes met.

All 21 dorsal fins snapped open, vivid with a multitude of colors and flashing with bioluminescent sparks that ran down the spines. The fins went flat, snapped open, flat, open, flat, open. Open, flutter, flat, snap flutter, snap...

The more agitated the oomboles were, the faster they talked

with their fins, and passing through the portal must have discom-
bobulated the oomboles beyond their capacity. It was like being
greeted to a psychedelic display of jazz hands viewed at ten times
the speed. The translation units built into the bases struggled to
transform the rapid chaos of colors and movement into words,
spitting out gibberish onto their screens. The screen belonging to
the globe on the far left crackled and went dark. A small puff of
smoke slipped from its edge.

I raised my hand. A wide length of carefully dyed fabric
segmented by plastic spines snapped open above me, held up by
Gertrude Hunt's tendrils. I went through the folding and snapping sequence, assuring everyone that currents were calm and
free of predators. We would have to rely on the communication
screens for anything more complicated but greeting species in
their own manner tended to calm them. It was a small gesture that
went a long way.

The oomboles quivered, slowing to a somewhat calmer frenzy.

I took them to their suite, which consisted of a constellation of
tanks connected by narrow channels. The largest tank was the
size of an Olympic pool, complete with plants, corals, and custom
lighting. The oomboles entered it, immediately formed a school
around the spouse candidate, a spectacular orange specimen, and
the fins stopped flashing.

The Donkamins were next. I braced myself.

For visually evolved species, sight was crucial. We evaluated
everything, from the suitability of a potential mate to our
offspring's health, by eye. We noted the skin tone, the condition of
the eyes, the sparsity or fullness of hair just so we wouldn't miss
that someone was deathly ill and would be able to avoid them in
time or administer medical treatment. We made millions of
assessments unconsciously during our lives, examining each
other, our pets, and other animals, because fearing a rabid dog
foaming at the mouth saved our lives.

Unfortunately, our perception was flawed. Our eyes had difficulties distinguishing between minor skin ailments, like ringworm, and a plague. Every year hundreds of people thought they saw a monster instead of a mangy coyote. Things that were just different enough often freaked us out, because when our rudimentary biological brain had no frame of reference, it interpreted everything as danger just to be on the safe side.

Donkamins tripped every human visual alarm sensor in existence. A relative newcomer to the interstellar scene, they were aggressively trying to expand and grab their own slice of galactic real estate. The first of their species had visited Earth roughly 200 years ago. An innkeeper urban legend said that the first innkeeper who opened the door to them took one look and blurted out, "Don't come in!" which was how they got their nickname.

The light within the portal spun. Twenty-one Donkamins entered the arrival chamber in an orderly procession. They were eight feet tall, hairless, covered with pale pearlescent skin, and unmistakably humanoid, although they were not even mammalian. Their tall, thin bodies stood upright on two appendages that resembled legs. Their shoulders sloped very sharply down, as if their clavicles had been broken, and just kind of dangled there. They had two upper limbs, long and reasonably arm-like, and two hands with seven very bony long fingers without fingernails. Their round heads sat on seemingly human necks.

I glanced at Sean. He had gone still like a statue.

To start with, Donkamins were scantily clad. Their clothes consisted of lengths of gossamer fabric, strategically tied at some odd place they considered aesthetically pleasing. Then came the nipples. They were pink, incredibly human, and arranged in two rows that ran down the Donkamin chests all the way to where a human groin would be. They were not technically nipples, but they definitely looked the part.

The chests themselves appeared to be deformed, as if someone took a giant trilobite shell and stuffed it inside the Donkamin body so the ridges protruded under the skin. Then came the faces. They had large eyes that would've made any barn owl proud. Their nasal openings were shielded by a smaller version of that trilobite shell, and their mouths were very wide and lipless. The effect was at once revolting and horrifying, and it wasn't even the worst part.

I took a step forward. "Greetings, Children of the Silver Star. Gertrude Hunt welcomes you."

The leading Donkamin opened his mouth, a bright red, wet cavity studded with conical teeth. The ridges in his chest slid, elongating, and his neck stretched forward in an arc, covering the eight feet between us until we were eye to eye. His owl eyes stared at me unblinking.

Yep, that was the worst part.

"Greetings, innkeeper," the Donkamin said. "We are pleased."

I led them to their rooms. Technically, it was Sean's turn, but he was still standing still, and I took one for the team.

The Kai were next. Short beings from a high-gravity world, they were covered in a natural armor of bony plates. They had six limbs and strange, snake-like faces with three protruding bottom fangs and pretty pink eyes. They were the first of the nonhumans to have brought a human-like candidate, a lean, beautiful male with silky blue hair, golden skin, and pink-colored irises. Clearly some genetic fiddling had taken place. The candidate's name was Prysen Ol, and he spoke all three languages of the Dominion flawlessly.

Strictly speaking, a human-like candidate wasn't required for spousal selection. Only the potential genetic compatibility mattered, and the economic and diplomatic benefits the union would bring. However, having a human-like spouse helped, something the oomboles and Donkamins had yet to figure out.

The Kai were a very formal species. They inquired about my health, Sean's health, the health of our respective parents and siblings, and informed us about their health and their relatives' medical issues. Sean barely had a chance to settle them into their quarters and get back in time.

The Dushegubs were next.

The portal swirled with light. A mass of dark tree roots slithered out of it.

I tapped my broom.

A gaping hole yawned in front of the portal. Two thick branches shot out of the ceiling, grasped the wriggling root ball and yanked it out of the swirling light and down into the hole. Tree limbs, trunks, and foliage plunged into the gap and the floor reformed itself. The Dushegubs were safely in their underground pit.

A lone human walked out of the portal. She was statuesque and very pale, with long golden hair that fell in ringlets around her shoulders, and big violet eyes. An elegant gown sheathed her frame, showcasing all the right things.

On the edge of my vision, Gaston raised his eyebrows.

"Greetings, candidate Unessa," Sean said. "Your delegation is already in their quarters. I will show you to your room."

She gave him a soft smile, the two of them went off, her high heels clicking softly on the floor.

"Trust is a wonderful thing," Tony said when they were out of ear shot.

I nodded. "It is. Since she is the Dushegub candidate, she will eventually try something, and he can neutralize her faster than me."

The portal flashed again. So soon?

Two beings emerged from the churning light. The one on the left was an otrokar, and a familiar one at that. Tall and lean, he held himself with the ease of a predator in a familiar territory. His skin was deep bronze, his hair dark, coarse, and short, and when it caught the light, it shone with vivid red. He surveyed the scene with sharp eyes, startlingly light green against his sun-scorched skin.

The last time I saw him, he had worn the full armor of the Hope Crushing Horde, a combination of braided leather and chitinous bony plates embedded with complex circuitry. Today he'd traded it for a lighter spacer armor woven of ballistic material that looked like leather but shielded like reinforced steel. A belt with pockets hugged his waist, supporting an array of wooden and bone charms dangling from it. A golden medallion, a sharp-rayed sun studded with jewels, hung from a leather cord around his neck, identifying him as the emissary of the Khan.

Now it made sense. These were the observers. Miralitt did say that they would pop through in batches between the formal delegations. One of the delegations was from a Southern otrokar clan. The Khan and Khanum were both Northerners and there were always tensions between North and South within the Horde. They had sent their son to see what happens.

Envoy or not, his knife was still with him, a long slender blade riding in a sheath on his thigh. He was deadly with it. Sean would just love this.

The other being was clearly a vampire. Vampire knights lived in their syn-armor, removing it only for the most private moments in the safety of their rooms, and she wore hers like a challenge. It was in excellent condition, so black it swallowed the light, and her long red cloak took it over the edge right into drama. She carried a blood sword in a sheath on her hip. A mane of brown hair dripped over her shoulders, inconveniently obscuring the house crest on her chest. Her face was beautiful and familiar somehow, although I was sure I had never seen her before.

The otrokar and the vampire stared at each other, and I saw the precise moment they both realized that whoever spoke first would get greeted first. The Horde and the Holy Anocracy were at peace, but their rivalry was alive and well. They opened their mouths at the same time.

"Greetings, honored guests!" I said before they decided to get offended and start a brawl.

The otrokar got there half a second earlier. "Winter sun to you. So good to see you again, Dina."

The vampire knight clamped her mouth shut. He shot her a triumphant glance.

Yes, we have met before and know each other. No need to rub it in.

"Winter sun to you also, Under-Khan Dagorkun. How are your mother and father?"

"The Khan and Khanum are well," Dagorkun told me. "My mother recalls you fondly and has tasked me with delivering this tea to you." He produced a small ornate box.

"I'm deeply honored." I bowed my head and let a tendril rise out of the floor and swipe the box from his hands.

The vampire knight rolled her eyes.

I turned to her. "Greetings…"

"No need for formalities," the vampire knight said. "My name is Alvina, Lady Renadra, Commander of the Krahr Vanguard, Daughter of Soren and Alamide."

Lord Soren? Oh. Oh!

"You may call me Karat," she said, hammering every word in like it was a nail in Dagorkun's coffin. "I am Arland's cousin. His favorite cousin. And I am your sister's best friend."

She pulled a small packet from the inside of her cloak. "Lady Helen sent these treats for the feline creature. She also sent you a hug and a kiss, but you will have to imagine it. I do not go around kissing random humans."

Karat tossed her hair back and triumphantly strode toward me, leaving Dagorkun behind.

———

THE THRONE ROOM WAS FULL. THE GUESTS MURMURED TO EACH other in a dozen languages and traded dirty looks. Gertrude Hunt was on high alert, ready to snatch anyone who stepped out of line.

If I were to draw the Throne Room, it would look like a narrow rectangle. At the top of the rectangle was the massive door through which everyone had entered. Sean stood by it, wearing his innkeeper robe and holding his spear. At the bottom of the rectangle was the throne platform, where I now waited.

Large screens ran along the perimeter of the room, placed where the walls met the ceiling and tilted toward the audience. A swarm of small mobile cameras, ranging in size between a walnut and a plum, zipped above the crowd. The event would be broadcast across the Dominion. The Sovereign's PR chief had installed a tight beam transmitter that actually shot the data from the inn through the portal to the Dominion to avoid any delay. I had no idea that kind of technology even existed. The cost had to be staggering.

The Dominion's etiquette dictated that nobody could sit higher than the Sovereign. We solved that problem by raising the throne platform to six feet high and making two seating galleries, one on each side of it. I filled the galleries with cushy ornate seats arranged in three rows, packed the observers into the gallery on my right, and stationed Gaston there to keep things calm.

I spared the Observer Gallery a glance. Karat and Dagorkun sat in the front row, with Cookie between them. They left a seat open for Caldenia on Karat's left. Her Grace was taking her time. I wished she would hurry up.

The gallery on my left remained empty. It was reserved for the Holy Ecclesiarch and his retinue and the Sovereign's attendants, except for Resven and Miralitt, who had their own designated places.

I looked across the room, searching for Sean. He was still at his post by the far wall. Between us, the 12 delegations waited. We had arranged them in two columns, 6 delegations per column, each group segregated from others by a short decorative wall. We put the four most volatile delegations in the first and last row, so both Sean and I could keep a close eye on them, and sandwiched the less troublesome delegates between them.

The row directly in front of me held the otrokars and House Meer.

The otrokar delegation was on my right, decked out in traditional otrokar green and Southern red. Otrokars biologically adjusted their bodies for their chosen role starting at puberty. For example, Dagorkun was a general and a strategist. He had aimed for versatility and a balance between speed, strength, size, and durability. The majority of the otrokar diplomats were strategists as well. One would expect most of the members of the otrokar delegation to look like Dagorkun. Only two of them did.

Of the 20 otrokar delegates, excluding the candidate, 6 were over 7 feet tall, with huge shoulders and massive chests, the bruisers who would charge into the fight first, smashing through the enemy's vanguard. Another 6 were lean and fast, likely swordsmen or other close quarters combatants, ready to become a coordinated whirlwind of steel, capable of precise and rapid carnage. Of the remaining 8, 3 were likely marksmen, 2 were medics marked by long green sashes, 2 looked like Dagorkun, and the last otrokar was a shaman in a ceremonial kilt, with an exposed torso, a mane of ruby hair so dark it was almost black, and a dozen thin leather cords and chains dangling with charms and pouches wrapped around his waist.

This wasn't a diplomatic party; this was a Southern otrokar warband. Even the two strategists looked battle ready. Their candidate, a tall, powerfully built warrior, might have lacked the bruisers' bulk, but he would snap any adult human male in half like a twig. He moved like a leopard, every rippling muscle perfect, and the way he glared at Dagorkun didn't bode well.

The Holy Anocracy delegation on my left didn't look any less menacing. The vampire society consisted of Houses, some large, some small, each with their own military force and territory. This delegation came from House Meer, an aggressive, formidable House with far-reaching ambitions.

House Meer and House Krahr, into which my sister was going to marry, were on the verge of becoming sworn enemies. Over the last few years House Krahr had grown in power, and House Meer was trying to keep them in check. During the Nexus peace summit, House Meer sent three knights to torpedo the peace talks, and Sean, in his role as Turan Adin, killed them in about two seconds, scaring the hell out of everyone. Very few people knew about Sean's alter ego, so I didn't worry about him being recognized, but the possibility did occur to me.

House Meer was not a fan of humans, inns, or me. The twenty of them loomed in their syn-armor like a solid block of darkness. Their candidate, a statuesque female knight with platinum blonde hair and the remarkably even skin tone particular to vampires, was sneering so much, her face was in danger of becoming stuck like that.

The fewer opportunities we gave House Meer and the otrokars, the better, which was why we put the Kai and oomboles in the second row as a barrier between them and everyone else.

The third row featured the two delegations from opposite ends of the Seven Star Dominion. They were the most likely to mind their manners, simply because they were representing the Dominion, but like all Dominion diplomats, they were also prone to murder, which was why we put the Temple of Desire and Donkamins in the fourth row to throw everyone off balance. Gaston referred to this strategy as eye candy and eye scary, and it seemed to be working.

The Temple of Desire was missing its candidate. According to their representative, Lady Wexyn Dion-Dian was indisposed after the transit and would join us shortly. I had glimpsed her only briefly. She rode in on an antigravity palanquin, hidden behind translucent curtains, a full fifteen minutes ahead of her scheduled time, and I passed her procession in the hallway as Sean led them to their quarters. Her attendants, both male and female, were also shrouded in shimmering diaphanous fabric that moved in the slightest breeze, delicately hinting that under all those gossamer-thin layers lay sexy bodies and amazing beauty. The Temple had elevated the skill of suggestion to a fine art.

The fifth row, behind the Temple and Donkamins, contained the feline Higgra and the elegant Gaheas, humanoid, with skin the color of amber and very long dark violet hair that reached to their knees. Of all the delegations, the Gaheas were the most striking. They looked breathtakingly beautiful, moved like flowing water, and spoke in melodious voices. They had also perfected psionic warfare and could melt a sapient mind with a focused thought. The bejeweled tiaras on their heads weren't there for decoration.

The last row held more troublemakers. Murder Beaks were on the right, closest to Sean. Avian, flightless, and armed with huge beaks and powerful clawed feet, this species would've given Earth's prehistoric Terror Birds a run for their money. They had a strong prey drive and killed for sport. Their name for themselves translated as Murder Beaks, and they insisted on the literal translation so the entire galaxy would know of their predatory awesomeness. Fortunately, they had tried to invade the Gaheas, who were their immediate neighbors in space. The Murder Beaks knew exactly what a focused mind wave could do to their brains. They minded their beaks and talons.

Finally, across from the Murder Beaks, the Dushegubs were a dark tangle of roots and limbs, shrouded in foliage, as if some nightmarish forest had magically sprouted in the corner of the room. They had large begonia-looking leaves, purple at the edges and brilliant blue in the middle, splattered with random patterns of the brightest Pepto-Bismol pink. Sean was standing across from them, and Tony had parked himself on the side, just in case they wanted to try anything. The gorgeous woman who was their candidate perched on a large Dushegub root like some dryad.

It was a lot. The variety was dazzling and confusing, but mostly very dangerous and anxiety-inducing.

The wall behind Sean parted, forming a tunnel. What was he doing?

Oh.

A huge lupine shape emerged from the tunnel and sat on his haunches by Sean. Sean lowered his hand. Gorvar sniffed his fingers and rubbed his shaggy cheek against Sean's hand.

At my feet, Beast let out a quiet growl, just in case the oversized wolf decided to run across the ballroom and attack me.

A low trumpet sounded. Gaston cleared his throat, his voice amplified by a microphone and spilling from the hidden speakers. We needed a Master of Ceremonies, and he had enthusiastically volunteered.

"Her Grace, Caldenia ka ret Magren," Gaston announced in a deep resonant voice. His High Galactic was excellent even without the translator. "*Letere Olivione, Dystim Adrolo,* She Who Controls Fate, the Light of the Midnight Sun."

Caldenia walked into the room. She wore a magnificent formal gown, deep green accented with silver. An emerald tiara crowned her spectacular updo. Her makeup was flawless.

The ballroom went silent as a tomb.

Her Grace had taken three steps forward when her eyes finally registered the glowing symbols of the Dominion on the arched ceiling above the throne. For a fraction of a second, Caldenia froze. It lasted a mere heartbeat, and I committed it to memory, because it would likely be the first and last time I saw Her Grace lose it.

Our stares connected. *I tried to warn you.*

The miniscule moment of shock ended. She glided forward, a calm smile on her face.

Gaston moved away from the Observer Gallery on an intercepting course, approached Caldenia, and offered her a graceful bow. She gave him a smile and rested her fingers on his forearm.

Gaston murmured something to her. Her eyes sparkled and she quipped something back.

What are you doing? Take her to her seat, quickly. We've talked about this.

The conversations resumed but at a markedly lower volume. Nobody had any idea what would happen next, us included. Sean and I had been given assurances, but no guarantees. I would protect Caldenia at all costs.

The trumpets blew a triumphant note. A man appeared at the entrance. His elegant white robe hugged his tall, muscular frame, its intricate embroidery luminescing subtly with pale gold. His skin was the darkest shade of black, with a shocking blue undertone as if someone had carved him out of onyx and dusted his cheekbones with sapphire powder. His hair, cut down to near stubble, was shaped with almost microscopic precision, and it shone with white, like swirls of the first frost on a window. His face was intelligent and long, his dark eyes bottomless, and when he strode into the room, there was no doubt that it and everything within it was his to command.

Caldenia froze again, her eyes wide.

"His Supremacy, Kosandion ka ret Maggran," Gaston announced next to her. "*Letero Kolivion, Dystim Arbiento,* Sovereign of the Seven Star Dominion, He Who Is Immune to Fate, the Light of the Morning Sun."

Caldenia's fingers on Gaston's forearm trembled. I had so wanted to spare her this, but she'd made it impossible.

Kosandion reached Caldenia. You could hear a pin drop.

"My dear aunt," the Sovereign intoned, his voice a clear baritone that carried though the entire room unaided. "I haven't seen you since you murdered my father. It's been too long."

Caldenia's face snapped into a mask. "Greetings, dear nephew. You look well. The throne agrees with you."

Kosandion nodded and ascended the twelve steps to his throne. Resven assumed his position by the throne and Miralitt parked herself to the right of the staircase.

Gaston gently steered Caldenia to her seat.

The Sovereign sat upon his throne. The glowing symbols of the Dominion above him pulsed with golden light and settled back into their light blue.

"I trust everyone has rested," Kosandion said, his tone announcing that he didn't require an answer. "Good. Let us begin."

[11]

Kosandion, the Sovereign of the Seven Star Dominion, arrived at the inn to begin the selection of his future spouse. He is assisted by Resven, his chancellor, and Miralitt, the head of his security. 12 spousal candidates made it through to this final selection. Now they have to introduce themselves to remind everyone who they are and what they stand for.

Kosandion was an excellent orator. His diction was perfect, his voice modulated to carry through the space without sounding harsh but conveying just the right amount of gravitas to underscore the importance of every word.

"We all know why we are here, but I shall reiterate for the record."

For Earth politicians, popularity was a major factor, but it wasn't everything. Plenty of people took office based on the strength of their personality or tough stance on a particular issue. Some of the politicians were nearly universally disliked but continued to be reelected for complex reasons. For the Dominion, a ruler's likability was vital. Kosandion knew that fact better than anyone. He had beckoned me over once he took the throne, and I stood only a couple of feet away. From this distance, the force of his magnetic personality was almost too much.

"We have gathered in this hall today to select my future spouse. After a long and careful consideration, twelve candidates have made the final cut. The parent of my future offspring is among you."

In the attendant gallery, the Holy Ecclesiarch was nodding sagely. Elderly, with the skin the color of old parchment and an elaborate headdress on his bald head, the spiritual leader of the Dominion seemed too slight for his luxurious vestments. He wore a silky white robe with an overdress embroidered with metallic brass-colored thread. A short, carefully draped cape covered his shoulders, reaching to mid chest, its deep neckline revealing a tall asymmetric collar. A rectangular jeweled medallion hung from his neck, indicating his holy status.

He looked ready to keel over, and I was watching him for any sign of fainting. He was led in by his acolytes shortly after Kosandion's arrival, and it had taken him a long time to cross the ballroom to the throne. At some point Kosandion became concerned and went down the stairs to escort him. I had suggested that we make the Ecclesiarch more comfortable in custom quarters from where he could watch the proceedings, but he had patted my hand and told me that this was the last duty he could do for the Sovereign, and he had never been one to abandon his responsibilities.

"Bringing a child into this universe is a grave and sacred task. A parent's obligation is far deeper than a simple contribution of genetic material. One must guide, educate, and love one's offspring, putting their needs above one's own. That is why the candidate who will become my spouse will be required to reside within the Dominion for a period of no less than twenty-five Dominion years. In recognition of this significant commitment, the Dominion will honor one request from the spouse or their sponsors."

And that was the deal in a nutshell. Prior to entering the spouse selection, each delegation was required to list a minor and a major ask. If they made it to the finale, the Dominion would honor their minor asks, but only one delegation would ever be granted their major request. It was the grand prize. The whole process provided the Dominion with an opportunity to negotiate some deals they wouldn't have been able to make otherwise. Some delegations made it to the finale for purely political reasons that had nothing to do with the qualities of their candidate.

A movement in the far end of the room drew my eye. The Dushegubs were getting a bit more agitated. Sean was openly watching them. Both he and Gorvar stared at the dark forest with identical expressions, like they wanted something to bite.

Looking around the room, it was clear which candidates thought they had a chance of winning. Most of the humanoids had taken care to match the Dominion's aesthetic: structured garments in tasteful shades, a lot of white, a lot of delicate embroidery. The otrokars were the exception, and the vampire candidate was in her syn-armor, but she had taken the time to add a cream cloak and to decorate her hair with big white flowers.

"Let us remind those who are watching of every being's origin and allegiance," the Sovereign declared. "We shall begin our introductions in a random order chosen by our host."

That was my cue. I tapped my broom. Sections of the floor under the delegations lit up, the pale glow bouncing from group to group until it stopped under the Gaheas. It wasn't really random, but nobody needed to know that.

A graceful Gaheas glided forward into the open space between the two rows of participants. He wasn't lean, he was lithe, with long limbs, perfect amber skin, and a face that was androgynous in its delicate beauty. He wore a stylized scale mail, a deep burgundy accented with white, more of a ceremonial garment than battle-ready armor.

"My name is Nycati of Gaheas. Should I be chosen, I shall

teach our offspring the beauty of the arts so their soul can reach harmony with the universe."

I bounced the light again and stopped it under the Kai. Prysen Ol moved forward. A full foot shorter than Nycati, he wore a pale blue robe with wide sleeves. It was cinched at his waist with a sash. His long blue hair streamed down his back. The Gaheas was a tough act to follow, but Prysen Ol held himself with quiet, calm dignity.

"My name is Prysen Ol. I represent the Kai. Should I be chosen, I shall love our child and share with them the teachings of ancient masters, the logicians and philosophers, so our offspring will seek understanding and harmony in all things."

Clearly, harmony was the theme. They must've been given talking points.

I moved the light around and let it pause under the Dushegubs. Their candidate hopped off the root on which she had been perching and strolled into the open, rolling her hips. Her dress, a slight flowing gown, seemed to be held up purely by the fullness of her breasts.

The Dushegubs, subtle like bulldozers. Humanoids like sex. Here's sex, now give us everything we want.

The woman tossed her hair back. The Dushegubs' roots stopped undulating. The killer trees held completely still, waiting to see if the prey took the pretty bait.

"I am Unessa of… *Creeeeak hisss hisss creeeeak knock.*"

And that's why we called them Dushegubs.

"Should I be chosen, I shall commit fully to ensuring our children will be conceived in love and care…"

Aha, and?

"… and I shall raise them to smother their enemies before they have a chance to root."

There it is.

"And harmony," Unessa concluded triumphantly.

"A harmonious smothering," Kosandion murmured under his breath. "Of course."

I tossed the light again. Let's see… It had to be the Horde or the Anocracy. If I waited too long, they would get offended.

My magic let me know there was movement in the Temple's quarters. I opened their doors and stopped the light under House Meer.

Lady Wexyn exited her quarters and was moving toward us at top speed. Sean glanced at me. His voice whispered in my ear through a tiny earbud.

"Do you want me to bar the door?"

"Nope."

Sean grinned.

The vampire candidate rearranged her face into a milder version of a sneer. "I am Bestata of House Meer."

Everyone was sticking to the brief and keeping the introductions simple. Normally she would've rattled off a list of titles and battle honors that was a mile long.

"Should I be chosen, I will raise our child in the finest tradition of my House. I shall make our child strong, powerful, decisive, skilled in the battle arts—"

The doors burst open, and Lady Wexyn appeared in the huge doorway. She was five foot nothing, and all of her was wrapped in a shiny golden gown and decorated with jewelry, as if someone had taken a 5-gallon bucket of precious accessories, tossed it at her, and most of it had stuck.

She wasn't simply curvy, she was voluptuous, with large full breasts, a round firm butt, and a soft tummy. Her naturally pale skin was sun kissed to a glowing tan. Her dark brown hair rode on top of her head in an elaborate ponytail that dripped curled locks onto her shoulders. A massive headdress crowned the front of her head, with the ponytail strategically threaded through it. It looked like a tree made of pure gold, complete with branches dripping with ruby flowers and supporting tiny, bejeweled birds. The whole thing added three feet to her height.

She opened her big dark eyes as wide as they could go and declared in a loud voice, "Your Majesty!!!"

Resven turned green.

Kosandion didn't miss a beat. "Lady Wexyn, what a pleasure to have you with us."

"You didn't wait for me, Your Majesty. Am I late?" She clasped one hand to her ample bosom. A dozen thin bracelets in every precious metal found in the galaxy clinked on her wrist.

"Only a little. Please join us."

"Thank you, Your Majesty!"

She swept into the room, somehow keeping the golden oak upright on her head. Unessa's hip roll was amateur hour. This was a master class. It was hypnotic. There was no way I could ever imitate that sashay. Not only did I not have the hips or joints for it, I didn't have the confidence.

Next to me Kosandion leaned his elbow on the armrest of his throne, rested his chin on his hand, and tried very hard to appear disinterested. At the Observer Gallery, Gaston was blinking rapidly. Tony leaned in a little to watch as she passed, and Sean was staring intently at her back. Hehe.

"Sean, pick your jaw up off the floor," I murmured with a small smile.

"She moves very well."

"I noticed."

"No, not like that. That thing on her head is real gold. Scan it."

I nudged the inn. Lady Wexyn was carrying fifty-two pounds on her head and thirty-five on her body. And she moved like a weightless butterfly. She reached her delegation with a dazzling smile, and they swarmed her in apparent joy. Someone clapped their hands. Someone squeed in a high-pitched voice.

Kosandion gave them another twenty seconds to settle down and turned to Bestata. "Please continue."

She glared at Lady Wexyn and ground out. "Harmony. In battle."

Kosandion nodded, and the vampire knight turned and stomped back to her House.

I moved the light around.

At the Observer Gallery. Caldenia sat very still, watching Lady Wexyn with an almost predatory focus, like an eagle sighting her prey. Karat pretended to look bored. Next to her, Cookie was smiling.

I stopped the white spot under the otrokars. Their candidate strode into the open. He truly was a stunning example of good genes and focused physical training. Perfect, hard muscle corded his large frame. His broad shoulders strained his chitin battle armor.

"I am Surkar, son of Grast and Ulde, Champion of my tribe, Gutripper, Blood Drencher..."

The vampires were rolling their eyes. Dagorkun was too. Clearly, following the directions or reading the room wasn't in Surkar's skill set.

"...Bone Crusher. I am not meek. When I am chosen, I will mold our child into a war machine. They will reap a bloody harvest of their enemies, until all who oppose them cower and tremble, too afraid to cry out."

"Splendid," Kosandion said with a completely straight face. "Thank you, Son of Grast and Ulde. Let us continue."

I flicked the light around to the first Dominion delegation. We still had six groups to go.

———

THE HIGGRA DIDN'T BOTHER WITH A HUMAN, LIKE THE DONKAMINS and oomboles. Their candidate was 3 feet tall at the shoulder, stood on four legs, and was covered with brilliant white fur splattered with flecks of gold and gray. She had an unmistakably feline face with big golden eyes, and fluffy paws hid dexterous fingers and razor-sharp claws. Her gums and tongue were a vivid

111

Prussian blue, her name meant 'cyanide,' and as usual, the Higgra insisted on the literal translations of their names. Cyanide promised to teach her children to observe the world and make sound judgements. In complete harmony, of course.

The Donkamins were next, and I'd confirmed my suspicions. The Donkamins didn't only freak out the Earth-born humans. They freaked out everyone. When their candidate strode into the open to deliver their message of scientific exploration and harmony, every humanoid in the room made valiant efforts to look elsewhere.

One of the Dominion's delegations was next. I'd started calling them Team Smiles and Team Frowns based on their expressions, and this one was the Smile one. Their candidate was an enthusiastic young woman, a typical Dominion citizen - taupe skin, big gray eyes, and soft, dark-gray hair, which she had styled in an asymmetric wave. From her looks alone, she could've been Resven's niece, and she gazed upon Kosandion with worshipful adoration. She mentioned unity and harmony twice in four sentences.

The Murder Beaks were next. Their candidate was a remarkably handsome stocky man with lemon yellow skin and brilliant green eyes. His wavy brown hair was sideswept in an artful curve. His name was Pivor. He smiled a lot, delivered his speech about cooperation between species and harmony, and returned to his place, obviously pleased with a job well done.

Humanoid skin came in many different variations, but there was usually a limit to how brightness of its pigment. Pivor stood out like a dandelion on a green lawn. It had to be the result of a dye, although why he would dye himself was anyone's guess.

The Frowns Dominion delegation presented an unusual candidate. She was tall and muscled like a gymnast, and she moved with a natural grace. Her skin was the deepest indigo verging on cosmos-black, her eyes were the color of coal, and her glossy dark hair, braided into a complex arrangement, rode on her head like a crown. An Uma, same as Kosandion's mother.

Seeing an Uma outside their world was extremely rare.

The Uma had been discovered a thousand years ago by Earth's time by one of the slimier galactic nations. The newcomers arrived bearing gifts and sweet promises, and it took almost twenty years before the Uma realized they were not being helped, they were being colonized. The invaders severely underestimated the Uma spirit. In less than a century, the Uma purged them from their planet and shut their doors to most galactic visitors. The lucky few who had been invited told a story of a beautiful world populated by fierce people.

The candidate, whose name was Ellenda, glared at the gathering. Her speech hit the talking points, but her tone seemed almost defiant. She mentioned progress and harmony and strode back to Team Frown with her head held high.

It was the oombole turn now. Their candidate, a fish that looked like someone had painted it with fire, treated us to a frenzied display of jazz fins, and their translation software was clearly having issues.

"... raised the offspring to seek safety and to swim in a way that doesn't shower those behind them in body fluids."

Right. Don't pee on your fellow citizens.

"Thank you, candidate Oond for this refreshing definition of harmony," Kosandion said. "I believe we have only one candidate left."

Lady Wexyn glided into the open and smiled. There was something so infectious about that smile. It made you want to smile back.

She leaned forward slightly, making the delicate birds on the golden branches of her headpiece tilt. "Do I say it now, Your Majesty?"

"Yes," Kosandion said.

Resven clenched his hands together, probably to keep from slapping one of them over his own face.

"I am Lady Wexyn of the Temple of Desire!" she announced.

We waited. Seconds ticked by.

"Lady Wexyn, would you like to tell us how you would raise our child?" Kosandion prompted.

She smiled wider, her eyes innocent and clear, like a night sky lit up by starlight. "Of course. I will love them most of all, Your Majesty. They would be my favorite."

It took Kosandion another five seconds to realize it was all he was going to get. "Thank you, Lady Wexyn."

She sashayed back to her people who swarmed her with whispered congratulations.

"On that note, we shall conclude the introductions," Kosandion announced. "Tomorrow we shall convene for the first of the final challenges. Rest well."

I glanced at Gaston.

He stepped forward. "We humbly beg you to join us for the evening meal."

I flicked my hand. The Dushegubs fell through the floor into their pit, where they would find six pig carcasses floating in a foot of dark water. We had asked the delegations in advance if they preferred to dine in public or in private. The Dushegubs didn't get a choice.

About half of the delegations chose private dining. The rest we divided between the three dining halls. I ended up in the Ocean Dining Hall, mainly because Kosandion took one look at the balcony facing the sea and determined that this would be his preferred view. Of the other dining halls, one offered a vista of our orchard, where Sean currently had his hands full with the otrokars and the Temple, and the third, overseen by Tony, presented a beautiful view of Saturn.

After this was over, I would have to think of the way to thank Tony. Without him, this whole thing would be a lot harder.

The Sovereign wanted to dine in privacy but still be seen, so I sectioned off a portion of the balcony with a see-through soundproof barrier and keyed it to Resven so a request from him would adjust the barrier's transparency. Besides him, five other groups were in the dining hall: the Holy Ecclesiarch with his party, House Meer, Team Smiles, the Gaheas, and the observers.

Everyone seemed focused on their meal, which was as expected considering who cooked it. I strode between the tables a couple of times to make sure everything was going smoothly and parked myself by the wall.

Team Smiles laughed, their faces and posture relaxed. Their candidate, the one who stared worshipfully at Kosandion during the ceremony, kept sneaking glances at the partition, probably hoping he would look her way. House Meer ate like they were in enemy territory, watching everyone around them. At some point they calmed down enough to talk, which I considered progress. The Gaheas were performing incredible fits of dexterity at their table. They ate with four utensils, holding them two per hand, and they sliced tiny pieces from their food like a team of superstar surgeons.

The Holy Ecclesiarch had barely touched his plate. He was looking a bit mournful.

I drifted over to his table and murmured softly. "Is the food not to your liking, Your Holiness?"

"Your hospitality is beyond reproach," he said.

"But?"

He looked at his plate of lean fish and vegetables arranged with such artistic flair, it should've been photographed for posterity. "It is beautiful. Alas, I have grown older."

The members of the Dominion's most numerous species experienced a diminished sense of taste in the final decade of life. It never went away completely, but for them the flavors became muted. The profiles of their meals grew spicier and bolder to stimulate their tired tastebuds. Any galactic chef knew this, let alone a Red Cleaver one.

"No worries," I told him. "I will be back."

I walked away to the wall, snapped up a transparent sound-proof barrier around myself, and pulled up a screen to the kitchen.

"Orro?"

He appeared on the screen, a looming dark mass of quills. Things must've been hectic.

"What's going on with the Holy Ecclesiarch's food?"

His spikes trembled. "I was given specific dietary requirements due to health restrictions. Mild food only, to avoid 'unnecessary strain' on digestive system." His voice told me exactly what he thought of that.

"His time is coming to an end, and mild food isn't going to make a difference. He has only a few meals left. I will take full responsibility."

Orro clapped his clawed hands together. "Then I will dazzle!"

"Go for it."

I dropped the barrier. Five minutes later Droplet emerged from the kitchen, dashed over to the table, swiped off his plate, deposited a new dish, and withdrew. The new plate held a fish that had been descaled, cooked, and sliced into sections. The sections were reassembled into the original fish shape, and the whole dish was soaked in a rich dark broth. The aroma of spices drifted on the slight breeze. The elderly man took a single bite and smiled at me.

Crisis averted.

I drifted through the dining room again. House Meer was about mid-way through their meal. The Smiles delegation finished the main course and moved on to their customary tea and dessert, which meant they would stay parked for another half an hour. Half of the observers had left. Only Dagorkun, Cookie, Karat, and Tomato remained at the observer table.

116

Tomato hailed from a republic neighboring the Dominion. He was green-furred, large, and a bit bear-like. His translation software had informed him that his name phonetically matched tomatoes, and upon arrival, he assured me that he was not a fruit.

I checked on Caldenia. She was in one of the terminal rooms, accessing the Gertrude Hunt news database. Gaston was with her. His mission for today was to stick to her like glue. I didn't want any surprises.

Karat saw me looking and waved me over. I approached their table.

"Your sister said you would provide all necessary information to me."

Thanks, Maud. "What can I clarify for you?"

She glanced in the direction of the semi opaque partition obscuring Kosandion and his party. "That man doesn't strike me as unintelligent. He knows who he's going to marry. Why is he bothering with this farce?"

The other three observers stared at me with rapt attention.

This would take a bit of time to explain. I glanced around the dining hall. Everything seemed calm. I summoned a chair out of the floor and sat.

"Ratings."

Karat blinked. "Their ratings? He's ranking them?"

"Not him. The entire Dominion. Everything that happens is being recorded and broadcast back throughout their territory. The citizens are watching it and vote in approval or disapproval."

"They vote on the likability of the spouses?" Karat raised her eyebrows. "Why? This shouldn't be a popularity contest. He is their monarch. It's his choice."

Trying to figure out how to explain a concept alien to most species was surprisingly difficult.

"Are you familiar with the Bluebug hivemind?" I asked.

Karat grimaced. "They are a massive pain."

117

"It." Tomato plucked some cherries from his plate with his alarmingly long claws.

"It, they, no matter." Karat shrugged.

"No," Dagorkun said. "That is precisely the matter."

"The Dominion isn't a hivemind," Karat said. "If they were, there would be no need for the broadcast. You would only need one of them here."

"You're right," I said. "They are not hivemind, but they are linked. It's not a telepathic link via intelligence. It's more of a collective empathy."

"I don't follow," Karat said.

I would lean on Sean for this. "Have you fought on Nexus?" I asked.

She nodded.

"There must have been times in battle when your force rallied. When things seemed lost, but you saw a single knight rise to the challenge. An act of bravery, a sacrifice, a display of courage, and suddenly the mood changed and those who had been dejected before became inspired. And then you charged in a single wave and felt..."

"Exuberant," Karat finished.

"Revived," Dagorkun added. "We have a word for it. *Kausur.* Collective courage."

"For the citizens of the Dominion, that feeling extends beyond the battlefield. It's a loose connection but it's always active. Even though there are different species within the Dominion, somehow they all feel a measure of this collective empathy. After a few years, those who emigrate to the Dominion also develop it. There is even a celebration to mark one's ability to sense the collective mood."

"That's horrific." Karat drained her glass. "I do not want to be plugged into anyone's feelings but my own. I don't like people. I don't want to like what they like. I make exceptions for family, but there are times when I can barely tolerate even them."

"Agreed," Dagorkun said. "When I give an order, I don't want to know if they like it or agree. I just need them to do it."

Karat shook her head. "How does their army not disintegrate under the weight of all those feelings? How ever do they fight?"

"Very well," Tomato said. "They're a machine, disciplined and united. Their morale is impossible to break."

"When they decide to resort to violence, it's because an overwhelming majority of them feel it's justified. They are united in their righteousness," I said.

"But they're still individuals," Dagorkun said. "There will be dissent."

"There is, and if the dissent grows too large, those united by it will abandon cause," I said. "The Dominion's civil wars are the bloodiest in the galaxy. It's not a matter of policy or interests. It's all fueled by emotion. Kosandion is a monarch, the executive head of their state. Their policies and laws are enacted by him, but they're dictated by legislative, judicial, and religious branches."

"So what happens if the Sovereign becomes unpopular?" Dagorkun asked.

"At first, it will produce a collective anxiety," I said. "People will become more irritable. You will see the rise in general rudeness, lack of patience, and disproportionately severe reactions to small annoyances. The people of the Dominion will sense the discontent among their peers and will want to disconnect from those feelings, but there's no escape. If the situation is allowed to worsen, the stress-related breakdowns will increase. Conception rates will drop, and miscarriages will occur more often, because the collective unhappiness indicates that now is not a good time to have a child and activates certain biological mechanisms to lower the birth rate. Their collective immunity will falter, making the population vulnerable to plagues. Brawls will break out in the streets, and there will be a sharp uptick in spree killers."

The vampire and the otrokar stared at me. Cookie smiled into his whiskers. He hadn't said a word this entire time. He just listened.

"Eventually, a chunk of the population will snap in self-defense, and someone will murder the Sovereign," I finished.

Tomato nodded. "We've watched it happen. It is the same for the Six Star Supremacy, the Dominion's sister empire."

The first time I had seen the collective empathy of the Dominion in action, I was sixteen years old. I had decided I wanted to go to college, and that morning I went to take my SATs. I had told my family in advance. I scheduled it. I paid for it. Everyone agreed to let me be. It should've been a quiet morning. The inn had about a hundred visitors. Klaus and Michael were off on a fishing trip with Dad. Maud and Mom were at home, holding the fort, and between the two of them, they didn't need my help with anything.

When I finished and turned my phone back on, I had three messages from Mom telling me to get home as soon as I could. I felt so annoyed. My family treated my entire high school adventure like it was a hobby or a fad. Something I did that wouldn't really matter. Meanwhile, in school, every teacher and coach preached college nonstop. You went to college, or you were a loser.

I had studied my ass off for those exams. I didn't even get a good luck or how'd it go?

I got home, sensed my mom in our garden, went there, and when I stepped outside, into my carefully nurtured botanical wonderland, I smelled this terrible bitter smoke. We were hosting a large group from the Dominion and the Six Star Supremacy. They were an extended family traveling on a sightseeing trip to celebrate their reunion. That morning, while I took my exams, they had set their hair and clothes on fire.

I walked through the garden among people smeared with ash, moaning and weeping, some catatonic, rocking back and forth, until I found my mother. Mom could handle any emergency the universe chose to throw at her, but that morning, she stood there, glassy-eyed, unable to stop their suffering.

It was the day Caldenia murdered Kosandion's father.

"Kosandion isn't just trying to score points," I said. "By involving the whole nation in his choice of a spouse, he is letting them feel like they matter. Even if their preferred candidate doesn't make it to the altar, their opinion still counted. They were engaged, they were given a voice, and they were a part of it."

"It goes deeper than that," Caldenia said behind me.

She had been heading our way for a bit now. I wasn't sure if she was looking for me or if she was just hungry. Apparently, she was looking for me.

The observers turned to her.

"Kosandion will choose his spouse, and he will make sure the Dominion feels it is also their choice. They will be loyal to that person because they have chosen them, and when the child is born, they will transfer that loyalty to Kosandion's heir. That child will be beloved and cherished, and the entire Dominion will be invested in their future. That is how dynasties persist and thrive."

Wow.

Caldenia looked at me. "If I could have a word?"

I rose. "Of course, Your Grace."

[12]

When we last left Dina and Sean, the introduction ceremony had finished and everyone enjoyed one of Orro's sumptuous dinners. Dina reminisced on the complete emotional breakdown the Dominion guests experienced at her parents' inn when they learned that Caldenia murdered her brother, Kosandion's father. The dinner ended with Her Grace wanting to have "a word" with Dina. Uh-oh...

"I wish to visit Lady Wexyn."

Not the word I expected. I had separated us by a soundproof partition, so I could still keep an eye on the diners, and I had to keep my expression calm, while Her Grace turned her back on them probably so they couldn't read her lips.

"May I ask why?"

"I wish to have a chat."

Her face told me that the only way to get more would be to honor her request and tag along. Unfortunately, I still had a busy dining hall to babysit.

"One moment."

I checked the other two dining halls. Sean's was still half full, but Tony was done, and he was moving my way. A moment and he came around the corner. I dropped the partition and approached him.

"Would you mind looking after this crowd while I run a quick errand?"

He gave me a smile. "That's what I'm here for."

"Thank you." I turned to Caldenia. "I will take you to Lady Wexyn, Your Grace. She may choose to not see you, and as you know, we guard the privacy of our guests."

"She will see me," Caldenia said.

And that didn't sound ominous. Not at all.

We strolled out of the dining hall and back into the Grand ballroom. The sun was setting, and as we walked, the chamber transitioned from day to night, mimicking the sunset at the Capital. The floor and walls began to darken, steadily gaining a blue tint. Astronomical symbols of the Dominion shifted to sunset-orange. On the left side, where the sky dimmed, a faint edge of the purple moon slipped into view, delicate and pale as if cut from tulle. It would grow solid by the time we came back.

Crossing the Grand Ballroom took some time. We passed into a long hallway interrupted by arched floor to ceiling windows showing a projected view of Texas sunset over the never-ending fields.

"You could simply do that thing you do," Caldenia waved her hand dismissively. "Instead of making us walk all the way."

"But then how would we clear the air, Your Grace?"

Caldenia rolled her eyes.

"Are the decorations to your liking?"

"They're adequate. Barely."

We kept walking. If I had to make this trip longer to accomplish this conversation, I would "do that thing" I did. We would keep walking until both of us said what we had to say.

"You should have told me," Caldenia said.

"I tried."

"You should have tried harder."

Sometimes the best defense is no defense at all. "You're absolutely right, Your Grace. It's my fault. I apologize."

Caldenia glanced at me. If looks could cut, I'd have a big gash right between my eyes.

"Your insincere show of meekness will not pacify me."

"Of course not."

Caldenia stopped.

"Are you tired, Your Grace? Would you like a chair to rest in for a moment?"

"The audacity!"

I simply waited.

"I had no idea you had it in you."

"I didn't. Not always, but I had a very good teacher."

Caldenia glared at me. "Yes, you did. And don't you forget it."

We resumed walking. She knew perfectly well that to tell her about the Sovereign, I would have had to cross the personal boundaries she had put in place. She would pardon me for respecting her wishes, but she would have never forgiven me for trampling on her freedom.

A part of her must've known. The description of the spousal selection had to have sounded familiar, so she must've suspected it and made a conscious or subconscious effort to avoid it. Caldenia was both perceptive and introspective. Her mind was as sharp as her teeth.

"Do you have any idea how much trouble this entire affair will bring?"

"Yes."

"I very much doubt it. You've jumped into the whirlpool, and you're in danger of drowning."

"If I do drown, would you throw me a rope so I can pull myself out, Your Grace?"

She arched her eyebrows. "Do we have that kind of relationship?"

"That's up to you, Your Grace."

I halted. The distant door at the end of the hallway rushed at us and stopped two feet from me.

"If any harm comes to the Sovereign, the Assembly will take my inn. If anything happens to one of the guests on my watch, I may as well surrender the inn, since I wouldn't deserve it."

"Are you threatening me with the loss of my safe haven?" Caldenia's eyes blazed.

"No. You are a guest, Your Grace. My very first one. Your well-being and safety are my first priority. I am simply advising you of facts. I hope that when things become dire, you would give me your guidance as you have in the past. Do you still wish to see Lady Wexyn?"

She tilted her chin up. "Yes."

I knocked on the door. "Her Grace Caldenia ka ret Magren to see Lady Wexyn Dion-Dian."

The door swung open, and a veiled male attendant with dark eyeliner, broad shoulders, and tan muscular arms invited us in with a bow. We followed him inside.

The door opened to the courtyard paved with pale brown stones. A brook wound its way around it, spilling into a wide pond. Beautiful Fortune trees leaned over the blue pond like slender women, dripping their long branches with lemon-yellow leaves into the water. An ornate wooden pavilion perched on the shore, cushioned in Fortune trees and ornamental shrubs. Within the pavilion, Lady Wexyn reclined on a chaise, sipping tea from a flower-shaped cup.

She had traded her spectacular golden tree for a small crown of glittering green jewels that was likely worth millions but seemed modest in comparison. A chocolate-brown, diaphanous skirt hid her legs, secured by a wide sash of lighter russet embroidered with gold. The sash wound around her hips, clasped in place with an elaborate golden brooch showcasing a green gemstone the size of a walnut. A pale, rose gold top wrapped her ample breasts, leaving the soft stomach bare. Another wide translucent sash, this one green, completed the outfit, draping strategically over her shoulders and waist. She was barefoot and a dozen thin bracelets and anklets decorated her wrists and ankles.

She saw Caldenia and rose in one fluid movement, dipping her head. Her dark eyes sparkled. "*Letere Olivione!* You honor me."

"Greetings," Caldenia said, her face radiating menace. Her Grace, joy personified.

Lady Wexyn lowered herself to the chaise. Everything she did was beautiful. She was like a gifted artist who painted with her body instead of a brush.

Attendants appeared, deposited tea and snacks on a side table, and withdrew silently like brightly colored wraiths.

Caldenia scrutinized Lady Wexyn, who sipped her tea and fluttered her eyelashes.

"You look like your mother. Has she spoken of me?"

"Yes, *Letere Olivione.* At length." Lady Wexyn nodded, her expression earnest and devoid of any subtlety.

"Then this will be quicker and simpler. If you interfere with my plans, I will kill every creature within your little Temple and explode the planet on which it perches."

Okay then.

"Oh my goodness!" Lady Wexyn opened her eyes as big as they could go.

Caldenia narrowed hers.

Lady Wexyn gazed back at her, a picture of innocence.

A few moments passed.

"Dina," Caldenia said. "Please leave us."

I looked at her.

"I won't harm her," Caldenia said.

Great. Now if I refused, she would take it as an insult. Caldenia had never broken a promise to me, but there was always the first time.

"Do you wish to allow Her Grace to remain in your quarters?" I asked.

"Yes," Lady Wexyn said. "It is a blessing to be in her presence."

Blessing was one way to put it. "Should you encounter any difficulties, call my name."

"I shall," she promised with a solemn expression.

Why did I get a sense that I was being humored?

The two of them were looking at me. Both guests requested privacy for their conversation. Not much I could do.

"Very well."

I walked away from the pavilion. Whether she liked it or not, Gertrude Hunt was Caldenia's chosen sanctuary. I just had to hope she remembered that.

———

THE PIT OF THE DUSHEGUBS WAS 50 YARDS ACROSS AND 200 YARDS deep. Even if they stood on top of each other, they couldn't climb out. Three feet of murky water enriched with nutrients flooded the edges of the hole's bottom. In the center, a small mud island offered a bit of dry land. Above, a high-powered light source simulated the lavender sun of the Dushegubs' planet, cycling between red in the morning, violet-blue during the day, and a deep purple in the evening.

It was night now, and the light had dimmed to an indigo glow mimicking the native fluorescent clouds. In this diffused light, the Dushegubs were mere shadows, a tangle of roots and branches slithering over each other like black serpents. Luckily for me, Gertrude Hunt had excellent sensors, and the view on my massive screen was crystal clear.

I leaned back in my chair, trying to relax. Everyone else was safely in their quarters for the night. I had locked them all in so nobody could wander. My feet hurt, and my head buzzed a bit, as if a swarm of bees was trying to settle inside my skull after a busy day of flying and collecting honey. Beast napped in her dog bed by the wall. She'd rolled onto her back, and her four paws lay limp, sticking out in the air.

Even my dog was worn out.

Sean slipped into the room and wrapped his arms around me. I leaned my head against his warm muscular forearm.

"Problems?" he asked.

"They should have formed a copse for the night."

Sean glanced at the screen. The Dushegubs were treading water in small groups, three or four trees in each one.

"They're up to something," I told him.

He let me go and stepped aside. My chair grew wider, flowing into a couch. I really enjoyed the extra power the guests brought to the inn. Reshaping furniture on the fly took barely any effort.

He sat next to me and put his arm around my shoulders. I rested my head on his bicep. We watched the wandering Dushegubs. They would slither a few feet, slide their branches and roots against the reinforced walls of the Pit, then slither a little further.

"They're testing it," Sean said.

"Yes, but why? It's concrete layered with space-grade flexi-steel. They'd need a high-powered drill to get through it. What could they be planning?"

"Shenanigans," Sean said in a somber voice.

I turned to look at him. "What?"

"Hijinks, mischief. They're up to no good."

I laughed softly.

"How is Caldenia doing?" he asked.

"She visited Lady Wexyn and promised her that if Lady Wexyn interfered with her plans, she would blow up her planet."

Sean raised his eyebrows. "Plans? What plans?"

"She didn't share that with me."

"That's concerning."

Two of the Dushegub groups came together by the far wall. I adjusted the angle so we could see them from the side.

"Why that wall?" Sean murmured.

"I put a dummy camera on the opposite side. They saw it and now they're trying to shield their plot from view."

"Sly dog, you."

"Thank you."

I snuggled closer to him. I hadn't seen him since dinner. After leaving Caldenia and Lady Wexyn, I headed back to the Ocean dining hall, but the Kai delegation informed me that one of their members had developed a twitch in his middle left limb, which was a matter of grave concern to the entire delegation, so I detoured to their quarters. After an hour of medical scans, it was confirmed that the twitch was a stress response, so I created a sensory respite area in their quarters where they could destress.

After that, Resven wanted to fight with me over the Holy Ecclesiarch's meal, which I shut down flat by presenting him with Orro's resume. A chef of Orro's training and experience had more than enough expertise to make sure his food didn't adversely affect digestion of elderly sislafs. That shut Resven up but didn't endear me to him in the slightest.

After that I received a request from the oomboles who explained to me that the water plants in their habitat failed to provide enough privacy. I doubled the number of plants, but they didn't like their color and felt there was not enough variety, so I sent Gaston out to the Baha-char to get different plants. They were now cycling in the quarantine tank, so I could add them to the habitat tomorrow provided they were free of disease and contaminants.

"How did it go with the otrokars?" I asked.

"Do you remember that cartoon we watched where Thor is an environmentalist?"

"The one where he kept peacefully protesting 'until he was provoked?'"

"That's the one. The otrokars want to be provoked. Very badly."

"Ugh."

We sat in silence for a couple of minutes.

"How likely is she to go after Kosandion?" he asked.

"Caldenia?"

He nodded.

"I don't know. I reminded her that the survival of the inn is at stake. Previously, when there were conflicts involving the inn, she was always a neutral third party. This isn't a neutral matter. It's family and painful memories. Kosandion is a reminder of why she lost everything and now lives in exile."

He frowned.

"What?" I asked.

"Wonder if she's considering going out in a blaze of glory. She's already infamous. Murdering Kosandion would make her a legend."

One of the Dushegubs split. Its thick trunk opened. The other Dushegub thrust roots into it and withdrew a large, industrial drill, the kind used in asteroid mining.

"Huh," Sean said.

"It's probably an old injury. They shoved the drill in there and glued the trunk back together with sap."

"And it didn't show up on weapon scans."

"Apparently not."

The Dushegubs struggled with the drill's controls. It was made for someone with slender digits rather than thick roots.

"If Caldenia wanted to go out in a 'blaze of glory' she's had plenty of opportunities to do so."

Sean shook his head. "But none like this. Killing her nephew, the Sovereign, on Earth, in an inn, live, or almost live on galactic television. It would be even bigger than killing her brother."

"I don't think she'll do it."

"She could though."

"But she won't."

The drill flashed with lights. The Dushegubs flailed their roots.

"Do you trust her that much?"

"I don't trust her. I trust her survival instincts. Sean, this woman ruled over six star systems. She gave it all up to come live at this inn where she drinks Mello Yello and tries to murder tomatoes in her garden with her lack of nurturing skills. She did it because it was the only way to survive. Her will to live is that strong."

"Why did she kill her brother?"

"Nobody knows."

Sean sighed. "And that's the problem. If she gave up six star systems to eliminate her brother, would she give up exile in the inn to eliminate her nephew?"

The Dushegubs planted the drill against the wall and turned it on. Sparks flew.

"I guess we'll find out," I said.

"True. It's not like we have a choice."

The only choice would be to exclude Caldenia completely by confining her to her quarters, and neither of us would do that.

Sean looked at the world a little differently than I did. I kept track of various possibilities, but I was decent at predicting what *would* happen. Sean concentrated on what *could* happen, and there was a vast difference between the two. It made us a good team.

The Dushegub closest to the hole got hit with a spray of sparks and slithered away, hissing up a storm.

"There's one thing that puzzles me," Sean said. "You're Kosandion. Your aunt killed your father and started an interstellar war. You see her, finally, after all this time, and you are civil to her. You are completely unbothered by her presence. Your heart rate doesn't rise, your pupils don't dilate, your breathing stays even. He wasn't pretending. He was cool as a cucumber. Why?"

I spread my arms.

The Dushegubs withdrew the drill and inspected the quarter inch deep hole they'd managed to make. Branches shook, roots slithered, and they put the drill back in.

"Far enough?" I wondered.

"Yeah," Sean agreed.

The leading Dushegub turned the drill on. An electric arc splayed out of the hole, hitting the drill dead center. The drill exploded. The miner Dushegub flew back, smoking, and landed on mud island. The rest of the killer trees chased it and tried to roll it into the water.

Sean smiled.

"People are complicated," I said.

He leaned over and kissed me. "At least these idiots are easy. Come to bed. We have a big day tomorrow."

I smiled at him, and we left for our bedroom.

[13]

What an eventful first day for the spouse competition! Long lost family, first impressions of the spouse candidates, and a flurry of guests keeping the innkeepers on their toes.

Let's take a closer look at the man in the center of it all.

I stood on the balcony in Kosandion's private quarters and watched Resven struggle to contain his irritation at my presence. Being included in a very private discussion of the Dominion's state secrets wasn't in my plans, but Kosandion requested my attendance during the breakfast, and here we were.

I had built the Dominion suite to remind Kosandion of the Palace. The trick wasn't to replicate his home but to nod at it subtly with the right shades and familiar contours. New experiences were an essential part of travelling. I tinted the colors slightly warmer, relaxed the geometric harshness, and threw a few unexpected shapes, like the asymmetric arches. The asymmetry showed in their haircuts and clothes, but a lot of the Dominion architecture was old and incorporating the new trend would give the suite some freshness.

133

My original design didn't incorporate a balcony, but after watching Kosandion contemplate the orange ocean during dinner, I moved his suite to Kolinda's door.

Once an inn's branch reached a new planet and the inn opened a door leading there, it would begin to root through that space, claiming a section of the world. Some rootings were tiny, barely enough for the human-sized door. Others were vast. Kolinda's rooting covered over one square mile. Gertrude Hunt's door opened onto a small island, a chunk of jagged rock that thrust from the depths of the ocean, and the entire island belonged to us.

I had oriented the Ocean Dining Room to the south-west, to take advantage of the sunsets. Kosandion's suite now faced directly south, giving him a beautiful view. I provided him with long balcony rising high above the water and equipped it with an array of patio furniture. He was only a hundred yards from the Ocean Dining Room, but an outcropping of rock hid it from his view, assuring his privacy.

I had installed a carefully calibrated barrier that put an impenetrable invisible wall along the balcony's perimeter. It shifted into a slightly less protective mode when anyone entered the balcony, so Kosandion got the sea breeze and sounds but not the monsters that hunted within the cool orange depths. Gertrude Hunt was swimming in alien beings' energy, like a glutton at a cake contest, and maintaining the barrier resulted in minimal drain.

Kosandion was on the balcony now, sitting in a comfortable chair with a breakfast spread on a patio table before him. The sun had risen above the jagged dark peaks on the horizon. The Sovereign watched the ocean, tracking a massive sea serpent as it slid under the surface, its spines the only warning to its potential prey.

His inner circle arranged themselves around him. Resven rested in a large, padded chair in front of me and to my right. Miralitt sat on my left, one leg over the other, as close to the transparent rail as she could get. Between them, in an identical chair, perched Orata, Kosandion's head of PR, although that was likely an inadequate title considering her duties and their importance. She had come through the portal this morning to deliver the voting results and would go back before the day officially started. Orata was curvy, young, and fashionable, with a purple tint to her medium-toned skin and silver-blue hair, and every time I looked at her, I thought of Prince Lotor from the *Voltron* anime.

In my defense, I had woken up twice last night, one time because the Dushegubs had climbed onto each other trying to escape the Pit and the other because the Murder Beaks had a fight, and I had to treat the injured parties while Sean confined all of them to separate cells within their flock arena. I could've used a couple more hours.

"The ratings are as follows," Orata announced, barely glancing at the holographic screen in front of her. "Behoun is in the lead with ten points over their closest competitor."

Team Smiles, the ones with the enthusiastic female candidate whose name I kept forgetting. They represented Behoun, the fourth planet added to the Dominion.

"The people like Amphie," Resven said. "They like her education and pedigree."

Orata nodded. "Indeed. They especially like her enthusiasm. Key words mentioned most are earnest, relatable, and attractive. She's trending well with parents."

"A nice girl. The kind you take home to meet the family," Kosandion murmured. "A safe choice."

He looked away from the sea serpent and pondered his plate. I wasn't the only one who had noticed his love of the ocean. Orro had outdone himself. I didn't know you could even make a pancake in the shape of an oyster shell and turn an egg into a pearl within it.

"Your breakfast is getting cold, *Letero*," Miralitt murmured.

Kosandion gave his plate a mournful look. "It's almost too pretty to eat."

"You need to keep up your strength." Miralitt held his gaze, making it clear that she wouldn't drop it until he took a bite.

Kosandion picked up a delicate two-tined fork and tried a small piece of the pancake. "Delicious. Continue."

"In second place, Prysen Ol with the Kai," Orata said. "The people view him as intelligent, dignified, and wise. He also trends well with parents. They feel he would be a patient and attentive father. His lowest rankings are in the under-twenty-five demographic. They find him boring."

Kosandion smiled. "Splendid. We should just marry those two to each other in a glorious spectacle of a wedding. Nearly every soul in the Dominion would be thrilled."

Resven sighed. "*Letero*, I implore you to take this seriously."

"I do. Think of the joy it would bring my people. Not to mention the ratings bonanza."

Orata's dark eyes sparkled.

"No," Resven told her.

"You're no fun," Orata murmured.

"We are not here for fun," Resven said. "We're here to choose the parent of an heir and the spouse of the Sovereign. This person will have an impact on our society for decades to come. Please concentrate on the task at hand."

Orata gave him a pointed look. "In third place, Lady Wexyn." She had punctuated *Lady Wexyn* to make sure it sank in.

Resven jerked, startled. "How? Why?"

"The people find her endearing. She's unpredictable and fun to watch. Those are direct quotes."

"That woman is chaos personified. 'Your Majesty'? Your Majesty! How many times have I gone over the proper forms of address? *Letero Kolivion* or Your Supremacy. How hard is it to remember?"

"I'm sure she does it just to spite you," Miralitt said.

"She doesn't have the presence of mind. Have you looked into her eyes? They are as clear as the summer sky. Not a cloud of thought in sight."

"The people think she is 'cute,' 'funny,' and 'breath of fresh air,'" Orata announced.

" 'Breath of fresh air'? She's a fart at a funeral." Resven realized what came out of his mouth and caught himself. "My apologies."

Kosandion waved them on.

"In fourth place, the otrokar," Orata said.

"Surkar, son of Grast and Ulde," Kosandion said.

"Yes," Orata confirmed.

Miralitt frowned.

"Key words?" Kosandion asked.

"Strong, decisive, and powerful."

"Well, he is all of those things," Kosandion agreed.

"His support among people 30 and under is 46% percent," Orata continued. "62% of people 20 and under are interested in civil and military service."

Resven raised his eyebrows.

Kosandion smiled again. "They see me as soft."

Orata cleared her throat. "Yes, *Letero*. The dominant chatter in the forums is that you are too civilized, and that the Dominion would benefit from 'warrior blood.' The Conqueror faction is making their usual noises about getting back to our roots."

"Have they forgotten the Assassination War?" Resven growled.

The Assassination War was a bloody conflict that sparked by Caldenia's murdering her brother. I was sixteen, in my junior year of high school. By Earth's biological metrics, Kosandion was only about five years older than me. He would've been around twenty-one. While physically an adult, socially he would've been considered a "youth," an equivalent to a human fifteen-year-old. Many factions in the Dominion thought he was unfit to lead. He proved them wrong.

"Most of the younger hotheads were children when that war

took place," Miralitt said. "Our people know you are a gifted commander. However..."

"The age of peace and prosperity our population enjoys thanks to your wise rule hasn't provided you with many opportunities to showcase your warrior side," Orata finished.

Smooth.

"Those who haven't experienced combat are easily impressed by a superficial show of physical power," Miralitt added.

"Surkar is impressive." Kosandion glanced at Orata. "Make a hard copy of the ratings for me."

"Yes, *Letero.*"

I had done some digging. The Hope Crushing Horde had settled a slew of planets, and Surkar and his delegation came from one of their frontier worlds. The power differential between Surkar and the Sovereign was enormous. With a single word, Kosandion could unleash an armada of ships that would block out the sun of Surkar's homeworld. No amount of muscles, flexing, or roaring would save Surkar's tribe from the hell that would rain down on them. And yet within the limits of this contest, Surkar was seen as stronger of the two.

Orata got up, placed a small data cube in front of Kosandion with a bow, and returned to her place.

He waved at her to continue.

"Then we have the Gaheas, followed by the oomboles."

"Really?" Kosandion asked.

Orata smiled. "The oomboles are bright and colorful, and a certain segment of the population thinks it would be funny if you married a fish."

Kosandion chuckled.

"House Meer is seventh, the Higgra are eighth, the delegation from Kyporo is ninth."

Team Frowns was from Kyporo, the sixth planet added to the Dominion. They were the ones with Ellenda, the Uma candidate. I would have thought the second of the Dominion's home teams would've ranked higher.

"A poor showing for Kyporo," Miralitt said.

"Ellenda comes across as unlikeable. The Murder Beaks are tenth, the Stranglers are eleventh, and the Children of the Silver Star are in last place," Orata concluded.

The birds, the Dushegubs, and the Donkamins. Apparently, nobody in the Dominion could pronounce the Dushegubs' proper name either.

"I expected the Children to rate higher," Resven said.

Orata sighed. "They are...uncomfortable to watch."

Figured.

"The Dominion doesn't want my child to bend their neck backward and address them with their face upside down?" Kosandion asked with pretended innocence.

"No," Orata said, her voice very firm.

Kosandion smiled and sipped his orange juice. He didn't look surprised by any of this.

In the ocean, a beautiful black fish leaped out of the water. It had to be the size of a whale, but it was built like a sturgeon with pike jaws. An enormous, scaled mouth followed it, the cavernous maw gaping. The fish twisted in one last futile effort to escape and fell into it. The scaled titan slipped back under the surface. The sea was once again still.

"Good work," the Sovereign said. "That will be all."

The three advisors bowed in unison and departed. Resven managed to get in one last warning look in my direction before the door shut behind him.

Kosandion pointed to a chair across the table. "Please."

I sat.

"Do you have any questions?" he asked.

"I don't want to impose, *Letero*."

"Please no titles. I have so few opportunities for informal conversations. Let's pretend we are friends."

Where was he going with this? "In that case, what's the real significance of the rankings?"

"As you know, the candidates face three challenges. The three least popular delegations are eliminated after each challenge until only three candidates remain for the final ceremony."

"I understand that." It was in their briefing. "How important are the rankings to you?"

"It's a complicated question." He didn't seem inclined to elaborate.

"Can you influence the rankings?"

He nodded. "To a degree. They are numbers produced by emotions and public opinion, and both of those are susceptible to manipulation. It may be as simple as editing a few seconds out of the footage or as complex as triggering the right person to say exactly the right thing at a completely unrelated event. As your world shows, one can come to the funeral of a friend, proclaim their purpose not to praise the deceased but to bury him, and then incite a revenge riot."

Not a reference I had expected.

Kosandion took another sip out of his crystal glass. "The public opinion can never be permitted to run freely. It must be nurtured, steered, and moderated. That's how dynasties stay in power."

Déjà vu.

"What about your personal preferences? Do they not factor in?" I asked.

"They do. But personal preferences are fleeting. I've had many partners over the years, male, female, humanoid and not, yet none of them remain by my side."

I had no idea if he was saddened by that, proud of it, or simply resigned to the fact. I wished Caldenia was here so I could take my cues from her.

"I am to be assassinated before the final ceremony is over," Kosandion said.

I almost did a double take. "How do you know that?"

"The same way I know many other things."

"Is this the real reason you wanted to move the venue to the inn?"

He nodded.

It would have been great to have that information before I put Gertrude Hunt on the line.

"Given my family history, it isn't exactly unexpected. You had to have at least considered the possibility, and if you hadn't, your highly trained significant other definitely has."

Sean would not like this. He wouldn't be surprised, but he still wouldn't like it.

"Do you know the identity of your potential assassin?"

He shook his head. "Not yet."

"One of the candidates?"

All of the candidates were guaranteed a one-on-one date with the Sovereign. Any other member of the delegations would have a lot harder time getting close to Kosandion.

"Most likely."

Twelve beings, half of them not human. One was a would-be killer. Which one? Or was it Caldenia?

"I trust you to keep me safe." Kosandion gave me a brilliant smile.

Sure, he trusted me, but not enough to share this assassination plot with me before we signed on the metaphorical dotted line.

Smacking the Sovereign of the Seven Star Dominion was out of the question. No matter how frustrated he made me feel.

"We will do our best, *Letero*."

Kosandion studied me. Looking straight into his eyes was difficult. He drew you in like a magnet.

"Regrets?" he asked quietly.

"Too late for that." We were committed now. "You know our reasons for hosting this event."

"Have you heard from the kidnapper?"

"No."

Six days had passed since we learned that Wilmos was taken through the portal gate from Baha-char to Karron. We had no idea if he was still alive.

"I have something for you." Kosandion flicked his fingers at the tabletop, and Gertrude Hunt obliged with a holographic screen. I had instructed the inn to summon conveniences on command for him. The screen flashed and turned toward me. An energy read-out, waves of blue and white.

"What is this?"

"Feed from our sensors on Karron. There are statis pods in the facility, designed to be used in case of a catastrophe. Each pod emits a signal when it's used. One of them came online 8 days ago."

"Thank you."

I had to show this to Sean. It wasn't the proof of life we both wanted, but it was something.

Kosandion nodded. "You're welcome. If I could impose on you for a small favor?"

I braced myself. "It's not an imposition. Your needs are my top priority."

Kosandion pushed the data cube with the ratings across the table toward me. "Make sure my aunt sees this."

[14]

The First Trial is about to begin. Will Gertrude Hunt rise to the challenge of hosting? Will we survive the candidates' wit? Let's listen in.

"Do you think the data is real?" Sean asked.

We were walking through the short dim hallway side by side. Beast trailed me, and Gorvar trotted by Sean's side. The two animals had decided to ignore each other's existence, concentrating on guarding us instead.

"Kosandion is Caldenia's nephew, so he's devious enough to manufacture this energy reading and use it to manipulate us. But why bother? He could've simply asked me to hand the ratings off to Caldenia. I would do it because he is a guest. Instead, he felt that there was a value attached to me running this errand, and he compensated me for my effort."

Sean's frown deepened.

I had taken the data to Caldenia right after my conversation with Kosandion. I found Her Grace enjoying a lovely breakfast on our back patio. I'd placed the cube on the table and told her Kosandion wanted her to have it. She raised her eyebrows and said, "He did, did he?" She scanned the cube with her reader, and then she smiled with all her teeth, and I'd been low-key haunted by that smile ever since.

We stopped before a dark wall blocking our way. Sean's eyes were still grim. I reached over and squeezed his hand. "I'm sorry."

He blinked.

"We don't know anything and it's eating at you." It was eating at me. "I know that you really want to go and look for him, and instead we have to do this."

"It's not that."

"Then what is it?"

"I don't like surprises. And I don't like being lied to. This was supposed to be straight forward: keep the candidates from killing each other. We were told that Kosandion would ignore Caldenia's presence. Instead, the candidates are trying to kill him, and Kosandion and Caldenia are scheming, either together or against each other."

"Nothing really changed," I said. "When we took this job, we knew we had to keep Kosandion safe. This assassination plot doesn't alter that. We also knew that Caldenia and Kosandion have a complicated history. Predictably, their present relationship is complicated."

He made a low growling noise in his throat. Gorvar's ears twitched.

"And that's exactly what I find surprising. What is the nature of their relationship? Is she plotting to kill him?"

"I don't think so?" I didn't sound very convincing.

"Of all the places in the universe, Kosandion picked our inn. Is he planning to punish Caldenia for the murder of his father? If I were him, I would provoke her until she snaps and does something unwise. It doesn't matter if she succeeds. As soon as she acts against him, you and I will have to expel her from the inn. She would be done. The bounties on her head are still sky-high. I checked."

I knew how he felt. One small mistake, and everything we've

built could come crushing down. We couldn't lose Gertrude Hunt. We just couldn't.

"This could be made much simpler if we just locked Caldenia up until it's over," Sean said.

"Sometimes you say things that make me wonder about you."

"No need to wonder. I'm a simple man. I love you and I will protect you. And the inn. Even if I have to murder Caldenia and everyone else to do it."

I stood on my toes and kissed him. "What if we don't murder anybody?"

The corners of his mouth curved. "No promises."

"Are we ready?"

"As ready as we're going to be."

I touched the wall in front of us with my broom. Glowing dots of light pulsed from the broom, drawing an outline of a huge double door in the wall. The once-solid surface split down the middle, and the two halves of the door swung open, letting a flood of sunshine bathe us.

A large empty arena spread before us, bordered by a raised amphitheater divided into fourteen sections, one for each delegation, one for Kosandion and his retinue, and the last for the observers. Each section was freestanding, raised thirty feet above the arena's floor, and separated from the adjoining sections by a thirty-foot gap. A short safety wall secured the sections. We had shamelessly stolen the idea from the Old Arena at Baha-char.

Ideally, I would have encircled each section by an impenetrable barrier, the same way I had secured Kosandion's balcony. Unfortunately, maintaining that many barriers simultaneously was beyond Gertrude Hunt's capacity. They also caused a distortion in Orata's cameras, and since the whole thing had to be recorded, I settled for the wide gaps and bringing Gertrude Hunt to high alert. If the delegates as much as twitched toward each other, the inn would pluck them right out of their seats and toss them back into their respective quarters.

In the center of the arena, I had raised a stage. Perfectly round and exactly 25 yards across, it sat about ten feet above the arena floor. When the candidates would need to enter it, I would make a ramp from their section directly to the stage.

"What about the moderator platform?" I asked.

We needed a moderator for the debate, and Sean had volunteered to make a special platform for him.

"I'm working on it," Sean said.

He raised his head to the brilliant blue sky and squinted at the sunshine. In reality, the arena was deep inside the inn. I had done some serious damage to dimensional physics. The sky above us was real, but if someone flew a drone over the inn, they would find only the worn roof of an ordinary ornate Victorian.

Even a year ago, expending that much energy would have been impossible for me. Each inn had a finite capacity for energy storage. A steady flow of guests was much preferable to the feast or famine scenario Gertrude Hunt had to endure for the last couple of years. Our reputation was spreading, and we'd had more visitors in the past few months than ever, each of them more troublesome than a typical inn guest but very much welcome. These guests allowed our inn a chance to grow, but its energy reserves were still insufficient to contain the massive influx of this event. Gertrude Hunt was overflowing with magic. It was a use-it-or-lose-it situation, so I used it to give the trials a wow factor.

Tony had shaken his head at the arena and told me I was working too hard. According to him, a college auditorium would've done the job. But the Dominion was broadcasting the spousal selection across multiple star systems. Their neighbors were tuning in, and the Innkeeper Assembly was watching it and evaluating our performance. Gertrude Hunt's reputation was on the line. As Caldenia once told me, life gave us few opportunities to put our best foot forward, so when a chance to shine presented itself, it was best to take it. A little bit of showmanship didn't hurt.

A chime pealed through the arena. It was time.

Sean tapped his spear on the floor. Huge screens descended from the clear sky, offering each section a chance to view the action up close.

I planted my broom on the stone tiles, formed a tunnel between the closest section and House Meer's quarters, and opened their doors.

———

"GREETINGS, MY FELLOW BEINGS!"

Gaston cut a striking figure in the middle of the stage. He'd changed into a stunning white and gray outfit, embroidered with silver-blue thread that complemented his silver eyes. It fit him like a glove while still projecting the air of what he called "gentlemanly menace." He had looked like a space pirate before. Now he looked like a space pirate prince who had done very well for himself.

His voice matched his new for-TV persona, resonant and smooth, as it blasted from the hidden speakers. It took him exactly four words to get everyone's attention. Sean, a few yards away at the edge of the stage, might as well have been invisible, despite his robe, his spear, and his tendency to loom.

"Welcome to the First Trial!" Gaston announced.

The 12 delegations cheered, stomped, and made species-appropriate noises. Even Kosandion in the chair to my right clapped politely. Gaston clearly missed his true calling.

"I know all of you have been waiting to find out how our contestants will showcase their talents today. Are you ready?"

The delegations roared to indicate they were most definitely ready.

"He's turning it into a spectacle," Resven murmured.

"It is meant to be one," Kosandion told him. "People love a good show."

"Today's challenge is...DEBATE!"

147

The alien equivalent of "wooo!" was rather loud.

Gaston waved them on, inviting more noise, then made a sweeping gesture that somehow brought instant silence.

"Our spousal candidates will face off in randomly selected pairs. Both candidates will be asked the same question. One will respond first, and the other will reply. The winner will be determined by a combination of popular vote, the Sovereign's opinion, and the feedback from our esteemed debate moderator."

He gave them a moment to digest and went on.

"Our debate moderator is truly a scholar of great renown. He has devoted himself to contemplating the mysteries of the universe. Beings from every corner of the galaxy travel thousands of light years to seek his advice."

The floor behind Gaston split, and an SUV-sized stone egg positioned on its side with the narrow end toward the center of the arena rose from under the floor on a metal stalk.

He didn't.

The metal stalk carried the egg up and stopped about fifteen feet above the stage.

Yes, yes, he did.

"Recipient of the Starlight Quill, Sage of the Great Tree, Vanquisher of the Sphinx, the First Scholar Thek!" Gaston roared.

The stone egg split in half lengthwise. The top half retracted, revealing the First Scholar in all his glory, holding his teaching stick, his hat firmly on his noggin with the glittering white feather attached to it. His two assistants dutifully stood behind him, looking down and playing the part of modest disciples.

"An egg?" I hissed into the mike.

"It's funny."

Ugh.

"He thought it was appropriate."

The arena greeted the First Scholar with resounding applause. He nodded to them, waving his hand-claw benevolently.

The original moderator had encountered unexpected travel delays because his second wife kidnapped him, and now his other four wives were having their own debate on the merits of rescuing him. We needed a substitute in a hurry, and the First Scholar Thek was the talk of the galaxy after the Sphinx escapade. Orata practically drooled when Sean suggested him.

They didn't have to twist Thek's wings. He demurred at first, but I had a conversation with Orata prior to her visiting him, and once she told him that it was a chance to illuminate millions of minds with the wisdom of his scholarship, he was all in.

"I keep waiting for his hat to slide off," Sean murmured.

He was right, the headdress should've slipped off his feathers by now. *"Whatever his disciples did, it seems to be working."*

"Maybe they glued it."

"I hope not."

The First Scholar preened at the show of support and waved his teaching stick. His voice rolled out of the speakers.

"Let us begin."

A line of delicate glass flowers sprouted from the stage floor below the egg. They looked like three-foot-tall dandelions, each topped with a white sphere the size of a basketball swirling with white and gold. One orb per candidate. When a candidate's name was called, their orb would descend under the floor so they couldn't accidentally choose themselves for the debate.

I bounced the white light between sections, highlighting their retaining walls, and stopped on Team Frowns. A small section of the front wall slid aside, and a ramp unfurled from the gap leading down to the bottom of the arena.

Ellenda rose. She wore a black robe with an elaborately pleated, deep hood. It was an odd choice. I'd noticed it when their delegation took their seats. The fabric of her garment was plain, almost coarse. It looked out of place compared to everyone else's formal wear.

The Uma woman descended the stairs, approached the orbs, and lowered her hood. Kosandion became very still. Her face and neck were splattered with gold paint.

I had encountered only three Umas counting Ellenda, and one of them had stayed at my parents' inn. He also wore the gold paint. I was six years old back then, and I told him he looked very pretty. My father apologized and later explained things to me. The Uma wore that gold paint when they were in mourning. Someone either died or was about to.

It was a safe bet that nobody in the arena recognized the gold for what it was. The Uma guarded their culture very closely. But Kosandion would know. They were his mother's people. Why was she here if she was in mourning?

"Choose your opponent," the First Scholar Thek prompted, indicating the orbs with a sweep of his wing. They looked identical.

Ellenda put her hand on the closest orb. Its transparent shell popped like a soap bubble, releasing a swarm of glowing golden insects into the air. They surged up, turned, streaked to the Murder Beaks' section, and hovered around Pivor.

Pivor rose with a big smile, bowed to the left, bowed to the right, grinned again, displaying even, white teeth, and made his way down the stairway that formed from his section. He crossed the arena and stood opposite Ellenda. They faced each other with ten feet between them. Tiny blue sparks by their ears announced their mikes being activated.

"The question the two of you must contemplate today is..." The First Scholar paused dramatically. "What is more important, happiness or duty? You have one hundred moments to consider your answer."

The arena fell silent. Seconds ticked by.

The First Scholar's egg turned white. The time to prepare ran out.

"Daughter of Uma," Thek said, "The floor is yours."

"Duty," Ellenda said.

The First Scholar turned to Pivor.

"Happiness," the Murder Bird candidate said.

Silence.

The First Scholar waited for a couple more breaths and turned to Ellenda. "You must defend your answer."

"Happiness is fleeting, subjective, and selfish. Submitting to and successfully carrying out your duty ensures the continued survival of society."

"Duty is equally subjective," Pivor answered. "If I see a child being chased by a predator, is it my duty to intervene?"

"Yes."

"But, by intervening I put my own survival at risk. I'm an adult who survived diseases and the perils of my own childhood. If I'm killed by the predator, would my death not be a greater loss to society than a child who has yet to mature? Could that child take my place and assume my obligations? What of my duty to my clan and family who depend on me?"

Ellenda didn't answer.

Pivor kept going. "You say that duty exists to ensure the survival of society. I say that the purpose of society is to create individual happiness. Every law of a successful society is designed to help its members attain that goal. We seek to guarantee safety, access to resources, individual rights, and we even guard mandatory leisure. Therefore, the pursuit of happiness is supreme over carrying out one's duty."

"I would save the child. I have nothing more to say." Ellenda pulled her hood over her head.

The First Scholar waited a few seconds, but the hood remained up.

"Very well," he announced. "Thank you both. You may return to your seats."

The two candidates rejoined their delegations. The white light bounced again.

One of the twelve delegates was an assassin. I was hoping for a peek at their cards during this debate. Some clue, something that might identify them as a killer. So far, Ellenda clearly didn't want to participate, and Pivor came off as selfish. Not particularly illuminating.

The light stopped on House Meer. Bestata rose, her black syn-armor swallowing the light. She had attached a white cloak to it, made of lightweight fabric. I angled the air current circulating through the arena toward her, and the cloak billowed behind her as she marched down her ramp. It was such a pretty cloak. It would be a shame to waste it.

"Dramatic," Kosandion murmured.

"Vampires often are. One time they visited this inn in secret, but they still had to introduce themselves, so they forcefully whispered their house creed at me."

Kosandion smiled.

Bestata reached the orbs and planted her hand on one of them without hesitation. It burst, and the glittering swarm veered to the Dushegubs and settled on Unessa's hair like a crown.

"Nice touch," Kosandion approved.

"Thank you."

Unessa sashayed her way to the arena floor. She wore a brilliant green gown that moved with every step, giving hints of the pale skin underneath.

"I pose the following question for your consideration," the First Scholar announced. "What is the purpose of your existence and why is your purpose superior to your opponent's? You have one hundred moments to consider your an—"

"Procreation!" Unessa said. She turned to look at Kosandion and smiled.

Bestata stared at her for a stunned second and looked at the First Scholar. "I am supposed to debate that?"

"Do your best," the First Scholar told her.

"There are other things besides procreation. Devotion, the pursuit of personal excellence, learning, gaining expertise, passing it on to next generation."

Knowing the First Scholar, that answer earned Bestata all the brownie points. She was talking about martial prowess, and he was thinking in terms of academic wisdom, but knowledge was knowledge.

"Honor," Bestata continued. "Pride in accomplishments. The glory of your house. A death that would be remembered. All of these are more important than simple copulation and reproduction."

Unessa smiled. She was likely going for sweet, but there was a rotten edge to it. She looked slightly reptilian, like a lizard about to snatch a grub.

"And if your people stopped breeding, who would do all those things?"

"My people haven't stopped breeding for thousands of years. It is an instinct. I do realize you've been brought up by logs but do try to think less like a stump."

Ouch.

A long shoot slithered out from the large Dushegub in the front row of their section.

Bestata kept going. "It is unfortunate that you have been raised for the sole purpose of trapping a male with your looks, but you don't have to be just pretty fruit on the vine."

She was killing it with puns.

The shoot coiled on itself in a tight spiral.

"At least I'm pretty," Unessa said.

"Thank the gods for that," Bestata snarled. "Nature had to give you something to compensate for your boiled egg brain."

The shoot snapped out, launching a projectile into the air.

Sean and I moved at the same time.

A pit appeared in the middle of the arena floor, sucking the projectile into itself. Long flexible tentacles erupted from inside the pit, grabbed the Dushegub, wrapped him up like a mummy, and pulled him into the hole.

The arena went silent.

A single breath passed, and then the stands erupted.

The Donkamins made a weird ululating noise. The otrokar stomped their feet. House Meer stood up and clapped, roaring. The oombole section turned into a 4th of July fireworks show with colors and fins flashing in a dizzying display.

The Dushegubs hissed and creaked in unison. Unessa wrinkled her nose and hissed at Bestata. The vampire knight sneered and bared her spectacular fangs.

Sean slid the pit toward the killer trees, the tentacles hovering straight up, waiting to snatch the next troublemaker.

I rolled my voice through the arena. I didn't scream, I didn't raise it, but it sounded loud, and it was everywhere.

"No interference with the trials will be tolerated."

The Dushegubs fell silent.

The First Scholar spread his wings, calling for silence. When the arena complied, he leaned forward and spoke to Unessa. "Do you have a rebuttal?"

Her eyes narrowed. "I wasn't told I had to bring one with me."

Bestata spread her arms and looked around at the audience.

"Very well," the First Scholar said. "This debate is concluded."

Unessa raised her chin and shot a triumphant look at the Dushegubs.

"You didn't win, idiot!" someone yelled from the otrokar section.

Kosandion covered his face with his hand, hiding his expression.

Unessa turned toward the First Scholar.

"While crudely voiced, the assessment is undeniably accurate," he told her. "Neither of you will be the winner of this debate."

She spun on her heel and marched back to her section, her hands clenched into fists.

Neither Unessa nor Bestata seemed likely to assassinate Kosandion. Subtlety wasn't their strong suit. If either of those two targeted the Sovereign, it would be a direct assault. The way he spoke about it suggested a cunning hidden enemy.

"Instead of attacking the question, the knight attacked her opponent," Resven said.

"She holds her in contempt," Miralitt said.

Resven raised his eyebrows, but Miralitt didn't elaborate.

Kosandion glanced at me. He was Caldenia's nephew, so he knew perfectly well why Bestata reacted the way she did, but he wanted a public explanation. Perhaps it was for the viewers at home.

"The Holy Anocracy prizes personal excellence," I told them. "They strive for a life of individual achievement. Bestata had to train and fight since she could walk. She knows she can kill Unessa in individual combat without even raising her heart rate. Now she also knows that Unessa's thinking is underdeveloped. From her point of view, the Dushegub candidate is a useless, pretty thing unworthy of her sincere effort. She refused to dignify her with an actual debate."

"What is your opinion of Unessa?" Kosandion asked me.

Put me on the spot, why don't you? "The way she speaks and what she says indicates that she was raised by the Dushegubs from an early age. Anyone who can survive that shouldn't be underestimated."

Bestata was confusing education and cleverness. Unessa might have had limited exposure to the humanoid society and its complexities, but she had rebutted Bestata's argument, even if she didn't know the proper word for it, while Bestata had nothing to counter with and resorted to insults.

Where did the Dushegubs find a humanoid child? Did they buy her? Did they steal her? Were there more like her?

It was time to bounce the light again. I stopped it on the Kai. Prysen Ol rose, swept his layered robe back with an elegant gesture, and descended the ramp. He always held himself with a quiet dignity. Even as he was walking now, his steps were small, and his right arm was bent at the elbow and held across his body. It was all very deliberate and restrained.

Self-control would be an excellent quality for an assassin.

Prysen Ol touched an orb. The insects spiraled out, floated over to the Gaheas, and danced around Nycati's purple hair, matching the golden diadem on his head. The Gaheas candidate stood up, a flawless movement, and took the ramp to arena floor.

An appreciative murmur spread through the spectators and died down.

"Interesting," Resven observed. "Those two appear well matched."

I had looked through the footage from yesterday's dinner, and something caught my eye. On paper, Nycati came from a scholar family, aristocratic, but mid-ranking, and all appearances indicated that he was selected to be their candidate for his merits and achievements. The head of the Gaheas delegation, Naeoma Thaste, was the equivalent of a duke, one step removed from the royal family. He outranked Nycati by a mile.

Yesterday at dinner, Naeoma made a disparaging remark about the Donkamins. Nycati looked at him for a moment, and the duke looked down. The Gaheas were psionics. They dueled by staring at each other. To look away was to back down, but to lower your gaze to the ground was like kneeling with your head bowed. Complete submission.

Only a prince could stare down a duke. Nycati was Gaheas royalty. I was sure of it.

A Gaheas prince, even if he had been raised in secret, would have survived dozens of attempts on his life. Most of them became efficient killers by adulthood, or they died. His delegation lied about who he really was. They could have done it because they secretly wanted to tie their bloodline to the leadership of the Dominion, or they could have done it because Kosandion was their target. Either way, Nycati's chances of being the assassin had shot up into the stratosphere.

The First Scholar surveyed the two men. "The question before you is as follows: Why are you here?"

"Before I can answer," Prysen Ol said, "would the Honored Scholar be so kind as to define 'here'?"

"Indeed," Nycati agreed. "It is a fair request. Does 'here' designate a physical location or a fixed point in time? Does it refer to our presence or our purpose?"

"How can we be sure that we are 'here' at all?" Prysen Ol added.

The First Scholar puffed to twice his size, looking positively giddy. His eyes sparkled. "The interpretation is entirely up to you. You have a hundred moments to compose your thoughts."

[15]

When we last left the Arena of the Trials, Nycati, the psionic space elf, and Prysen, the scholar representative of the hypochondriac Kai, were asked a simple question: why are you here? They are now trying to answer it. Grab a coffee and get comfy. It might take them awhile.

" ... However, applied meaning runs in tandem with applied ethics, therefore, the meaning and definition of a concept, perceived through the lens of that view set, must be considered in situational context."

Prysen Ol shook his head slightly. "Your mistake is in seeking to apply multiple definitions to a singular concept. Should we not be concerned instead with focusing our search on a single, albeit broad, principle that captures varied iterations of a concept in an effort to distill its essential meaning?"

They had been at this for half an hour. Not only could they not agree on what 'here' meant, they couldn't even figure out by what parameters to define it. Most of the audience had zoned out. The otrokars were playing bone dice. The Dushegubs' branches had drooped together, braiding into a canopy. Unessa had curled up under it and was taking a fine nap. The Kai had formed a shield wall with their bodies, which normally happened when they were traveling through the wilderness and had to rest while guarding against predators. Resven had anchored his elbow on his arm rest, leaned his chin on his hand, and nodded off. Kosandion had given up and was reviewing some complicated-looking documents on his personal screen.

"Help..." Tony whispered into my ear. "Eyes closing... Can't resist..."

I pulled up a small screen. Tony was up in the hidden tower above the stands, getting the bird's eye view of the arena. He looked like he was halfway into a coma.

"You're an ad-hal. Use your badass training."

"There are limits to my power."

I flicked my fingers at the screen, accessing the kitchen. Droplet popped up on it, her cute squirrel tail raised behind her. "How can I assist you?"

"Could I please have coffee in travel mugs?"

"How many?"

"Four."

Kosandion glanced at me. The Uma I knew were fond of caffeinated drinks, and Dominion citizens frequently drank tea.

"Make it five," I said.

Resven's chin slipped. He jerked awake, blinking his eyes.

"Six. Cream and a little sugar in all." We needed the calories.

"Coming right up."

Nycati pondered the sky. "Agreed. Let us for the purpose of this discussion, narrow our viewpoint to a specific circumstance governed by a general principle. How shall we define this circumstance?"

"I suggest we begin at the most fundamental baseline. Let us define 'here' as a set point within the space-time continuum."

"It may seem tempting, however, time is subjective and immeasurable. It's passing slower or faster, depending on one's perception..."

"It seems to be passing pretty damn slow right now!" the head of House Meer announced, his deep voice booming like an alarm gong.

"We've been here forever!" someone shouted from the otrokar section.

Gertrude Hunt chimed in my head, announcing Orata coming through the portal. I pulled up a small screen showing the arrival chamber. She stepped out of the portal and made the universal motion for 'wrap it up.' Unlike the opening ceremony, the debate was being broadcast almost live with only a minute or two delay. The ratings had to be dropping.

A small table emerged from the floor, bearing six coffees in metal insulated tumblers of various colors. I took one and offered it to Kosandion.

"Thank you." He opened the tumbler and sipped. "Delicious."

It was interesting how he never simply accepted a gift or a favor. He always thanked you and then made sure to indicate that he valued your gift.

I handed the blue tumbler to Resven. He gave it a suspicious look, unscrewed the top, and took a drink. His eyes widened.

I kept one tumbler for myself and sent the rest through the floor to Sean, Gaston, and Tony.

"You are a saint," Tony said.

Sean saluted me with his tumbler.

"Nectar of the gods," Gaston murmured.

"...so how can we define 'here' if time is constantly flowing, since a single instant in which we anchor our definition will end in that moment?" Nycati wondered.

Prysen Ol smiled. "That concept is predicated on the belief that time actually passes, that it moves and, further, that said movement is measurable. I will concede no such thing. In fact, I reject entirely the notion that time can be reduced to infinite numbers. Rather, it's best expressed through finite numbers.

There is a limit to their precision, for nature is inherently random, chaotic, and imprecise."

First Scholar Thek clapped his clawed hands in delight.

Orata held her hands in front of her, palms up, fingers spread, as if trying to bring an invisible melon to her face. The Dominion's gesture for pleading. She was begging me to end it.

I accessed the First Scholar's earpiece. *"We have to cut this short."*

"But it's so invigorating," he whispered.

"My time is finite!" another knight yelled from House Meer. "Every moment that passes, or doesn't, saps my will to live."

"We concur," the Donkamins announced in a chorus.

"You know why you're here?" Surkar jumped to his feet. "To win!"

Applause broke out through the arena. He raised his arms, accepting the ovation, and flexed his award-winning biceps.

"And the debate goes to the otrokar," Kosandion murmured.

I turned the First Scholar's egg white.

"Alas," the First Scholar announced. "We are out of time. It has truly been a pleasure. Please return to your seats."

"Who won?" someone from Team Smiles yelled.

"Who cares?" a female otrokar yelled back. "We all lost."

Gaston stepped forward. "We shall resume the trial after a short recess. Please take advantage of the refreshments to regain your strength for the second half."

Refreshment trays sprouted from the floor.

On my screen Orata exhaled happily and went back through the portal.

"What's the schedule of the dates after the debate?" Kosandion asked.

"Oond of the oomboles, followed by the Donkamin candidate," Resven said.

"Has it been announced?"

"No, *Letero,*" the chancellor said.

"Switch Oond with Ellenda," Kosandion said.

"Yes, *Letero*."

Sean was still down in the arena. I whispered into the mike. *"Hey."*

"Hey," he said, his voice warm. *"What's up?"*

I hesitated. This was kind of stupid. I could see him. He was right there. But we've been so busy these last few days. Normally we spent our time together. We weren't glued at the hip, but we usually ate together. We did chores together. At night we settled into a comfortable room I made for us off our new joint bedroom, and we played video games or watched TV with Beast and Olasard.

We hadn't been able to do any of that. I felt like I barely saw him, which was somehow worse than not having him here at all, like when he went on his excursions with Wilmos. I missed him but saying it out loud seemed too needy.

"Are you okay?"

"I miss you," he said.

"I miss you, too."

"Young love," Gaston purred.

"Disgusting," Tony said with mock derision. *"If it wasn't for the mission, I would mute you both."*

A trumpet-like sound pulsed through the arena, announcing the end of the break.

———

Surkar of the otrokars stared at Oond in his fishbowl. This was clearly not the opponent he would've preferred. Too bad for him. The orbs had been set up at random. Even I didn't know which was which.

"Am I supposed to debate a fish?" he demanded.

"Xenophobia has never led anyone to a path of enlightenment," the First Scholar told him.

Surkar raised his eyes to the sky briefly, as if inviting the sun to witness his tribulations. He was about to debate a space fish, and their discussion would be presided on by a space chicken. This was not a trial appropriate to his stature. His hero-of-the-Horde image was taking a bit of a beating, but throwing a fit about it would make him look like a fussy baby and he knew it.

"Ask your question," he growled.

"What is best in life?" the First Scholar announced. "You have one hundred moments to consider."

Oh, sweet Universe. *"Sean, I know it was you,"* I whispered.

"I have no idea what you're talking about," Sean said.

"We just rewatched that movie a month ago."

"Let's see what he says."

Surkar straightened his shoulders, as if he was going into battle on familiar ground and just noticed a gap in the enemy's line.

"To crush your enemies," Sean mumbled in a horrible imitation of an Austrian accent. *"See them driven..."*

"He isn't going to say it. There is no way." There were few things that I was willing to bet my life on, but Surkar of the Hope Crushing Horde not having seen *Conan the Barbarian* was one of them.

The First Scholar's egg turned white.

"Victory," Surkar announced.

Oond spread his fins and let them float down gently like delicate veils thrown into a breeze. His translator flashed, and a soft voice issued forth from the speakers in the base of his fishbowl. "Safety."

"Victory is the only way to achieve safety," the otrokar champion growled. "Crush your enemies."

Sean made a strangled noise in my ear. Tony snorted.

"Slaughter their armies. Drive them back. Force them to submit. Fill their hearts with fear and dominate their minds, so they tremble at the mere mention of your name. That's how you ensure safety."

Oond's fins wavered back and forth. "Untrue."

Surkar glowered. "What does a fish know of battle or honor?"

Oond's fins unfurled, twisted, and snapped. "I know of deep water. I have tasted the darkness so thick and cold, it blinds all senses, a place without a current where no direction exists. I have witnessed the things who live within it. I have seen the jaws of monsters who span the length of the ocean. I know the value of safety. No matter how powerful you are, there are enemies one cannot crush."

"Spoken like a coward."

"You seek to belittle me. Have you swum in the deep water? Can you kill a leviathan?"

Surkar shrugged. "Fine. How do your people obtain safety? Enlighten me."

"Within the ocean, there are vast corals reefs. A coral grows slowly through the efforts of tiny creatures, and yet over the years it spreads and shelters other lives. Fish dart around it, playing and feeding; mollusks crawl, cleaning up the ocean floor; dozens of species feed, live, and reproduce within its growth, and, should a predator appear, they will withdraw within the coral's sturdy walls and most of them will survive. If you wish to secure safety, you must become a coral. Help others. Make yourself indispensable to them. Show them that apart you struggle but together you prosper."

Surkar sneered. "That's the way slaves are made. Make yourself indispensable, and those who are stronger will chain you to serve them. Why should they respect you or care about your well-being, if they can simply force you to do their bidding? Without the power of retaliation, none of your talents matter. You will become the lowest of the low, doomed to a wretched existence. No. My people will not live like this. I cherish my freedom. I will not set it aside. I will not cower."

"Untrue."

"I don't lie, fish. I have no need. I'm strong enough to force others to suffer through the discomfort of my true words."

"Kill your enemies," Oond's translator said, its voice soft and sad. "Murder parents. Slaughter offspring. You cannot grow safety this way. You grow memories. They sprout deep in the bellies of the survivors, like sea urchins covered in spikes. They hurt and hurt until those you have crushed return to crush you and rip the source of their pain out."

Surkar bared his teeth. "They will regret it."

"And then the eggs of pain will be sown again. In turn your people will grow their own anguish and will seek revenge. And so it will go, a cycle of pain never ending."

"The crucible of revenge makes us strong," Surkar said. "I had six siblings. The war took four. Only my brother and I remain. We are the strongest of our clan. By achieving victory, we proved our right to live."

Tiny sparks of light ignited along the oombole's fins and body. Oond turned within his fishbowl, drawing a complete circle. It was a breathtaking sight, yellow and red lights sliding through his layered fins, graceful and beautiful. He raised his fins, lowered them, and turned again, like a living flame.

The arena watched in hushed silence.

The mesmerizing fins flowed. The light pulsed, gentle and beautiful.

"What is he doing?" Surkar asked.

"He is dancing for you," Sean told him.

"Why?"

"You are a child of pain," Oond's translator said. "You have suffered. This is a small gift. A moment free of anguish."

Surkar stared at him for a long moment. "A pretty dance. A pity that dances don't win wars. I'll give you a piece of advice: when the enemy comes for the lives of your children, gather them and run away to your coral. Don't waste time on dancing."

He turned to the First Scholar. "This farce is over."

"Very well," the First Scholar said.

"Do the oomboles have professions in the traditional sense of the word?" Kosandion asked.

"Yes," I told him. "Oond is an ookarish, an exceptionally beautiful being whose job is to dance for those who are aggrieved."

Cyanide was next. The beautiful sleek Higgra padded into the arena on her big paws, looking very much like a mythical cousin of a terrestrial snow leopard.

Most species evolved appendages that allowed them to manipulate tools. The Higgra did not. They still walked on all fours, sitting on their haunches or lying down in specialized tool chairs when they had to do something intricate. Their digits were dexterous, but it was their claws that truly made their tool-use possible. Long and curved, they allowed for extreme precision. A Higgra could pluck a yolk out of an egg and carry it across a mile of rough terrain without breaking it. It was theorized that the Higgra didn't evolve at all but had been enhanced by some advanced civilization lost to time. Their origins were one of the mysteries of the galaxy.

Cyanide sliced one of the remaining three orbs with her claws, as her own orb dropped out of view. The insects tagged the Donkamin representative. He came to stand next to her on the arena floor.

"Are you bound by Fate?" The First Scholar inquired. "This is your question. You have a hundred moments to contemplate."

Cyanide didn't bother with waiting for 100 moments. "Yes. That which shall be, will come to pass."

The Donkamin twisted his neck to the side, stretching it to two feet. My stomach tried to crawl out of my body.

"We are the architects of our future. Fate is an empty concept."

Cyanide smiled, showing her blue gums and gleaming white fangs.

"If everything is predetermined, why should one try to do anything at all?" the Donkamin candidate demanded.

"Of course, one should try. The future is unknowable, and we are blind to what's to come. Our life is a test by which we are measured. To earn your fate, one must prove they are worthy of it."

"There is no evidence that fate exists."

"There is no evidence that one has a soul, and yet here we are."

"I have no soul," the Donkamin candidate stated.

"Then I shall not speak with you any further, soulless one. Our dialogue would be pointless."

Cyanide turned around and went back to her seat.

Okay. That was over quick.

The First Scholar waited until everyone was seated and spread his wings. "The final two candidates may come to the floor."

Two ramps unfurled from the Team Smiles and the Temple sections. Amphie was the first on her feet. She'd practically jumped up. A long purple gown accented with geometric white and black embroidery wrapped her figure. The color was beautiful and deep but desaturated rather than vibrant. It was less of a ball gown and more of a formal state dress befitting the spouse of a Sovereign. Her dark locks crowned her head in an artful arrangement—not a hair out of place. Black sandals decorated her feet. It was all very tasteful and dignified.

Lady Wexyn also wore purple, but hers was an unrestrained celebration of amethyst. Her translucent gown flowed at the slightest breeze, iris-purple in the center, then transitioning to a fiery rose, and finally turning an exuberant yellow. Her hair was pulled back from her face into an elaborate rose secured with a spiky golden ornament that looked like stylized sun rays. The long slit of her dress opened as she walked, giving everyone a glimpse of her tan, round thigh. A dozen anklets tinkled with tiny bells as she moved, and when the breeze swept the hem of her gown aside, I saw that she was barefoot.

They stood side by side, an elegant, somber inhabitant of a

palace and the woman of light and color who would've been at home in a flowering meadow.

"The question before you is as follows: what is love?" The First Scholar asked. "You have 100 moments."

Sean hummed a familiar tune into my ear. I picked it up. It was catchy and I was really tired.

"Don't hurt me..." Tony joined in.

The egg turned white.

"Love is complex," Amphie said. "It is at once an abstract concept, yet it has the power to affect living beings. Its impact is irrevocable and those who experience it are forever changed and often scarred, and yet, despite the pain they endured, some of them have no regrets. One can say that love is a process of elevation, a transformative journey from baser animalistic urge to a near-spiritual purity of feeling, from the compulsion to possess to the enlightenment of self-sacrifice, a transcendence that no longer requires mutuality but exists independently of the object of desire. It can be a passionate longing, or appreciation rooted in respect, or it can be unilateral and impartial, as the love of a deity for its followers or a ruler for their subjects."

The First Scholar nodded.

"Love raises questions," Amphie continued. "It is healing and yet it can also harm. One must love oneself, but too much self-love causes one to compromise their ethics and become blind to their own flaws. One could say love is a quest to complete oneself, seeking virtue and beauty in others that we lack within ourselves. Love exists in opposition to reason, for when we love someone, we ignore their faults, allowing their moods and wellbeing to affect our own. While it is the root of charity, it is also a kind of madness. In conclusion, love is a layered phenomenon that must be examined in a specific context, for it is too broad for generalizations. Its power is immense, its impact is lifelong, and it warrants further contemplation."

The First Scholar nodded again and looked at Lady Wexyn.

She smiled back at him. A soft blush touched her cheeks. She glanced up at Kosandion. "Love is what I feel for His Majesty."

Resven slapped his hand over his face. Amphie stared at Lady Wexyn with an open mouth.

"He is my favorite, and I will never love anyone else in the same way."

Lady Wexyn gave Kosandion a little wave and smiled.

[16]

When we last left the inn, the debates were finished, and the ~~Book Devouring Horde~~ Dominion citizens were busy voting for their favorite in the official ratings. Meanwhile, Dina desperately tried to figure out the identity of the assassin targeting Kosandion. Unfortunately, the debates proved less than illuminating.

The Dushegubs stared at me. 'Stared' was a figurative term in their case, as their eyes were hidden in the crevices of their bark. They planted themselves, standing straight and stretched their branches to take up as much space as possible. Their limbs slithered and slid over each other, reaching for me like dark nightmarish tentacles, ready to grab and constrict. The wood creaked and groaned as they moved, suggesting the sound of human bones snapping.

Sean, next to me, didn't seem impressed. I wasn't impressed either.

Everyone else had already been dispatched to their quarters, including Unessa. In three hours Kosandion would go on his first date, which would be with Ellenda, and everyone else would be invited to an early dinner, but until then the delegates would stay locked in. We'd had enough socializing for one day.

The largest Dushegub stretched his branches at me, holding them above me like fingers of enormous hands ready to snatch me off my feet. The translator attached to his bark hissed and spoke in a low male voice.

"Proposition. You stop interfering or we kill you and break your house-tree. Do you want to discuss?"

This was not my first Dushegub rodeo. "You follow rules, or we kill all of you, go to your planet, and kill your saplings with fire."

The leader creaked, rocking side to side.

"Fallacy: you do not leave your tree. You cannot go to our planet. Submit or we kill you. Do you want to discuss?"

"I will kill you here. He will go to your planet." I pointed at Sean.

Sean showed them his teeth. The arena floor parted, displaying a clump of weeds in a flowerbed. Two nozzles shot out from the stone. The first unloaded a spray of hardcore off-world weed killer on the plants. The weeds shriveled. The Dushegubs drew back. The second nozzle clicked and spat out a jet of flame, turning the withered weeds into a miniature torch.

"We kill. You die." I crossed my arms on my chest. "No need to discuss. Return to your pit."

The Dushegubs creaked and hissed.

I tapped my broom on the stone floor. A low sound pulsed through the arena, rattling my bones. The Dushegubs were sensitive to vibration and sounds. That was how they identified their prey.

The trees scooted back.

"Submit."

The Dushegubs moved together into a clump, folding their branches. I opened the floor under them and funneled them down a slippery chute into their pit.

Sean laughed.

"Sadly, this isn't the end of it. They are single-minded assholes. I surprised them this time, but they will come back with something."

"What happened to their fellow tree ruler-breaker?"

I turned around. The First Scholar was right behind me, while his two assistants hovered from a respectful distance. He was supposed to have been escorted home by Gaston, who was nowhere in sight.

"Was it harmed?" the First Scholar asked.

"No," Sean said. "I dropped her back into the Pit."

Dushegubs were gonochoric, with male and female trees. Telling them apart was pretty much impossible, but only females produced the spore pods.

"Their spore pods aren't lethal," I explained. "They cause a temporary stupor. They hurl them at distant prey to knock it out so they can get close and eat it."

Had the pod landed, Bestata would've taken a nap. But then, with vampire metabolism, it might have only slowed her down, and then we would be treated to a stunning impersonation of Paul Bunyan done in knight armor with vampire weapons. A primed blood sword would cut through an adult Dushegub in two or three swings.

"We keep all our guests safe. Even the pesky ones," Sean said.

"Speaking of guests," the First Scholar said. "Could the inn accommodate three more? I wish to see how this contest plays out."

"We would be delighted to have you with us," I told him. "But what of your lectures?"

The First Scholar sighed. "Steering the development of young minds is an arduous and draining task. One should rest to be most effective, and a few days of self-study and personal contemplation would be beneficial to my students."

I still had the koo-ko coop in storage, but it would be way too large. I carved a new set of rooms in the observer wing and began shaping them into a small habitat. What was it he liked last time? Millet. That was it. I'd need to let Orro know.

Sean's cell rang. He took it out of his robe and looked at it. "Marais."

Officer Marais had been moonlighting as our security guard. He had a ton of leave built up, so he had taken a week off to guard Gertrude Hunt. He also did not share that fact with his wife. I had a feeling there would be hell to pay.

Sean listened for a few moments.

"I'll be right there." He hung up and turned to me. "We have protesters."

"What?"

"Some sort of Dominion religious group is protesting in front of the inn. They have an issue with the spousal selection."

"In broad daylight?"

I pulled the feed from the street-facing cameras onto the nearest big screen. Three people stood in front of the inn, just outside of the boundary. They must've used skin tints because their skin shades looked terrestrial enough. Their high-tech signs, projected from small metal rods and glowing neon, did not.

"I've got this," Sean told me.

He took off toward a wall. The inn made an opening for him.

I waved the screen off.

"Is this urgent?" the First Scholar asked.

"No worries, Sean will handle it." I finished furnishing the room and opened a passageway to the observer wing. "Let me show you to your rooms."

We walked down the hallway. This was my chance to pick his brain. We still had a hidden assassin to deal with.

"What is your opinion of Nycati?"

"Intelligent, eloquent, and well educated," the First Scholar said. "Alas, not a true philosopher."

"Why?"

"Nycati shares the same shortcomings as Amphie, although hers are more apparent."

"I thought she did well."

The First Scholar shook his head. "She had good teachers. They taught her how to find knowledge and how to retain it, but they failed to ignite the spark of original thought. It is true that familiarizing oneself with the thoughts of those who came before us is the foundation of philosophy, but it is only the first step. The next step is to develop one's own view. A much more terrifying endeavor."

"Then Amphie lost?"

"Without a doubt. What question did I ask?"

"What is love?"

The First Scholar nodded. "Exactly. I asked them for their definition of love. Amphie simply announced that love was complex, regurgitated what she was taught about it, and walked us back in a circle to her thesis. She never answered the question."

"And Lady Wexyn?"

The First Scholar's eyes lit up. "Such a beautifully concise demonstration of Tessidect's Principle. He was one of the foundational philosophers that came out of the Omega Centauri Cluster about a thousand years ago. Tessidect proposed that love, in essence, is binding. Whether reciprocated or not, it creates a relationship between a being and the object of their desire, forming its own microcosm. A miniature universe of our own making, subverting all aspects of the time-space continuum. When you are in love, your perception, your inner equilibrium, even your sense of time and place is altered."

Interesting. I never thought of it that way.

The First Scholar continued, waving his stick as he walked. "Since every being is unique and unlike any other, so too their love and the microcosm it creates are unique. It cannot be defined, but only experienced."

True. I had been in love before I met Sean, but my relationship with him was unlike any of the others. It was... It was different, and I couldn't quite put it into words.

"In two short sentences, Lady Wexyn distilled the very essence of this concept: her love cannot be explained, only felt; it is unlike any other; and she prefers it to all prior loves she has experienced. I should have expected nothing less from the disciple of the Temple of Desire. After all, their education is exquisite."

There was a lot more to Lady Wexyn than she showed to the world, although a certain long-suffering chancellor would likely tell the First Scholar that he was giving her way too much credit.

"But Prysen Ol is the true find of the bunch. Did you notice he quoted Sequatist? I know of many scholars who would shrink away from even mentioning that name. A planetphage, a superorganism traveling from planet to planet, devouring all life to support its own, yet aware and tormented by its existence, cursed, reviled, and finally destroyed, and here is this young man who not only had the courage to quote its exploration of one's purpose, but to expand on it, adding his own observations. I'm almost certain he comes from the Sa Monastery. His arguments have their particular relaxed yet refined approach."

"Could he be an impostor?"

"Impossible. He must've devoted himself to study from early childhood. I have seen scores of young aspirants, and this man has put in the work."

If Prysen Ol was a true scholar, that made him less likely to be an assassin. Not impossible, but not as likely.

Right now, my money was on Nycati. But then there was also Lady Wexyn, who had a unique grasp of ancient philosophy, "moved well," and warranted a visit from Caldenia.

And Ellenda, who was now wearing mourning paint possibly because she knew she was about to murder Kosandion and would not survive the aftermath. The candidates were promised to have a one-on-one date with the Sovereign, but it was not a guarantee. A candidate could be eliminated before their turn for the date ever came about. Ellenda was lagging in the rankings, so she put on the mourning paint, knowing Kosandion would recognize it and react. Now she would have her date and the perfect opportunity to target him...

We reached the new quarters I had just made. I opened the door. A comfortable room waited for us, not too large, not too small, its walls lined with tree branches offering convenient perches. Three house-nests protruded from the walls in a triangle around the central shallow pool. The middle nest was larger than the others and decorated with colorful pebbles. Three windows, each with an individual perch, flooded the room with sunshine. Two other smaller rooms branched off to the sides, one a bathroom and the other a study.

"Wonderful," the First Scholar murmured. He waved his wings at his assistants.

They closed in. One of them gingerly pulled several large pins from the First Scholar's feathers, the other grasped the headdress and plucked it from his head.

The older koo-ko sighed in relief, sat at the edge of the pool, and dipped his taloned feet into the water. His feathers fluffed up, puffing him to twice his normal girth.

I opened my mouth to wish him a good stay.

The inn chimed in my head. Someone was trying to open a communication channel from Baha-char.

The inn sprouted a screen for me, and I took the call. A woman appeared, wrapped in a shawl, so only a small sliver of her face was visible. Her skin was variegated, a color pattern you normally saw on a brindled dog or a tortoise cat, and dotted with tiny diamond-shaped protrusions. No, not protrusions, thin scales. She was clearly a type of human, and yet she had scaled skin. I had never seen anything like it.

"Are you the innkeeper?" she whispered, her voice urgent.

"Yes."

"The Sovereign is in danger. One of the candidates is not who they claim to be. Meet me at the glass stall on Curved Street. I will wait for half an hour. No males."

The screen went dark.

———

I MARCHED THROUGH THE INN IN MY TRAVEL ROBE, A NONDESCRIPT gray garment, worn and slightly tattered. Sean marched next to me, looking like a thundercloud about to erupt with lightning.

"It's not safe."

"I'm bringing my energy whip and my broom."

The broom, reshaped into a staff for ease of carrying, was in a Velcro sheath on my back. The energy whip was on my belt under my robe. Squeezing it would release a seven-foot-long filament that could cut a human's head off the body, instantly cauterizing the wound. I'd been practicing with it, and I'd gotten good enough to not need the glove that I used to wear with it. The glove was the only thing the whip wouldn't cut, but it also hurt my hand when I wore it.

Sean's face turned into a harsh mask. "That's not enough. I'll go instead."

"You'll go and nothing will happen. She said no males."

"I don't care what she said."

"I'm getting that."

"You are the only female innkeeper here. If they wanted to isolate you, this is the perfect way to do it. Send a woman who pretends to be scared, so there is no possible way you would bring backup."

"I *am* bringing backup."

The door in front of me swung open, and I walked out onto the terrace where Karat, Gaston, and Dagorkun were drinking tea and watching Cookie chase a yellow butterfly in the orchard. It felt like the beginning of a joke. A knight, a warrior, and a spy walk into a bar...

"And here come our lovely hosts," Gaston said. "Uh-oh. I don't like those expressions."

The two fighters came alert like sharks sensing blood in the water.

"Is there trouble?" Dagorkun asked. "Please let there be trouble. I have a lot of pent-up frustration to release."

"Lady Karat," I said. "Would you fancy a short trip?"

Karat's eyes narrowed. "What kind of trip? Would it require primed weapons?"

"Probably."

She jumped up. "Let's go! I'll get my sword."

Karat ducked inside, into the common room, and jogged to her quarters.

"See?" I told Sean. "Backup."

He growled. "Fine."

"I must protest!" Dagorkun rumbled.

"Girls' trip," I told him. "No males."

"I should come," Cookie called from the orchard.

How in the world had he even heard us?

"Cookie, you're a male."

Cookie smiled into his whiskers. "A very quiet, very sneaky male that no one will notice."

A speculative light appeared in Sean's eyes.

"No," I told him.

Karat emerged onto the balcony. She wore a long dark cloak that hung open in the front, giving a glimpse of a massive sword strapped to her thigh. She pulled the cloak closed and raised her hood. "Ready."

———

KARAT AND I HURRIED THROUGH BAHA-CHAR'S CROWDED STREETS. We had about fifteen minutes left.

"Why Curved Street?" Karat grumbled. "Couldn't she have picked somewhere closer?"

"You'll see when we get there."

We passed another alley, turned into the next one, and emerged onto Curved Street. It wasn't so much a curve as a horseshoe, with narrow alleys branching off from both sides. Tall, terraced buildings rose everywhere, connected by breezeways, bridges, and colorful canvas shade sails. Shoppers clogged the alleys.

"I see," Karat said. "It's a warren."

"Yes. Easy to run away and disappear."

"If she runs, should I chase her?"

"No. We came here in good faith. She will say what she has to say, or she won't."

The glass stall sat in the middle of the U, visible from far away because of a tall mast that protruded from the entrance, rising above the street at an angle like an oversized fishing pole. Glass doohickeys, ornaments, wind chimes, prisms, and suspended vases in every color and shape hung from it, glittering and shining in the light.

We stopped directly under the mast. Shoppers moved past us in a steady current. Across the street, a group of short, hairy creatures that looked like a hybrid of a monkey and a donkey enthusiastically bargained with a tachi weapon shop owner, climbing onto each other to better screech in his face. The insectoid tachi was remarkably patient with their silliness.

"We're being watched," Karat said.

I felt it too, a focused gaze scrutinizing us with desperate intensity.

Moments dragged by.

A spot of light fell on Karat's cloak and slid toward me. I raised my head.

The building that housed the weapons shop was shaped like a backward L. Its bottom floor was the widest. On the right side, the building rose three stories high. On the left, a large roof terrace stretched from its second story over the top of the remaining first floor. A narrow stone staircase squeezed between the left end of the terrace and the next building, the only access to the terrace from the street.

On that terrace, a lone figure wrapped in a shawl stood by the stone rail, holding a small mirror in her hand.

"We're invited," Karat said. "We passed inspection."

"Seems so."

We crossed the street to the narrow stone staircase. The terrace sat forty feet above the street, too far to jump. If we went up there, the staircase would be the only way down.

Karat eyed the stairs. "Your sister informed me that you are not a fighter. If there's trouble, hide behind me."

"Thank you for that generous offer."

"It wasn't a suggestion."

She really was Maud's best friend. They were exactly the same.

The terrace was empty except for the woman with the mirror. As expected, it offered only two exits, the stairs that we took and a door leading inside the second floor of the weapons shop. The door was open, and something stood just inside, hidden in the gloom.

"A combat droid," Karat murmured.

"How can you know that? It's too dark to see."

"I smell the lubricant and cooling fluid."

Vampires.

Karat halted. I stopped too. The woman watched us for a moment, then approached. She moved very quietly. She came within three feet of us and held out a small tablet. On it a familiar face grinned. The haircut was different, the clothes didn't match his current image, and his smile had a vicious edge, but there was no doubt.

"His name, his true name, is Cumbr Adgi. His father rules the Vagabond fleet of the Muterzen meteorite belt."

"Pirate," Karat spat out. "I hate pirates."

"He was raised in luxury bought with the misery of many others. He's sadistic and merciless."

The woman pulled her hood down. Tiny scales sheathed her face. With her large, dark eyes and delicate features, she would have been beautiful by any standard. A large scar crossed the left side of her face, stretching diagonally from her nose to her jaw. The edges of the scar were red and ragged. Another scar clasped her neck, old and thick from repeated wounds. It was the kind of scar a dog might get if it strained against a collar with spikes on the inside.

"I was altered for him. To please him. The scales are his fetish. He did this." She pointed to the scar on her face. "And this." She pointed to her neck.

Her eyes told me she wasn't lying. They brimmed with pain and cold anger, a kind of fury that had burned like a fire but had been repressed for so long, it crystalized into ice. This woman suffered in ways I couldn't even imagine. People said the eyes were the windows to the soul. If that was true, her soul was raw.

Karat was perfectly still, like a statue.

"There is a price on the Sovereign's head. It's enough to buy a whole fleet," the woman said.

"But it's not the money, is it?" I asked.

"No. He wants to outdo his father and his siblings. This act would bring him great prestige and honor among those he seeks to rule one day."

"He's aiming for the pirate throne," Karat said.

The woman nodded and put her hood back in place. "Now you know where to look. You can verify everything I said. I ask only that you do not kill him. He and his father owe me a debt for the deaths of my parents."

"Do you think you can collect what's owed?" I asked.

"All I need is a small window of opportunity. A shot." The

woman bared her fangs. They were long and slender like those of a cobra.

"You know where the door to my inn is," I said. "If what you say is true, tomorrow would be a good time to linger outside of it."

"I have no reason to trust you," she said.

"I know her and her sister. They do not lie. You will have your shot. Don't waste it," Karat said.

The woman turned and walked away, disappearing into the building. The door slid shut behind her.

We started for the stairs.

"Do you believe her?" the vampire knight asked.

"Trust but verify," I murmured. And I knew just the person who could get me the information I needed in a fraction of the time.

A cold, nasty feeling bloomed in my spine, as if icy, rotting slime dripped onto the back of my neck. Revulsion squirmed through me. I knew this magic.

"Stop!"

Karat froze with her foot an inch off the ground.

A creature moved up the stairs. Its long, tattered robe, so much like my own, swept the stones as if it floated rather than walked. Wide sleeves hid its hands, and the inside of its deep hood was darkness.

Karat put her foot down and pulled her sword from her thigh. Bright red light burst from the hilt, running through the veins within the blade. The blood weapon whined, priming.

The corrupted ad-hal emerged onto the terrace and faced us, blocking our escape. The light caught the bottom half of its face, and I saw the outline of a pale, leathery jaw. We had nowhere to go. The staircase and the building next to it were in front of us. The weapons shop was behind us, and I highly doubted the mystery woman would let us in.

The creature raised its right arm. Its sleeve fell back, revealing a monstrous hand clenched into a fist. The corrupted ad-hal opened its long, clawed fingers. A clump of longish hair fell onto the stones, black shot through with gray.

Goosebumps slid up my arms. *Wilmos.*

"Someone you know?" Karat asked, her gaze fixed on the creature.

"Yes. This thing shoots lightning. Don't try to block it."

A phantom wind stirred the corrupted ad-hal's robe. Fetid magic condensed around it, like a nauseating cloud.

"Is he alive?" I asked it.

The ad-hal didn't answer.

"What do you want? What can I trade you for his life?"

The magic pulsed, so intense I almost gagged.

Something leaped off the roof of the building in front of us. It plunged through the air and smashed into the ad-hal.

The werewolf woman. Oh no.

She ripped into it, stabbing the robe in a frenzy with two blood-red knives. The ad-hal grabbed her and flung her off. She flew, smashed into the building behind the staircase with a crunch, and slid down.

The creature's magic sparked, spawning orange lightning between the fingers of both hands. It leveled one ball at us and the other at the werewolf woman.

"Stay behind me!" Karat barked and charged.

The werewolf woman rolled into a crouch on the stairs and leaped at the ad-hal.

The creature hurled the twin lightning balls. I lunged left, Karat lunged right, and the blinding sphere tore between us. The second ball caught the werewolf in midleap. She'd tried to twist out of the way, but it splashed over her side and back in a burst of white flame. She screamed, the sound of pure agony, and collapsed onto the terrace, writhing in pain.

My body remembered being hit with that lightning. It felt like being thrust into the center of a star, drowning in an unimaginable, searing, unbearable pain that set the marrow of your bones on fire. It had almost killed me. The echo of that pain rolled through my body. Fear filled me, pushing out everything else.

Not again. No, never again.

The lightning ball aimed at us, curved, and streaked to me like a heat-seeking missile.

I dashed to the side, spurred by panic, ripped the energy whip off my belt, and squeezed it. The filament burst out in a shower of yellow sparks. I snapped the whip. The tip caught the ball of lightning. The impact reverberated through my arm, and I threw myself to the ground.

The orange sphere exploded with white fire. The magic blast wave punched me, pushing me backward across the stone. The overload of revolting magic stomped on my ribs, and my heart screamed in my chest. Pain drowned me. I swam out of it, gagged, sobbed, spat blood out of my mouth, and rolled upright.

Karat sliced at the corrupted ad-hal, insanely fast, her sword an extension of her body. The creature raked her armor with its claws. She roared and kept swinging, fast, precise, leaving it no opening to gather its magic.

The werewolf woman staggered to her feet, gripped her knives, and lunged at the ad-hal, looking for an opening. They tore at the creature from opposite sides. It darted between them like a rag on a clothesline dancing in strong wind.

I wasn't fast enough to keep up with either of them. If I tried to attack, I'd hit one of them with the whip.

A long streak of blood drenched the side of Karat's face, wetting her hair. The werewolf's right side was a mess of holes and smoldering clothes. The black hardsuit she wore underneath showed through the gaps.

Karat thrust. The ad-hal spun, turning its back to her, and her blade missed by an inch. The werewolf saw an opening, dove in, and slashed with both knives. The ad-hal jerked aside, avoiding the slash, and lunged at her in the split second her arms were apart. Its clawed hand caught the werewolf just under the sternum. The creature ripped its hand upward, carving flesh and clothes with its claws in a spray of blood. The werewolf screamed.

Karat slashed at the ad-hal. The creature slid out of the way, but the blood blade caught the edge of its robe. A piece of the fabric flew, cut free. Karat grinned, her face a terrifying grimace, and launched a frenzied attack. Left, right, swing, cut, slash, I could barely follow.

The werewolf darted in, stabbing.

Magic spun within the ad-hal's robe.

"Run!" I threw my arm up, pushing my magic in front of me like a shield.

Karat ignored me and stabbed at the ad-hal.

Magic erupted from the creature like a shockwave from a collapsing star. The foul torrent hit Karat and the werewolf, tossing them behind me like they weighed nothing, and smashed into my shield. The air in front of me flashed with turquoise. Orange lightning smashed at the screen of my magic. It felt like a thousand red-hot needles pierced me in a single moment. My arm went numb.

The fetid magic died.

Out of the corner of my eye I saw Karat convulsing on the ground. The werewolf sprawled on her back, making small wheezing noises.

The ad-hal hovered in front of me. A black stain spread through its robe, from the hood to the hem, as if it had shed its skin, exposing its true nature underneath.

I felt it. There it was. The corruption. The awful, wrong, cosmic *thing* that wanted to infect, consume, and smother.

Wisps of orange lightning snaked over the former ad-hal, rising up, as if the creature were caught in an invisible dust devil. This thing with clawed hands and a monstrous jaw used to be a person. A human just like me. Now it was a husk, a host for the corruption within, and that corruption would kill me, then it would kill Karat and the werewolf. None of us would get out alive.

Memories flooded me. Fighting a creature just like this one, almost dying, bringing its body to the inn, learning it was my brother's best friend, and then watching the corruption within it leak out and escape. It crawled inside my inn like some disgusting parasite. It tried to infect Gertrude Hunt and Tony, while I could do nothing, helpless and torn from my own body by the death of the tiny inn I'd tried so hard to save.

I had killed that intruder. I had purged it from my inn. I was an innkeeper, and I would purge this one. It was my duty.

I pulled the broom from my back and planted it in front of me. Magic streamed around me, spiraling from my body and tugging at my hair.

The corrupted ad-hal snapped its hands up.

I pushed my magic out into the building under me. It streamed through the stone of the terrace into the first floor below, growing from the soles of my feet like roots of a tree.

Twin balls of lightning flared in the ad-hal's hands, fed by its magic. It clamped them together. The glowing clumps connected, merging into a blinding sphere churning with energy. More lightning clasped it, sliding from the creature's robe.

"Dina!" Karat yelled behind me. "Get away from it!"

I wrapped my magic around me and the broom like a cocoon, binding us.

The brilliant sphere broke. A beam of orange lightning streaked toward me, mottled with dark magic.

I gripped my broom, pulsing my power through it.

The beam tore at my magic screen, trying to drill through it, scalding, burning, biting… The strain gripped my spine, crushing my vertebrae, so heavy it felt like I would crumple and collapse. The magic tore at me, trying to push me back, but I was anchored. My roots were deep. I would not be moved.

The beam flared with pure white.

186

Agony vibrated through me, radiating from my chest to my fingertips. I tasted blood and held fast.

The beam sputtered.

I waited, filled with pain.

The lightning died.

"My turn."

I fed everything I had into my broom. The shaft split in my hand, sprouting tentacles of brilliant turquoise. They surged to the creature and gripped it in a vise, wrapping over its robe.

The corrupted ad-hal screeched. Its power flared, coating my tentacles, fighting against me. I gritted my teeth and squeezed. Killing wasn't enough. I had to contain it. It would not infect anything else.

The lightning dashed up the tentacles to the broom and bit at my hand. It felt like someone flayed me with an electric razor blade.

I didn't scream. I didn't rage. I just squeezed, harder and harder, trying to wring it out of existence. Nothing it could do to me would make me stop. If the sky cracked and fell on me, I would keep squeezing.

The creature screamed, flailing. Its magic ripped at me, and I felt the corruption within it rage. It burned with fury and frustration, a torch at its own funeral. It had been thwarted, and it knew it, indignant at being bound.

The former ad-hal jerked, frantically trying to rip itself free. My magic pushed against it, spreading from the tentacles, wrapping it up tighter and tighter. It shrank under the pressure. Its robe collapsed into a clump.

I kept squeezing.

The body of the former ad-hal was gone. It was just a blob of pure corruption now, viscous, liquid, but still bound by my power.

It wailed in my mind, enraged and helpless.

I reached deep within, to the bottom of my soul, and sent the final terrible pulse through my broom. My magic crushed the foul blob in its fist. It burst and rained onto the terrace, splattering the stone and the three of us with foul-smelling goo. Its magic was gone. It was just rotting fluid now.

I pulled the tentacles into the broom and wiped the disgusting sludge from my face. Behind me, Karat staggered to her feet.

[17]

When we last left our inn crew, Dina, Karat, and the werewolf fought the corrupted ad-hal. The Sovereign's date with Ellenda is looming ever closer. Will our trio get back to the inn in time for Dina to fulfil her role as an innkeeper and will they survive that journey? Stay tuned for the next exciting instalment... Okay I will stop now.

The door leading from Baha-char to Gertrude Hunt swung open, and Karat and I staggered through it, smeared with blood and fetid fluids and carrying the unconscious werewolf between us, her arms draped over our shoulders. We took a step down the hallway and ran straight into Sean.

"God damn it," he snarled, grabbing the werewolf woman out of our arms.

"We don't have time for this. She's critical, and Karat is injured."

"I'm perfectly fine." Karat gave me a trademark vampire-knight sneer.

Of course, she was. The left side of her face was the color of a pomegranate, she was taking short shallow breaths, and her armor would need hours of repairs. Vampires didn't bruise easily. She either took a hard hit or landed on her face.

I opened the tunnel to the medward in the floor. Sean lifted the werewolf like she was a child and started down. "Once this is handled, we will make time."

It sounded like a threat.

The moment Sean lowered the werewolf into the nearest med unit, it unfolded like one of those three-dimensional greeting cards. Scanners slipped out from under the bottom of the bed, sliding diagnostic lights over her body, and robotic arms sprung from the frame, stripping her clothes. The results of the scans flashed above the unit. Three broken ribs, shredded lung, internal bleeding... Oh wow. The corrupted ad-hal had sliced right through her hardsuit and her ribs like they were tissue paper.

Ironically, hardsuits were considered soft armor, soft being a relative term. There were many variations of it, but the essential requirements dictated that it was flexible, close fitting, and able to stop a typical blade. I could hack at the werewolf woman all day with an ordinary knife and not leave a mark. One look at her chest told me her suit was beyond repair.

Karat touched the House Krahr crest embedded in her breastplate. Her syn-armor came apart at the seams. She lowered it to the floor. Oh. It was worse than I thought.

Normally, getting a vampire out of their armor was an impossible task. They took it off only in the privacy of their quarters, for rest and intimacy. For them, the armor was a second skin that kept them safe, and sometimes they fought to keep it on even when severely injured. Karat dropped hers without any hesitation.

It was an unprecedented show of trust. Of course. She was Maud's best friend and I was Maud's sister. Karat trusted me to keep her safe.

The vampire woman winced as the last of her armor slid free.

The dark gray suit Karat wore underneath was thankfully blood-free.

"If I fall asleep, wake me up," she said. "I can't miss the Sovereign's dates."

"We will," I promised.

She climbed into the unit, and it sprang into action. The scan flashed on the holographic screen above the bed. She had a broken rib, and there were early signs of sepsis.

Sean stepped in front of me, his face harsh. "Dina. Decontamination shower."

I touched the nasty goo drying on my skin, looked at my stained fingers for a second, and went to clean up.

Ten minutes later, I emerged with clean hair and skin and wearing another robe over my shorts and T-shirt. The runoff from the shower drained into a tank under the floor. The fetid slime I washed off my body felt inert, but I heated the tank until the dirty water evaporated and then flushed the reservoir with acid just to be on the safe side.

Karat was napping in her med unit with a dreamy smile on her face. Sean was staring at the werewolf woman, Gorvar sitting by his side.

I came to stand next to them. "How is she?"

"She'll live."

"Karat will be happy. She'd carried her most of the way."

"Tell me," he said. "All of it."

I did.

He looked up at the ceiling, his face unreadable.

"I'm sorry," I told him.

"For what?"

"I had no idea she would jump from the roof and start a fight."

It had been a priceless opportunity to communicate with Wilmos' kidnapper. I didn't even know if the corrupted ad-hal could speak or understand me, but I would've tried my hardest.

Every crumb of information was precious. It killed me that I didn't get anything more out of the corrupted ad-hal.

Sean exhaled. "Nothing it could tell us would be worth you getting hurt."

"I wasn't hurt."

"I smelled your blood when you came in, and I can feel the way the inn is hovering around you. How much magic did it cost you?"

"More than I thought I had," I said quietly.

Sean looked at the werewolf woman, his face grim. "She shouldn't have started that fight."

"Have you met her before she showed up at the inn for the first time? Maybe on one of the trips with Wilmos?"

"If I did, I don't remember."

It didn't surprise me. When werewolves encountered Sean, they either stared at him with worshipful eyes, hit on him, or tried to fight him. He made it a point to interact with his people as little as possible.

"She really cares about Wilmos. She risked her life for him," I said.

"That doesn't make her special. Every werewolf I know cares about Wilmos," Sean said. "If you're a werewolf and you have a problem, you come to see Wilmos. He will either fix it or know someone who will."

"The way he fixed your problem by sending you to Nexus?" I shouldn't have said that.

Sean faced me. "Back then I wanted three things: to learn about werewolves, to learn about the galaxy, and to learn about myself. I wanted to know how far I could go, so I'd asked him for the most dangerous job he had. He thought it was a bad idea. Tried his best to talk me out of it. Told me that he hadn't brought my parents up from babies just so I could get myself killed because I thought my father saw a bigger moon."

I hadn't heard that werewolf idiom, but the meaning wasn't hard to figure out. Nothing Earth could throw at Sean could compare to the kind of combat his parents endured. He'd wanted to know if he could measure up. I would have to apologize to Wilmos.

"Is that what his projects are about? Helping random werewolves?"

"It's either removing a threat or getting money. He never keeps any of it. It all goes out as soon as it comes in."

"I had no idea Wilmos was the werewolf fairy godfather," I murmured.

Sean barked a short laugh. "You should call him that when we rescue him."

"And you sure she isn't Wilmos' family?"

He shook his head. "He doesn't have any. Unless you count the alpha strain. A chunk of his DNA is in all of us."

Sean glanced at the female werewolf.

"You really don't like her," I told him.

"She barged into the inn and then put you in danger."

"We've discussed this before. There will be times I will be in danger."

"I would like those times to be less frequent. This was avoidable."

"I stand by my decision. I've met the woman in the shawl. There was no way she would ever set foot in the inn or let me change the location of the meeting. You should have seen her eyes, Sean."

"I don't care about her eyes."

The line of his jaw hardened. He stepped closer and kissed me. I tasted Sean, and the forest inside him swallowed me whole. The trees closed in, sheltering me, and the scarred wolf who lived in there wrapped himself around me to keep me safe.

The kiss ended, and I looked up at him. He hugged me to him, his strong arms warm. There was no place safer.

"Were you worried?" I asked softly.

"A little."

I leaned my head against his chest. "I was worried too."

In Sean's perfect world, we would live happily ever after in complete safety and nothing bad would injure us. But even he knew that a future like that wasn't just unrealistic, it would be boring. Even before we were together, he was a werewolf soldier looking for adventure, and I was an innkeeper who took it upon herself to police the neighborhood. We'd had multiple chances to get out and settle into a more peaceful life, and we'd rolled right past them. We didn't look for trouble, but we didn't back down when it found us.

"I'm okay," I told him.

He kissed me again.

"If you keep doing this, we're going to miss the Sovereign's date," I murmured.

"It would be worth it."

"We can't. He might get murdered."

He sighed. "Do you believe your informant?"

"Yes. And I know how we can quickly verify it."

He frowned. "Cookie?"

I nodded. Clan Nuan's information network was one of the best in the galaxy. Cookie wanted Lady Wexyn to win. If the pirate candidate got eliminated as a result of this, Lady Wexyn would face less competition.

"If he can confirm this, I would do something right."

Sean bared his teeth. "You did everything right. You kicked ass. You beat a corrupted ad-hal outside of the inn. That's fucking amazing."

It was kind of amazing. And I shouldn't have been able to do it.

The first time I had put that much effort into using my magic outside of the inn, I ended up gasping for breath in my car outside of Costco. If Sean hadn't found me, I would've died. The second time we fought Michael, and I almost died then, too, but not because of the magic drain. Actually, now that I thought of it, I had committed a lot more magic to that fight than I did to the one in Costco, and I'd managed to hang on to consciousness.

This time, I killed the corrupted ad-hal and then came home. I was tired, but I was still talking and walking.

Did my power grow without me realizing it?

"If I was the one who kidnapped Wilmos, I would be worried right now," Sean said. "This did not go the way they expected."

No, it didn't. "I wish I knew what the hair meant. Is it 'hurry up and come get him' or is it 'do as we say or he's dead?'"

"No way to tell."

The only way to find out was to finish the spouse selection and get to Karron.

The inn chimed. 30 minutes before the Sovereign's first date. I sighed and went to wake Karat up.

———

THE BROADCASTING SCHEDULE OF THE DOMINION HAD A DEFINITE pattern. Formal occasions of little interest, like the reintroduction of the candidates, were the most edited and presented to the audience with a significant delay. The trials were almost live, with only a few minutes of lag to make the emergency adjustments. The dates with individual candidates were practically in real time.

Nothing could go wrong.

When Orata realized just how much power the innkeepers had over our environment, she'd hopped up and down in excitement. Thanks to Kosandion's PR chief, every candidate was asked their preferred theme for their date. Ellenda had chosen trees. No other guidance. Just one word: trees.

I took them to the orchard.

Back when I was growing up in my parents' inn, I was responsible for the gardens. They were my favorite part of innkeeping, and the massive magnolia tree that ruled over the other trees and flowerbeds had been my crowning achievement.

I'd been an innkeeper for about four years now, and Gertrude Hunt's orchard was a place of beauty. From the street, it looked like any typical backyard garden you might find in a house with a bit of acreage. Ornamental shrubs, a few apple trees, some oaks. If you worked your way through the bushes, you would run into my camouflage wall, a tall barrier designed to perfectly mimic the shrubs around it. Very thin and undetectable from the street, it changed with its environment and ran all along the property, keeping the actual orchard out of view.

Kosandion waited in the inner orchard now, the one nobody except the guests and us ever saw. Tall apple trees flanked a wide stone path. They had finished blooming, and their branches bore tiny fruit. The sun shone through the green leaves. Flowers grew between the trees and along the path's edges, raspberry-colored coras, purslane in every shade from pink to lemon yellow, zinnias bursting with magenta, pink, and crimson, and finally, in brightly lit spots, red yuccas. Ruby-throated hummingbirds hovered near the tiny yucca blooms. The air smelled of flowers and summer grass.

"Could you put up the screen please?" Orata whispered through my earpiece.

I had my doubts about the screen. The date seemed like it should be a private affair, but Kosandion had asked me to defer to Orata's wishes.

I moved my hand, and a massive branch slipped through the canopy and grew a screen on it. The view of the Ocean Dining Hall appeared on it. We had packed all the delegates into it, with snacks and refreshments. The live feed from the date was projected onto several massive screens, so they would see every moment in real time.

Sean parked himself at the back wall of the dining hall. He wore a gray robe and turned his usual spear into a staff for the occasion. Originally, he was going to chaperone the date, but I was too tapped out to handle a dining room filled with that many creatures right now.

And right now he didn't have Tony for back up. In the few minutes before the date, I had explained the fake spouse candidate and the corrupted ad-hal encounter to Tony. He'd left the inn to look at the scene of the fight. Very few things could knock a smile off Tony's face, but that one did. Michael was his best friend. Tony wanted revenge. He didn't talk about it, but his eyes said plenty.

A stir ran through the delegates in the Ocean Dining Hall. Everyone turned.

Karat entered the room.

Repairing syn-armor was a delicate art requiring years of practice. Karat didn't have time to fix it, so she didn't bother. Her once pristine black armor was scuffed. A big rip crossed her chest, and two smaller ones marked her ribs. The injury to the left side of her face had faded from bright red to a less fresh but obvious bruise, and she wore it like a badge of honor.

Dagorkun turned purple, from jealousy or curiosity, I couldn't tell.

Karat raised her chin and marched to the observers' table. House Meer practically dislocated their necks trying to get a better look.

"Quite an entrance," Kosandion murmured next to me.

"Look at Bestata's face," I said.

Bestata's eyes narrowed. She focused on Karat like a tiger who just saw another tiger bleeding from its wounds and was desperately trying to figure out what kind of predator made them.

Six tiny globes, about the size of a walnut, rose into the area, floating around us and above. Orata's cameras.

"You are live," Orata said into my earpiece.

Right. No more private conversations. I muted the sound on my screen so it wouldn't interfere.

The back door of the inn opened, and Gaston emerged,

leading Ellenda into the light. She still wore the gold paint and her rough-woven dark garment. Her expression was flat.

Tony melted back into the dark entrance. He would be going back to the Ocean Dining Hall to help Sean.

Ellenda approached Kosandion. He inclined his head a couple of inches. "Welcome, *kalenti*."

Ellenda bowed her head slowly. No response. Off to an awesome start.

"Shall we walk?" he asked.

"Yes."

The two of them strolled down the path, leaving about a foot of space between them. I followed a couple of steps behind. Orata's orbs followed. My screen did too, sliding along the path.

"What branch do you hail from, *kalenti?*" Kosandion asked. His voice was calm and light. Reassuring with its warmth.

"My people come from Sahava."

"The land of cliffs and dark forests, where the glowing ava flowers bloom in the deep."

A little bit of life came back into Ellenda's voice. "Yes. Have you ever been?"

"My mother took me there when I was young. We spent four days in the House on the Cliff. I remember sleeping in the spider cocoon hammocks suspended over the raging sea. I thought it was the best bed ever invented." Kosandion chuckled softly.

"I'm surprised. The cocoon hammocks scare outsiders."

"I'm not an outsider. I'm a child of the Dominion and a child of the Uma. One doesn't exclude the other."

"I meant no offense." Caution iced over her voice.

Kosandion offered her another smile. "I took none."

They reached the pond where the stone path curved around the water. The pond took up a whole acre, a shallow, crystal-clear body of water with a large flat rock jutting out a few feet from its left shore. Little fish darted in the cool depths, and brilliant water lilies bloomed on the surface. Stone benches along the path offered places to rest. This was Sean's favorite spot. When the inn had a lull of visitors, we came here to swim in the pond, sunbathe on the hot rock, and drink beer.

Kosandion and Ellenda continued down the path.

"Do you truly mean that?" Ellenda asked softly. "Are you a child of the Uma?"

Kosandion pulled his left sleeve up and raised his arm. A row of intricate white tattoos shot through with gold marked his dark skin.

Ellenda stopped and turned to face him, a resolute expression on her face. He pivoted toward her. They stood on the path, perfectly still, the same straight posture. In that moment, the two of them looked like they belonged to the same people.

Ellenda took a deep breath.

I braced for an attack.

"Tell me what troubles you, *kalenti*. You can tell me anything."

"Anything?" she asked.

"Anything at all. This is our moment. My time and my attention are yours."

Ellenda exhaled and shut her eyes.

If she moved a muscle in his direction, I would drop her right through the floor. I had expended a lot of magic, but it wouldn't take much, and my reaction time was just fine.

The Uma woman opened her eyes. "Do not choose me."

On the screen behind them, the Ocean Dining Hall went perfectly still. Nobody moved.

"What do you mean?" Kosandion asked.

"Do not choose me. I don't want to be your wife."

Oh wow. I did not expect that.

"My branch owes a debt to the Kyporo outsiders," she said. "I came here to repay it."

Duty over happiness. Of course.

"My presence was required. I don't want to marry you. I don't want to stay in the Dominion. Don't try to take my freedom, because I will defend it with my life. So please don't choose me."

A silence fell. Birds chirped in the trees, a fish broke the surface of the water and splashed, but the two people in front of me were perfectly still and silent.

On the screen, the faces of the Frowns delegation looked contorted, some with alarm, others with outrage. Their leader clenched his fists on the table.

A subtle change came over Kosandion. He seemed larger somehow, formidable, majestic, no longer a man but an embodiment of power.

"What is it you truly want, daughter of the Uma?" he asked.

Ellenda opened her mouth and then spoke, as if jumping off a cliff. "I want to go home to my planet and the man I love."

"It is done," the Sovereign said.

There was a resounding finality to his voice. Goosebumps ran down my arms.

"Innkeeper, take Ellenda to the portal. Once she passes through it, the Dominion will chart a ship to take her back to her homeworld. No citizen of the Dominion will ever trouble her or her branch again."

On the screen one of the Frown delegates, a man wearing white and green, stood up and walked down the aisle to the door.

Where the hell was he going?

The man reached the table where the Holy Ecclesiarch sat with his entourage.

A transparent column shot out of the ground, sealing the holy man and his retinue inside. Wind jerked their hair as Sean flushed the inside of it with fresh air. At the same time a second column caught the man from the Frowns delegation, cutting him off from the dining hall. He jerked and collapsed.

I turned the volume back up, and the sound roared in, beings jumping to their feet.

Sean leaped over the tables and landed in the middle of the

room, his gray robe flaring around him. The staff in his hand split, releasing a brilliant green spear head. His mouth opened, and he roared in the deep snarling voice of an alpha-strain werewolf. It was the same voice that had thundered over the battlefields of Nexus.

"Freeze!"

The three hundred creatures in the dining hall stopped as one.

When we last left the inn, Kosandion's date with the Uma candidate, Ellenda, did not go to plan, and her delegation made a move against the Dominion's Holy Ecclesiarch. Will Dina and Sean manage to eliminate the dangers gathering around the Sovereign? In this week's episode of Sweep of the Heart...

The prisoner hung from the ceiling of the throne room, his body wrapped in the inn's restraints. The Kyporo delegation stood under him, grim-faced and ready for some sort of action if only they could figure out what that action might be. Calling them Team Frowns in my head no longer seemed appropriate.

The rest of the delegates had been asked to return to their quarters. Only the Sovereign faction and the observers remained. The feed was going live to the entire Dominion. Kosandion was making a point: he had nothing to hide, from his people or from the rest of the galaxy.

He sat on the throne now, his expression harsh and cold, watching the massive screen behind the prisoner. On it, Tony led Ellenda to the portal. Her head was held high. They stopped before the round gateway. She turned, looked back at the camera, and gave us a brilliant smile.

The lights on the rim of the portal flashed, the green glow swirled, the Uma woman stepped into it, and her presence vanished from the inn.

Kosandion looked at Sean. "What happened?"

"That man tried to kill the Holy Ecclesiarch," Sean said.

"How?"

"Poison. A microcapsule sealed inside his tooth. He bit it and exhaled the poisoned vapor."

And Sean sensed it despite being forty feet away. Hundreds of innkeepers had watched him crush that assassination attempt. Not even one would disagree with a simple fact: Sean Evans was amazing.

"The antidote is already in the prisoner's system," Sean continued. "He will survive."

"Unfortunate," Kosandion said. The word landed like a brick.

The leader of the Kyporo delegation, a spare, ascetic-looking man, stared at Kosandion with open hostility.

The Holy Ecclesiarch smiled. Every time I had seen him, his kind face all but shone with benevolence, but in this moment his expression changed, as if a different man rose from the depths to the surface. Shrewd. Smart. Powerful. It was there for a mere fraction of a second and vanished back into a soft caring smile. Something wasn't right about this.

"Well," the holy man sighed. "At least I'm still important enough to be murdered."

"Obviously, Sar Ramin had a lapse in judgement," the leader of the delegation ground out. "We had no idea he held such extremist views."

"How quick you are to throw your people into the fire, Odikas," Kosandion said.

"He is young and impressionable," Odikas said. "A group

should not be penalized for the actions of one individual, nor should it bear responsibilit—"

"I thought you were a man of vision," Kosandion said, his voice harsh.

His pose was relaxed, almost languid, but the intensity in his eyes was frightening. His body signaled that he didn't condescend to view Odikas as any kind of threat, and his face assured that retribution was coming, and it would be swift and brutal.

"Alas, I was wrong, and you are blind. What is it you said about my father? A weakling controlled by a woman, wasn't it?"

"Yes," Resven confirmed, his voice so buttery you could spread it on toast.

"You brought an Uma woman here, because you thought I missed my mother so much, I would forget my duty, lose my mind, and throw away the nation's interests for a chance to bed someone who looks like my parent."

The Kyporo delegation collectively winced. Yes. Ew.

The cavernous room was so quiet, you would hear the proverbial pin drop.

"Did you plan to use her to influence my policy decisions, or was I supposed to die once the heir was born, so you could pull her strings and play at being regent?"

Odikas clenched his teeth.

"How long was I supposed to remain alive? Would you have given me the courtesy to see my offspring being born?"

No answer.

Kosandion shook his head slightly. "The Uma value their freedom beyond everything else. You forced Ellenda to come here against her will. If I had chosen her, she would either have killed you or killed herself. All those years you blamed my mother for the reforms my father implemented, and yet you never took the time to learn anything about her people."

The gray skin on the older man's cheeks turned darker. Odikas looked a hair from losing it.

Kosandion glanced at Resven. "Explain it to him."

"You knew Ellenda was in danger of being eliminated when you saw the preliminary rankings," Resven said. "She refused to debate, so you counted on the date to save you. The moment she reclaimed her freedom, your plans collapsed, so you sent your favorite subordinate to murder the Holy Ecclesiarch in hopes that his death would force us to void the selection and begin again. It is painfully obvious, and yet you're making excuses, as if the whole world has lost the ability to reason, and you are the only one still thinking."

A grimace twisted Odikas' face. He bared his teeth.

Resven stared at him, derision plain on his face. "It's not the plotting. It's the sheer, obnoxious stupidity of it that irritates me. A man of grand ambition yet meager talent should at least strive for hiring a capable adviser."

Wow. I had no idea Resven had it in him. There had to be some history there.

"You!" Odikas choked out.

"Look into the sensors, Odikas," Resven said. "We are here to witness the funeral of your career. At last, the Dominion is watching just as you always wanted. All eyes are upon you. Are you not pleased? Was it everything you hoped it would be?"

Odikas clenched his fists, choked by his own outrage.

"The Kyporo delegation is disqualified," Kosandion said. "All their asks and honors are void."

"You can't do that!" one of the delegates shouted.

Kosandion looked at him. It was like being on a dark cliff and suddenly having the bright beam of the lighthouse fall upon you.

"For the citizens at home, tell me, Chancellor, can I do that?"

"Absolutely," Resven said. "The law gives you that power, *Letero*. The Kyporo delegation knows it does. They have read the contracts and signed them prior to their arrival."

Kosandion glanced at me. "These people are no longer part of the selection. The Dominion thanks our gracious hosts for their patience in delaying their expulsion at my request. I do not dare to abuse their hospitality any longer."

I would have to find a way to thank Kosandion. The innkeepers at home were likely wondering why we hadn't taken any action. He spelled it out in the most deferential way.

My broom split in my hand, revealing its bright blue inner light. The delegates from Kyporo focused on me.

"You've attempted to kill another guest on the inn's grounds. Your guest status is withdrawn. Your belongings wait by the portal."

The wall at the back of the throne room split, revealing the portal room. The screen showed the Kyporo delegation's quarters. I collapsed them. Walls folded as if they were coke cans being crushed. Stone columns disintegrated, flowing like melted wax, absorbed back into the inn. Wooden furniture snapped, shattered, and was consumed by the floor. It was a waste, since Gertrude Hunt expended more energy making it than it would get back, but it was worth it. The reputation of the inn was on the line, and the galaxy needed a reminder. Within our domains, we were supreme. We would not tolerate any breach of rules.

The inn opened a hole in the ceiling by the portal and vomited the delegates' possessions out, packaged into clear plastic-like bags. Had they all participated in trying to kill the Ecclesiarch, I would've dramatically expelled them, hurling them into that portal, but only one of them actually carried out the assassination attempt. Besides, I had a feeling Kosandion had more to say.

The Kyporo delegates stared at the growing bag pile, owl-eyed. Things were happening way too fast.

The last bag fell. The inn had purged them.

Miralitt stepped forward. "Prime Councilor Tair Odikas, you stand accused of conspiring to assassinate a citizen of the Dominion, intent to cause grievous harm to a member of the religious order for the purpose of interfering with their duties, bride-purchasing, sapient-being trafficking, and violation of the Second Covenant."

Ten guards in pale armor emerged from the portal and marched toward us.

The First Covenant of the Dominion spelled out the individual's rights. The Second Covenant established the federal government, its powers, limitations, and vital functions. Violation of the Second Covenant was a catch-all charge that covered a wide variety of offenses. It was also the main charge against Caldenia.

Miralitt had just branded Odikas a traitor, and the Dominion's Capital Guard showed up to take him into custody in all its menacing glory.

The dam that contained Odikas' rage finally broke.

"You're not fit to rule!" he snarled. "Your father *was* a weakling, and you are weak just like him. The abomination who murdered him is right there." He stabbed his finger in Caldenia's direction. "And you sit in that chair as if all of us have forgotten her colossal sins."

Caldenia rose and strode toward Odikas. Uh-oh.

"You think you've won? Ha!" Spit and word flew out of his mouth. "Who are you to judge me? What have you accomplished? What are your achievements? A feeble offspring of a feeble father, soft, indecisive, and spineless. Your very existence impairs our great nation. You should've never been allowed to take the throne. If I had my way, I would've smothered—"

Caldenia stopped in front of Odikas. Her hand shot up, and she drove her razor-sharp nails into the soft tissue right under his jaw. Blood spilled from his mouth.

Well, shit.

Odikas clamped his hands on Caldenia's wrist, trying to pry himself free. She raised her arm.

Odikas' feet left the ground.

Wow.

Caldenia wasn't even straining. Odikas hung from her talons, bleeding from his mouth. I had seen her slice through aluminum cans with her nails.

A female delegate lunged forward to help.

Caldenia glanced at her. Her voice cracked like a whip. "Have you forgotten who I am?"

The Kyporo delegation cringed. The woman ducked and backed away.

Her Grace examined Odikas like he was some sort of gross bug. "You always were an odious toad, Tair. Dumb as a rock, to borrow the local expression. I warned you before to mind your mouth."

Odikas gurgled. More blood came out.

"Your Grace..." I started.

"I haven't killed him yet, Dina. I've only shredded his tongue. The day is yet young."

Odikas made a tortured noise. I needed to stop this.

"Aunt," Kosandion said softly. "Perhaps this one time due process might be a better path forward? Out of consideration for the patience of our gracious hosts?"

Caldenia sighed and dropped Odikas. He landed on the floor. She smelled his blood on her fingers, gave him a small, refined sneer, and shook it off.

"Thank you," Kosandion said.

He motioned to the guards, and they grabbed Odikas and hauled him to his feet.

Sean glanced at the prisoner still suspended from the ceiling. The inn's tendrils unrolled, lowering the captive onto the floor. He took a deep breath and blinked, clearly disoriented. The guards closed in, and two of them sandwiched the would-be assassin between them.

"Form a column," one of the guards ordered.

The delegates obeyed without a word. The guards led them to the pile of their belongings. Each of the delegates grabbed a single bag and one by one, they walked through the portal.

I had no idea what the innkeepers watching this would make of it.

"We'll reconvene tomorrow," Kosandion announced.

I opened the doors to their quarters. Kosandion strode off, his people behind him. Gaston offered Caldenia his arm. They walked away. He said something and Caldenia laughed softly.

Sean approached. I took his hand. He squeezed my fingers.

"You are awesome," I whispered.

"No, just fast."

The observers walked past me toward their quarters. Karat made big eyes at me. Dagorkun was grinning. Cookie was next.

I pulled the floor under Cookie's feet toward us. To his credit, he didn't jump in surprise. The floor brought him to us and stopped.

"A word?" I asked.

"Of course." Cookie nodded.

"We need some information," Sean said.

Cookie fluffed his tail and squinted his eyes. I had seen that exact expression on Nuan Cee's face. It meant trouble.

"Tell me more," Cookie purred.

It was two hours until midnight. I sat on the terrace of the Ocean Dining Room savoring a cup of oolong tea and gently rocking in a rocking chair I had stolen from our patio. Sean sat in the other chair, drinking decaffeinated coffee. It was late and he didn't want to be wired. Beast napped by the rail, while Gorvar had somehow climbed on top of the other table and lay there, his tongue out. He liked being high up.

The deep amber ocean of Kolinda shimmered with bioluminescent sparks, as if the setting sun had bled its glowing lifeblood into the waters and now it flickered in the depths. The air was warm and smelled of salt and sea.

To our left and slightly behind, the interior of the Ocean Dining Hall glowed with honey-colored light of its chandeliers like a giant garden lantern. It was quiet and mostly empty. The floor to ceiling wall of glass that separated it from the terrace was almost invisible.

Just inside the Ocean Dining Hall, Orro slumped in a big chair at a round table, an exhausted heap of dark quills. The taller of his assistants had curled up on the floor, the other crawled into a chair and passed out. Droplet had pushed two chairs together, climbed onto them, and wrapped her fluffy tail like a blanket around herself. None of them noticed me quietly reshaping the chairs and the floor under them into comfortable loungers so they could stretch out. The food on their table remained mostly untouched.

It had been a long day. All remaining delegations decided to discuss Kyporo's expulsion, and all of them wanted to do it over dinner in their individual quarters at different times. The kitchen staff was exhausted.

I was exhausted too. After we dealt with Odikas and the Kyporo delegation, Kosandion went on a date with the Donkamin candidate. The candidate had requested a "plain room with nothing in it," which was exactly what I provided. Kosandion and the Donkamin stood for an hour inside the empty room, discussing scientific advancement. It was intellectually boring and visually disturbing.

On the way back, the Donkamin candidate nearly collapsed in the hallway. I caught him before he fell to the floor. Apparently, Donkamins didn't do well when they were separated from their group, and they also found us grotesque and incredibly disgusting. Once I delivered the candidate to his rooms, they asked me for a purifying pool so they could wash my molecules off the candidate's body. The purifying liquid was complicated and took forever to make.

The ocean shimmered. Amber lights in front of us, warm

yellow glow behind. Sean and I sat in the narrow strip of shadow and watched the waters under an endless sky, studded with alien stars and so deep that looking at it for too long filled you with vague unease.

My earpiece chirped steadily, delivering a successive assortment of the Dominion's news broadcasts into my ear. The fall of Tair Odikas was the talk of the nine star systems.

Olasard padded out of the dining hall on his fluffy paws and hopped into my lap. I put my tea on the small side table between my and Sean's chair and stroked the cat's back.

According to the newscasts, the saga of Tair Odikas stretched back many years, long before Kosandion was born. Four centuries ago, Kyporo faced a crisis. The planet's population had outpaced its natural resources while its space technology was in its infancy. Kyporo joined the Dominion to save itself.

Before the unification, Kyporo had a rigid, striated society with sharply defined social castes, while the Dominion adhered to the belief that every citizen had the same rights. The integration of Kyporo was slow, difficult, and took centuries. Officially the castes had been abolished, but the citizens of Kyporo had good memories.

Odikas came from a long line of patricians, the highest caste of Kyporo. His great-grandfather was the Prime Councilor, revered and venerated, and on the rare occasions he had condescended to leave the hallowed halls of the Grand Council and stepped into the street, among the commoners, people of lesser castes knelt and touched their foreheads to the ground.

No matter how much education and cultural exposure they had, some people craved to be bowed to.

Odikas followed in the footsteps of his ancestors, climbing to the post of the highest elected official, resisting change, and doing his best to block the Dominion's attempts to integrate the planet. His highest aspiration in life was to resurrect the old customs. He wanted to step outside his palace and see an ocean of bent backs with not a single person daring to meet his gaze. He would've rebelled if he could, but the Dominion managed Kyporo wisely, leaving them with little military autonomy, and the public sentiment among the younger generations wasn't on Odikas' side. Once the genie of freedom came out of the bottle, it was hard to put it back in.

For the forty years he was in office, Odikas flirted with separatism, made grand pronouncements about national identity and independence, and hated Kosandion's father, who had removed the last vestiges of the old social system. When Caldenia murdered her brother, the Dominion was already facing an external threat from an alien species and domestic unrest on several fronts. His death struck the seven star systems like a meteor, causing numerous fractures. Odikas had taken full advantage of that. Kyporo was the last planet to accept Kosandion as the Sovereign, and Odikas and his faction continued to be a massive pain in the ass through his reign. Until today.

Sean pulled the earpiece out and put it on the side table between us. I took mine out as well.

"I scanned the Holy Ecclesiarch when he went to his quarters."

Sean glanced at me.

"He's in perfect health," I said. "I mean he is elderly, but there is nothing inherently wrong with him. He could live another decade or two. You don't seem surprised."

"He doesn't smell like a sick man on his deathbed."

"Do really sick people smell different?"

"Usually."

"I think Kosandion knows. I think this whole thing with the deathly ill Ecclesiarch is a sham."

"He's using us to clean house," Sean said. "The Ecclesiarch's illness is a pretext to bring everyone here and isolate them from their allies back at the Dominion. Now he can deal with them one by one."

"You think there will be more like Odikas?"

212

Sean nodded. He was contemplating something.

"A penny for your thoughts?"

"Kosandion is dangerous. For Odikas it wasn't just politics. It was personal. Kosandion recognized it, so he backed Odikas into a corner and gave him just enough rope to hang himself."

"He is Caldenia's nephew."

"And that's what worries me. I'd like to know in advance if he's planning to settle more scores."

Olasard stretched in my lap and turned over. We'd been so busy, I had neglected our usual cuddles, and he was determined to get all the petting he was owed. I scratched his chin.

"I can ask Her Grace. If anyone knows, she would."

"Would she tell you?"

"I don't know, but the worst she can do is say no."

Sean pondered the ocean. "Every time George gets involved, things get complicated."

"If things weren't complicated, there would be no need for George. That's the whole point of him." I sighed.

"Kosandion should just marry him and be done with it."

"The galaxy wouldn't survive. Also, George is already married, and Kosandion isn't foolish enough to fight Sophie for him."

The inn tagged me. The Higgra delegation wanted to talk. I pulled up a screen to their habitat. With the Dushegubs, I didn't bother, I just projected the disembodied voice, but the Higgra would want a visual.

The habitat appeared on the screen, a dense space of real and synthetic trees interrupted by jutting rocks with smooth tops and conveniently placed soft perches. Cyanide sprawled on the nearest perch, her huge white paws dangling over the side. Her golden eyes focused below my face and widened.

"Why did you pick him up?"

I glanced down at Olasard.

"I didn't. He jumped into my lap on his own."

"Why?"

"He wanted attention."

Olasard tilted his head to give me better access to his jaw and flashed his emerald-green eyes at Cyanide.

The two cats stared at each other.

A minute passed.

Another.

"Is there something you wanted?" I asked.

"Yes." Cyanide frowned in a weird cat way, her muzzle going slack, her forehead wrinkling.

Olasard kneaded my knee with his claws gently and looked at me. I held out my hand. Gertrude Hunt dropped a brush into it, and I began gently brushing his soft gray fur.

Cyanide lifted herself up on her forelegs and leaned all the way into the screen.

Olasard purred.

"What was it you wanted?" I prompted.

"It's not important."

The call cut off.

Okay then.

Sean narrowed his eyes, looking up into the sky above Kolinda's ocean.

"What's the matter?"

"Something is coming."

I looked in the direction of his stare. A white star detached from the heavens above the horizon and streaked toward the inn, slicing through the air at shocking speed.

Sean bared his teeth. "A Muterzen pirate cruiser."

I let Olasard off my lap, stood up, and planted the broom into the floor. Its shaft split, exposing its glowing inner core. A shoot of the inn slid through the floor and wrapped itself around the staff, binding us into one.

The cruiser was clearly visible now, a big, strange shape, as if six giant barrels had been bound together into a space caltrop bristling with weapons.

Behind me Droplet let out an alarmed screech.

The two forward-facing barrels ignited with brilliant red.

I sank my consciousness into the inn, merging with Gertrude Hunt, and raised the void field.

The barrels flashed. Twin warheads shrieked through the air toward us. Time slowed, and I watched them spin as they hurtled straight for the inn.

A phantom breeze stirred the hem of my robe.

The warheads met my invisible void field and detonated. A wall of blinding white fire drenched the space in front of us. Water exploded straight up, like a tsunami, flowing over the invisible dome above us, all of it silent.

The inn didn't shudder. The air current didn't change. The lights didn't flicker. No sound penetrated. The terrace and the hall behind us remained as tranquil as ever. I had spread the void field over the entire island.

Out of the corner of my eye I saw Droplet standing on the table. Every hair on her body stood on end. She looked like a cartoon squirrel who'd been electrocuted. The two assistants cowered behind her.

Orro opened one eye, glanced at the incoming cruiser, yawned, waved at Droplet with a limp hand, and fell back asleep.

Sean got up and pulled off his robe. He wore a dark combat suit underneath. The subcutaneous armor that masqueraded as his tattoos expanded, sliding in a black wave over his neck. He held a knife with a green-edged blade. His eyes were clear and bright.

The water drained down. Alien fish and long serpentine creatures rolled and slid over the void field dome, tumbling back into the orange depths.

Sean pulled a thick inn branch out of the floor. It wound around him.

"I need a hole," Sean said.

Being in love with a werewolf: enjoying unwavering support

interrupted by moments of intense terror. This was a terror moment. He trusted me, and I had to trust him.

The cruiser hovered right in front of us. They couldn't believe it. They had come in for a closer look.

I split the void field, parting it like pages of a book.

The branch grasping Sean snapped, flinging him into the air. Gorvar jumped up on his table and let loose an eerie, hair-raising howl. Sean landed on top of the cruiser and stabbed it.

Yep, that's exactly what I thought he would do.

The knife carved through hull steel like it was butter. Sean's body broke, expanding into a large shape in a blink. Dark fur sheathed his head. He grasped the edge of the ballistic plate with his clawed hand and tore it off. It fell into the water, and he dropped into the hole he made.

I reinstated the void field and sat back in my chair.

Gorvar kept howling.

The cruiser hovered in place. They had to have seen him cut his way in. They thought they could either kill him or neutralize him.

"Awoooo!!!"

"Come here," I called.

The big wolf leaped off the table and ran over to me.

"He will be fine," I told him, petting his furry shoulder. "This is what he does."

The lupine beast sat next to me and stared at the cruiser. I did, too. Judging by the size, it had a crew of anywhere between 50-100, and all of them would be armed and used to close-quarters combat. Sean had his claws and a knife. I exhaled slowly, trying to vent my anxiety with it.

Gertrude Hunt moved the screen it had sprouted for Cyanide in front of me. I looked at it. A call from Cookie's quarters. I accepted the communication, and the little lees appeared on the screen.

"Good news," he said. "Everything your contact told you

checked out. I have independent verification from multiple sources. He is a pirate prince."

The cruiser shuddered. The void field ate the sound, but it looked like something might have exploded.

"That's great," I said.

"Does he have access to any outside communications?" Cookie asked.

"No. He is completely isolated."

Cookie nodded. "That's good. That's very good. They can't warn him."

The cruiser listed to the right and began to spin in slow motion, moving away from the inn.

"Why would they know to warn him?" I asked.

"There were complications."

The cruiser was upside down now, its barrels turning randomly.

"You promised to be careful."

Cookie looked taken aback. "I'm always careful. But they were very alert. I think they know that we suspect, or they suspect that we know."

"You don't say."

The cruiser broke in half. Explosions flashed in the gap. The stern half slid and plunged into the ocean, sending another massive wave toward us. Watching it all without the sound felt surreal.

"I wanted to warn you in case they attempt to attack. Forewarned is forearmed."

"Thank you, but your timing sucks."

I turned the screen so he could see the remaining chunk of the cruiser slowly slide toward the waves.

"Ooooooooh," Cookie said.

Tony came striding out of the dining hall and said in a great imitation of an English accent. "I felt a great disturbance... Oh hell."

The remaining half of the cruiser landed in the waters and broke apart.

"Did you fire at it?" Tony asked.

I shook my head.

Tony looked around. "Where is Sean?"

"Take a wild guess."

He stabbed his finger at the fracturing hull of the sinking cruiser. "Is Sean in there?"

I nodded.

"How...?"

"He used the inn to throw himself at it."

"Does he know you have anti-aircraft weapons?"

"He does. He installed half of them. He is making a statement."

Tony landed in Sean's chair. I dismissed Cookie's screen and watched the underwater explosions flash.

"Does he do this kind of thing a lot?" Tony asked.

"Define 'a lot.'"

"I'm sorry," Tony said. "This must be very stressful."

"Not as stressful at it is for the pirates inside. He is slaughtering them in there."

"That's not what I meant," Tony said.

"I know. Thank you for caring. It is stressful, but I picked him, and I have no regrets."

We sat quietly for a few moments. The cruiser was almost completely submerged now. Only a corner of the hull protruded above the waves. The sea around the wreck churned, as the local wildlife realized there were delicious meaty bits inside.

Sean was a good swimmer. I held on to that thought like a life preserver.

"I spoke to my dad," Tony said. "We are more popular than the Super Bowl. Everyone is watching."

There would be more excitement tomorrow. "Did he have any advice?"

"He says we're doing great. He's surprised we haven't killed a Dushegub yet."

It had become my personal goal to get through this mess without losing any of the guests while they were on the inn's grounds, Dushegubs included.

"Two more challenges left," Tony said.

"Yes." The talent challenge was next. "Do you think he will hand out roses tomorrow at the elimination ceremony?"

Tony cracked a smile. "We can only hope."

A bright red flash announced another explosion. I sighed.

"Do you want me to go help him?" Tony asked.

I shook my head. "It's a matter of trust. I have to trust that Sean wouldn't take on anything he couldn't handle."

Tony nodded, rose, patted my shoulder, and walked away.

Five minutes later I dropped the void field and watched human Sean climb up onto the balcony. He was wet from head to toe, but otherwise uninjured. He straightened and grinned. I put my arms around his dripping body and kissed him. His face was cold, but his lips were warm, and he tasted just as I remembered. He squeezed me to him. Gorvar whined, circling around us.

"Sorry," Sean breathed into my ear.

"That wasn't cool."

"It was a little bit cool."

"No."

"Admit it, you were impressed."

I shook my head.

He laughed and there was no better sound.

[19]

When we last left our fearsome innkeeper duo, Sean had taken down the pirate vessel that attacked the inn's branch reaching out to the planet of Kolinda. But mysteries remain: how did they know that Gertrude Hunt had a door leading to the planet and where it was? What was their motive? Who is the pirate prince masquerading as one of the candidates? Stay tuned to find out. Maybe.

I opened my eyes. The slanted ceiling above me was shrouded in gloom except for a narrow rectangle of moonlight coming through the top of the window. The clock on the wall told me it was just past one. We'd gone to bed thirty minutes ago, after locking everyone in.

"What is it?" Sean asked.

"Caldenia."

There was a tiny pause as he checked where she was. "How the hell...?"

"Gaston or Tony."

My money was on Gaston. I had given both of them temporary privileges to open doors to guest quarters, because we needed all of the manpower we could get, and they ended up escorting various groups of guests back and forth. As the first, the longest, and the most special guest of the inn, Caldenia had access to all common areas and could roam freely, but it would have taken either Gaston or Tony to unlock the doors to the otrokar delegation's quarters and let her in there.

I got up. "She's been in there for twenty minutes. I'm going to get her."

"I'll go."

"I've got it." I leaned over and kissed him. "Rest. You've done plenty. I need to talk to her anyway."

"We should lock her in," he grumbled.

"She would be mortally offended."

I got up, took my robe off the hook, and slipped it on. Nobody needed to know that I was wearing only underwear and a tank top underneath. Finding my sandals seemed too hard, so I stuck my feet into a pair of flowery Crocs Sean kept making fun of, took my broom, and headed to the otrokar section.

I had made the otrokar quarters for the peace summit that freed Sean from being Turan Adin. At the time, it housed the Khanum, who was Dagorkun's mother, and her delegation. All otrokar tribes had similar requirements: private bedrooms for the leaders and the shaman, communal bedrooms for the warriors, a large common area with a sunken fire pit, and a secondary meeting area with another fire pit, where the leaders could hold private meetings. Tailoring the rooms to the current otrokar delegation took ten minutes. I had adjusted the colors to reflect the Southern sensibilities, added another bedroom, and called it a day.

At this time of night most of the otrokars would be in the common area, probably playing dice or telling stories before going to sleep. The Hope Crushing Horde had robust oral traditions, born at the time when their nomadic tribes traversed their homeworld following the seasonal rains. They would ride their vicious savok mounts all day and then camp, cook their food by the fire, and recount stories of heroes from long-gone ages.

The modern Horde warriors rarely grilled their meals over an open flame, although they tried to do it every chance they got, and the skies above them usually shone with unfamiliar stars, but some traditions remained sacred. The same stories that had once echoed over the plains of the ancestral planet were now told in the hulls of massive spaceships on the way to their next interstellar conquest.

I swept the quarters with my senses. As expected, most of the group was in the common area, but two beings chose a more private setting, on the balcony overlooking the orchard. One of them was Caldenia. The other was...Surkar, the otrokar's spousal candidate.

I approached from the orchard side. I had put a barrier in place, so the otrokars could view the orchard, but they couldn't jump down into it. I had no such limitations. The barrier slid over me like it wasn't even there, and I paused in the shadows, directly under the stone balcony. I had gotten poisoned on this balcony and almost died, and then Sean had sold himself into eternal servitude to the Merchants to save me. Fun times.

A fire burned in the pit above me. The inn had a strained relationship with fire, and it was acutely aware of the small knot of heat and flames. The night breeze brought a faint scent of red tea. The Khanum preferred wanla, a stronger, coarser version she'd called "poor people's tea," but this smelled like a more refined, expensive variety.

Caldenia was talking in a low voice. The last time she had used that tone, a Draziri warrior betrayed his commander and tried to murder him in the middle of the battle.

Gertrude Hunt offered me a branch. I stepped on it and the inn lifted me up, dissolving the seemingly solid stone above my head. I rose out of the balcony like a wraith.

The balcony had no lamps. The illumination came from the

fire pit and the soft light of the common room behind it. Her Grace sat half in shadow, flames dancing over her face, and sipped her tea from an ornate clay cup. She had abandoned the elaborate evening gowns in favor of her Earth clothes: a pair of gray jeans, white T-shirt, and a black leather jacket, which was entirely too warm considering the lingering heat.

She almost never wore anything like that. In fact, I was sure these were the only jeans she owned, because I bought them for her years ago when she came to the inn, and I had never seen them since. Even when she visited with her friends from the subdivision across the street, she usually chose a dress. She must've felt the rugged nature of the jeans would make the right statement to Surkar.

To her left, Surkar wore a kilt, soft boots, and nothing else, letting the light of the fire highlight what he believed to be the galaxy's best chest. Sean's was better.

Caldenia's tone was sardonic and slightly bitter. "...His father was the same. Let's just say that their deductive powers leave much to be desired. Some people simply must be confronted with the obvious."

Surkar nodded, his face thoughtful. The two of them were completely at ease, two conspirators murmuring over the fire.

Lingering here any longer would be eavesdropping.

"Your Grace," I said.

Surkar jerked. *That's right, fear my stealthy ways.*

"Alas, my babysitter has arrived." Caldenia set her cup down. "I suppose you've come to fetch me to my rooms?"

"You're free to access all common areas of the inn at any time, Your Grace. However, that privilege doesn't extend to the private rooms of other guests."

"She was invited," Surkar said, his voice hard.

"Be that as it may, visiting hours are over for everyone's safety."

"She is welcome to stay as long as she wishes," the otrokar said.

"Don't fuss, dear. I will go." Caldenia rose. "Rules are rules, after all. I'll leave you with this parting thought: strength begets strength. If you desire something, make it known. Reach out and seize it."

Surkar nodded as if he heard something profound. Caldenia, the Tony Robbins of the galaxy.

Her Grace fixed me with a look and sighed. "Lead the way."

I pushed with my magic. A staircase sprouted from the balcony leading into the orchard. Caldenia took it. I followed her, dissolving the stairs behind us.

We walked down the flagstone path through the orchard gardens. The moon had hidden behind a cloud, and the darkness leeched colors from the plants, painting the flower beds in a dozen shades of black, charcoal, and hunter green. I sent a pulse down the path. Cream-colored globes ignited next to it, illuminating the stone just enough to see.

"Is my nephew awake?" Caldenia asked.

I checked. "Yes."

She sighed. "I may have to speak to our lovely chef. Kosandion will sleep very little for the next few weeks. He will need enhanced nutrition."

"Why?"

"Because of Odikas, of course."

"I thought it was settled." Kosandion already won.

She gave me a short laugh. "Oh no, my dear. Removing Odikas was only the opening salvo. Now the real fight begins."

"I don't follow."

"Power abhors a vacuum. With Odikas gone, the members of his Conservative Alliance will scramble to climb onto his now-empty throne, shoving and kicking each other out of the way. This is a gambit years in the making. The boy planned it beautifully and executed it well, but now he must maneuver pieces on the game board to push the right candidate to the top without anyone realizing they have been manipulated."

Oh.

"My money is on Senator Dulvia of Tar. She is aggressive and power-hungry. Of all of them, she wants it the most, yet she's shrewd enough to realize that she is the least qualified for it. That sense of hidden inferiority is priceless. If she ascends, she'll spend years stomping out any opposing factions in the conservative block. She will go after anyone brighter than her to destroy the competition before it has a chance to blossom into a threat. By the time she consolidates her power base, Kosandion will have everything in place to steer her in the direction of his choosing, and the Conservative Alliance overall will be weaker, less creative, and easier to handle. Dina, you have a strange expression on your face."

"I'm relieved that I am who I am."

"And not my niece?" Caldenia smiled.

"Yes."

"You are a child of innkeepers. You were born into this life, and your every experience contributed to your education. By the time you reached adulthood, you were an expert innkeeper. Kosandion and I were born to be fit to rule well. I do not mean this in a pompous way of entitlement. I mean it as a statement of fact. We were genetically enhanced with a careful selection of traits that made us capable administrators and nuanced leaders. We were educated in the way of governance from the moment we opened our eyes. We are highly specialized, skilled workers, bred for the purpose of leading interstellar nations, and we have an added incentive of painful death in case of failure that drives us to excel."

"The responsibility must be crushing."

Caldenia sighed. "It is, at times. But then this is what we do. And let's face it, tearing down your enemies is a great deal of fun. You are a picture of restraint, but a part of you enjoys flexing your power when the occasion requires. Kosandion is much the same. An embodiment of self-discipline and decorum until it's time to stab and rip the still-beating heart out of the chest of his enemy. It's just that his stabs take a great deal of work and much preparation."

The boy planned it beautifully... There wasn't just admiration in her voice. There was familial pride.

"I have some bad news for Kosandion," I said.

Caldenia stopped. "How bad?"

I paused. We'd come to an intersection of several paths, where they joined into a round patio.

"Politically difficult."

"Tell me."

I did.

Midway through, Caldenia started pacing. It was a violent movement, fueled by rage. She'd picked up a small branch somewhere, about the width of my finger, and she flicked her thumbnail across it as she walked back and forth, slicing perfect little sections off with each slide of her thumb. She was like the proverbial caged tiger, flicking her tail, looking for an opening.

I finally finished.

"You must tell him now."

"I was planning to tell him in the morning."

She stopped and glared at me. "No. Now. The sooner he knows, the better. I realize you have no obligation to share this information, and your innkeeper's duty is to let him rest, but it is a matter of his political survival. Do this for me, please."

"Okay," I told her.

"Right now."

"Right now," I promised. "Do you want to come?"

"No. It is best that I interact with him as little as possible. But tell him this: *Olivio teseres tares.* He will know what it means."

———

I KNOCKED ON THE DOOR LEADING TO THE SOVEREIGN'S QUARTERS. Next to me Sean looked alert and fresh-faced, as if he'd had a full night of sleep instead of 30 minutes.

"Enter," Kosandion called.

The door slid open, and we did. The Sovereign looked up from the transparent screen in front of him. Nothing changed in his face or posture, but somehow it became instantly clear that he knew an emergency had occurred and was ready for it.

Sean placed the data cube in front of him. I pulled two chairs out of the floor. We sat. A moment later the floor parted, and a small table grew like a mushroom, holding a carafe of coffee, three mugs, and an assortment of creamers and sugars.

"Coffee?" I asked.

Kosandion didn't seem to have heard me.

Sean poured two mugs, one for him, one for me. Sometimes coffee was truly a life-saver.

The results of Cookie's fact-gathering appeared on the screen. Reports, video footage, testimonies... Ten minutes into it, Kosandion stood up, walked over to our table, poured himself a cup of coffee, dumped sugar into it, and went back to the screen. His face showed no emotion, but a storm had to be brewing inside. The Muterzen pirate had barely covered his tracks. Everything in his dossier indicated that long-term planning and attention to detail never made it into his bag of tricks. He was impulsive and careless. His assumed identity might have passed a superficial check, but the top candidates were rigorously vetted. The moment Kosandion's people started to dig, the warning bells would've gone off.

If it was negligence or incompetence, the blow would've been bad enough. Kosandion would look like a fool who was unable to hire the right staff and properly supervise them. An inept leader who allowed a notorious criminal accused of monstrous atrocities to come within one step of becoming a parent of the Dominion's next ruler.

Sadly, it wasn't just incompetence. It was much worse.

Cookie's briefing ran its course, and the recording of Sean vs Pirate Cruiser rolled on the screen. Kosandion viewed this grand epic with the same dispassionate expression. His own private view of Kolinda was directed at a different section of the ocean. If he had been out on the balcony during the attack, he might have seen some flashes to his far right, but the void field ensured that he would've heard nothing.

On the screen Sean tore into the pirate vessel.

Kosandion's eyebrows rose a millimeter.

The cruiser broke in half.

"Once Clan Nuan started digging, the pirates realized that their prince's cover was about to be blown," Sean said. "Since we cut off all communications between the candidates and the rest of the galaxy, they couldn't warn him. They chose to attack the inn. Entering our solar system wasn't an option, so they opted for Kolinda. If the inn functioned like a typical hotel full of VIPs and was equipped with a portal, as soon as the attack began, the guests would have been immediately evacuated. The pirate prince is a scumbag, but he isn't stupid. The Muterzen crew counted on him putting two and two together and slipping away in the chaos."

"Whoever fed them the intel about Gertrude Hunt does not understand how the inns operate," I added.

Kosandion leaned back and studied both of us. "There is more?"

Yes, there was.

Sean put a small dark crystal onto the table in front of Kosandion. "Their log."

Somehow, in the middle of all that killing, Sean had paused long enough to retrieve the cruiser's log. It showed the entirety of their communications, every incoming and outgoing message, and all their maneuvering. I'd been thinking about it, and I was pretty sure that getting that log was the reason he'd launched himself at the spaceship in the first place.

"They moved into Kolinda's orbit three Earth days ago and immediately started scanning the surface, looking for energy anomalies," Sean said. "We maintain a protective shield over the terrace and the balcony. It gives off a slight energy signature. Since Kolinda isn't inhabited by a sapient species and has no industry, we stood out like a sore thumb."

"They knew the inn had a door here, on this planet," Kosandion said.

"Not only that, but their vessel was ordered to Kolinda nine hours before the first spousal candidate entered the inn," I said.

Kosandion's mouth turned into a hard line.

The candidates and their delegations had no idea which inn they were going to until they arrived at Gertrude Hunt. The Dominion had insisted on secrecy.

"When that order was issued, only three people from the Dominion knew that Gertrude Hunt had a Kolinda door," Sean said.

Kosandion himself, Miralitt, and Resven. Miralitt and Resven had come to tour the inn, and we took them to the Ocean Dining Hall. They saw Kolinda. Miralitt had asked me about it. She wanted to know if it was a weak point in our security. I gave her a detailed explanation.

A wolf stared at Kosandion through Sean's eyes. "How much do you trust your people?"

The Sovereign's expression turned dark. The change was so sudden, I had to fight an urge to get out of my chair and back away.

"More than two of my people knew," he said.

He touched the screen. It pulsed with blood red.

"Who are the others?" I asked.

"Orata," he said. "Resven gave her a summary of your inn's capabilities and his impressions of it. One she would have shared with her staff."

Oh.

Orata's face appeared on the screen. Her silver-blue hair was tousled, and a wrinkle from a pillow creased her cheek.

Kosandion pulled up the pirate's face on the screen. "Who vetted this man?"

Orata blinked, and alarm sparked in her eyes. "Vercia Denoma."

The name landed like a Molotov cocktail, splashing the three of us with its explosive fire.

Neither Sean nor I knew much about the inner workings of the Dominion, but that name was mentioned in just about every broadcast. Vercia Denoma, a scion of a prominent Dominion family, renowned for their political and humanitarian contributions, stunning, educated, elegant. A year ago, she began a relationship with Kosandion, and seven months ago it ended. There was wild speculation that she would enter the spousal selection and equally loud disappointment when she did not. The Dominion media had given her a nickname meant to describe her unique beauty and complex charm. They called her *Aalind Voun*. That's how I remembered her name. *Aalind Voun* translated to "Special Snowflake."

Kosandion's voice could have frozen a supernova. "Bring her to me."

———

VERCIA DENOMA WAS A TRULY STUNNING WOMAN. HER SKIN WAS A light taupe, and her hair was a deep shade with a touch of cinnamon, unusual for the Dominion. The pale orange gown draping her tall, slender frame complemented both. Her features were sharply cut, forceful rather than delicate, an echo of the aggressive beauty particular to the Dominion's upper class. This same genetic pool had produced Caldenia all those decades ago, but where Her Grace was a *tour de force*, Vercia was an ice princess. She held herself like her spine didn't know it could bend.

She came into the throne room behind Orata, flanked by four Capital Guardsmen in full armor. While Orata had traveled to Vercia's home and detained her, both Resven and Miralitt caught up on the crisis. They watched her enter, Miralitt cold and unfeeling like a block of marble and Resven staring with burning hostility.

Sean and I stood to the side in our robes with the hoods up. To an outside observer, the two of us looked faceless, silent, and motionless. This drama would need to play out without interference. Strictly speaking, we shouldn't have been here, but I had gotten paranoid about Kosandion's safety. Sean had always been paranoid, so it worked out.

Vercia raised her head and hit Kosandion with a punishing stare. Even sitting down, Kosandion was tall, and the raised platform of his throne put him six feet above Vercia's head. She managed to look down on him all the same.

This wouldn't go well.

"I see you've finally caught on," she said. Her voice was deep, her delivery confident. She didn't seem even a slight bit nervous. No, she'd been looking forward to this confrontation, and now she relished it. Everything she had done was deliberate.

Kosandion had turned into a statue. He sat motionless, as if he and his throne had merged into a single entity that was the Sovereign. When he spoke, his voice was even and measured. "Why?"

"Five months, Kosandion. And here I am, in the exact same position I was prior to our liaison." She glanced at Orata. "I should have her job. That was the least you could have done in the way of compensation."

Orata bristled.

The Sovereign's voice turned cold. "I wasn't aware a relationship with me required compensation."

"Oh please. A relationship with the Sovereign, the man who will give you an entire five percent of his attention. A man who is

231

never available, who is absorbed in work, who makes it clear on the first encounter that he places limits on feelings. A man who explains that you're good enough for sex and occasional casual conversations but that he will never commit to more. Whatever crumbs of his attention he doles out will be on his terms and schedule. What was that phrase you used? 'Managing expectations to avoid misunderstandings' and 'incapable of a serious relationship.' What woman wouldn't be delighted?"

Resven opened his mouth. Kosandion tapped his armrest with his index finger, and the chancellor's jaw clicked shut.

"You pursued me," Kosandion said. "I agreed to meet with you to discuss it. I was honest with you, and you assured me that what I offered was enough. You were not forced. As I recall, you were *enthusiastic.*"

A muscle jerked in Vercia's face. Her control slipped. Caldenia would've never allowed herself a lapse like that.

"Before we slept together, I was a rising star," she squeezed out. "After, I became an incompetent fool who had access to the Sovereign for 5 months and failed to garner any political advantage from it. You've turned me into a laughingstock. When Parseon and you were over, he became a Third Rank Minister."

"That promotion was in place before their relationship started," Resven said. "Minister Parseon petitioned to delay his confirmation, because his duties would preclude him from visiting the Capital for the first two years. You can find the record of it in the governmental archives in Section—"

"Oh, shut up." Vercia grimaced. "It's too late to play nursemaid to the orphan, Resven. Your little boy is fully grown. He is capable of speaking for himself."

"You're an uncultured woman. You bring shame to your family," the chancellor spat out.

"Not for much longer. Soon my family and everyone in the Dominion will know that brushing me aside comes with a price."

I had many partners over the years, male, female, humanoid and not, yet none of them remain by my side. Poor Kosandion.

Vercia tossed her hair back with an impatient jerk of her head. "Let's cut to the chase. You can do nothing to me. I've covered my tracks, and you have no proof. Only the accusation of incompetence might stick, and once this beautiful mess becomes public, everyone will see my actions for exactly what they were: a deep, calculated stab to the heart. My career will soar, while you'll nurse your wound and try to recover some semblance of respect in the public eye."

"A pirate," Kosandion said. "A despicable criminal. You allowed him to enter the selection and then you passed confidential information to his associates, endangering everyone here. Do you even know what he has done?"

She smiled. "Every single bit of it. Mass murder, rape, slavery. He has done everything a man can do when he's given weapons, fast craft, and money without any strings of moral guidance. He is reviled even by his peers. That's why I picked him. It had to be sickening, Kosandion, otherwise it wouldn't have the necessary impact. I've dropped enough hints to the right people. Go ahead. Try to hide it. It will explode in your face. Every gory detail of his atrocities will be splashed over the Dominion's screens. The tower of your pitiful arrogance brought down low in one swift cut. I'll cherish it."

Orata took a step forward. "I can fix it."

Kosandion glanced at her.

"Please, *Letero*. She is my subordinate. Let me fix it."

Kosandion considered it. "You have till tomorrow's elimination."

Orata nodded, her face sharp, and tapped her earpiece. "Selerian, wake everyone. Yes, *everyone*."

Kosandion turned his head slightly. Miralitt nodded to the guards. "Confine Public Servant Denoma."

"On what grounds?" Vercia demanded.

233

"Breach of protocol. Failure to greet the Sovereign, failure to call the Sovereign by title, and interfering with a Public Servant with intent to disrupt his duties."

"What?" Vercia drew back.

"The Office of Chancellor is responsible for maintaining the record of the Sovereign's life and must provide that record on demand to public," Miralitt said. "You accused a public official of improper conduct in front of the Sovereign, which constitutes a demand for information. Chancellor Resven is duty-bound to immediately disclose where that information can be found. By telling him to shut up, you prevented him from performing his duty, which constitutes suppression."

"That's absurd!"

"Take her out," Miralitt said.

The guards marched Vercia back to the portal. I watched them vanish into the glow.

"Dismissed," Kosandion said.

Orata and Miralitt left the room, the PR chief all but running to the portal and the security chief heading to her quarters. It was only Kosandion, Resven, Sean, and me.

Kosandion's expression cracked. An emotion twisted his face, a mix of resignation, dull ache, and deep intense loneliness. A bitter fatalistic acceptance.

The older man knelt in front of Kosandion and took his hands in his. "I am so sorry, *Letero*. So sorry."

Sean took my hand. We withdrew quietly and went upstairs to our bedroom. We took off our robes, and then I crawled into bed next to Sean and hugged him. I didn't want to feel alone.

Sean wrapped his arm around me. For a little while I lay awake, reassured that we were okay by the warmth of his body, and then I slipped into my dreams.

When we last left the inn, we learned that Kosandion's former lover betrayed him. Oh Kosandion. So considerate, so handsome, so lonely. If only he had someone to comfort his troubled heart. Now Orata, his PR chief, is trying to put out that fire. But breakfasts do get cold, and even innkeepers have to eat...

The Dushegubs woke me up again around 4:00 am by trying to dig into the bottom of the Pit. Normally, I'd let them tire themselves out, but I was exhausted, so I made them a very large screen and then put the *Leave It to Beavers* documentary on it. It was a PBS production with a lot of footage of beaver tree-cutting and dam-building. Horrifying guests went against the innkeeper policy, but the Dushegubs were really testing my patience.

Sean woke me up at 5:00 am by getting out of bed, and when I asked him what was happening, he kissed me and told me to go back to sleep. When I finally crawled out of our bed two hours later, the bedroom was empty. I found him outside talking to Marais. Marais had discovered a couple of the Dominion paparazzi trying to film the inn at dark o'clock, apprehended them, and turned them over to Sean, who tossed them out into Baha-char while I slept. Now they were discussing what to do if more of the celebrity stalkers showed up. I left them to it and took myself to breakfast.

Most of the delegations once again opted for a private meal, so I went straight to the observer quarters. They had talked Tony into letting them eat on our back patio, and when I came out, I found Dagorkun, Karat, Tomato, Tony, and Gaston, all situated around the big outside table enjoying Orro's version of the traditional American breakfast. If the traditional breakfast included serving sunny-side-up eggs in little baskets made of French-fried potatoes and bejeweled with beads of crystallized but delectable ketchup and maple syrup.

The moment I sat down, Droplet emerged from the kitchen, placed a plate with my own egg in a basket and a cup of coffee in front of me, and vanished back into the kitchen. The table was so full of food, it was a wonder it didn't break. I stared at the spread for a long moment, struggling with decision paralysis, then put a couple of sausage links on my plate, added some fruit, and took a sip of my brew.

Mmm, delicious caffeine.

"I thought you preferred tea," Tony said. His plate was the size of a Thanksgiving platter, and he was putting food away like he would never get a chance to eat again. There was a reason he was Orro's favorite visitor. Well, aside from Gaston, that is.

"I do. Tea isn't cutting it right now."

"Dushegubs?" he asked.

"Mhm. And paparazzi. And pirates. Which one of you let Caldenia into the otrokar quarters last night?"

Gaston raised his hand. *"C'est moi, je suis coupable."*

Tony rolled his eyes.

Why was I not surprised? "You are supposed to watch her, not cater to her whims."

"I have a dual mission, to assist you and to assist the Sovereign. George, and the Office of Arbitration, want the spousal selection to go smoothly."

Of course, George wouldn't let it go.

"Watching Her Grace is truly an honor and a privilege," Gaston said. "Her plotting is sublime. When I grow up, I want to be just like her. If she was taking apprentices, I would immediately pledge myself on bended knee. Sadly, she isn't interested at this time. I've asked."

That's just what we needed, Gaston underfoot.

"That is a spectacularly terrible, no good, awful idea," Tony said. "That woman can dissect you with two sentences. You'll never recover."

"And that's precisely why I would want to be her apprentice," Gaston said.

"What was that language you used?" Karat asked.

"French. A version of it, my lady," Gaston said.

Oooh, "my lady." Someone had caught on to vampire etiquette. Dagorkun frowned.

"Does your planet have more than one language?" Karat asked.

"It has many. I learned to speak French and English at the same time. They are both my mother tongues. Does your planet have other languages?"

She shook her head. "No, we have various dialects, but they are all distributaries of the same linguistic river. Your other language sounds interesting."

"Would you like to hear more?" he asked.

Dagorkun's frown deepened.

"Yes. I think I would."

Gaston leaned forward.

"Âme sentinelle,
Murmurons l'aveu

De la nuit si nulle
Et du jour en feu.

Des humains suffrages,
Des communs élans
Là tu te dégages
Et voles selon."

He had a really good voice, deep and resonant, and somehow French seemed to suit him.

Tony rolled his eyes again.

"What does it mean?" Karat asked.

Gaston made a small, elegant gesture with his hand. "It's a poem by Arthur Rimbaud. It speaks of the eternity one finds in the moment the setting sun touches the ocean or two lovers make a whispered promise. It's a quest for unlocking infinity in an instant and carrying it forever in your memory as a defense against the inevitability of torment."

I stopped eating and looked at him.

"It's true," he said.

"Fascinating," Karat said. She anchored her elbow on the table and rested her chin on the back of her hand. "Tell me more."

The muscles on Dagorkun's jaw stood out.

Karat turned toward me to reach for the small jar of jam and winked.

Oh. Oh! She was doing it on purpose.

"What would you like to hear?" Gaston asked.

"Oh, I don't know." Karat smeared a bit of jam on a tiny bagel shaped like House Krahr's crest. Orro had really outdone himself. "Does the Horde have any fascinating poetry, Under-Khan?"

Dagorkun unlocked his jaws. "Yes."

"Would you recite some for us?"

"No."

I drank my coffee to keep from laughing.

"Aww, how disappointing." Karat fluttered her long eyelashes.

The inn tugged on me. A communication from House Meer. I waved my hand, so nobody would be startled, and Gertrude Hunt delivered a screen showing Bestata to me. The vampire candidate wore a stripped-down version of armor, the kind knights wore during training. I pulled the practice weapons out of storage.

"I wish to speak to Lady Renadra."

Well, since we are using the official titles instead of first names...

I looked at Karat. "Do you wish to speak to Lady Emindra?"

"Yes."

I moved the screen to her.

The racks of practice weapons rose through the turf of the lawn. They were the exact size and weight of the standard vampire weapons but made from a different material and their edges were dull. Being hit with one of those still hurt.

"Do you fancy a brief exertion this morning?" Bestata asked.

Karat's eyes flashed. "Always."

"I suppose someone will come to escort me to your location?"

"Yes," I said.

"Excellent. I look forward to a bit of exercise."

The screen went blank. Karat rose. "I'll be right back."

I turned to Gaston. "Would you mind fetching Bestata?"

He gave me a shallow bow. "It's my pleasure."

"Thank you."

Gaston left the table.

"How did you know she would say yes?" Tomato asked. "You brought the weapons before they even agreed to fight."

Orro had served him small cubes of raw steak. Tomato pierced them with his claws, dipped them into a saucer of spiced honey, and gently popped them into his mouth one by one, taking a long time to chew each piece.

"I recognized the training armor she wore. Every time Bestata appears in public, she is in full formal mode. There was only one reason she would call while wearing practice armor. She wanted to spar, and there was only one person among us she would challenge."

"But how did you know Karat would accept?" Tomato asked.

"A vampire knight of Karat's standing never backs down from a challenge by a rival house. This is Bestata's chance to get a feel for Karat's skills. Karat knows it and is happy to demonstrate she isn't worried about House Meer's intelligence gathering. Also, Karat is just like my sister. She can't resist the sword. If there is one in the vicinity, her hand starts twitching toward it."

Dagorkun drank his tea. He was clearly brooding.

"Why didn't you recite *By the Light of the Moon, by the Trail of Blood?*" Tony asked.

He waved it off. "It didn't occur to me at the time."

"Can you explain Surkar to me?" I asked. "You are here to observe him. Why is he here?"

Dagorkun sighed. "When the Horde claims a planet or builds a space station, the settlers are chosen through a complex algorithm. It takes into account seniority, achievements, needs of the colony, and individual preferences. It also ensures that the population of the colony is diverse and equally represented. No one clan can claim a numbers or specialist majority. The colony's survival requires cooperation; everyone must set aside their ancestral differences and blood feuds and work together to thrive. In a few decades, as the newer generations rise, they begin to think of themselves as being from that colony rather than being from the Tribe of the Northern Wind or the Tribe of the Southern Gusts, and if any troublemakers pop up, they usually enlist and are shipped off into the Horde bootcamps, where they learn unity or die. That's how the Horde remains cohesive."

It made sense. If the Horde was a garment, it would be Joseph's coat of many colors, sewn together from thousands of scraps. Each color was a tribe. Each tribe had a long and bloody history. If all of Earth's ethnic groups came together, we would barely account for a single sleeve of it.

Keeping this multitude from fracturing had to be a monumental task.

Tony pretended to be absorbed in his food, but I could tell he was listening to every word. This is exactly the kind of knowledge the innkeepers went bonkers over. His father would want a full report.

"This system has worked in 11 colonies so far over eight planetary systems," Dagorkun said. "And then we have Harra, which is where Surkar is from. Somehow when this little planet was settled, 80% of the settlers came from the South. 48% of those came from the Tribe of the Gar, which happens to be Surkar's tribe."

"Someone tampered with the algorithm," Sean said, emerging from the kitchen.

Marais walked in behind him. He looked haggard.

Sean pulled a chair out for him. Marais sat. Sean poured him some coffee and put a plate in front of him.

"Yes," Dagorkun said. "We don't know how they did it, and we didn't catch it for five years. The few Northerners that ended up on Harra kept having bad luck. Surprise mud slides. Power grid failures. Stray meteorites hitting their vital installations. That sort of thing."

"Nothing you can prove," Sean said.

"No," Dagorkun said. "What we can prove is increased emigration. Northern veterans who have bled and earned their land are cashing out and getting off planet. And now Surkar and the gang are here. Every delegation gets main and minor asks. I need to know what their asks are."

Marais looked like he was falling asleep.

"Hector, go home," I murmured.

He shook his head. "I just need a minute."

Next time we hired him to do anything, I would write his work hours and mandatory downtime into a contract and make him sign it.

Karat walked out onto the porch wearing practice armor, strode to the practice rack on the grass, chose a sword, and tossed it six feet up. It spun, and she snatched it out of the air.

Dagorkun blinked.

"If Surkar is chosen as the spouse, and they ask for a military alliance between Harra and the Dominion, would the Horde go to war?" I asked.

"Yes," Dagorkun and Sean said at the same time.

A war between the Horde and the Dominion would be catastrophic. The Office of Arbitration would want to prevent it at any cost, as much as they would want to protect the stability of the Dominion itself.

I could almost see a translucent specter of George looming over us. He must've wanted so much to be here, nudging things on the right track with a gentle hand, but he couldn't.

Bestata and Gaston emerged from the kitchen. Bestata ignored the existence of our table, making sure that all of us registered that we were beneath her notice. It bordered on insulting.

Gaston invited Bestata to the grass with a flourish. The tall blonde knight strode to the practice rack.

"How old is this thing?" Karat asked, examining the sword in her hand. "They don't make guards like this anymore."

"Old," I told her. "It was gifted to the innkeepers by a descendant of the Holy Anocracy's great hero many years ago."

Originally, I thought these weapons were a couple of centuries old, but then Maud asked me about them after she sparred with Arland. She thought the weapon set was a lot older, so when things calmed down, I dug through the Gertrude Hunt archives until I finally found a mention of it. The set was brought to Gertrude Hunt by one of my predecessors, who inherited it from a much older, now destroyed inn.

Once I figured out where the weapons came from, I immediately took the set of practice daggers from the rack and put them into a special box for my niece. Helen would flip.

Bestata condescended to look at me. "Which hero?"

I'd dealt with many vampires over my life, but none of them had sneered at me as much as Bestata had. I wasn't sure if it was just her default expression, but there was a limit to my patience.

"Press the black dagger-shaped switch on the side," I told her.

She examined the weapon rack. Her fingers found the switch.

A hologram of a giant dark-skinned vampire woman tore out of the rack. She wore ancient armor with ornate metal pauldrons and a cuirass sitting over the syn-armor, a style that came from a time when vampires didn't fully trust the new technology and stubbornly held on to their metal for a century too long. A scar crossed her face, ripping through her lip. Her eyes blazed.

The vampire raised a huge axe to the sky and roared, displaying frightening fangs. Bestata and Karat shied back on pure instinct. Marais jerked awake and jumped to his feet.

"*I, Sileta of House Korsa, Daughter of Lorsan and Delendine, Granddaughter of Olasard the Ripper of Souls, gift these weapons to this inn,*" the vampire declared. "*May the descendants of our great nation use them to better themselves during their travels. Let their weapons strike true, and let their will never falter. Let them bring death to all Mukama across stars and time!*"

I sipped my coffee.

The recording vanished.

Sean looked at me.

That's right. You thought you knew all my secrets. You haven't even scratched the surface, buddy.

I smiled and gave him a little salute with my coffee cup.

"This is a holy relic," Bestata hissed.

"No, it's just a practice weapon rack with a long history," I said. "Does Lady Emindra feel unequal to the challenge?"

Bestata glared at me. "My skills are beyond contestation."

Karat chuckled.

"Splendid," I said. "All of us look forward to witnessing you honor your ancestors. The spirit of Olasard's granddaughter is watching. No pressure."

———

KOSANDION DECIDED TO HOLD THE ELIMINATION IN THE ARENA.

Outside of the inn, a bright sunny day was in full swing. Inside, a late evening painted the sky above the arena with blues and purples, and in the west, a splash of brilliant pink diluted with gold gently smoldered into night. I had recorded a spectacular Texas sunset and was now projecting it on the ceiling. The air was pleasantly warm. A simulated evening breeze fanned the delegates in their seating sections.

At the south side of the arena, an enormous stone doorway opened to a short passage leading to the portal glowing with pale green light. I stood just inside of it, out of view. Gaston waited next to me. He'd chosen another space musketeer outfit, this one a deep hunter green, and he topped it off with a brimmed hat with a ridiculously fluffy black feather.

At the north end, directly opposite the doorway, a stone crag thrust from the bottom of the arena. It had two small seating sections on each side and a stone staircase that led all the way to the top, crowned with a stone throne. Behind the throne, eleven enormous banners, each representing the remaining delegations, hung from seemingly empty air, stirring gently in the breeze. There was a spot for the twelfth banner, between the second and third banners from the right, but it was obviously missing.

Between the throne and the doorway, in the center of the arena, the raised stage waited. I had lifted it a bit higher and added some fog for atmosphere. Dark mist swirled along the bottom of the arena, sliding around the stone stage, lapping at the walls of the delegations' sections, and flowing to the throne crag and back, like a turbulent sea. Occasionally tiny motes of golden light emerged from the mist and floated up slowly until they melted into the evening air.

It was as if the throne crag and the stage had risen from a bottomless chasm shrouded with mist. But the mist was barely three feet deep. I had bought it from Cookie, and he gave me a slight discount, which made his followers clutch their metaphorical pearls. It was still not cheap, but worth it. Orata had asked for "maximum drama." No innkeeper would shy from that challenge. We lived for this stuff.

The arena hummed. The last delegation had been seated fifteen minutes ago, and they were getting antsy.

There was some minor commotion in the observers' section. I pulled a screen up to take a closer look. Two of Cookie's helpers dashed about, pretending to spar with two long daggers. Dagorkun looked like someone stomped on his foot, but he had to endure it, so he just let all the pain go to his face. Next to him Karat smiled and clapped her hands.

The smaller of the lees leaped into the air, bringing his dagger down in a sweeping cut. Oh! They were reenacting Karat and Bestata's bout this morning. They must've seen the footage.

I knew Bestata was in trouble when Karat asked me to record their sparring session, because she wanted "an instructional video for Lady Helen." All vampire houses prided themselves on their melee skills, but House Krahr had taken personal combat to new heights.

Like all vampires, House Krahr treasured their children. They knew for decades that they would have to send them to battle on Nexus, where anomalies made aerial warfare impossible, and so they turned Arland and Karat's generation into expert ground fighters. My sister described her future husband as "a killing machine" and meant it, which Arland would've taken as a huge compliment.

This expertise came with a hefty price tag. Concentrating on ground combat meant less time for education in other aspects of warfare. For example, Sean warned me that if Arland ever had to fight a space battle without an admiral to guide him, he would lose. But it did make for remarkable duels.

I split the screen and checked Lady Bestata. The red streak across her face was barely visible now. I had convinced her to spend a couple of hours in the medward, because having a spectacular bruise across one's face highlighted on the Dominion's screens would've been a bad look. The welt on Bestata's face could be healed, but the wound to her pride was permanent. Karat had killed her three times during that duel.

"A remarkable woman," Gaston observed over my shoulder.

"Which one?"

"Both of them. Although Lady Karat is much more engaging."

Aha. Engaging.

The inn chimed in my head. It was time. I dismissed the screens and grasped the arena with my power. This would require careful timing.

"Go," I murmured to Gaston.

He touched the brim of his spectacular hat, flashed me a serrated-tooth smile, and marched through the doorway.

I flicked the lights on. Twelve clusters of flood lights, positioned at the ends of 100-foot poles along the perimeter of the arena, came on and tilted down, illuminating Gaston in the passage. We had gone full Monday Night Football.

The solid ground ended at the doorway's threshold, but Gaston didn't slow down. For a moment his foot in a dark brown boot hovered over the empty air, and then the first section of a stone bridge rose out of the mist to meet it. He took a firm step onto the stone. A row of small round lamps ignited in the rail of the bridge like runway lights guiding a plane to safe landing.

A hush fell onto the arena. Gaston kept walking. The light chased him, as if trying to catch up, all the way across the bridge and onto the central platform, where it dashed along the round stone rail, forming a complete circle. Gaston greeted the delegates with an elegant bow and a hand swish that had likely required ballet training in childhood.

The arena erupted in stomps, hoots, and applause. Gaston welcomed it all with another bow.

The noise swelled, then began to ebb. Gaston raised his arms and the commotion died. He smiled, the huge screens by each section zooming in on his face, and called out, "**Let us begin!**"

A massive bell rang through the arena.

At the base of the stone crag, Kosandion emerged from under the floor. He wore a brilliant white robe trimmed with deep blue. A long indigo cloak hung off his left shoulder. He looked majestic.

The light in the stone rail in front of Kosandion ignited, and the glow dashed all the way up to the throne. Kosandion started up the stairs. I added a bit of wind, and his cloak flared as he climbed.

The floor of the side sections parted. Nobody paid it any mind, because Kosandion was still ascending, and the entire arena missed Miralitt, Resven, and Orata emerging on the left and the Holy Ecclesiarch and two of his acolytes on the right. Orata looked in my direction and grinned. Apparently, the level of drama was sufficient.

Kosandion sat on his throne. A hundred feet above him, a constellation of the Dominion star systems sparked into light, suspended in midair. The silver radiance spilled over him. He looked like a glowing god ready to sit in judgement of mere mortals.

A hush fell.

Sean stepped out from behind the throne like a shadow in a dark gray robe. It was his turn to babysit.

Gaston turned to Kosandion and waited. The Sovereign moved his hand. Gaston bowed and turned back to the arena. His voice boomed.

"**Twelve candidates journeyed here for the Final Selection. One, brought here against her will, bravely reclaimed her free-**

dom." He pointed to the missing banner. **"Eleven candidates remain. Today we must say goodbye to two more. It is heart-wrenching to part with them, but the Dominion has voted. Their voices guide us tonight."**

Gaston paused, solemn.

"The first delegation to leave us is..."

The arena held its breath.

For a man who grew up without commercial breaks, he definitely had a thing for dramatic pauses.

"The Children of the Silver Star," Gaston announced.

I highlighted the Donkamin section and extended a ramp from their section to the center of the raised area below. The twenty-one Donkamkins rose and moved in an orderly line to join Gaston, the ramp folding behind them.

It was hardly a surprise. They had been notified this morning that they had garnered the least amount of votes from the Dominion. They had time to pack and prepare. There was always a chance that they would do something rash as a parting shot; however, it went against the way the Donkamins had conducted themselves so far.

The Donkamins faced the throne.

"Children of the Silver Star," Kosandion said, his voice clear and strong. "You have honored us with your presence. We are grateful for the precious gift of your time and effort and for a chance to meet your civilization. What do you ask of the Dominion?"

Ah. The minor ask.

One of the Donkamins spoke. "The Silver Star wishes to exchange knowledge with the Dominion. We ask for the establishment of a scientific embassy on Teplaym."

Teplaym was the Dominion's most scientifically advanced planet.

"Granted," the Sovereign said. "May the sharing of knowledge and exchange of ideas benefit both of our societies for centuries to come."

He rose and bowed to the Donkamins. The Donkamins swiveled back. Their feet remained planted, but their heads, necks, and other parts twisted in weird directions. It was a display of respect that no Earthborn person could watch without flinching. I fought a shudder.

"A round of applause for our departing friends," Gaston requested, and the arena obliged.

Twenty-one Donkamins turned, swiveled at everyone for the last time, and finally started across the bridge toward the portal.

Once this was over, I would expand the Donkamin entry in my innkeeper files. I had learned a lot about them, and any additional information about the guests benefited the inns. I had already started, and my contribution so far amounted to a single line in all caps: "DO NOT LIKE TO BE TOUCHED."

The Donkamin delegation reached the doorway. The leading Donkamin's neck spiraled out and paused six inches in front of me.

"Thank you for your hospitality, innkeeper. Be well."

"Gertrude Hunt is honored by your presence. It was my privilege to host you."

The Donkamins walked into the portal. As the last of them exited, I held the portal open, and a new group of visitors arrived —Vercia Denoma, flanked by four Capital Guards. She shot me an ugly look.

"And now for our final elimination of the day." Gaston turned to the stone crag and held his hand out.

Orata rose and stepped forward. I lit the platform perimeter, and the massive screens zoomed in on the PR chief.

"My name is Orata Tavan. I serve the Dominion as the Sovereign's Liaison. My left hand touches the Sovereign, my right touches the Dominion's people, and it is my sacred duty to bring them together."

Nicely put.

"When my office vetted the candidates for the selection, we discovered a terrible crime. One of the candidates was not who they claimed to be."

The arena had gone completely quiet.

"Every delegation brought the best of the best, the exceptional, the honorable, the worthy. But this candidate was the worst of the worst. Dominion, what I'm about to show you is horrific. But you must see it for yourself, so you can do your civic duties and render your judgement."

On the screens, Pivor of the Murder Beaks beheaded a child with a swing of his sword. His skin was a deep lavender, and his hair was long, straight, and dark, but it was unmistakably him. The smile was a dead giveaway.

"Behold, Cumbr Adgi ar'Muterzen," Orata announced. "The third son of Gar Por ar'Muterzen, and fourth in line to lead the Vagabond pirate fleet. We know him as Pivor."

In the Murder Beak section, Pivor tried to rise, but the floor swallowed his feet. I pulled the floor directly under him up, and his chair carried him fifty feet into the air, above the seats, leaving him trapped on top of a stone pillar. He gripped the armrest, trying to pull his feet free, but the inn held him tight.

The screens flashed with strategically selected shots, a gallery of Pivor's atrocities.

The Murder Beaks screeched. I had interacted enough with them over the years to recognize the specific tone of their shrieks. It wasn't a protest, it was surprise and outrage. They hadn't known.

The morbid gallery kept rolling. Orata had removed the sound from the footage, and watching it in silence made it more horrifying somehow.

"When this vile deception was discovered, we faced the question of how to proceed. It would be a simple matter to reject his candidacy and expel the delegation sponsoring him."

Technically nothing she said was a lie so far. She just didn't specify when exactly the deception had been discovered.

Vercia was frowning. Yes, I had no idea where Orata was going with this either, but apparently this was a cue because the guards started marching down the bridge to the central section, Vercia between them.

"However, one courageous member of our team, the one who was responsible for vetting his candidacy, made the decision to permit him to continue. She felt she had a duty to take this chance to expose his atrocities to the entire galaxy at just the right time, when everyone's attention would be on the event, so all would be aware of exactly what he has done."

Again, not a lie.

"Dominion, that public servant is Vercia Denoma. She is our hero."

I directed the nearest spotlight onto the platform. It caught Vercia in its radiance. I zoomed the screens on her face. She was doing a stunning impression of a deer in headlights. The guards around her snapped to attention. I had seen them do this exact move in Kosandion's presence. They were her "honor guard."

"It is thanks to her tireless efforts that we can now stand here, see these crimes for ourselves, and witness justice being done. I brought this to you today to remind you to be vigilant. Evil is insidious. It can worm its way into your inner circle and stab you in the back."

Oh wow.

"If it wasn't for Vercia's efforts, we might have been unaware of the evil that is Cumbr Adgi. She is the reason he has reached this moment and the reason I can now expose him to all of you. Everything that follows is thanks to her. Today we honor you, Vercia Denoma. The Dominion owes you a great debt."

Orata bowed. Behind her Resven and Miralitt bowed as well.

Pivor's father indulged his children. He spoiled them, and he was in the business where a terrible reputation was an asset. He couldn't afford to look weak or suffer disrespect. If anything happened to his offspring, he would retaliate. It was simply good business, and Orata had just told him exactly who was responsible for his son's downfall. Orata hadn't just thrown Vercia under the bus. She'd picked the bus up and dropped it on Vercia's head.

The fear in Vercia's wide-open eyes told me that she understood exactly what had happened.

Kosandion's voice echoed through the arena. "Cumbr Adgi ar'Muterzen."

I spun the stone pillar, so Pivor faced the throne.

"Do you have anything to say?" Kosandion asked.

Pivor grinned and this time it looked psychotic. "Fuck off, you dumb prick. You want a piece of me, be a man and get it yourself."

Kosandion's face was glacial, as if carved out of an iceberg. "Cumbr Adgi ar'Muterzen, you are hereby expelled from the selection. Your sponsor is disqualified. Their asks will not be honored."

"I have something to say," the largest Murder Beak shrieked.

Kosandion nodded.

I moved the lights onto the Murder Beak section and slid Pivor's pillar toward it, far enough to stay out of reach. The largest bird rose. She was huge with rust and crimson plumage. Her enormous beak could crack a cow's femur in half. I had seen it happen, because Orro served them bovine bones when they felt peckish and wanted a fun snack.

The leader of the Murder Beaks took a step forward and stepped onto the rail bordering their section. The wicked spurs on her legs were sheathed in razor-sharp metal, and they glinted in the light of the arena. Her talons gripped the stone and squeezed, chipping it. She glared at Pivor with the unblinking focus of a predator.

"Go back to your father, pirate. Give him my message. Your skulls are soft. Your brains are delicious. We are coming."

She opened her beak and let out a deafening shriek. Every

feather on her body stood erect. Pivor was thirty feet away from her, but he jerked back in his seat.

"The Dominion acknowledges the vow of vengeance," Kosandion said. "We do not bear the Murder Beaks any ill will and hold them blameless in this affair."

"Fight me, you fucking asshole!" Pivor howled, twisting in his seat. "Fight me."

"Sadly, someone else has a prior claim," Kosandion said. "Innkeeper, we are finished."

Sean raised his hand and his voice whispered through the arena, quiet but heard by every creature there.

Your welcome is withdrawn.

The architecture of the inn folded above the doorway, spinning, collapsing, and a door rushed at us and flung itself wide open, revealing Baha-char's sunshine. The roots of the inn spilled from the ceiling, yanked Pivor off his chair, and hurled him through the door. It slammed shut.

The feed on the screen showed Pivor landing on the big stone tiles paving the alley. He rolled, stopped, spat into the dirt, and got up, his chin jutting into the air. He adjusted his clothes...

A familiar woman dropped from the upper balcony, wrapped in a shawl.

He squinted at her.

She pulled her shawl back, revealing the faint outline of scales on her face.

"Do you remember me, Cumbr Adgi?"

He laughed.

"You beheaded my father." Long orange blades slipped into her hand from within the shawl's folds.

"You starved my mother to death."

She started toward him.

"You butchered my sister."

He kept laughing.

"You violated my body."

"And enjoyed it," he said.

"Today is the day I cleanse my soul of this blood debt."

"Bring it on!"

She charged him. He danced out of the way, impossibly quick for a human, and swung at her. She dodged. Pivor's fist connected with the wall of a building, cracking the stone. That explained why he wanted to fight Kosandion.

He shook the dust off his hand and grinned. "Come on! I'm waiting! Come on, come—"

She slipped close to him with deadly grace and spun her sword over his left forearm. Pivor didn't even register it until his fist slid off his arm and fell to the ground. He bellowed and charged at her.

It took almost two minutes for him to die. She painted the alley with his blood, carving pieces off of him bit by bit, and when everything was done, she gouged out his eyes with her bare hands, cut off his head, pulled her shawl over her face, and walked away, melting into the current of shoppers on the busy street at the mouth of the alley.

Vercia's honor guard turned as one and exited the stage, heading down the bridge, past me, toward the portal. She looked after them, looked at Kosandion, then back at the screen where pieces of Pivor littered the alley. Desperation twisted her face. She marched to the bridge at a near run. Nobody except me paid her any mind. There was no need to arrest her or charge her with anything. She was a dead woman walking.

Vercia saw me and swallowed. "I want a room."

"We have no vacancy."

She spun around and waved at the arena, incredulous.

"We are full, Lady Denoma." I pointed to the portal. "Please, return to the Dominion."

She clenched her hands and fled to the portal. The green glow swallowed her.

Good riddance.

I took a moment to savor the cleaner air and turned to the arena. We needed to wish the Murder Beaks goodbye, put everyone else back into their quarters, and prepare for Kosandion's date this afternoon. He would be having a one-on-one with Cyanide, and I had no idea how it would go.

[21]

In our last thrilling instalment, the identity of the pirate prince was finally revealed. He was exposed and purged from the inn to Baha-char, where the woman whose family he murdered exacted her revenge. It wasn't swift, but it was bloody.

Vercia got her just deserts when Orata dumped the entire responsibility for the Muterzen pirate prince into her lap. Vercia realized that she has a space cruiser sized target on her back and attempted to request a room at the inn. The request was denied. Mmm, so satisfying.

Now the guests are in their chambers and the long-awaited date between Cyanide and the Sovereign is beginning. Are you suffering from sweltering summer heat? Read on, for relief is only a few words away.

Gertrude Hunt had a dozen branches. Some we used often, like the one leading to Baha-char. Some, like the desert door, were used once in a while. The rest stayed mostly shut, and half of the time I forgot we even had them. However, today one of those forgotten branches got its chance to shine.

Cyanide made three requests with regard to her date: she

256

wanted to be up high, she wanted a new view, and she wanted something soft to lie on. Like most big cats, she didn't fancy walks unless it was the only way to get a delicious snack. We managed to deliver on all three counts.

Kosandion surveyed the rustic alpine lodge. To be honest, rustic was a relative term. It wasn't rustic as in "Grandpa built a little cabin out of whatever timber he found handy." It was the luxury kind of rustic, a modern homage to a Renaissance Jagdschloss that sometimes occurred when too much money met the need to roleplay as a medieval Bavarian aristocrat hosting a hunting party.

The lodge was sixty feet tall, with a gabled ceiling made of faux-redwood boards in a rich beautiful brown. The floor matched the ceiling. In front of me, a wall built with rough square slabs of gray stone housed a massive fireplace. A fire crackled within, radiating warmth. Thick timbers, stripped of their bark but left naturally round, thrust from the wall above the fireplace, supporting a narrow second story walkway. Matching wooden columns rose to the ceiling to meet thick beams.

The wall on my left was redwood and stone. The walls on my right and behind me were floor to ceiling glass, set into a faux-redwood frame. Beyond the glass lay an alien planet. A winter wonderland stretched as fast as the eye could see.

We were high up on a mountain slope under a sky smothered with pale clouds. In the distance, on the left, a white peak rose from the forest, jagged and sharp, a sign of a young mountain range. Just beyond the windows, the ground dropped, rolling to the valley below. Alien trees blanketed the steep slope. Their branches, sheathed with long, fluffy needles and coated with snow, cast blue shadows onto pristine white powder. It was one of the most perfect winter landscapes I had ever seen. You could almost hear the crunch of the snow underfoot just by looking at it.

"Where is this?" Kosandion asked.

"I don't know. There are no artificial signals coming from this planet. No radio waves, no energy readings. When that happens, the only way to identify the location is by taking an image of the night sky and running it through a galaxy mapping unit, but I've never seen the stars here. It is always like this—a long blue winter under an overcast sky."

Theoretically, we could get a small craft through the branch's door and fly up past the cloud cover to capture an image of the stars, but it would be dangerous and there was no need for it.

Kosandion crossed his arms and gazed out the window. He'd traded his Sovereign robe for a two-piece outfit that reminded me of the stylish Senator-wear designs from Nigeria: narrow hunter green pants and a matching shirt with an asymmetric hem that ended almost at his knees. The Senator shirts tended to be cut a little loose, while Kosandion's tunic, embellished with the Dominion's geometric embroidery, was perfectly tailored to accentuate the breadth of his shoulders and his narrow waist.

Kosandion's body looked elegant, but his face looked troubled. It wasn't his expression, it was in the eyes, a kind of weary introspective distance.

"How much trouble will Vercia's mess cause you?" I asked.

"More than I would've preferred," he said. "The Muterzen fleet is an immediate threat, but the Murder Beaks should keep them occupied. Still, contingency measures must be implemented."

"What about her family? Will they make things difficult?"

"The Dominion's politics are complicated. There will be quiet inquiries. Those who are perceptive enough will discern that show for what it was—a good save and a swift punishment. In the immediate future, her family will lobby for federal protection."

"Will you grant it?"

He shook his head. "The penalty for impeding a public official is a tiered charge. The more power one has, the steeper the punishment. An ordinary citizen shouting over Resven would have gotten a warning and a small fine, but Vercia was a highly placed officer in the Liaison Corps. If the Justice Corps proceeded with the charges, she could have faced a prison term. She resigned last night, hoping to avoid it. Now she is no longer a servant of the people, therefore she is ineligible for the additional federal security. This will not endear me to her family in the slightest. They will bide their time waiting to stab me in the back, and I will spend the next couple of years slowly removing them from positions of influence."

He fell silent. First, Odikas and his Conservative Alliance looking for a leader, then the pirates, Vercia, her well-connected family, and all on top of the spousal selection and other matters pertaining to running the Dominion, which didn't stop just because he was trying to find a partner. He had a lot on his plate.

"Her Grace asked me to tell you something. I meant to do it last night, but things were hectic."

Kosandion raised his eyebrows.

"*Olivio teseres tares,*" I told him.

He smiled.

"What does it mean?"

"'Fate needs a mason,'" he said. "It's an old saying."

She told him to become the architect of his own destiny. Interesting.

I felt Cyanide approach. It was time to put on a show for the viewers many light years away.

"Your date is here, *Letero.*"

The doors in the far wall opened, revealing Tony and Cyanide walking side by side. The big, white cat saw the winter outside, opened her blue mouth, and panted once. I didn't know enough about the Higgra to interpret that.

"Greetings, candidate Cyanide," Kosandion said.

"Greetings, Sovereign of the Dominion."

Tony retreated and shut the door behind him.

Cyanide padded to the fire. I had made her a long, ergonomic version of a cushioned chaise lounge, large enough for her to stretch out. Kosandion got a comfortable stuffed chair. I had put a couple of small tables here and there, but I kept it simple.

Cyanide examined the lounge and looked at me. "Sit here."

I glanced at Kosandion. He frowned.

I sat on the edge of the lounge. Cyanide leaped onto it and flopped herself on my lap, all two hundred and fifty pounds of her.

Ow.

Big golden eyes stared at me. "I require attentions," Cyanide announced. "All of them."

Kosandion raised his eyebrows.

"And the brush," Cyanide said.

Whatever made this date go smoothly.

I reached out, and Gertrude Hunt pulled one of the brushes from the stables. They were soft with dense bristles, originally designed for the beasts of burden the Merchants sometimes brought with them, and I had sterilized them after each use. The brush landed in my hand, and I began working through Cyanide's fur. Her eyes widened, flashing dangerous gold, then half closed, and she turned her head, presenting me with the corner of her jaw. Just like Olasard. Except he barely weighed seventeen pounds. If this went on for too much longer, my legs would go numb.

Silence ensued.

Cyanide made a soft rumble in her throat. It was too deep to be a purr and not violent enough to be a roar, more like an internal contented cough.

"Do you wish to tell me of your planet?" Kosandion asked.

"No."

Well, this was going swimmingly.

He tried again. "What would you rather talk about instead?"

Cyanide turned over on her back, her fuzzy paws level with my face. I glided the brush along her chest. Long claws shot out of her paws and withdrew.

"If I marry you, can I bring this human with me to serve me?"

"No," Kosandion said.

"A pity."

Cyanide made her coughing noise again.

More silence. Kosandion really needed an image boost, and his spousal candidate was flat-out ignoring him. How to salvage this...

Kosandion pulled out a small gadget, squeezed it, and it projected a tablet in front of him. He began scrolling through the documents.

A minute passed. Another.

What was going on?

"You should tell her about our arrangement," Cyanide said, stretching to get a better brushing angle. "Or she won't focus on attentions."

"Is that wise?" I asked.

"This date isn't broadcast live," Kosandion told me, still absorbed in whatever he was reading. "Highlights only."

"I thought all dates were live like Ellenda's."

Kosandion put the tablet device on the side table.

"Ellenda didn't do well in the voting, but her presence guaranteed high ratings," he said. "My mother was a mysterious, inscrutable figure for most of her stay in the Dominion. She spent twenty-two years there, and by the time she returned to her planet, most people knew just as little about her as they did when she first arrived. For the Dominion's citizens, Ellenda was a chance to get a better understanding of the Uma, my mother, and my heritage. The Higgra do not generate the same level of interest."

I thought that the spouse had to stay for a period of 25 years... Oh. Kosandion was twenty-one when his father died. His mother must've left when he ascended the throne. Was it voluntary? Did she want to go home?

"I do not care about the Dominion's interest," Cyanide rumbled.

"What do you care about?" I asked.

"The neural nets," Cyanide said. "And Clan Sai."

Clan Sai, the Merchants who claimed the Dominion as their territory. This was getting convoluted. Officially, the Merchants had no territories, and many of them competed for the best trade partners, trying to outbid each other. But they always strived for a monopoly, and once a Merchant Clan grasped a region in its claws, it was difficult to shake them loose. According to Cookie, a century ago, Clan Sai managed to push out the other three Merchant Clans vying for the Dominion, and they had been highly protective of it ever since.

"What's a neural net?" I asked.

"There is a special plant that grows on our planet," Cyanide said. "A fur lichen den, formed by the long tendrils of the fur lichen plant colony. Many organisms coexist within the fur lichen, some microscopic and others large enough to be visible by even a human eye. The Fuzzy Worms feed on the many creatures of the fur lichen den and craft their webs within it. We harvest the webs and weave them into neural nets with our tools and claws."

"The neural nets are the best solution for regeneration of the nervous system," Kosandion said. "Once they're implanted, the healing is miraculous. People whose paralysis resisted every other treatment regain the use of their limbs within days. Transplants, nanotherapy, artificial neurons, nothing else comes close."

"We want to sell them to the Dominion," Cyanide said. "But the Sai are blocking our way."

"The Sai have moved a ship into the orbit of the Higgra planet," Kosandion explained. "They're pressuring the Higgra to use them as intermediaries for the sale. The Higgra have applied for a direct trade agreement with the Dominion; however, Clan Sai indicated that they are not above using their other trade agreements as leverage."

"If you buy directly from the Higgra, the Merchants will pitch a fit and stop supplying you with other goods?" I guessed.

"Precisely," Kosandion said. "According to the federal guide-lines, a thorough review of the potential impact must be conducted by the Commerce Department, which could take years."

"So, you're cutting out the middleman and the bureaucracy by using the Higgra's minor ask." I brushed Cyanide's throat.

"Yes." Kosandion smiled. It was a sharp and cold smile. "I don't react well to blackmail."

A lot of things suddenly made sense. I kept brushing. Cyanide rumbled, her eyes closed. In the fireplace a log popped, sending sparks into the flue.

"If Clan Sai suddenly canceled their trade deals, it would put the Dominion's economy into a difficult position," I said. "If only there were another Merchant clan willing to step into the gap. Someone with a lot of resources, able to react to the situation quickly. Someone who might have sent a representative to observe this spousal selection."

Kosandion chuckled. "By the end of this affair, we will make you into a proper Dominion politician, Dina. Let me know if you ever consider a career change."

"No thank you," I told him. "I'm happy right here, doing what I do now."

Cyanide rumbled and turned on her side. Kosandion picked up the tablet and resumed his reading.

Outside the snow began to fall, fat fluffy snowflakes drifting softly to the ground. For the next half hour, I brushed the big cat and watched the snow, while the Sovereign caught up on his paperwork.

———

Tony ambushed me as soon as the Higgra's date was over.

"Dad wants to talk to you." He thrust the phone at me.

My heart made a pirouette. Most innkeepers avoided personal phone calls. Even getting a phone number of an innkeeper was a sign of trust, and it was understood that direct communication was only for emergencies. What was bad enough for him to call me?

Brian Rodriguez looked back at me from the screen. "Have you gotten anything from Lachlan Stewart?"

"No. I don't know who he is. Should I know who he is?"

Brian heaved a sign. "How much do you know about the Loch Broom Inn?"

"Um... It's an old castle in Scotland. Very remote. They specialize in large-scale events."

Loch Broom was off the beaten path, and its beautiful but severe landscape meant that human visitors were rare. If you wanted to have a destination wedding on Earth, or a diplomatic summit, or a convention, Loch Broom Castle was your venue. It wasn't the only inn catering to large-scale events, but it was one of the better known.

"Lachlan runs Loch Broom Castle. He is fourth generation, old, and crochety. Also stubborn like a goat."

"Okay."

"He wants to adopt you."

"What?"

"He's eighty years old, and he's been looking for a successor. His oldest is an ad-hal, and her kids live off-planet. His youngest took over a small inn in Bulgaria just to get away from him. His kids don't want to deal with their grandfather either. Lachlan's been watching the coverage of the selection, and he's decided you are worthy."

The walls around me creaked in alarm. In the innkeeper world, adoption could take place at any age, provided the "parent" was at least twenty years older than the "child." Once adopted, the "child" would be considered a rightful heir to the "parent's" inn. But I wasn't an orphan. This was ridiculous.

"I already have parents."

"That was pointed out to him. He says that according to our guidelines, enough time passed that they can be declared dead soon..."

"They are not dead!" They were missing.

Brian nodded. "I know. We told him. He is determined to get you and Sean over to Scotland. He says you have 'the vision.'"

A wall to my left parted and Sean came out of it, looking ready to fight somebody.

"It doesn't matter what he's determined to do. I'm not leaving Gertrude Hunt. The Assembly can't separate us, I won't—"

Sean put his arm around me and leaned over my shoulder to pin Brian with a stare.

Brian raised his hand. "Dina, if Lachlan reaches out to you, he might make it seem that this has been decided and you must leave your inn and go to Loch Broom. I'm telling you right now, as a representative of the Assembly, you don't have to do what he says. If he tries to bully you, call me. You're doing a good job where you are. You've bonded with your inn. Nobody is going to remove you unless a catastrophe happens. So don't worry about it, and if he calls, tell him no. Okay?"

"Okay. Thank you for the warning."

"Let me talk to Tony, please."

I handed the phone to Tony, and he walked away, muttering something.

Sean hugged me. "What happened?"

"An elderly Scottish innkeeper wants to adopt me." I shook my head. "What's next?"

"Next, you're going to sit down for at least 15 minutes and eat something. Come on."

He sat me down at the kitchen table, and Droplet brought me food. I took exactly two bites of the most delicious burrito I had ever tasted, and then the inn tugged on me. The werewolf was awake.

————

I FOUND THE WEREWOLF IN OUR HIGH-TECH MED UNIT. SHE MUST'VE heard me come in, but she gave no indication of it. I approached the bed. She looked at me and didn't say anything.

I pulled up a chair and sat. Her color was much better, and she seemed alert. Around us the walls were a nebulous charcoal, swirls of darker and lighter gray. Karat had an aversion to the sterile white, so I had adjusted it to her preferences.

Gertrude Hunt pulled on my attention, announcing an incoming call from Gaston. I took it.

"We have a slight problem," his disembodied voice said from the empty air about eight feet up.

The werewolf sat up and squinted at the source of the voice.

"What is it?" I had dumped, that is delegated, the responsibility for the 2nd Trial, the talent show, onto Gaston and Tony. They should be at the rehearsal now.

"One of the talent demonstrations is in poor taste."

"What do you mean?"

"I personally find it distasteful," he said.

What would Gaston find distasteful? Orata warned me that the candidates were allowed a lot of latitude when displaying their talents. Even if one of them were to light themselves on fire, we couldn't interfere.

"Is it dangerous to other guests?"

"No."

"You have to let them do it. If we block any of the candidates from demonstrating their talents, they could claim we prevented them from becoming a spouse."

"Understood."

266

He broke the connection. We sat in silence for a couple of minutes.

"You win," she said finally.

I waited.

"I saw you kill that thing before I passed out. You're stronger than me, so you win."

"I never was in competition with you."

She looked away.

"What's wrong with your ossai?" I asked.

She gave me a dark look.

"You didn't go into a wetwork form during the fight," I told her. "And your rate of regeneration is lower than that of a typical werewolf."

The ossai were a marvel of bioengineering. A programmable synthetic virus, it was the reason werewolves could bounce up tall trees, murder their opponents with insane speed and accuracy, and change shape. The werewolves had three forms: the human form they called OPS; the OM form, a quadrupedal animal shape they used for scouting and covert action; and the wetwork form, a huge human-wolf monster, which they used in combat.

Werewolves changed forms without thinking. It was instinctual like breathing. Sean had shifted into the wetwork shape when he'd attacked the cruiser and then shifted back, probably without conscious effort.

She didn't. The corrupted ad-hal nearly killed her, but she had stayed human.

"What's wrong?" I repeated.

The werewolf sucked the air in and let it out slowly. "Activation failure. In your boyfriend, the ossai are linked into a single bionet. They communicate with each other. My ossai don't. Sometimes chunks of them link up, and I get a boost, but most of the time they fail."

Oh. Like a faulty fluorescent light. When Sean flipped the

switch, the light came on instantly and was blindingly bright. When she flipped the switch, it pulsed and flickered.

"Can your ossai be fixed?"

She shook her head. "I hoped so, but Wilmos said no."

Sean was right. She had a problem, and she went to see Wilmos. Except this time he couldn't help.

The werewolf shrugged. "It took me three years to make my way to him, and in the end, it was for nothing. My parents are normal. Apparently, this just happens sometimes during fetal development."

"You fight well."

She gave me a bitter smile. "I like how you didn't say the second part out loud. I fight well—for a defective werewolf."

"Only things can be defective, not people."

"Spare me."

There was a lot of self-loathing there. Arguing with her would only provoke hostility.

"Wilmos said that if I find a strong werewolf, the kids would be normal. If at least one parent is fully active, and the fetus is monitored and treated in the womb, the activation failure usually doesn't reoccur," she said.

"Is that why you fixated on Sean?"

"I asked Wilmos who the strongest werewolf was. He said Sean but he was taken. I never run away from a fight."

"No, you just run into it without thinking."

She glared at me.

"I was talking to the thing that took Wilmos, and you attacked it before I got anywhere."

It took a few seconds to sink in. She slumped against her pillow.

"You know where Wilmos is," she finally said. "What's there to talk about?"

"Why they took him? Is he alive? What do they want?"

She looked at the ceiling. I could see it in her face: she realized

268

that she screwed up. It wasn't the first time, and I could tell it was getting old for her.

"Have you ever seen Sean fight?" I asked her.

"Fight? No. I barely got to talk to him. The first time, he threw me out of your inn. The second time he came out to get the guy with weird teeth and told me to stay out of his way."

I flicked my fingers. A screen appeared on the wall. On it, a battle raged across the barren hellish landscape. Armies clashed, vampires in black syn-armor, otrokars in battle suits, and the Merchant mercenaries in tactical gray.

"Nexus," I told her.

A clump of fighters burst on the right and a single figure tore out into the open. He was seven feet tall and clad in obsidian black. The armor coated him like a second skin, flowing over his muscular body, completely seamless. It turned into clawed gauntlets on his oversized hands, into boots on his feet, and into a hood on his head. Inside the hood was darkness. Ink-black darkness that looked back at you.

The fighter ripped into the soldiers, moving with insane speed. The two green-edged blades in his hands sliced, stabbed, and cut with relentless, controlled fury.

The werewolf woman stared, open-mouthed.

"Nexus killed all of Sean's predecessors. Every Turan Adin before him died," I said.

Nuan Cee had given me this recording after the Peace Summit. I never knew why. It just arrived one day to the Baha-char door, a small datacube inside a little box with Clan Nuan seal on it. I had watched it twice so far, and I'd cried every time. A familiar heat warmed the back of my eyes. I had to hold it back until I got my point across.

"Consider the kind of willpower required to wake up every morning and fight through hell, then heal your wounds, and do it again. And again. And again."

The vampire and otrokar warriors moved as one, their blades

slicing, creating a deadly whirlwind with Sean at its center, their own fighting forgotten. Blades flashed, and then the ring of weapons and fighters broke, and he was through, splattered with blood. He didn't feel like Sean. He felt like a force, as if the rage and the bloodlust that emanated from the fighters had coalesced into a humanoid form and tore through the battlefield.

I wiped the tears from my cheeks.

"Why are you crying?" she asked me, her voice quiet.

"Because he is inside that."

"I don't understand."

"He was protecting the Merchant fort. He didn't fully understand what was required of him until he arrived there. He found refugees, families, children, the elderly. Creatures who had no place to go. Their lives depended on him. He couldn't leave. There was no escape, so he killed a part of himself, the one that was kind and funny and was bothered by hurting others, and became that. I cry because I know what it cost him."

She looked back at the slaughter.

"It took him a long time to come back," I told her. "Do you understand now? I haven't trapped him here. I'm not guilt-tripping him into staying or keeping him from being the best werewolf he can be. No force in this galaxy could make Sean do something against his will. I knew him before he was Turan Adin, I saw him with the armor on, and I was there when he took it off. He stays here because he loves me, and I love him."

She looked at the battle. "Please turn it off."

I dismissed the screen. We sat in silence for a few moments.

"Your wounds should heal in another couple of days. Do you have a place to go? Where is home?"

She gave a short, bitter laugh. "A small room a block away from Wilmos' shop. I've been living there for the last six months. When he didn't have werewolf guests, I went to hang out at his shop and listen to his war stories. Hanging on to scraps of other people's glory because I don't have any of my own."

Sean had viewed the recording of our fight with the corrupted ad-hal, and according to him, she was well trained and knew what she was doing in a fight. Despite her activation issues, she was faster and stronger than an average human. A lot of security forces would be happy to have her. Failing that, she could make a good living as a mercenary.

None of that mattered. Her self-esteem was nonexistent. She seemed to tackle every problem head-on, without strategy or planning, trying to power through it on sheer will and physical persistence. It must have worked for her in childhood. She probably learned that even if her ossai misfired, if she just ran fast enough, hit hard enough, and didn't quit, she could hold her own. But the older she grew, the wider the gap between her and other werewolves became. She was likely almost as good as everyone in early childhood, but by mid-teens she would've started to lag behind, and by the time she became an adult, she probably realized that no matter how hard she tried, she could never keep up.

If she continued on the same path she was on now, she would die fighting. Heroically, but probably needlessly. She needed to feel competent, to be in a place where her skills were valued, so she could stop seeing herself as a failed werewolf. I needed to talk to her more, but it was almost 10 pm, and I had somewhere else to be.

"What's your name?" I asked.

"Derryl of Is."

I waved my arm. The wall in front of us opened into a new room with a floor-to-ceiling window that offered a soothing view of our pond. I slid the medward bed into it, lightened the walls to a comfortable, soothing blue-gray, and added a screen, some furniture, and a plush rug.

"Things are not as bleak as they look, Derryl," I told her. "You still have a couple of days to recuperate. Rest. We'll talk again."

———

I KNOCKED ON THE DOOR OF THE GAHEAS' QUARTERS. THE DOOR opened slightly, giving me a narrow view of a female Gaheas. Like most of her people, she was tall and willowy, with amber skin and long, dark hair put away into an elaborate arrangement on top of her head. When Gaheas felt at ease, they let their hair down, literally. With the exception of their candidate, not a single one of them let themselves have a L'Oreal moment after that first opening ceremony. They considered themselves to be in enemy territory.

"A calm night to you, innkeeper," the Gaheas said. "How can I be of service?"

"A calm night to you as well. I have a small gift for Nycati."

"Now isn't a good time," the guard said.

"On the contrary, now is the perfect time. It is the end of the 4th Phase, and if we wait another half an hour, it will be too late."

I raised my hand and made a small gesture, gently forcing the door to open a bit wider. Behind me Gaston carried a large trunk. I lifted the lid so she could see the shimmering fabric inside.

The woman's eyes widened. She stepped aside, inviting me to enter with a sweep of her hand. I walked in, with Gaston right behind me.

The interior of the Gaheas' common room was perfectly round. While they recognized the need for straight lines in technology, when it came to their living arrangements, they considered corners inauspicious. The floor was smooth and gray, like soapstone. The walls were slightly curved, forming a gentle dome overhead, and made of burled wood and smoky resin. On their native planet, the resin would be polished quartz, seamlessly fitted to the wood swirls, but we had to make the quarters in a hurry, and the tinted resin was a quick and easy substitute.

The entire delegation had gathered in the center of the room, clustered around Nycati. They turned as one at my approach, their stares hostile. Hands went to weapons, which in their case meant they simultaneously touched the ornate tiaras and diadems on their heads. Duke Naeoma Thaste, the official head of the delegation, stepped forward, body-blocking Nycati from my view.

"What is the meaning of this intrusion?"

I waved my arm. The dome above us opened like a flower bud blooming. The view of the night sky spread above us, the moon bright like a silver coin. A small red spark ignited in the wall to the left, projecting a translucent red circle with a complex border upward, centering it on the light of a very distant star. An equally complex array of light painted the floor with twenty-one spaces arranged in three concentric circles. One in the center, three in the ring around it, and the rest along the outer rim.

The Gaheas stared at me, unsure. I raised my hand, indicating Gaston's trunk. The female guard who'd greeted me at the door gently lifted the fabric out of the chest. It unfurled into a shimmering metallic sash, and the light of the array reflected on it and fractured into a rainbow of colors.

Everyone went still. It was a royal stole.

The moon of Gahea dominated its night sky. Several times larger than Earth's satellite, Gahea's moon rotated very slowly on its axis, and as it turned, it changed colors, flowing from one phase to another. The phases dictated every aspect of the Gaheas' calendar. Their passage of time, their holy days and rituals, even the selection of the most auspicious day for marriage, birth, battle, and the signing of contracts — everything depended on the moon.

Today marked the end of the 4th Phase, the conclusion of the Gaheas' winter. It was a holy day. Failing to carry out the correct rituals meant bringing ill fortune for the next six Gahean months, until the 10th Phase, the middle of summer, the date of equal spiritual potency when the effect of neglecting the 4th Phase rites could be negated.

The phase rituals were complex. It was vitally important that proper formalities were observed, especially the correct attire. However, the Gaheas hadn't brought a royal garment for Nycati. It would have been an obvious tell of his identity, which they were desperately trying to hide. Now the lot of them didn't know if they should kill me or thank me.

Nycati murmured something, too quiet for me to hear.

Naeoma Thaste stepped aside. Nycati strode forward, stopped before us, and raised his arms. Carefully, with great reverence, the guard carried the stole to him and knelt, offering it in her outstretched hands. The duke approached, picked up the stole, and draped it over Nycati's shoulders.

"How did you know?" the hidden prince asked.

"I am an innkeeper. It is my sacred duty to see to the security and comfort of everyone within the inn."

I put a bit of emphasis on that "everyone."

"Understood," Nycati said.

I bowed my head, and Gaston and I retreated, leaving the chest on the floor. The doors shut behind us, and we walked down the long hallway back to the throne room.

"What the hell was that all about?" Gaston said. "That was a very near thing. One wrong word, one wrong gesture, and we would have had to make a very undignified exit."

"Nycati is secret royalty."

"The best kind. I take it, they're hiding his pedigree?"

"Yes. Except their society is hung up on etiquette, and the duke slipped up a couple of times and treated their candidate with too much deference. The gap in rank was obvious."

"And you wanted them to know that you know. Any particular reason?"

"Nycati has a date with Kosandion tomorrow, after the 2nd Trial. If he tries anything, I won't just restrain him, I will expose him, and I wanted them to understand that."

"And you brought me along to demonstrate that not only you know but other people are aware of his lineage as well. Killing you would be pointless and killing me would be difficult."

"Yes."

274

Gaston let out a rumbling chuckle. "Have you ever considered a career in skullduggery, Dina?"

"Everyone is offering me a job lately."

"You're doing so well. That's how it works. Do you find any of the offers tempting?"

"None at all. I don't need a new job, I just want people to stop making the one I have more difficult."

Gaston laughed.

I waved goodbye to him and headed straight for my bedroom. Tomorrow would be another busy day and I needed all the rest I could get.

[22]

Ah, it is that time again. The wonderful FrInnDay, when we come together to learn of the latest happenings in Gertrude Hunt and pass judgement on the silly beings within. Welcome, honored guests! During our last happy meeting, we learned more about Derryl of Is, the lone female werewolf with a 2×4 chip on her shoulder, and watched Dina remind Nycati that innkeepers are a power unlike any other. Today we bring you the Trial of Talent.

Warning: the following chapter contains a brief description of animal cruelty. The Universe is vast and not everyone abides by the same standards.

T he light of early morning illuminated Kosandion's private balcony and the bags under his eyes. He took a sip from his coffee mug and looked at it.

"Why is this so sweet?"

"Because you didn't sleep last night," Sean said. "You need the sugar."

Kosandion frowned at him and took a big gulp.

Orata fidgeted in her seat. "Perhaps, a booster..."

"No," Kosandion said firmly.

Orata looked at Resven. The Chancellor spread his arms.

"At least some drops for the eyes," Orata said. "Just for the optics."

"What's wrong with my eyes?"

"They're bloodshot," I told him.

Kosandion hadn't slept for almost forty-eight hours. The night before last he dealt with Vercia's betrayal. We'd gone to sleep close to 2:00 am, and he was still awake. When I had gotten up 2 hours later to deal with the latest Dushegub caper, he hadn't gone to bed. Last night was the same. Orata had let it slip that the Conservative Alliance was proving to be a thornier issue than anticipated. Other political factions had entered the fray, and things became "a little complicated."

Kosandion had paced a few times during the night because it helped him think, and Gertrude Hunt woke both Sean and me up every time he moved too much, which was why the two of us decided to join him for the morning briefing.

I read somewhere that lack of sleep was cumulative. After this event was over, and we got Wilmos back, I would sleep for a week. Unlike Kosandion, I couldn't stay up for 48 hours straight without some chemical help.

Kosandion held out his hand. Orata jumped up, put a small vial into his fingers, and went back to her seat. The Sovereign put two drops into each eye and firmly set the vial on the table.

Resven approached, picked up a dish with one of Orro's beautiful muffins on it, and held it out to Kosandion as if he were a two year old.

"Please take a bite, *Letero*."

Kosandion just looked at him.

"Sleep or food," Miralitt said. "You must have at least one."

Kosandion picked up a muffin and took a small bite. "Let's move on to the ratings."

Orata looked like she'd bitten into a lemon. "Surkar is leading across all categories with an average of 17 points."

Kosandion chewed his muffin. "Of course he is."

"It's that damn show." Orata waved her arms.

"What show?" Sean asked.

She glanced at Kosandion. He nodded.

Orata tapped her tablet and tilted the holographic screen toward us. On it a panoramic shot of a battlefield rushed toward the viewer, following a bird of prey that swooped down over the field. Bodies in armor littered the bloody ground. Here and there, individual duels still raged, the fighters tripping over corpses. The view zeroed in on a large warrior in antique Dominion armor. He climbed over a hill of the dead to a rock jutting from the bodies. Atop the rock, another fighter splattered with blood roared, brandishing a spear.

The challenger made it to the rock and ripped off his damaged breastplate, revealing a shockingly muscular chest. Miralitt raised her eyebrows.

The two men clashed. Weapons rang, striking each other. They danced across the crag, cutting and slicing. Finally, the challenger leaped and buried his sword in his opponent's throat. The wounded man clasped his neck, spat out a torrent of blood, stumbled about, waved his arms, seemingly forgetting that there was a blade in his throat...

The hero leaped and kicked the pommel of the sword, driving it into the man and knocking him off the cliff. Miraculously, all the soldiers on the field stopped to watch the body fall. It landed with a meaty thud.

The hero pulled off his helmet. He looked remarkably like the Dominion version of Surkar. If not for the obvious differences in size and pigmentation, they could have been cousins.

"I'd watch that," Sean said.

Kosandion rolled his eyes.

The hero grabbed a flag, pulling it from under the corpses,

triumphantly planted it by his feet, and bellowed. *"Warriors! Comrades! Look! The tyrant is dead! Let his death serve as a warning to those who dare claim our freedom!"*

"'Claim our freedom,'" Orata muttered. "It's not even good writing."

"They're not watching it for the writing," Miralitt said.

"No, but they are watching. In huge numbers." Resven glanced at Orata.

She covered her face with her hands.

"I swear on this field watered with the blood of our battle-kin that my blade shall not rest until every threat to our liberty is vanquished. As long as my heart beats in my chest, I will stand for justice and peace."

The camera panned to the few warriors standing among the carnage below.

"That's a lot of peace," Sean said.

"Yes, they had a large budget," Orata said. "They even got Samrion for the lead. He's an intellectual, nuanced actor. He usually does mystery and intrigue shows. We talked before the production. He was very apologetic. Apparently, they paid him an obscene amount of money. I don't know what they were feeding him to get him to that size..."

"Who are 'they' and when did they have time to put all of this together?" I asked.

"They are the Enforee family," Resven said. "They own one of the largest video channels, and they opposed the *Letero's* succession. They lost and now they're bitter."

"The identities of the spousal candidates were made public seven months ago," Orata said. "They put it together pretty quick. A tight deadline but not impossible."

The hero gripped the flagpole and waved it around, flexing.

The message was clear: the Dominion needed a warrior to safeguard its freedoms and lead it to glory, and Kosandion wasn't it.

"How do they benefit from Surkar winning?" Sean asked.

"They don't," Kosandion said. "Selecting Surkar as a spouse would involve the Dominion in the Horde's internal squabbles. He brings very few benefits and lots of problems, problems which will keep me occupied and distracted. It's one of the many stones they hurl into my path hoping I will trip on one of them."

I wasn't a Dominion politician, but even I understood that the only way to neutralize Surkar was to shatter his image as an invincible warrior, and I had no idea how Kosandion could do that. He couldn't exactly order Miralitt to march into the arena and kick his ass.

"What are the rest of the rankings?" Kosandion asked.

"Amphie, Lady Wexyn, Bestata, Prysen Ol, Oond, Nycati, Cyanide, Unessa," Orata reported. "The show gave Bestata a boost as well, and Oond, who was up right after the debate trial, is now down. Also, they really didn't like Cyanide's date. They thought it was boring, and she was entitled."

She was a cat.

Resven nudged the second muffin toward Kosandion. Kosandion broke it in half and bit into it.

"Is everything ready for the 2ⁿᵈ Trial?" Orata asked. "Do you need anything?"

"No, we have it covered," Sean said.

We did have the arena covered. The rest was up to the candidates, and there was no telling what they would come up with.

"WELCOME TO THE 2ⁿᵈ TRIAL!" GASTON ANNOUNCED. "ARE YOU ready?"

The cacophony of whistles, creaks, stomps, applause, and howls confirmed that the delegates were indeed ready.

We had reshuffled the seating arrangements, eliminating the Donkamin, Murder Beak, and Team Frown sections, so everyone sat closer to the stage. Kosandion was back in his section, and we hid his throne mountain under the arena's floor. The door to the portal was shut, and the bridge that connected it to the stage was retracted. The mist was gone too. It was expensive and I was saving it for the elimination ceremonies.

Gaston, who was whipping the crowd into an excited frenzy from the center of the stage, was practically glowing in his blindingly white outfit. When I asked him how many clothes he'd brought with him, he told me he grew up in a swamp wearing rags and he was overcompensating. I didn't know what to make of that, so I made an excuse and walked away.

Kosandion watched the pre-show with a dispassionate expression. He was on his third cup of coffee, and I told Orro to cut him off before he became jittery.

I did a quick sweep of the arena. Everyone was where they were supposed to be. The Holy Ecclesiarch and his retinue were in place, the observers' section was in order, and all of the delegations were present. Tony was above the arena. Today he would be handling the special effects.

Sean parked himself near the Holy Ecclesiarch. Apparently, the elderly man specifically requested his presence. His Holiness was still pretending to be decrepit. His performance was suffering at the moment since he and the First Scholar were engaged in a spirited debate, and he was waving his arms with the vigor of a man half his age.

Sean looked at me. To everyone else his expression would be perfectly neutral, but I knew better. This was his long-suffering look.

One of Cookie's helpers, a petite merchant with sable fur and bright green eyes, jumped up and down in the observers' section, waving her little paws at me. She could have just requested a call, but she didn't, which meant she wanted to tell me something personally. I extended a narrow bridge to the observers' section, barely a foot wide. A human would've walked very carefully across it. The little lees scampered over it like it was solid ground.

She reached me, dropped a piece of paper into my hand, and dashed back.

I retracted the bridge and checked the note. On it, in Caldenia's graceful hand, was written, *"It is vital that W goes last and the oaf right before her. Please indulge me."*

I glanced at Caldenia. Her Grace nodded at me.

Now she was passing me notes as if we were in class and had to hide from the teacher.

I surveyed the sections. Surkar sat in the first row, in the center of the otrokars' section, wearing a long cloak. Not a typical garment for the otrokars unless it was winter. Lady Wexyn was in her expected place, veiled head to toe in a glittering golden fabric.

What was Caldenia up to? Whatever it was, the order of contestants didn't really matter to me. We would take a break between candidates 5 and 6, and Bestata had to be candidate 6, because Tony had told me her talent required some setup. There was no harm in letting Surkar go next-to-last and Lady Wexyn after him. If anything weird happened, Sean and I would handle it.

I tapped my earpiece. *"Time to start things up."*

"Please welcome our first candidate!" Gaston boomed and exited the stage by dramatically sinking into it.

I bounced the white light and stopped it under Team Smiles. A ramp unfurled from the edge of the section to the stage. Amphie rose. She wore a silver dress accented with pale gold flowers that flowed over her body like a glittering stream. A narrow ribbon of hunter green wove through her hair, a nod to Kosandion's outfit during his date with Cyanide.

Amphie descended the ramp, crossed the stage, and came to stand in the center. A slow melody filled the arena, quiet at first, but growing louder. Amphie opened her mouth and sang, her voice surging through the music. Behind her a glowing vine with two shoots, one emerald and the other silver, emerged from the edge of the stage. They wove around each other, spiraling, growing leaves, sprouting buds, branching and twisting, as if nourished by her song.

Super subtle. She couldn't have made it more obvious unless she finished it off with a neon sign that said *Kosandion and Amphie sitting in a tree, k-i-s-s-i-n-g*. Gaston and Tony had rehearsed with the candidates yesterday, and now I understood why Tony called her a simple soul afterward.

The song reached a crescendo. Amphie delivered the final ringing note and fell silent. The vine behind her bloomed with golden flowers.

"Lovely," Kosandion said.

It sounded like a genuine compliment. Maybe with all the conflicts and crises he had to resolve, raising a child with Amphie was beginning to look appealing. She clearly adored him, they were both from the Dominion, and it promised to be uncomplicated.

The arena offered applause, and Gaston reappeared to cordially escort Amphie back to her seat.

I bounced the light again. Prysen Ol was next. He came down dressed in another blue robe, looking humble and handsome.

He cleared his throat and announced. "I've composed a poem to celebrate this once-in-a-lifetime occasion. I humbly offer it to you."

He took a deep breath and began. "The darkness is vast. The universe is cold..."

The poem lasted five minutes. It was beautiful, and it spoke of every star being a sun to someone. At the end of it the Holy Ecclesiarch teared up, and the First Scholar rested his wing on his chest over his heart and had to take a moment.

Oond was next. He performed a dance, and by the end of it I needed a moment from the sensory overload.

Cyanide sang the song of her people, which was long and very yowling. The Higgra delegation were overcome and joined in toward the end.

"I can't take it," Sean whispered into my earpiece. *"It's like a room full of cats being slowly strangled."*

"Be nice."

"She's an expert weaver. Why didn't she make something?"

"Because she doesn't give away her secrets to the enemy."

My poor werewolf. I could practically feel his eyes twitching.

By the time Cyanide finished, most of the audience had reached a breaking point. Bouncing the light again was a relief. I settled on Unessa. We needed something to wake us up, and she was unlikely to sing. Somehow, I just didn't feel that Dushegubs put the same value on fine arts as we did.

Unessa practically ran down the ramp with a bounce in each step. Hmmm.

A portion of the stage, twenty feet across, dropped down in a perfect circle and came back up, carrying a big cage. Inside it, green lizards squirmed and hissed, each about the size of a large house cat.

Unessa strode to the cage, pulled a small door near the top open, and snatched a lizard out. The screens around the arena zoomed in on the reptile. A bright red crest snapped erect along its spine. It tried to claw at Unessa, but she held it tight by its throat with one hand and pulled its mouth open with the other, revealing long, sharp teeth.

"Venomous," Unessa announced. "Sharp teeth. Very fast."

She dropped the lizard back into the cage. A giant screen descended from the ceiling with a digital timer, the 00:00 in bright red.

What was she...

A bell rang through the arena. The numbers on the timer flashed. The cage collapsed, and fifty lizards dashed in all directions. Unessa plucked the nearest one off the floor, quick like a striking snake, and in one smooth motion twisted its head off.

Oh, dear Universe.

She dropped the dead body and snatched the next lizard. It

screamed in terror, like a frightened puppy, and she snapped its neck, dropped it, and grabbed another one.

Oond's people flailed in alarm, their fins snapping to communicate a predator warning. The otrokars went silent. They were careful hunters, concerned with preservation and management of the animals whose lives they took, and they never murdered for sport. This...this atrocity went against every hunting tradition of the Horde. It was just a pointless slaughter, and the lizards were screaming, dashing, and climbing over each other to get away from her. They didn't sound like reptiles. They sounded like small mammals gripped by sheer panic.

Another lizard. Another.

"Stop her!" Kosandion growled.

I dropped the stage around Unessa, leaving her standing on a stone pillar. The surviving lizards scattered through the arena. The Dushegubs creaked and hissed in outrage.

"I warned you," Gaston said into my ear.

He had. I made my voice do that loud, unsettling whisper thing, sending it to every ear in the arena. *"**The Sovereign thanks candidate Unessa Sybate for her demonstration.**"*

A large Dushegub charged to the wall of their section and fell through the floor as Sean sent it back into the Pit. The rest of the trees creaked and shook their branches but stayed in their spots.

Unessa counted the lizard bodies with her finger, pointing at each, and looked up at the timer. "Twelve in seven seconds!" And then she smiled.

"It's time for a short break!" Gaston announced and escorted her back to her seat.

Tables with refreshments sprouted in each section.

Kosandion looked angry. I had never seen that before, not when he dealt with Odikas, not even when he found out about Vercia's betrayal. Unessa's display of animal cruelty caught him by surprise. The anger radiated from him like heat from asphalt in the summer.

I should have asked Gaston to be more specific when he mentioned it. But even if he had, nothing Unessa had done was forbidden under the terms Orata had provided to us. The point of the Talent Trial was to reveal the abilities of the candidates. It was meant to be a surprise and a display of skill. We all knew what Unessa's special talent was. She had told us during her introduction. She was good at smothering.

I gathered the remaining lizards into an enclosure under the arena. Gertrude Hunt's database identified them as Tumma Fangsinkers. They were, indeed, very venomous. They were also microchipped by their trader. As soon as the trial ended, I would ask Gaston to take them right back to Baha-char to the Tumma trader who'd sold them to the Dushegubs.

The Dushegubs had trained Unessa like a terrier going after rats. Except that she didn't even rank as a pet. We felt affection for our pets. Dushegubs felt nothing for Unessa. A sickening feeling washed over me. I had a pretty good idea about what would happen to her if she didn't become the spouse.

Kosandion had stopped her, offending the Dushegubs and breaking the tradition. There would be political ramifications, because even breathing too fast had consequences in the Dominion when you were a public figure. I didn't think he cared. I checked his face. Nope, he didn't.

Tony was moving things around below. No trace of the stage remained, the floor of the arena once again empty. Stone pillars, each just large enough to support a human foot, emerged from the stone tiles, rising to different heights. The shortest was fifty-five feet tall, the tallest three feet higher, with a few feet of open ground between them.

Tony grouped the pillars into a twisted path that veered left, then right, then left again. Three platforms appeared, flanking the trail where it curved. Each platform supported a long pole protruding above the trail with three bags filled with sand attached to the top of the poles on long ropes. The bags rested on the platforms.

Obviously, an obstacle course. High-risk, entertaining, and, best of all, no small animals were likely to be harmed. Perfect.

"Ready?" Gaston asked me.

I hid the tables with refreshments. *"I can't wait."*

"And we're back! Please give a warm welcome to our next candidate, Lady Bestata of House Meer."

Bestata approached the first pillar, jumped, catching it with her hands, and climbed to the top, standing on one foot.

"For this demonstration," Gaston announced, **"we will need volunteers."**

The entire otrokar section stood up.

"We will only need three. Please pick among yourselves."

A brief scuffle ensued while I made the individual bridges from the otrokar section to the platforms. Three otrokars emerged and took their places on the platforms.

"As Lady Bestata makes her way to the other end of this treacherous path, please do your best to knock her off the pillars and down to the floor of the arena using the sandbags available to you."

"A savok from my stable to the first person to bring her down!" Surkar roared.

There were few things the otrokars prized more than savok mounts.

"Only using the sandbags!" Gaston added. **"She must touch the ground for your throw to count. Are you ready, Lady Bestata?"**

She tied a length of black cloth over her eyes. "Ready."

The crowd murmured in appreciation, anticipating a good show. Kosandion leaned forward, his face showing only interest. No traces of outrage remained. It was still there, he was just hiding it.

A bell tolled. Bestata unsheathed two long, slender swords and leaped onto the next pillar, running across them like they were solid ground. The crowd cheered.

She dashed toward the first bend in the pillar path. The otrokar on the platform next to it grabbed the first bag and swung it at Bestata. She shied back, poised on the toes of her left foot, leaning dangerously back on the pillar, her swords held out at her sides for balance. The bag whistled in front of her. She sprinted forward, and the bag swung back like a giant pendulum, hurtling through the spot she just left.

The second bag missed her by half a second. The third went too wide, spinning a full foot away from the vampire knight. Another moment, and Bestata was out of range, running toward the next platform.

The next otrokar, a large red-haired female, bet on strategy rather than speed. She spun the first bag, sending it in a circle toward Bestata, grabbed the second bag, aimed it slightly to her right, and let it go. The first bag curved, slicing through the air. Somehow the vampire knight sensed it coming and leaped to a pillar on the side, right into the path of the second bag.

The crowd froze.

The second bag flew toward her, straight at her chest. Bestata swung her left sword. The black blade whined, priming, and the bag plunged to the bottom of the arena, sliced in half, its sand spilling like victory confetti.

The spectators roared.

Bestata sprinted. The otrokar swung the third bag, but it was too late.

In the observers' section, Karat leaned forward, laser-focused on Bestata, clearly reevaluating her threat potential. Dagorkun shook his hands and bellowed in his battle voice, "Throw the damn bag! Don't swing it, idiots, throw it!"

The third otrokar, a lean, powerfully muscled older male, clearly a veteran, must have heard him. I was pretty sure people all the way in Dallas probably would've heard him if I hadn't soundproofed the arena.

The veteran grasped the bag with one hand, leaned back like a javelin-thrower, and let it loose. The bag tore through the air and smashed into Bestata just as her right foot touched the next pillar. The bag exploded into a fountain of sand. For a torturous half second, she teetered on the verge of falling fifty feet to the sand floor below.

If she fell, it would hurt. A drop that large would damage even a vampire in syn-armor.

If she fell, I had to catch her.

Bestata leaped backward, her arms spread like wings, turning her fall into a jump. Her right sword plunged to the ground. She threw her right arm out, above her head as she flew, and just as her body began to fall, she caught another pillar with her hand and clung to it.

The crowd screamed, House Meer in triumph and Surkar's delegation in outrage.

"He hit her, he hit her square in the chest! It's over!" Someone howled from the otrokar section.

"No part of her touched the ground!" House Meer screamed back.

The veteran otrokar on the last platform hefted the second bag, took aim, and threw it. Bestata flexed her arm and leaped straight up, onto the pillar. The bag smashed against the stone, missing her by a hair.

Bestata charged forward, leaping with inhuman grace.

The veteran snarled, grabbed the rope of the last bag, and jerked it down. The top of the pole snapped. He caught it, ripped the rope from it, tore the bag off, and swung the rope like a lasso.

Bestata was almost to the final pillar.

"*Cheater!*" I hissed into my earpiece.

"*Do I stop it?*" Gaston asked.

"*No,*" I growled.

"Let it play out," Sean said.

The otrokar hurled his lasso. Bestata twisted like a dancer on one foot and sliced through the rope with shocking precision. Before the crowd realized what had happened, she jumped to the last pillar and pulled off her blindfold.

House Meer surged to their feet, cheering. Karat stood up, raised her hands over her head, and clapped. Next to her, Dagorkun stared at Surkar, held his right hand out, palm to the floor, and brought it down, as if pushing an invisible lever. A Horde gesture usually reserved for younger people and subordinates who brought shame to those around them. It meant, "It's over, and nothing you can say will fix it."

Surkar clenched his fist and pounded his chair with it.

The veteran screamed, venting his rage. Bestata pointed her sword at him and motioned him forward. He started toward the edge of the platform. *Oh no, you don't.* I pulled a tendril from the inn. It grasped him around his waist and deposited him back into the otrokar section.

It took another five minutes to get the arena back to its previous state and to get everyone to calm down and take their seats. Finally, the stage was back, and I stopped the white light under the Gaheas. Nycati made his way to the stage. He held a string instrument in his hands, somewhere between a lute and a zither.

Oh good. Hopefully this would be elegant and soothing, and everybody would calm down and catch their breath.

"I am but a simple student of music," Nycati said. "Please forgive me for offending you with my inferior talent today. I was prepared to play one of our classics, an ancient melody that many before me have played with much more skill than I could ever hope. But I have been inspired. I bring a new melody to you today, one that has never been heard before. I dedicate it to Lady Bestata."

Bestata startled in her seat.

Kosandion sat straighter.

Nycati paused, holding the instrument in his left hand, his right hovering above the strings, and strummed it. A deafening electric note tore through the arena and broke into a rapid complex chord, so loud it vibrated in my chest.

Oh damn.

The song soared in the arena, furious, fast, struggling, fighting, falling back and returning even harder, beautiful and lethal, like a vampire knight swinging her blade. It built and built, until I couldn't take the pressure anymore, and finally triumphed, spilling into a heartbreaking crescendo, so moving and profound there were no words for it.

The final sounds died, fading. My cheeks were wet from angry tears. The arena was completely silent, as if all of us conspired to mourn the song's end. Bestata looked shellshocked. Her eyes were wide open, her face pale, her hands clutching her sword as if it were a lifeline. Nycati nodded to her.

I would never forget this.

The Gaheas prince turned and went back to his seat.

"**Amazing!**" Gaston boomed. "**Where else in all the galaxy would we be entertained like this? Friends, when we are old, we shall wow our descendants with the legend of this day.**"

I had to do my job. I wiped my face with my sleeve. I was neither calm nor soothed. I felt restless and upset, as if something precious had been torn away from me, and I had to get it back. All the emotions from the song still roiled inside me, and I wanted to punch something to let the excitement out.

"**Please welcome our next candidate,**" Gaston prompted.

I bounced the white light between the otrokars and the Temple of Desire and stopped it on the otrokar section. *Here you go, as requested, Your Grace.*

Surkar stood up and tossed his cloak off his shoulders. The crowd gasped. In the Team Smiles section, Amphie turned plum-red.

Surkar wore a Southern kilt, boots, and nothing else, just as he had been around the fire talking to Caldenia. It wasn't a ceremonial formal kilt adorned with stitching and leather belts. It wasn't even a casual kilt otrokars sometimes wore to informal occasions like dinners with extended family. No, this thing was tattered from years of wear and at least two inches too short. He had shown up to a black-tie event in his inside-the-house sweatpants.

I glanced at Dagorkun. He covered his face with his hands and swore something harsh and angry into them. Karat reached out and patted his shoulder.

Surkar pulled a large, curved knife from the sheath on his kilt. Technically, it was probably a short sword. It was shaped like a knife, but it was bigger than the largest Bowie, more like a machete. He swung it, flipped it from hand to hand, spinning it over his fingers as if it were attached to him by a magnet, and descended to the stage.

I had asked Gaston what Surkar's talent would be, and he said, "Sword dance." Surkar's face didn't read dance. It read murder.

He stopped directly in front of us and pointed to Kosandion with his sword. "You! Face me if you dare, Sovereign."

What?

"Prove to me that you're worth my time," Surkar bellowed. "Or will you hide behind your throne and your servants like a weakling?"

"...His father was the same. Let's just say that their deductive powers leave much to be desired. Some people simply must be confronted with the obvious."

Caldenia. She had convinced him that he needed to demonstrate his physical superiority in the most obvious way possible. And now he was here, in his kilt, challenging Kosandion who wasn't even worth dressing up for.

"This is what happen when Caldenia talks to people," Sean growled into my ear. *"She better know what she's doing, or I'll wall her in her room until she forgets what the sun looks like."*

"Well, Sovereign?" Surkar demanded.

My heart hammered in my chest. *Don't accept, don't accept, don't accept...* If he went down there, there was no way for us to keep him from getting hurt. She knew our inn was on the line. She knew why we were doing this. Why would she put us in jeopardy? Why would she put her nephew into the arena with an otrokar champion? Was I wrong? Did she want to kill Kosandion?

Kosandion stood up. Resven carefully, almost reverently, removed the robe from the Sovereign's shoulders. He wore a black suit underneath. It wasn't armor, it wasn't combat grade, it was just clothes, a form fitting garment that clung to him offering no protection at all.

Kosandion held out his hand. "Knife."

Miralitt stepped forward, produced a knife, and put it into his hand. It was a black fixed blade with an upswept profile, about seven inches long, with a simple handle.

"I need a path, innkeeper," Kosandion said.

I did not want to make him a path. I wanted him to sit his ass down right back on that throne.

"Dina," Kosandion said.

Argh. Fine. I let Gertrude Hunt sprout a narrow ramp curving from our section to the stage below. Kosandion nodded and started down, unhurried and calm.

There was no way around it. Nothing we could do.

He reached the stage. I left the ramp in place. Just in case.

The two men squared off. They were the same height, but the otrokar was at least fifty pounds heavier. His shoulders were broader, his legs were like tree trunks, and when he flicked the short sword, muscles bulged across his huge back.

This would end badly.

Surkar charged, swinging his blade in a simple overhead stroke. It was basic but fueled by his superior strength and guided by years of experience. He was an unstoppable force, sinking his mass and momentum into that swing.

Kosandion caught his wrist, pulled him forward, moving with the strike, and hammered a kick to the side of Surkar's right knee. Cartilage crunched, the sound amplified by the dozen screens zooming in. Surkar's leg folded, and the power he'd put into his strike drove him to his knees. Kosandion twisted Surkar's arm and dislocated the shoulder with a brutal snap.

Oh.

Surkar's mouth gaped in shock. It wasn't supposed to go like this, and his mind was still catching up to reality.

Kosandion drew a thin line across Surkar's neck with his knife, barely nicking the skin, plucked the sword from the otrokar's weakened fingers, and examined it.

"Thank you for this gift, son of Grast and Ulde. I shall keep it as a memento of this meeting."

The Sovereign turned and started toward the ramp.

In the observers' section, Caldenia beamed, her face ferocious and filled with pride.

The arena erupted, electrified. Kosandion ascended the ramp back to his seat, his back to the spectators, and his face was grim and cold.

Surkar finally realized that he had been beaten. He looked about, glassy-eyed. I could see it in his face—it really happened, and everyone saw it. It didn't just shake him. It shattered his world. Everything he held true about himself and his place in this life was proven false in a space of a second.

"*Sean?*" I whispered.

"*I got him.*"

Surkar sank into the floor of the stage. It swallowed him, closing over his head, and I felt Sean moving toward the medward.

"Please give a warm welcome to our final candidate," Gaston announced. He didn't even try to address what just happened. Good call.

Kosandion took his throne. His expression was hard as if

carved from stone. Beating Surkar had given him no joy. It hadn't even vented his anger.

Lady Wexyn stood up. Soft music filled the arena, the melody sad and full of longing. She walked down the ramp from her section to the stage, swaying gently in tune with the melody. Her golden veil slipped off, flaring behind her like the wings of a beautiful butterfly. She let it fall at the edge of the stage. She wore an amber-colored robe embroidered with golden thread and studded with red gemstones. Her hair was an artful cascade decorated with a golden spiderweb, flowers of precious metals, and a tiara gleaming with gems. Bracelets sheathed her arms.

She brushed her right wrist with her fingers, and the bracelets tumbled to the floor onto her veil. She brushed her left, and the rest of the ornaments rained down. She removed the tiara off her head and dropped it onto the golden fabric, discarding it as if it were made of foil. One by one, she pulled the flowers out and let them fall. The delicate gold web came off, and she shook her head, letting the waterfall of her dark hair loose. She touched her embroidered robe, and it slid off her. She stood clad in a simple blue and white gown with a wide skirt and loose sleeves. A gentle breeze stirred, and the nearly weightless fabric moved.

Lady Wexyn stepped out of her golden slippers and spun across the stage barefoot, her hair flying, her body swaying to the music. Her dress floated around her like a cloud. She moved with an unbelievable beauty, ethereal and at once very human. Her dance fought against everything that was bleak and dark. In the world that was anger and discontent, she was a soothing light, indestructible and powerful like love and hope. It was a gift, and it was meant for only one person.

Kosandion sat very still.

There were hundreds of beings in the arena, and yet none of us existed. It was only the two of them. It was their moment, and I held my breath so I would not disturb them.

[23]

It's FrInnDay again, and the Trial of Talent is over. There were smother-ings done in poor taste, beautiful dancing, poetry, and harsh lessons in underestimating your opponent. One must never listen to Caldenia unless one is absolutely sure she is on their side. Was Kosandion impressed with the candidates? Did he appreciate his aunt's schemes? After all, she did murder his father. Who knows the heart of the Sovereign? It is a mystery wrapped in an enigma, beating in a rather muscular chest. Let us see what happens.

As the delegates filed out of the arena, taking the tunnels to their respective quarters, Kosandion leaned toward me and said, "I've heard my aunt takes frequent walks." I confirmed that, indeed, Her Grace enjoyed her daily stroll, to which he said, "I should like to walk as well. It's good to stretch your legs after so much sitting." I nodded, stepped away, reached out through the inn, found Caldenia, who was on the way to her quarters, and quietly shared Kosandion's newfound love of moderate exercise with her.

Now Kosandion pondered the trees by our pond while I waited a few yards away, watching over him, and Caldenia, who had taken an opportunity to change clothes, was moving through the inn toward us.

Sean stepped out of the bushes. He was taking the whole "traverse through walls" thing to a new level. It was honestly easier to just use an established door, but popping out of random places appealed to him for some reason. I held out my hand, and he quietly squeezed it.

"How is Surkar?"

"Healing. I sedated him."

"Should we worry about him retaliating?"

Sean shook his head. "He knows when he is beaten. We talked before he passed out. He is coming to terms with it."

"I don't understand why he opened with such a straightforward attack."

"Because it worked for him many times before. If you give an average person a gun, and someone of Surkar's size charges at them with a sword, most people will forget about the gun and try to get out of the way or throw their hands up to protect themselves. It takes training to overcome that instinctual response. Even if Kosandion had a shield and tried to block, the power differential is too high. Surkar would have broken the shield and Kosandion's arm."

"Kosandion clearly has training."

Sean sighed. "As Surkar found out. I asked him if it ever occurred to him that a person of the Sovereign's status, with genetic modification and unlimited resources, would have access to the best combat trainers available."

"What did he say?"

"He said, 'Why would he need them? He has an army and bodyguards. He doesn't look like a fighter.'"

"The species prejudice tripped him up," I said. "The otrokars are so specialized that you can tell at a glance who is a range fighter and who is a front-line bruiser. Kosandion looks like he'd be a strategist or a tactician at best."

"Yes," Sean agreed. "Surkar judges his opponents by size and what they are wearing. Vampire knights are warriors because they are large and wear armor. Kosandion doesn't look like a warrior, and Surkar discounted him as a physical threat. In his head, he would crush Kosandion like a gnat, and then the Dominion would love him so much for it, they would force the Sovereign to take him as a spouse."

"So Surkar was planning to beat up a man he thought was a civilian and clearly no match for him? And he thought people would love him for it?"

"Basically."

"Doesn't exactly portray him in the best light."

Sean shrugged. "It was dawning on him when I left. If he'd stopped to think about it, that challenge would've never happened, but he hadn't, because Caldenia filled his head with fog and nonsense. She never suggested that he challenge Kosandion. She just led him to that door, showed him the shiny world on the other side, and he jumped through it on his own."

A door opened in the distance. Caldenia was incoming.

"Your favorite person is on the way."

Sean made a low rumbling noise.

I shivered. "So scary."

"Do you want me to babysit them so you can take a break?" he asked.

I shook my head. "Caldenia is more comfortable with me. I have a feeling this will be a difficult meeting."

Caldenia rounded the bend of the path. She wore a pale gown with a trumpet silhouette and a bateau neckline that cut in a horizontal slash just under her neck. The narrow sleeves were translucent, made of fabric that resembled tulle, and a small cape fell in graceful folds from her shoulders to her knees. The metallic fabric shimmered slightly as she walked, neither pink, nor beige, nor lavender, but on the crossroads of all three. It was a conservative dress that communicated power and maturity without reading old.

It was also a style she almost never wore anymore. Her national origins echoed in it. She looked like the head of state she used to be.

The inn chimed, and we simultaneously paused. The Dushegubs had decided to pummel the walls of the Pit. Sean squeezed my hand again and marched down the path. Sean had just about enough of their acting out, and the Dushegubs were about to learn the meaning of regret.

Caldenia and he passed each other on the path, heading in opposite directions. She raised her eyebrows at him and approached me.

"He seems rather annoyed," she said.

"You permanently damaged Surkar."

"I did no such thing."

"You broke his spirit."

"Then it wasn't that strong to begin with. Pain is the best teacher. Whether he learns his lesson is of no interest to me."

"Shall we walk, Your Grace?"

She glanced in Kosandion's direction, took a slightly deeper breath, and slowly started down the path. Her nephew continued to study the trees. Caldenia drew even with Kosandion, and as she passed him, he turned and started walking, keeping her pace. They strolled down the beautiful path without saying a word. I followed a few steps behind.

Birds sang in the branches. A fish splashed in the pond.

Gertrude Hunt let me know that Resven and two members of his staff left the inn via the portal. Resven had been glued to Kosandion since they'd arrived. This was the first time he'd left the inn. Tony was by the portal, probably waiting for the chancellor's return.

"Have you heard of Sees Lathen, Dina?" Kosandion asked.

It was amusing how nobody expected me to do my homework.

"Many thousands of years ago it was a galactic Empire. It survived for generations, ruled by a single family, but eventually it fractured in two. One half gave rise to the Seven Star Dominion and the other to the Six Star Supremacy."

"You are well informed," Kosandion said. "It was a difference of ideology. The Dominion favors a constitutional monarchy with an elected government that shapes its laws and a royal head of state who presides over the executive branch. While the Supremacy favors..."

He let it drift.

"Tyranny," Caldenia said dryly. "A civilized version of an autocratic government where the ruler's power is absolute in theory and constrained by political considerations in practice."

"How does that work with the collective consciousness?" I asked.

"Very well, actually," Caldenia said. "The ugly truth about democracy is that it breeds anxiety. The responsibility for the government is shifted onto the body of the citizenry, who often lack the awareness and knowledge necessary to make informed decisions. They are tasked with electing their officials, they stress over it, they fall into despair when their side loses and act like their lives are over, and then when the government they elected inevitably does something they don't want, they feel betrayed. There is no constancy in leadership, the policies vary wildly from one administration to the next, and one never knows where the nation shall be in ten years' time. It is chaos."

Nice try. "Democracy protects the rights of an individual. Tyranny protects only the select few and not very well."

"Tyranny provides stability and rules. Follow the rules, and you will be safe," she said.

"At the cost of personal freedoms," I said.

"You would be surprised how many beings will gladly trade their freedom for safety."

"Not me," I told her.

This wasn't the first time Caldenia and I had clashed over politics. I had seen a lot of the galaxy, and I'd witnessed the kind of horrors a tyrannical government brought. I would take chaos and freedom over stable shackles any day. Yes, it was messy and inefficient at times, but I could vote, I could run for office, I could criticize our government without fear of persecution, and that was priceless.

Caldenia shrugged. "As paradoxical as it is, authoritarian displays tend to stabilize the public. The citizens find a strong, frightening leader reassuring. The tyrant is a monster, but it is their monster, and they take pride in their power."

"To be fair, the Supremacy practices a limited tyranny. The Parliament of the Supremacy is also an elected body," Kosandion told me. "Sometimes they murder incompetent tyrants."

Caldenia shrugged. "Well, one has to throw the rabble a bone, Dina."

This was the strangest conversation. They were both talking to me without acknowledging the other person existed.

Resven returned and brought two people with him. They weren't the same as the two who left. It must've been a team swap. We had given Resven, Miralitt, and Orata a lot of autonomy when it came to their own people, because they changed their staff depending on the situation, and none of us had time to approve every personnel member they brought over. We'd asked them to keep their personal team at three members or less.

"The ruling families of the Dominion and the Supremacy grew apart over the many centuries," Kosandion said, "Yet each followed a similar method of selecting their rulers. At first, it was calculated marriages and natural birth, then a ruler with multiple partners and many children in hopes that one would prove suitable to govern, and finally genetic modification. A single heir bioengineered to lead the state and its people."

Of which both people in front of me were prime examples.

"A century and a half ago, there was a biological attack on the Dominion's ruling family," Kosandion said.

Caldenia gave him a sharp look.

"The perpetrators were found and eliminated, but the damage had been done. A vicious hereditary disease ravaged the bloodline, threatening to permanently end generations of careful genetic selection. It wiped out three quarters of the family. For thirty years the ruling family struggled to carve it out of their genetic code, but it came back again and again. It killed the children and destroyed hundreds of embryos in the natural and artificial wombs."

I had never heard of that. It was not in any of the Dominion or Supremacy documents.

"The bloodline of the Supremacy carried an immunity to that disease, attained through careful spousal selection and pure chance," Kosandion continued. "The Supremacy benefited from a strong Dominion, which served as a buffer between it and the Hope Crushing Horde. A secret agreement was reached under the pretense of paying homage to the ancient unity of bloodlines. Caldira ka ret Magren, the Empress of the Supremacy, agreed to carry two heirs of Sovereign Rebastion to term. To ensure the full transference of immunity, no artificial womb would be used. The embryos would be implanted, one at a time, and she would carry her children to term within her body."

"She loved her children before they were born and even more after. How could she not? A child who shares heartbeat with their mother..." Caldenia fell silent.

Sadness flickered in Kosandion's eyes. There was more to this somehow.

Kosandion resumed his story.

"The creation of an heir is a complex process. The heir is not conceived but crafted. Whether the gestation takes place within the mother or within an artificial womb, the genetic makeup of the heir is radically different from their siblings. The heir's purpose is to rule."

Made sense.

"Raising the heir, providing them with education and guidance demands full attention from the parents. Even if the heir's parents are in a committed and loving relationship, they delay having more children until the heir is on the cusp of adulthood. And those other children are not heirs, nor will they ever be. If the heir dies, another enhanced embryo carrying the desired set of genes will be created and in time, a new heir will be born."

"It seems like a very lonely childhood," I said.

"By design. The heir's first priority is the nation," Caldenia answered.

Kosandion nodded. "Too much attachment to one's siblings can lead the ruler to make decisions based on emotion rather than logic."

"The age gap also ensures that the other children will not compete for power. Although they will be no match for the heir, some do try despite their shortcomings." Caldenia sounded harsh. "Unfortunately, when you raise a tyrant to exercise their power at will, rules go out the window, even if they're sensible."

"Caldira agreed to bear the heirs only if they could be raised together until the youngest reached ten years of age. The Dominion had no choice but to agree. Two heirs were born, a female and a male two years apart. They were raised together as brother and sister, and their mother doted on them both. They had the best education, they shared the greatest tutors, yet their curriculums differed drastically. The older, female child was raised to be the future Empress, while her younger brother was to become the Sovereign."

"When they were twelve and ten," Caldenia said, "they were torn apart with the expectation that they would never see each other again outside of the rare state function."

Wow.

"Years passed," Kosandion continued. "The female child became the Empress and eventually gave birth to an heir. Her daughter died when she was fifteen, assassinated by a separatist faction. A decade later she tried again. Her son lived into his thirties, insisted on personally leading a fleet into war, and died doing so."

Oh. I didn't know. Caldenia's public file never mentioned family. Her face was devoid of all expression. She looked like a mannequin.

"Her brother became the Sovereign and lost three heirs. When his fourth heir was in adolescence, the Sovereign and his wife had two more children, conceived in the natural way, a boy and a girl. The heir was judged to be old enough to be permitted unlimited access to his siblings."

"What about his aunt?" I asked. "Did he ever see her?"

"Four times," Kosandion said. "First, she visited secretly when he was born. He doesn't remember that visit for obvious reasons, but he was told about it. The second time was when he was three and very sick. She sat by his bed, held his hand, and swore to murder everyone in the room if he didn't survive. The third was when he was twelve. She had come for the Ten Year Summit between the Dominion and the Supremacy, and late at night she met him for five minutes under heavy guard to tell him that she was proud of him and his accomplishments."

Caldenia gazed at the pond, as if she had gone deaf.

"What about the last time?" I asked.

"It was years later. The Dominion faced civil unrest. In theory, everyone agrees that the realm must evolve or die. In practice, people resist change because it threatens their way of life. They have the luxury of not worrying about the future of the nation. They care only about their survival in the here and now. Not everyone supported the Sovereign's reforms, no matter how much they were needed. A plot was hatched to kill him, and he was infected with a biological agent that resurrected the dormant genetic disease. It was never fully eradicated. It had just been suppressed."

Caldenia crossed her arms on her chest and stopped by a bench facing the water. Her nephew stopped next to her. They stood five feet apart, not looking at each other.

This was all so sad and terrible.

"The Sovereign knew he was dying," Kosandion said. "If the true cause of his death was discovered, as it would be, the fitness of his heir would be called into question. The genetic weakness of the previous generation was too well documented. The Dominion, which already faced an external threat from a foreign power and was experiencing a civil crisis, would fracture even further. The heir was still very young, half a year from adulthood. He lacked a power base sufficient to avoid a civil war."

"They would've killed him," Caldenia said, her voice harsh and tightly controlled. "They would've murdered the heir and the other two children and then they would've clawed their way to the throne over their bodies."

"The Sovereign had to die in a way that would hide all signs of the disease. Someone had to kill him and take credit for it. The Sovereign couldn't be murdered by some random nobody because that would make the dynasty look weak. He couldn't be killed by someone from within the Dominion, because that would make his entire faction look incompetent in failing to detect this threat and endanger his son's ascension."

I didn't like where this was going.

Kosandion stared at the pond. "The assassin had to be someone powerful. Someone frightening. Someone with the means and the motive, who could make this murder so loud, so outrageous, that the entire Dominion would unite in sympathy behind the heir. Instead of a weakling who failed to anticipate and resist a threat, the late Sovereign had to become a martyr, his name a battle cry."

The hair on the back of my neck stood up.

"The Sovereign asked his sister for help for the very last time. And she came."

"Of course, I came. He was my baby brother," Caldenia said quietly. "In the end, family is all we have."

"The fourth time my aunt visited me, I watched her poison my father," Kosandion said. "Resven had brought me to witness it. I stood in a hidden passage and watched it so that later on, I could stand before the Dominion and name my aunt as his killer with honesty and sincerity. The Dominion would feel my anguish and my sorrow and know they were true."

"I am so sorry," I told them.

"Keep your pity," Caldenia said. "I knew the consequences."

I had never seen Caldenia so fragile. In this moment, she seemed made of glass, as if a careless touch would shatter her. She'd given up her throne and plunged two nations into conflict to save her brother's children. And knowing her, she hadn't hesitated for a moment.

Tony, Resven, and the two visitors crossed the inn and were coming down the path toward us.

Kosandion smiled, a bitter parting of lips. "It cost my aunt everything. She had been feared before, but now she was reviled and despised. Her decades of careful governance had been forgotten. The Supremacy, shocked by the outpouring of collective grief from the Dominion, turned against her. She fought to hold on to power, but eventually she abandoned that struggle and fled."

Caldenia gave him a long look, and the fragility evaporated. "And yet, I'm alive and doing quite well. The entire galaxy has been trying to separate me from my head for years, yet here I am...what is the saying, dear? Living my best life."

Kosandion finally turned his head and looked at her. "I am glad you are well."

She looked back at him. "No need to get all solemn about it, my dear. Don't forget, I have seen you in swaddling clothes. Not only am I doing well, but you still seem to require my aid."

Kosandion bowed. "Thank you for Surkar."

"It was a small thing. Don't bend your head. You are the Sovereign."

"And you will always be the Empress."

Her Grace snorted. "The empress of what? I left those fools with a strong nation that functioned like a well-oiled machine. In less than a decade, they managed to fracture it into three puny kingdoms, one of which came to you begging to be taken in."

"In fairness, they brought us wonderful mineral wealth," Kosandion said, his eyes hiding a smile.

"I don't mind that you helped yourself—galaxy knows somebody should have saved them from themselves—but I don't understand why you left the other two unattended. You should convince them to join you, my dear, by whatever means are necessary. Frame it as a rescue of the Dominion's dear brothers and sisters. It would help your image and give the military something to do before they get antsy and start dreaming up a coup. Nothing ventured, nothing gained..."

Two kids came down the path and stopped. A girl around fifteen or so and a boy a couple of years younger. Caldenia saw them and fell silent.

"They know," Kosandion said softly.

She didn't answer him.

"Would you like to say hello, aunt?"

She swallowed. "Yes."

Kosandion offered her his arm and led the Empress to meet her niece and nephew. I stayed where I was, giving them the privacy they needed.

Nobody was in danger here.

[24]

When we last left the warm embrace of Gertrude Hunt, Sean departed to put out the latest Dushegub fire and Kosandion and Caldenia had a lovely chat. But the spousal selection marches on, and now Kosandion must date. Mandatory flirting. Ah, the lives of galactic rulers. So eventful. So busy. So tragic.

But life goes on. Let's check in and see what is happening.

I dragged my hand over my face. "Sean is a werewolf. He is new to this whole innkeeper thing. But you are like me. You were born into this business. You know better."

Tony didn't even have the decency to look apologetic. "They are uninjured. No harm is being done to them. They just can't move."

On our back lawn, hidden from view by the house, five Dushegubs stood frozen in weird poses, arranged in a picturesque manner. They must have really pissed Sean off because he got Tony to freeze them in place.

"Harm doesn't have to be physical. It can also be emotional."

"Dushegubs don't have emotions. Besides, I think this looks festive. Just view them as holiday decorations."

"For which holiday?"

"Halloween. It's only 3 months away."

Ugh.

Something was happening by the driveway. Something involving raised voices. I concentrated. Marais, standing just inside the boundary. He wouldn't have stepped on the inn's grounds unless he wanted to alert us.

"This conversation isn't over," I said. "I'll be right back."

"No worries. They're not going anywhere."

I went out of the inn the old-fashioned way, through the front door and down the steps to the driveway. Beast followed me, ever so vigilant.

At the bottom of the driveway Marais stood next to his cruiser. A dark-haired plump woman faced him, her arms crossed over her chest. Her face was in profile, but there was no mistaking that body language.

"You lied to me."

"I didn't." Marais didn't sound convincing.

Uh-oh.

"You said you were going to work. I went by the station, Hector! They told me you were on vacation!"

She sounded really angry.

"I have a side hustle."

Wrong choice of words.

"You have a side something, alright."

"It's a job, Donna."

"You are a workaholic. In the past three years you took one vacation, and I had to twist your arm to do it. Do you expect me to believe that you voluntarily took vacation time to work another job?"

"As you said, a workaholic..."

"You are parked in front of someone's house!" She shook her

head. "Stop lying to me. How could you do this to me? To us, to our family?"

Marais held his hands up. "It's not what you think."

"I don't know what to think anymore. I thought we were a team. I thought we talked to each other. It was us against the world. Now here you are sneaking around. Lying to me, to our kids, to your job. What happened to you?"

Hector's marriage was exploding in slow motion in front of me. Someone had to throw themselves on that grenade, and Hector wasn't going to do it, because deep inside he was still the Officer Marais who promised to keep our secret. He looked desperate.

I started down the driveway.

"I love you very much," Mrs. Marais said. "But I can't deal with cheating or lying. I won't."

"Donna, please…"

"You know what hurts the most? It's not even the cheating itself. It's that you were so unhappy that you looked for comfort with someone else, and I had no idea." Her voice caught. "You didn't trust me enough to let me know."

There was so much hurt in her voice. Ouch.

Marais looked like he wanted to fall through the ground under his feet.

A green Honda passed by, the driver craning his neck to get a better look at what was happening. They were standing right next to Marais' cruiser. People were conditioned to pay attention to police cars. It was a minor miracle that nobody from the subdivision across the street had shown up to watch the show and film all of this with cell phones. I had to get the two of them off the street.

"Enjoy your vacation. I hope it was worth it."

"Mrs. Marais?" I called out. Beast danced by my feet, barking. She sensed two people being agitated and wasn't sure if she was supposed to bite somebody.

The woman turned to me. Oh crap, crap, crap, crap.

"You!" the Costco lady squeaked.

I had the worst luck in the world.

Donna Marais pointed at me and strained. She must've had a lot of things to say all at once and they caused a traffic jam, because nothing came out. She just pointed with her mouth gaping.

Marais blinked, looking back and forth between us. "Do the two of you know each other?"

"It's her!" Donna spat out. "I told you. The monster in Costco! That's her. The woman that disappeared! Is that who you're sleeping with? What the hell is going on?"

"We are not sleeping together. I hired your husband."

Her face told me she did not believe a word I said. "Hired him to do *what*?"

There was no way around this. "Come inside, please."

"I'm not going in your house! I'm going to stay right out here, and someone better explain things to me."

Marais took her by the arm and said, "Trust me."

"Let go of me, you bastard!" she growled.

I really felt for her, but if I tried to reassure her here, not only would she not believe me, but she could decide to leave. She came here ready to challenge Marais and the person she thought he was sleeping with. It was much better to be a little combative. She would follow me if she thought I would give her that confrontation.

"Would you rather go inside and find out exactly what is going on, or would you rather stay outside here and keep making a scene for the whole neighborhood?" I asked.

Like throwing gasoline on the fire. Mrs. Marais drew back and gave me an angry stare. "I don't like you."

"That's fine, but I'm trying to explain things. After I'm done, I'll give you a can of beans you can throw at me."

She glared at me. "Five minutes. That's all I'm giving you."

"Five minutes is plenty."

She marched up the driveway. Marais and I struggled to keep up. We reached the door. I held it open and the two of them went inside.

I had to keep this as professional and impersonal as possible. The more business-like I was, the more it would reassure Donna that there was absolutely nothing between Marais and me. The customary innkeeper tone when meeting new guests was best here: courteous but slightly distant.

Caldenia emerged from the kitchen, still in her beautiful gown. "Here you are. Did you know that smoking meat with Dushegub logs gives the flesh a unique flavor? I just found out. This is very exciting. I couldn't help but notice you have five on the lawn. They must have done something to warrant a rigorous pruning."

Donna stared at Caldenia.

"We are not pruning guests to use as fuel for a BBQ," I said.

"I spoke to Orro, and he's on board."

"No," I said firmly.

"Are you her mother?" Donna demanded.

"Heavens no. I am her guest. Her first guest."

Her Grace smiled, showing Donna all of her beautiful, pointed teeth. Donna took a small step back.

"No pruning. That's final. Please follow me." I started down the hallway to the throne room.

The inn tugged on me, and I opened a door to the Merchant rooms. Cookie popped through it in all of his fluffy cuteness.

"I wish to reserve a dining hall for the fourth week of the next month."

"Which one?"

"The Ocean one. My grandmother has been watching the selection and she wants to visit. She specifically asked for me to escort her." His fur fluffed up. He danced around me, unable to contain himself. The lees revered their elders, and Grandmother

Nuan Re was Clan Nuan's most respected elder. To be able to host her was a massive boon.

I smiled at him. "Congratulations, Nuan Couki. What a great honor!"

"I know." His eyes sparkled. "May I have the dining hall?"

"Of course. Please let Orro know your preferences."

"Splendid!"

He dashed ahead of us. I opened the doors ahead, and he streaked into the throne room heading for the kitchen.

"What the fuck is going on?" Donna whispered to her husband.

"A lot," he said. "It's not usually this busy."

"Is this a movie? Hector, was that a little kid in a costume? Who's the scary old lady?"

We entered the throne room. It took Donna a couple of seconds to realize that the massive room could never have fit into the Victorian she saw from the street. Her eyes opened wide. She grabbed Marais' arm, holding on tight. He patted her fingers gently.

Gertrude Hunt tugged on me. I pulled a thirty-foot screen to the Pit out of the floor. A huge Dushegub waved its branches at me.

"Proposition: return those you took, or we kill you, we break your inn, and we smother your dog creature. Do you want to discuss?"

I flicked my fingers. Wooden branches shot out of the wall, wrapped around the Dushegub, and yanked it into the wall. I pulled it through the inn toward me. The floor split and the murderous tree emerged, wrapped in Gertrude Hunt's coils.

Donna shied back. "That's not CGI. Hector, that is not CGI."

I threw my voice down the hall. "Tony?"

"Yes?" his disembodied voice replied.

"I have one more ornament for the lawn. It's in the throne room."

"I knew you would see things my way. On it."

I turned back to Marais and Donna. "This way, please."

They followed me into the Ocean Dining Hall. Outside, past the outdoor terrace, the orange sea glittered in the sun. As if on cue, a massive, scaled creature raised its dragon head from the amber waters, snapped its jaws, and dove back down.

I pointed to the nearest table. "Please make yourself comfortable."

Donna froze. "I can smell the ocean."

"Let's sit," Marais told her.

She let him lead her to the table.

Droplet emerged from the kitchen. "Welcome, honored guests."

Donna just gaped at her.

"Chef wants to know if this is your captain and if your badge is on the line," Droplet asked Marais.

I had tried to explain the difference between film and reality to Orro, but he stubbornly refused to acknowledge it. It didn't help that Sean kept showing him buddy cop movies and calling them "Angry Captain Documentaries."

"She's my spouse," Marais said.

Droplet's fur stood on end. She ran to the kitchen, calling out, "It's his wife! Bring all the doughnuts!"

"Brace yourself," Marais said and yelled, "She likes strawberry!"

"What is all this?" Donna sounded almost desperate. "Who are you?"

"My name is Dina Demille, and this is Gertrude Hunt," I told her. "We are an inn that caters to a particular kind of traveler. We're hosting a spousal selection for the head of one of the galactic nations, and we hired your husband as extra security. I apologize if this has caused you concern. Secrecy is paramount to us. Officer Marais has the means to handle any problems he encounters, and he is very good at what he does."

"You're arresting aliens," Donna said in a small voice.

"Only sometimes," Marais said.

Donna stared at him.

"Mostly I cite the law, threaten them with a really deadly gun, and then they go away. It's very safe."

Donna blinked and looked at me. "A deadly gun?"

"It vaporizes things. On a subatomic level," he told her. "I'll show you later."

It was probably safe to smile now, so I did. "Gertrude Hunt is honored to count you among our visitors. Please make yourself at home. It's a lot to take in, and it's easy to get overwhelmed, so try to relax. You are safe here. Call my name if you need anything."

A procession of servers carrying platters marched out of the kitchen, led by Orro bearing a mountain of doughnuts on a crystal serving dish.

I got out of the way and went to handle my other problems.

———

AMPHIE'S DATE WITH THE SOVEREIGN WAS THE MOST TIRING experience. She was supposed to have a date after Nycati, but Kosandion requested the switch, and after spending an hour in Amphie's company, I could see why. He wanted to jump the biggest hurdle first. The second elimination ceremony was tomorrow afternoon, followed immediately by the Third Trial, which was why we were packing the remaining dates into today and tomorrow morning like sardines.

Amphie had chosen the gallery for her date, one of the pre-made environments I specifically created for the selection. I had taken a page out of every heist movie's playbook and built a some-what cliché museum room: large, with a high ceiling featuring a beautiful skylight, walls of frosted white glass, and a floor in a mosaic of creams and white. I'd pulled various alien items out of storage, arranged them on pedestals with some strategic lighting, and finished it off with a small vala tree.

The tree was a gift from Lord Soren, Arland's uncle. I loved it to pieces. It was my baby, and I moved it from its special spot in the vampire wing and gave it the royal treatment it deserved: its own focal point directly under the skylight where its blood-red leaves glowed against its black branches. It grew from a patch of moist soil dotted with mossy rocks, with the traditional House Krahr stream winding around through a shallow streambed. The stream continued through the room, creating a natural separation between sections.

It was a serene environment, designed to inspire quiet moments and contemplation. Amphie attacked it like she was in a fight for her life. She steered Kosandion from item to item, offered a quick factoid about its function or origin, asked him a question, and then eagerly hung on every word.

About ten minutes into it, I realized it wasn't about Kosandion. It was a performance for the Dominion's citizens, designed to show off her comprehensive education and understanding of galactic cultures. Periodically, she would make a small joke, just a little wink that said, "Yes, I'm educated but aren't I also clever and charming?"

It felt very A-student to me. As if she were called out by the professor to stand next to him in front of the class, and she was committed to proving to everyone that not only could she converse with him, but she could also impress him.

It was incredibly draining, and I didn't even have to keep up my end of the conversation the way Kosandion did. I kept hoping she would run out of clever, but more kept coming and coming, until finally after an hour, she was forced to exit.

Now I was escorting her to her quarters through a long hallway, with Beast leading the way. Nycati was next. He had also chosen the gallery, and I would pick him up as soon as I dropped her off. Normally either Tony or Sean would've brought the candidate to me while I remained with Kosandion, but Amphie's date was broadcast in its entirety, and they both had to babysit the delegations in the various dining halls.

Hopefully nobody would get poisoned this time.

I had sealed the gallery with Kosandion inside to give him a few minutes to relax. The inn was watching him, but I was still paranoid.

"How do you feel it went?" Amphie asked.

"It's not my place to offer an opinion," I told her.

"You are with him all the time. You've earned his trust. Does he talk about me?"

She was barking up the wrong tree. "Gertrude Hunt prides itself on confidentiality."

Amphie's eyes narrowed. The hint of a different person shone through, a driven, cut-throat woman focused on her goal.

"You sit in on their strategy sessions. There are no cameras here. Nobody would ever know if you chose to share a few drops of information. Help me, and I promise to compensate you. If I become the spouse, I will have unprecedented influence on the Dominion. You and your inn won't regret it."

I stopped before the door to her rooms. "We've arrived."

She gave me a frustrated stare. "You truly don't know what's good for you."

I flicked the door open.

"Will you tell him?" she asked.

"I keep confidence of my guests. All of them."

Amphie marched through the doors, and I shut them behind her. Beast woofed once softly by my feet.

"I agree," I told her, and we headed down the hallway to Nycati's quarters.

I never fully bought Amphie's earnest act. Every selection candidate was extraordinary in some ways, the best each delegation could offer, and the Dominion was a place of nuance and political maneuvering. Amphie was projecting an earnest sincerity that bordered on naivete, which was absurd because nobody would send an innocent into this process. The preparation for selection began as soon as the Dominion realized that Kosandion would be able to keep his throne. Even if she had started as a sweet young flower, years of education and preparation would have shaped her into a clever, ruthless political operative.

Amphie was ambitious. There was no question about it. She didn't want Kosandion, but she definitely wanted the power that came with being the spouse and the mother to the future heir. And she wasn't above holding that future power over my head. Being blacklisted by the Dominion would damage Gertrude Hunt's standing.

I had no idea what Nycati wanted.

We were still nowhere near figuring out the identity of the hidden assassin. At first, I thought Pivor was it, so I breathed a sigh of relief. But then it occurred to me that a hidden assassin would've been less sloppy. Kosandion's information indicated that the assassin was a highly skilled professional. Pivor had barely covered his tracks. I'd asked Kosandion's thoughts, and he agreed with me. Pivor was a curveball out of left field. Someone still wanted to murder Kosandion.

And we hadn't heard anything more from Wilmos' kidnappers. I felt like a skier midway up the slope of a steep mountain, eyeing the buildup of snow at its apex. Eventually it would break and become an avalanche, and I wasn't sure we could dodge it.

I didn't want anything bad to happen to Kosandion, and not because we would lose Gertrude Hunt.

Nycati had chosen a white robe that floated around him like a cloud, a striking color against his amber skin. A silver ornament, shaped like a melting snowflake, rested on his long hair. He gave me a brisk nod, and we proceeded down the hallway without a word.

Gaheas royals lived dangerous lives, and they remembered debts, those of others and their own. I knew his secret, which gave me power over him and made me his least favorite person. He would retaliate to reclaim that power. I just didn't know how or when. He had requested a game of Dominion chess with the Sovereign. Dominion chess was played on a twelve-sided board with 60 different pieces. It was insanely complex, and a single game took forever. Maybe his revenge was to bore me to death.

We stepped into the gallery. Orata's cameras were already floating, recording our arrival.

"Candidate Nycati," Kosandion said.

"Greetings, Sovereign."

I pulled a small table with the chessboard out of the wall.

"Shall we?" Kosandion nodded to the chess board.

"One moment."

What moment? No moment. Sit at the table and play chess.

Nycati gave me a smile. "It occurred to me that staying at the inn is a once-in-a-lifetime chance for new experiences, so I wondered if I could impose on our host and ask for a different setting."

Aha. I nodded. "What did you have in mind?"

"Something unique and extraordinary. I want to see something I would otherwise have no chance of witnessing in my lifetime."

Not just something he hadn't seen but something he would never see in his lifetime. This had to be his stab at revenge. He thought he could stump me. The entire Dominion was watching and so was the Innkeeper Assembly and half of the galaxy.

Kosandion raised his eyebrows.

I had to make this good. The floor under our feet shifted, carrying us up. I raised my hand, and the wall in front of us fractured, spinning to the sides.

"Your wish is granted."

A large room opened in front of us, the tall ceiling supported by square wooden columns, unstained so the rich grain of the wood was clearly visible under the resin. The floor flowed like a river, with currents of malachite and brown onyx twisting as they flowed to the dais at the far end of the room. The walls were the same stunning wood as the columns. Metal screens in shades of silver and white gold showed odd creatures with gemstone eyes. Elegant paintings hung on the walls.

The dais supported a throne. It was a rough, simple seat, carved from a translucent white stone traversed by blood-red veins. They spread through the stone, sparse in some places and dense in others, and the throne glowed in the light streaming through the massive open doorway and large window.

Beyond the doorway, a balcony of polished gray stone wrapped all the way around the room, sheltered by an over-hanging roof held up by massive stone columns. The vast plain that rolled into the distance was so far below, the sea of grass and isolated copses of trees looked like a miniature built by an artisan crafter.

The detail was breathtaking. No two columns were the same,

no two stone reliefs mirrored another. But it wasn't just about the detail. Stepping into this space was like entering an entirely different world, completely foreign and yet so cohesive, so refined that being in it was effortless. It was as if you suddenly found a better version of a room, where everything was in its most natural place, and you too became a part of it. Leaving it filled you with regret.

The two men held still, taking it in.

"What is this?" Kosandion asked finally.

"The Seat of Drífan Liege Adira of Green Mountain."

Shock slapped Nycati's face.

The Drífen were one of the great mysteries of the galaxy. Their entire solar system existed within a dimensional rift, and it was deeply magic. The sun, the planets, the moon, the plants, the animals, the beings inhabiting it, everything existed within this magical biosphere, connected and shaped by it. The Drífen didn't trade with the outside worlds. They didn't exchange emissaries, although some of them traveled through the galaxy for their own secret reasons. The only way to access the worlds of Drífen would be if one of the planets wanted you there, and then it would summon you whether you liked it or not and make you its own.

Sean and I hosted a Drífan Liege during Treaty Stay, an innkeeper holiday, months ago. Her emissary showed us a holographic projection of her throne room, which the inn recorded. I had made her quarters with elements from that image, but the throne room haunted me. Before Adira left, I'd asked her permission to replicate it. I didn't have to, but it felt right at the time. She agreed.

I'd been working on this space for almost half a year, tinkering with it when I had a moment. I'd started over three times, but I finally got it close. It still wasn't perfect, and it would likely never be finished. For one, the topography outside was all wrong. The Green Mountain view was that of mountains sheathed with forests. I wanted the height, so I built it in Wancurat, one of our lesser used doors, on top of a giant fossilized megatree.

"Will this cause any difficulties?" Kosandion asked.

I let a banner unroll from the ceiling directly behind the throne. On it, Adira stood in all her glory, the image of her painted onto the canvas by one of her retainers with shocking accuracy. A spiderweb-thin script shone with crimson across the banner. The letters squirmed on the fabric, twisting into Old Galactic.

"I, Adira, the Liege Lord of Green Mountain, gift this scroll to Dina of Gertrude Hunt. May it hang in a room worthy of it so the might of Green Mountain shall become known across the galaxy."

When in doubt, always get the permission in writing. I pulled the chess board out of the floor, set it on a low table and offered two floor cushions to Kosandion and Nycati.

They played chess for the next hour. Both were expert players. It was a surreal experience, to watch two very different men, both highly intelligent, both driven, sit in this serene space, completely absorbed in their game and yet seamlessly fitting into the room. Perhaps that was the true magic of Drífen. It was a place that collected strays from a dazzling variety of cultures and species and made them feel like they belonged.

When the hour was up, with the game reluctantly abandoned, and Orata's cameras deactivated, Kosandion and Nycati walked onto the balcony. They stood side by side, looking at the plain far below.

"Are you sure?" Kosandion asked.

"Yes."

"There will be no going back."

"I know," the Gaheas prince said.

"Do you really want it?"

Nycati shrugged. "Does it matter? Did you want it?"

"I didn't, but I didn't have a choice. You can walk away from it."

"So can you. You can ask our innkeeper to open a door into some distant place, walk through it, abandon everything, and disappear."

"The Dominion would be thrown into chaos."

Nycati's face was somber. "My people are in chaos now."

"If I didn't know, you would have been my choice," Kosandion said.

"I'm honored," Nycati said.

A gust of wind tugged on his hair. The Gaheas prince brushed it off his face with an impatient jerk of his fingers. "A logical choice, but not the right one."

Kosandion continued watching the scenery.

"You have been kind," Nycati said. "I may never get a chance to repay this kindness, so let me humbly offer this small piece of unwanted advice. We are focuses of larger forces. Duty. Honor. Survival. And yet, there are times when we must claim something for ourselves. Not because of duty, but because we require it to keep on living. Don't miss your chance, *Letero*."

"I'll take it under advisement," Kosandion said.

———

IT WAS ALMOST 9:00 PM, AND I WAS SO TIRED, I COULDN'T SEE straight. We had just finished Bestata's date and were about to start date number I-couldn't-even-remember, Surkar, and there was one more after that. Starting with Amphie, we had launched straight into the date marathon without any breaks, one candidate after another. Nycati was second, then Oond, then Prysen Ol, Unessa, followed by Bestata... Today turned out to be an insane day that lasted forever, and tomorrow wouldn't be much better.

I glanced at Kosandion. He leaned against the wall of the gallery, his eyes closed. How in the world he could keep going was beyond me. After a whole day of standing, my feet cried when I put any weight on them.

The inn chimed in my head.

"Showtime," I told Kosandion.

He pushed from the wall and opened his eyes. Orata's cameras came to life like a swarm of annoying mechanical insects.

The door slid aside, and Sean emerged with Lady Wexyn by his side. She wore a pale blue robe dress, nearly transparent and embroidered with large white blossoms, over an inner white robe and harem pants. A single silver ornament held her hair back from her face, gathering it into coils atop her head. For her, this was downright subdued.

The two of them reached us.

"Where is Surkar?" I asked.

"He refused the date," Sean said.

Refusing the date meant he withdrew from the selection. "Are you serious?"

Sean nodded.

"What about his small ask?"

"It's forfeit," Kosandion said.

I knew Surkar was proud, but that seemed shortsighted.

"My apologies for the sudden change in schedule, Lady Wexyn," Kosandion said. "I hope it wasn't too jarring."

"It wasn't your fault, *Letero*."

"Where would you like to go?" Kosandion asked.

"To the amber sea," Lady Wexyn said.

Easy as pie. I opened the door in the side wall. The four of us walked through it, down a short hallway, and emerged into the Ocean Dining Hall. It was mostly empty. Only one table was occupied. Karat, Dagorkun, Cookie, and Tony sat around it with Marais and Donna. Donna made big eyes at us as we crossed to the terrace.

I sealed the terrace door behind us, ensuring that we wouldn't be disturbed.

"Could we get closer to the water?" Lady Wexyn asked.

We were on top of an island, a solid chunk of rock protruding high above the shallow ocean. There was no beach. The walls of the island, sheer and nearly vertical, weren't suitable for walking on either. I would have to make something.

I tapped my broom. A section of the terrace dipped in front of us, sinking and flowing off the cliff like melting cheese, with a stone staircase forming as it touched the honey-colored waves. A small beach materialized at the end of the staircase, lined with smooth pebbles and sea glass, hugged on one side by the stone of the island and washed by the gentle surf on the other three. A tree rose out of the pebbles, its leaves a bright, lemony yellow. I had stolen it from Lady Wexyn's quarters. Its branches curved over the beach in a graceful bow.

There. Romantic enough.

Lady Wexyn smiled. "We'll need a blanket."

One of the inn's tendrils snapped out of solid rock and hung a blanket on the tree branch. Kosandion offered his arm to Lady Wexyn. She rested her fingers on it, and they strolled down the staircase to the beach. Sean and I waited at the top of the staircase, giving them a little distance.

"Do you wish to tell me about your life in the Temple of Desire?" Kosandion asked.

Lady Wexyn took the blanket off the tree and spread it over the pebbles. "Sit with me, *Letero.*"

"Very well."

They sat side by side.

"Are you tired?" she asked.

A hint of fatigue slipped through Kosandion's mask. "It's been a long day."

"It has. Does this hour belong to me?"

"Yes," he said.

"Then we don't have to talk, *Letero.*" She smiled a serene, easy smile. "We can just sit here and watch the waves."

I had the inn pull a couple of firm outdoor cushions out of storage and quietly slid them over to the couple. Lady Wexyn winked at me, moved her cushion closer, and leaned back against it.

For several seconds Kosandion sat next to her, unmoving, and then some of the rigid tension drained from his spine. He reached for his cushion, adjusted it to his liking, rested his arm on it, and let his gaze drift out over the water.

Sean and I were near the top of the staircase, with Kosandion and Lady Wexyn about thirty yards in front of us and fifty feet below. Going down there would be intruding, but letting the Sovereign out of my sight wasn't an option.

A section of the rock slid out of the sheer wall, forming a small natural terrace to the right of us. A chunk of it curved, flowing into a smooth stone bench. I glanced at Sean.

"He's safe," he told me.

"What makes you think that?"

"Trust me. We can keep an eye on them from here."

Standing on top of this staircase staring down at them felt stupid, and I was so wiped out. Besides, he said the magic words. I did trust him.

I landed on the bench. Sean sat next to me and put his arm around my shoulders. I leaned into him. He was warm. It felt so nice.

"Tired?" he asked.

"Exhausted. You and I can't go on dates anymore."

"Why?"

"Date is a dirty word."

He smiled. "That bad, huh?"

"Yes." I snuggled closer to him. "All of them were bad, but Prysen Ol and Amphie were the worst. He kept going on and on about obscure philosophical and ethical issues. I almost fell asleep standing up. She talked for the entire hour, super intense and tiresome, and then tried to bribe me on the way back to her quarters. At least Oond's dance was pretty."

Although a whole hour of jazz fins was really too much.

Sean's body tensed. "Bribe you with what?"

"Unspecified favors which she would provide when she became the spouse. She wasn't really clear on that part, but she did threaten to blacklist us if I didn't go along."

Sean cracked a smile.

"When you smile like that, you look like you're plotting murder."

"Not always."

"What's the deal with Surkar?"

"He's being strategic. They were in it to win it. He knows he's done, so he's cutting his losses."

"Why? They won't get anything now. They'll leave empty handed."

Sean stroked my shoulder with his fingers. "So will Dagorkun."

"I don't follow."

"Surkar and his people must have had a plan. The spouse-thing fit into it somehow, and whatever that plan is, they really don't want the Khan or the Khanum to know about it. Dagorkun is smart. He doesn't need much to put things together. Disclosing their minor ask might give away their hand, so Surkar would rather keep his mouth shut and go home with nothing."

Huh. I gave Surkar too little credit. It was a smart move. Dagorkun was free to suspect as much as he wanted, but without evidence, he could prove nothing.

"Do you think there will be a civil war within the Horde?"

"It will never get that far," Sean said. "Judging by their history, the Horde will find a new enemy soon, someone dangerous and vicious. And then Surkar and his tribe might find themselves on the front lines. Nobody wants to admit it, but part of the reason the Nexus war lasted so long was because the Horde needed a meat grinder. Their numbers are growing faster than they can manage. Nexus thinned those numbers and hardened the survivors."

"But the Khanum was desperate to end it."

"The Khan and the Khanum are not the only voices the Horde listens to. There are a multitude of tribes, the elders, the shamans, the bureaucrats, the honored generals who had distinguished themselves... Many of them saw Nexus as the necessary evil."

He fell silent. There were a lot of dark memories there.

On the beach, Kosandion lay on his back, rested his head on Lady Wexyn's thigh, and closed his eyes. The ocean lapped at the pebbles with a soft whisper.

"Unessa's date didn't last long," Sean said.

"No. How much did they show you?"

"Nothing. The feed was delayed by about ten minutes, then they announced that she was feeling unwell and wished to return to her rooms. I sensed she was with you and Kosandion for at least fifteen minutes, so what happened?"

I sighed. "She showed up in a see-through dress and nothing else. He tried to get her to talk about her childhood and how she came to the Dushegubs. It was like talking to a tree. She kept smiling, and then she pulled her dress over her head."

Sean laughed. "At least she is direct."

"So is Bestata. Apparently, House Meer is all about a new strategic military alliance. Not as part of the Holy Anocracy. Just them by themselves and their new best friend, the Dominion."

"The Warlord would just love that," Sean said.

House Meer had been excommunicated by the Hierophant of the Holy Anocracy, meaning they were barred from participating in religious events or holding federal positions in the government. They had dishonored themselves by refusing to fight on Nexus, but they were still a part of the Holy Anocracy and subject to their laws and the mandates of the Warlord.

Technically each vampire house was free to make their own alliances; however, the Holy Anocracy as a whole already had a treaty with the Dominion. By trying to form an additional alliance on top of the official one, House Meer would be superseding the authority of the Warlord. They were playing a very dangerous game.

"That's how wars start," Sean said. "All the little secret agreements. If Bestata became the spouse, and House Meer went to war with another house or with one of the other powers, the Dominion would be dragged into it."

"He's too smart to pick her."

"He might not have a choice. Tomorrow is Game Day."

The elimination followed by a nine-hour trial. I sighed. "Yay."

"I can tell you're excited."

"You know what? I am excited. One more day, and then he has to pick one of them. I don't care who it is at this point. That's his problem. I just want to rescue Wilmos."

Sean kissed me. "I think you pushed yourself too hard."

"I mean it. I don't care."

"You care about everyone all the time. You even care about what's going to happen to Unessa."

"They will probably eat her." The Dushegubs were pragmatic. They didn't feel affection, and Unessa was a source of nutrients. Since they didn't need her anymore, they would...recycle.

Sean squeezed me to him. "They won't get the chance."

"Do you know something I don't?"

"Quite frequently, yes."

I rolled my eyes.

He looked terribly smug. "What is it you tell me when you pull some surprise out of thin air? An innkeeper has their secrets."

"I'm too tired for secrets. Ask me anything, I'll tell you."

"Do you love me?"

"That's not a secret. Everyone knows I love you."

"Even when I throw myself at pirate ships?"

"Even then. Although please don't make it a habit."

We sat together and watched the ocean until the date ended and we could finally go to bed.

[25]

The dates are over and Kosandion is refreshed after the gift of Lady Wexyn's time and care. It's the second elimination ceremony at the inn. Oh the pageantry, the sites, the drama... Hark, do I hear a ship sinking?

W e were back to the arena for the elimination ceremony. The previous elimination went well, so I saw no need to change the layout. Everything was the same: the miniature mountain topped with Kosandion's throne jutting from the arena floor at the far end, the enormous banners of the remaining delegations suspended from the invisible ceiling behind it, the raised center stage shaped like a plateau, and the narrow bridge that led from it directly to the portal chamber. The only difference was, instead of parking myself by the bridge, I ended up in the observers' section.

I had woken up with a slight fever and my head felt heavy, as if someone had poured lead into my skull without me knowing. Sean promptly freaked out and dragged me to a med unit, which diagnosed me with the beginning of a common cold, calibrated the right cocktail of antivirals, and injected me with it. Within a couple of hours, my head cleared up, my fever vanished, but Sean insisted on me "taking it easy," which amounted to chasing me off to sit in a comfortable chair and eat snacks while Tony took my spot by the bridge.

I didn't fight Sean on it. As much as I hated to admit it, I was running on fumes. The sheer amount of magic that flowed through me every day as I moved things and beings around without any regard for the laws of physics was enough to tire out any seasoned innkeeper. Combined with lack of sleep and the constant low-level sense of anxiety that hung over me, the strain wore me out. I could either rest today and jump back in tomorrow, or I could heroically insist on working and risk collapsing. Kosandion was perfectly safe with Sean by his side, and Tony was more than capable of handling any problems that popped up on his end.

I leaned back in my ridiculously comfortable chair. Caldenia sat on my left, and Karat on my right. We had gotten through Kosandion and his people making their entrance, and once the Sovereign assumed his throne, Gaston delivered his introduction. He was dressed in rust and white for the occasion with a brilliant red feather in his hat, and the giant screens above each section were giving him all the close ups. Orata must've decided that he was "an asset."

"It's my unfortunate duty to announce that the first delegation leaving us today are the Higgra," Gaston solemnly proclaimed, exuding regret with every fiber of his being.

"He's a born showman," Her Grace said next to me.

"He does enjoy it," I said.

The images of Cyanide rolled on the giant screens, as the Higgra delegation made a circle around the stage with Cyanide in the lead and stopped directly in front of the throne.

"Noble Higgra," Kosandion said. "We are fortunate to have experienced the wonders of your civilization, and your memory will be cherished for years to come. What do you ask of the Dominion?"

"We desire to trade our neural nets with the Dominion and

only the Dominion, unhindered by any other parties," Cyanide answered.

"Granted," the Sovereign said. "The Trade Bureau shall draft the agreement immediately. Please allow me to extend the Dominion's hospitality to you and your people while you await the necessary documents."

"We accept and we are honored," Cyanide said.

"We look forward to centuries of prosperity together."

The Higgra crossed the bridge and disappeared from view. I felt them enter the portal and then their presence was gone from the inn. Their banner disappeared.

Well, that was easy.

Gaston made some regretful remarks and moved on. "**...The second delegation leaving us are...the valiant otrokar.**"

The otrokar delegation entered the stage. They wore their battle leathers and they jogged, keeping a steady, relentless pace that ate up miles, which the Horde warbands used when they had to cover long distances on foot. They had formed up like a warband too, with Surkar in the lead, the heavier fighters on the flanks, shielding the auxiliaries and ranged units in the middle.

I tensed. On the right, in the seat next to Karat, Dagorkun leaned forward like a wolf sighting his prey. Caldenia seemed perfectly indifferent. A small smile curved Karat's lips.

Uh-oh.

I leaned toward her. "What did you do?"

"What makes you think I did anything?"

"The last time you smiled like that, Gaston turned himself inside out reciting French poetry."

Her smile widened slightly. "Lady Dina, you give me too much credit. I assure you, Surkar will not be serenading me with sonnets."

Vampire humor, ha ha. I gave her a side-eye.

The warband halted in front of the raised throne, gathering around Surkar, as if expecting an assault at any moment.

"Surkar, son of Grast and Ulde, champion of your tribe," the Sovereign said, each word landing like the blow of a hammer. "Do you wish to withdraw?"

"I do."

"Do you understand that your withdrawal prohibits the Dominion from granting your minor ask?"

"I do."

"The Dominion regrets this decision, but it is yours to make. We wish you a safe return to your homeworld."

"I wish to ask a favor," Surkar said.

"Speak."

"I would like to remain at the inn to witness the next delegation's departure."

If Dagorkun focused any harder, Surkar would develop laser burns on his face.

"Are you trying to set him on fire with your mind, Under-Khan?" Karat asked, her voice mild. "Is this some secret talent of the otrokar?"

Dagorkun ignored her.

"I have no objections, but it is not up to me." Kosandion turned to Sean.

"You may stay," Sean said in his scary innkeeper voice.

Karat shivered. "I hate when you do that."

"That's the point," I told her.

The majority of the otrokar jogged down the bridge to the portal chamber. Only Surkar and the shaman remained on the platform.

What were they up to?

"A surprising turn of events!" Gaston boomed.

The remaining delegates made various noises, ranging from faint outrage to approval, confirming that yes, the turn of events was surprising and they were conflicted about it.

"That brings us to the final candidate departure of the day."

The center of the stage sank and came back up, carrying the

Dushegubs and Unessa. Tony had returned the lawn ornaments to the Pit last night. He'd also mentioned that the Dushegubs had had difficulty accepting their elimination. He tried to explain it to them three times, and they just hissed back.

"I find it hilarious that he didn't even try to pronounce their proper name," Caldenia said. "You have to admire a man who knows his limits."

Kosandion stared down at the trees, his face glacial. "The Dominion thanks you for your participation in the spousal selection. We are saddened by your departure. What do you ask of the Dominion?"

The Dushegubs didn't respond. Seconds ticked by.

Gaston stepped forward. **"You lost. State your ask and leave."**

Sometimes simplicity was the best policy.

The Dushegubs flailed their branches. The largest tree stretched its limbs toward Gaston like a nightmarish, menacing octopus, then pivoted toward the throne.

"Statement: Our candidate is the best. Proposition: chose our candidate and send others away, or we destroy the Dominion. Do you wish to discuss?"

As controlled as Kosandion was in his Sovereign persona, he failed to hide the flicker of irritation that crossed his face.

"The Dominion fears no enemy. Our military, technology, and resources are superior to those of your civilization. Attacking the Dominion means the extinction of your species. Leave peacefully, and I will grant your minor ask. Declare war, and you will die now, and your planet will die tomorrow. Make your choice."

The hair on the back of my neck stood up. Kosandion meant every word, and it mattered very little to him which way they chose.

The Dushegubs braided their branches, creaking and hissing. Unessa stood alone, a hint of uncertainty on her lovely face.

"Proposition," the largest Dushegub announced. "We leave, and Dominion builds a gate to Ugobuh. Do you wish to discuss?"

A green planet appeared on the screens with a description flashing by it. The Dushegubs wanted to colonize the other habitable planet in their system. Their spaceships were clunky, so an interplanetary gate would be the best way to do it, but what would the Dominion get out of it? Kosandion didn't do things without a reason. He had permitted them to progress this far, so there had to be something he wanted out of this interaction besides their entertainment value.

"The Dominion will build a gate to Ugobuh if your civilization agrees to mine and supply the Dominion with all pulsar requarzite found there. Do you wish to discuss?"

Pulsar requarzite was an essential component of most energy weapons. Now it made sense. According to the description, Ugobuh was hot, swampy, dangerous, and generally inhospitable to most humanoid life. Mining on it would have been an expensive nightmare.

For the first quarter of their lives, Dushegubs remained stationary, their roots burrowing deep into the soil. They were organic miners, pulling the minerals out with their roots. They also took everything literally. If they said yes to this, they would dig in that planet until every last ounce of requartzite was extracted and safely stowed away in Dominion warehouses, because Kosandion didn't want some requartzite. He wanted all of it. No sane creature would ever attempt to steal any of it with the carnivorous trees prowling the planet.

Not only would he get his mineral, but the Dominion would control the gate. They would be able to shut it down at will, severing all travel between the two planets. They would hold it over the Dushegubs to keep them in line.

There were times I was very grateful for Earth's special status.

"We agree," the Dushegub leader announced.

And they had gone for it.

The Dushegubs turned to leave.

"Wait!" Surkar's voice rang out.

"What is he doing?" Dagorkun growled under his breath.

"What happens to her?" Surkar pointed toward Unessa.

"She has failed. We will consume her to recoup our resources," the leading Dushegub said.

Unessa went white. The arena snarled in outrage.

"Statement: she is ours!" the Dushegub hissed.

"I wish to purchase the female." Surkar held out a sack.

"Inquiry: what do you offer?"

Surkar tossed the sack to the Dushegub leader. The tree snapped it out of the air, ripping it in half. Golden spheres, fuzzy like dandelions, tumbled out. Baderi fungus, filled with rare nutrients. The Dushegub equivalent of the rarest caviar, a delicacy. He just dropped enough of it to ensure the survival of an entire acre of young Dushegub saplings. To the Dushegubs, it was nearly priceless.

"Statement: she is yours."

The Dushegubs exploded into action, snatching the fungus and stuffing it into the cracks in their bark. In seconds it was gone, and the trees slithered their way to the portal and out of the inn.

Surkar looked at Unessa. "You are free. You can come with me if you wish. You will be safe. No one will abuse you."

"Do you wish to go with him?" Kosandion asked.

Unessa gave Surkar a long look.

"Are you strong?"

"Yes," Surkar confirmed.

"Are you rich?"

"Yes."

"Do others serve you?"

"Yes."

Unessa looked at the Sovereign. "I wish to go with him."

"The Dominion has no objections. Does the inn?"

"No," Sean said.

The arena erupted in applause. Surkar offered Unessa his

uninjured arm. She held on to him. They made a victory lap around the stage, followed by the shaman.

"Damn it all to all known hells," Dagorkun swore. "He was beaten and humiliated, and now he's a hero again. That lackwit couldn't come up with that move in a million years. Who helped him? Who? When I find out..."

"It was me," Karat said.

Dagorkun froze.

"I told him how to put this together."

He turned his head slowly to look at her. The shock and betrayal on his face was almost comical.

"Why?" Dagorkun squeezed out.

"Why not?" Karat sneered at him. "I do not owe you an explanation, Under-Khan. Our nations are at peace, but we are hardly allies. Consider it a small reminder."

Holy crap.

Dagorkun surged to his feet and marched off. I barely had enough time to open the door for him or he might have just walked through it.

"I thought you and Dagorkun had...something?"

Karat gave me a short laugh. "No. Dagorkun and Gaston had something. I am a vampire knight. I've seen this kind of farce play out many times before. This was a competition between two men who disliked each other and decided I would serve as the winner's prize without consulting me. Me, my wishes, my feelings were quite incidental to the entire affair. The Under-Khan is a smart man. I simply showed him he isn't as smart as he thinks he is."

"None of them really are, dear," Her Grace said.

Below us, Gaston waved his arms. "**Six candidates are gone. Six remain. We have said our farewells to the departed and now we must begin the 3rd Trial.**"

The remaining six candidates entered the stage: Amphie, Bestata, Oond, Nycati, Prysen Ol, and Lady Wexyn. A massive round table emerged from the center of the stage, sixty feet in diameter. Six chairs flanked it at even intervals. A terminal appeared in front of every chair, enclosed by privacy screens. The center of the table ignited, projecting a huge planet into the air.

Gaston grinned. "**WELCOME TO GAME DAY!**"

———

When Her Grace first arrived at the inn, she devoured popular culture, absorbing everything about Earth like a sponge. She watched countless documentaries, learned four languages, read thousands of books with ridiculous speed, and within six months, she could pass for a local provided she hid her teeth. Toward the end of that half year, she showed me a tablet with an advertisement for a computer game on it. It was the latest iteration of *Civilization* being offered at a steep discount, and within a day she was playing it.

Civilization started the player off with a small group of settlers, which it plopped at a random spot on the map. The settlers founded their first village, scrounged for resources, reproduced, began to grow crops, developed new technologies, created their first religion, and from that tiny seed, a mighty civilization grew, guided by the player all the way to the space age. That is, if the other civilizations didn't destroy it first. Warfare was an integral part of the game. One could play against AI or human players, and Caldenia had done both. She had beaten that game on Deity difficulty more times than I could count and moved on to *Stellaris* and other similar games, but *Civilization* remained her first love.

The Dominion had their own *Civilization*, a staggeringly complex and elaborate simulation called *Progress*. But to the Dominion it wasn't just a game, it was a national sport, complete with tournaments, professional teams, and very lucrative contracts. Playing it required an advanced understanding of economics, civics, military strategy, and resource management.

The game was constantly evolving, changing as the Dominion expanded its knowledge base.

For their third trial, the six spousal candidates had to play the Sovereign edition of the game, the most intricate version, and they had to do it on the highest level of difficulty. The game would last 9 hours, at the end of which their civilizations would be scored on a variety of criteria, everything from military might and population numbers to happiness and cultural richness.

The candidates with the three highest scores would move on to the final selection. Those with the lowest scores would be eliminated. Up to this point Kosandion and his team had subtly manipulated the public opinion, but this trial hinged on pure skill.

The candidates took their spots around the table, all except Oond. The Dominion provided him with a humanoid assistant, who followed the oombole's instructions through an earpiece. The game began and six groups of settlers landed in different regions of the planet.

The first hour went about the same for everyone. All six candidates feverishly tried to build up their population, so they could expand and grab bigger chunks of territory. Everyone had some clashes with computer generated rival tribes and roaming bands of barbarians.

By the second hour, the civilizations began to diverge. Bestata, Nycati, and Prysen Ol heavily invested in their military. Amphie concentrated on technological progress, while Oond and Lady Wexyn sank their resources into culture and religion. Lady Wexyn generated scores of scouts and sent them all over the map.

In the third hour, Amphie and Bestata had a minor clash over a valuable source of copper. Prysen Ol shifted his priority to developing a unique cavalry unit, Oond's nation became a theocracy, and Nycati, who had landed on a vast fertile steppe between two mountain ranges, set about conquering all of the budding AI-generated civilizations around him. Lady Wexyn unleashed a swarm of caravans and began trading with everyone.

We were in the eighth hour now. They had about 45 minutes before the game ended and the scores were tallied. I had eaten two sandwiches and drunk two cups of tea and a cream soda. I couldn't remember the last time I had spoiled myself that much.

Karat returned to her seat after another trip to the bathroom. "I don't understand how they can hold it for this long."

"If they leave, the game will continue without them," Caldenia said. "Five minutes away from the game could put everything at risk. Victory demands sacrifices."

"I suppose being a fish does offer some advantages in this situation," Karat said.

"But that advantage is offset by not having hands," I told her. "Oond has to explain what he wants done instead of simply doing it."

"He doesn't seem to be suffering," Karat said.

The holographic representation of the planet above the table was tinted with six different shades, representing the six territories controlled by the players. Oond's orange territory spread over his continent, infringing on Bestata's right side.

"The game is unfair," Dagorkun pointed out. He had returned to his seat after half an hour. Some sort of internal struggle must have taken place and Dagorkun must've resolved it and settled on a course of action, because he seemed relaxed and well at ease, as if the incident with Karat had never taken place.

Caldenia gave him an outraged look. "In what way?" she demanded.

"Amphie is from the Dominion, where this game is a national sport. She has years of practice," Dagorkun said.

"Well, those years were clearly wasted," Caldenia said. "She's made the one mistake she couldn't afford. It is a basic rule of any galactic warfare. Never get into a land war with a vampire. Especially during the Feudal period."

Karat chuckled.

The war between Bestata and Amphie had raged for almost

two hours. The vampire knight had built several fortified castle cities, leaving a small gap by one of her major rivers. It offered a straight shot to her mountain range and the limestone caves within. The caves were a source of saltpeter, potassium nitrate, the primary component of early gunpowder. Amphie failed to find any in her part of the map, so she had amassed a horde of horse archers and invaded.

Bestata beat a retreat, drawing Amphie's army deep into her territory, and then her fortified cities vomited armored knights who plowed into Amphie's horse archers, ripping through them like they were paper. Bestata destroyed her opponent's supply chain and a third of Amphie's army died of starvation.

Now the war had shifted into Amphie's territory, and Bestata had taken three of her cities and was laying siege to another two.

"Honestly," Caldenia sneered. "I had expected a better showing."

"Do you play, Your Grace?" Dagorkun asked.

"I was the Grand Champion of both the Dominion and the Supremacy for thirty years."

"Was that because of your skill or your reputation?" Karat asked.

The two of them were playing with fire.

Her Grace gave them her best predatory smile. "Any time the two of you would like to find out, you know where to find me."

She hadn't played *Progress* since she had arrived at the inn. The reminder of everything she had left behind must've been too painful.

A pulse of gold light rolled through Grand Prelate Oond's territory. His Magnanimousness had completed yet another ziggurat, to the delight of his worshipers.

"The Gaheas is throwing the game," Caldenia noted.

At some point during the match and probably without knowing, Nycati had decided to follow ancient China's approach to fortifications. He had built two massive walls connecting his mountain ranges, and then he sat on his steppe, breeding horses, building palaces, and developing poetry, music, arts, and medicine. He traded with Lady Wexyn, whose caravans by now reached every corner of the planet, and fought off two attempted invasions by Prysen Ol, but he showed no sign of expanding.

"His civilization seems to be doing well," I murmured. "His approval rating is high."

"The isolationist policy never works long term. One must interact with other cultures to progress, otherwise, they will surpass you. As a man of his lineage, he knows this. He had two chances to invade on favorable terms, and he deliberately ignored both."

A man of his lineage, huh? I leaned closer to her. "When did you know?"

Caldenia shrugged. "Immediately. It's blindingly obvious. Their attempt at secrecy was earnest and would've worked, except that I have eyes and a brain."

A warning chime sounded through the arena. Fifteen minutes left.

My earpiece came to life with Sean's voice. *"Kosandion says that no matter what happens next, we should let it play out."*

What did that mean? Nothing good, that's what that meant. *"Remind him that we are responsible for the safety of our guests."*

"I did. He says he takes full responsibility. He has cleared it with the Innkeeper Assembly."

And when, exactly, had he had a chance to do that? *"It doesn't matter what he cleared. This is our inn."*

"It's a matter of the Dominion security and his safety."

"And you're going along with this?"

"If something happens to him, we lose the inn. I will secure him. Whatever happens between the candidates is fair game."

I would have liked to argue, but I had let Kosandion fight Surkar with a knife despite all of my better judgement.

343

Caldenia leaned toward me, her voice discreet. "What's happening?"

"Your nephew is anticipating something, and he doesn't want us to interfere."

"About time," Caldenia said. "I was beginning to worry we'd miss the show."

A loud bell tolled through the arena. The game was over. The five candidates stepped away from the table and retreated to use the various facilities. Oond's humanoid helper stood up, bowed to him, and exited the stage. Oond rolled his high-tech fishbowl to the section of his delegation, where he was greeted by an enthusiastic fin display.

"You're looking a bit pale for a human," Karat said. "Here, eat some cookies. It's about to get exciting."

"No, thank you."

I didn't want cookies. I wanted peace and quiet and the orderly elimination of three additional candidates without any show or excitement.

"The scores have been tallied," Gaston announced, his microphone-amplified voice carrying through the stands. "Candidates, please take your places."

It took them five minutes to get there, and I could barely sit still from all the anxiety. The six candidates lined up. Nycati in a plain white outfit, Bestata in her black armor, Oond in a gorgeous veil of his orange fins, Prysen Ol in his trademark blue robe, Lady Wexyn in a translucent sage green kaftan style dress with a forest of golden accessories sprouting from her hair, and Amphie in a silver gown. They faced Kosandion, who sat upon his throne with all the dignity of a man who ruled an interstellar nation.

Three would go, three would stay. Almost there.

"In sixth place, finishing with the lowest score," Gaston said, **"is...Nycati of Gaheas."**

Nycati's rankings appeared on the screens. His people were happy and well fed, and his population numbers were robust, but his tech score lagged behind other contestants. His military, although numerous, was armed with outdated weapons, and his culture was too homogenous. His nation had stagnated.

When Nycati played chess with Kosandion, he had built up his resources and then he attacked, unleashing a chain of assaults and planting traps all over the chess board. By the time Kosandion repelled one attack, the next one already would be in progress. Caldenia was right. The secret prince deliberately lost the game.

"Another hundred years, and he would be conquered," Dagorkun murmured.

"Or not," Karat said. "As long as one has a strong foundation, the nation won't fall."

"Evolve or die, Lady Karat," Dagorkun said, his face impassive. "But you should persist in your xenophobia. The longer the Anocracy remains a closed nation, the better it is for the Horde."

"Is that so?" Karat flashed her fangs.

Dagorkun leaned back, a wistful look on his face. "One day the Anocracy will wake up, look outside of its own navel, and see the Horde's banners on every side. Mmm, I live for that day."

"No worries, Under-Khan. On that day, you will see me with my sword on your doorstep."

"Children, will you two be silent?" Caldenia snapped.

"You have conducted yourself with dignity and confidence," Kosandion was saying. "We are truly privileged to have been graced with your presence. It is with great regret that the Dominion must bid you farewell."

"The privilege was mine," Nycati said. "I have been warmed by the light of the Dominion, and I will treasure its memory in the depth of my heart."

Caldenia turned and gave me a look. "I rest my case."

Kosandion nodded. "What do you ask of the Dominion?"

Nycati raised his head. "Twenty-seven years ago, King Krolli held the throne of East Gaheas. He was betrayed. His uncle, Toliti, rebelled against him, led his troops into the Crystal Palace, and slaughtered the royal family. He claimed the throne and began a bloody reign of terror and repression."

Typical. In the Gaheas kingdoms, the royal bloodlines played musical chairs with thrones, and whoever was left standing when the music stopped usually died.

"Two people escaped that massacre," Nycati continued. "The first was the king's nephew, the youngest son of his second brother. He was only two years old. The boy was smuggled out by one of the rebels secretly loyal to the king."

And I knew just who that boy was.

"The second was Artonnda, the king's third consort. He had been entrusted with a priceless treasure of the royal line. The Wrath of Fire, a weapon and a crown, genetically linked to Krolli's line. When His Majesty realized that the palace was lost, he tore the Wrath from his head, thrust it at his consort, and pushed Artonnda into an escape shuttle, instructing him to keep the crown safe at any cost. His Majesty remained behind with his family while Artonnda escaped to the Dominion. There he offered the crown to the Sovereign in exchange for safe haven."

The arena was so quiet, you could hear a pin drop.

Nycati's voice rang out. "Today I ask the Dominion to return the Wrath of Fire to me."

Silence stretched for a long, torturous breath.

"Your request is granted," the Sovereign announced.

Resven rose, holding a carved wooden box in his hands.

Sean formed a stairway between the stage and the throne crag. Nycati marched up the stairs, each step a resolute statement. Resven met him halfway.

The screens zoomed in, capturing every minute movement in great detail.

Nycati opened the box and took out a circlet. It was a delicate half-moon of pale metal, two arms of twisted metal branches with fine leaves linked by a thin chain in the back. In the middle, where the branches met over the wearer's forehead, a large jewel glinted with white fire. Something one of Tolkien's High Elves might have seen in a dream.

Gingerly, Nycati raised the circlet in front of him and looked at it.

"Why is he hesitating?" Karat murmured.

"It will kill an imposter," Caldenia said. "The Wrath of Fire will accept him only if he belongs to the bloodline."

Nycati's entire life culminated in this moment. If it were me up there, standing with the crown of the family I never knew in my hands, I would be wondering if the people who had raised me had been lying to me all along. There would be no do-overs.

Nycati took a deep breath and placed the circlet on his head.

The jewel flashed with red, as if a miniature volcano erupted in its depths. Nycati's body jerked back, rigid. His arms flexed, his hands clamped into fists. He raised his head to the sky and screamed, his eyes swirling with gem fire.

A surge of magic shot from him, straight up, like a banner being raised, so intense my teeth rattled in my jaw.

Gertrude Hunt quaked, shuddering. I planted my staff into the floor and pulsed my magic through the inn, comforting, soothing, reassuring.

A pillar of glowing fire engulfed Nycati, humming like a high-voltage wire. He was screaming, his face a twisted mask of pain, but no sound came.

I strained, spinning my power around him, trying to minimize the impact.

The magic blinked and vanished. Nycati stumbled, suddenly released, caught himself, and raised his head.

The gem had turned a rich amber, swirling with deeper shades of golden brown. The exact color of Nycati's eyes.

The white robe slid off the prince's body, revealing pale battle armor underneath.

"The Dominion greets the Isarott," the Sovereign said.

And Kosandion had just officially recognized him as the ruler of East Gaheas. There would be war.

Nycati opened his mouth. Magic rolled from him, a whisper of tightly contained power. "The Isarott greets the Dominion."

He turned and descended the stairs. The Gaheas delegation rose as one and followed him down the ramp from their section, across the bridge, and to the portal. A few more breaths and they were gone.

"We will take a short recess!" Gaston announced.

———

"IN FIFTH PLACE, FINISHING WITH THE SECOND LOWEST SCORE," Gaston said, "is...**Lady Bestata of House Meer.**"

Bestata's scores appeared on the screens. The strength of her military was off the charts compared to Nycati's. Her knights were well trained and disciplined, her bowmen had technologically advanced weapons, and her fortresses were a marvel of military engineering. But all of that came at a cost. Her population was literate and had a good grasp of mathematics, but her arts and humanities were practically non-existent. She'd invested the bare minimum into religion, which somehow made her medicine and life expectancy lag behind. Her economy was stumbling. Her population was disciplined and patriotic, but they were not happy.

I really thought she would've scored higher, given that she was clearly winning the war with Amphie, but the Dominion must've placed a lot of value on quality of life.

Bestata wasn't happy either. Her trademark sneer was back, and she looked like she wanted to cut someone's head off. House Meer formed up behind her, as if they were about to storm Kosandion on his throne.

"Wars are expensive," Dagorkun said.

348

"Especially the way she fights them," Karat said. "This has been most illuminating."

"Would you like a recording of her game?" I asked.

Karat's eyes sparked. "I wouldn't like it. I would love it. You know who else will love it?"

"Lord Soren?"

She grinned and nodded. "My father will be most pleased. Why, he might even crack a smile."

"You should make preparations in case his face breaks."

She chuckled.

Dagorkun leaned around Karat to look at me.

"Of course, Under-Khan, I will send you home with a copy as well."

"Thank you. My mother will find it very useful."

"Honoring one's parents is paramount," Karat said.

"Yes. It is our sacred duty."

They shared a look.

House Meer had managed to achieve the impossible. The Horde and the Holy Anocracy would unite for a chance to kick their asses.

"What would you ask of the Dominion?" Kosandion said.

Bestata unclenched her teeth. "House Meer desires only one thing, one that only the Sovereign can grant us."

"Here it comes," Dagorkun murmured.

"3, 2, 1," Karat whispered.

"A pact of mutual protection between House Meer and the Dominion!" Bestata declared.

Caldenia sighed.

"It is within my power to grant. That is not in question." Kosandion paused. "However, House Meer lacks the authority to enter into such a pact."

Bestata opened her mouth, but Kosandion was still talking.

"House Meer is part of a nation. An agreement between that

nation and the Dominion already exists. You are pledged to the Holy Anocracy. Make a different request."

"So the word of the Dominion means nothing?" Bestata snarled.

Dagorkun sucked air in through his teeth.

"Too far," Karat said in a sing-song voice.

An incoming communication tugged on me. I opened a screen and listened to it. Uh-oh.

An older male vampire stepped forward. "We were promised a boon. You must grant it. Those were the conditions."

Resven stood. "Incorrect. You were promised an ask. The conditions of the contract which you have signed clearly state that the Dominion will consider all reasonable requests. Your request is not reasonable. Such a pact would be immediately void. Furthermore, it would bring the Holy Anocracy and the Dominion into conflict."

"That is irrelevant!" Bestata crossed her arms.

"Petulant child," Caldenia hissed.

"Grant our request!"

Karat rose and bellowed, her voice carrying through the stands. "Enough! You dishonor us all!"

Bestata spun toward her. "If House Krahr has a grievance, let them come down here and seek redress!"

Karat's hand went to her sword.

Sean chuckled in my ear. *"Let them fight."*

Sometimes I wondered if he actually understood this whole innkeeper thing.

The portal activated. Here they are.

"Lady Karat," I said in what she called my scary-innkeeper voice. *"Take your seat."*

She glared at me.

"Another party has a prior claim."

Nine vampires marched across the bridge to the stage, the leader in front and the rest in pairs behind her. Vampire knights grew larger and more grizzled with age, but these knights were on another level, huge, broad-shouldered in their black armor, their swirling red cloaks making them seem even larger.

Karat's expression went slack, and she dropped into her seat. Shock slapped Bestata's face.

The newcomers stopped as one. Their leader, an imposing middle-aged knight with dark gray skin and piercing blue eyes, stared at House Meer and raised her arm, holding a scroll in her fist.

"An order from the Warlord," she thundered.

House Meer took a knee.

The Warlord's herald pressed the side of the scroll with her thumb. It snapped open, unfurling, the parchment dotted with the black glyphs of the Holy Anocracy's script signed in red by the Warlord and marked with his sigil. I tossed the video message I had received five minutes ago onto the screens. The scroll was for House Meer, the proof of an official order. The video message was for everyone.

A massive older vampire in ornate armor stared at House Meer. Menace and authority radiated from him in equal parts. This was just a recording, but there was so much power and dominance in his eyes, I felt an urge to bow my head just so I wouldn't have to hold that gaze.

"House Meer," the Warlord intoned. It sounded like an accusation.

House Meer collectively flinched.

"Hasten to the High Castle, so you may witness the executions of your preceptor and your marshal while I ponder the fate of your house."

The screens went dark.

The vampires didn't blush and typically didn't pale. But Bestata's face turned an odd ashen shade, as if she had instantly become deathly ill.

351

"She's doomed her uncle and her aunt," Karat whispered in awe.

"Surely she bears no responsibility?" Dagorkun said. "Her house sent her here. She was ordered to do this."

"You don't understand." Karat's face turned sad and mournful. "House Meer refused to fight on Nexus. Cowardice is a sin, therefore they were judged by the Hierophant for that transgression. She is merciful, so she excommunicated them and hoped they would heed her warning. Instead, House Meer sent Bestata here with that ridiculous demand. That is treason, and traitors are judged by the Warlord. One does not look to the Warlord for mercy. He is not a forgiving man. He watched them, and as soon as Bestata and her knights entered the inn and had their communications stopped, the Warlord must've seized the marshal and the preceptor of their house. Nobody could warn her. If only she knew what had happened, she could have asked for something else, and her aunt and uncle might have lived. When she uttered those inane words demanding a pact, she swung the sword that will behead them."

The herald retracted the scroll. "Join us in our journey to High Castle."

It didn't sound like a request.

"Can she request sanctuary?" Dagorkun asked.

Karat shook her head. "She won't. The fate of their marshal and preceptor is sealed, but there is still a slim chance that her house might endure. She will go to High Castle to beg for the lives of her people on her knees."

The herald's knights parted, forming two lines.

Bestata turned toward Sean and Kosandion. Her lips were bloodless. "Thank you for your hospitality, innkeeper."

Sean nodded.

Bestata swallowed and strode between the two columns of the herald's knights. Her people followed in a silent, grim line.

"The Warlord thanks Gertrude Hunt for safekeeping House

Meer, so they may be in good health for their judgement," the herald announced. "We bid you farewell."

She turned and followed the rest of the knights across the bridge. I tracked them to the portal until they were gone.

"We will take yet another short break," Gaston said.

*Game Day, Game Day! Clap with us! Oond the oombole is our fish, if he
can't do it, you can only wish! Wooo! ::shakes the pompoms::*

Doesn't make sense, but it rhymes!

F our candidates stood on the stage, awaiting their scores.
Oond floated, seemingly serene unless you were familiar
with the oomboles and caught the slight shivering of his fins and
erect tail. Amphie looked confident, her shoulders held back, her
spine straight. Next to her Prysen Ol simply waited, his face a
handsome blank. Lady Wexyn smiled, looking innocently clueless.
During the break, her forest of golden hair decorations had been
pruned to a single kokoshnik-like golden comb modestly studded
with grape-sized purple jewels.

The arena fell silent. Orata was milking every last drop of
drama out of the elimination, because the crowning of a rebel
Gaheas king and near-complete destruction of a vampire house
simply weren't thrilling enough.

A large central screen, positioned above the exit to the portal,
came on, showing a table with four rows and multiple columns

labeled with *Progress* scoring categories: culture, medicine, science, etc. The final column was marked "Total Score."

"**It is my privilege and honor to now announce the results of the game,**" Gaston proclaimed. "**In third place...Oond of the oomboles!**"

Oond's name popped up in the third row down, as the scores in his columns populated. The oomboles broke into their version of applause, and I had to look away because the visual cacophony of waving fins and colors was worse than staring into a strobe light.

The side screens above the delegate sections displayed a detailed breakdown of his statistics and strategies. His population was happy, his economy was solid, if a little less diverse than it could've been, and the unique Witness military units he'd engineered had no trouble defending his realm. Oond had managed to go through the entire game without invading anyone. Instead of relying on brute force conquest, Oond would sidle up next to the settlement he wanted to annex and send his missionaries in. The missionaries would build schools, hospitals, and temples. They would employ people. He would spend a couple of generations indoctrinating the populace and then they would voluntarily join him.

However, he failed to account for the inherent tribalism of humanoid creatures. His mono-religion created room for bias and discrimination against the less or differently devout. As his science advanced, so did free thinking, because science hinged on questioning everything, and a god-king couldn't afford to be questioned. He had to suppress certain branches of the natural sciences to keep civil unrest down, and that took a big chunk out of his score.

"**In second place...**" Gaston boomed, "**...Prysen Ol of the Kai!**"

Prysen Ol's name appeared in the table on the big screen, in the second row from the top. His statistics and scores replaced Oond's on the side screens, offering a detailed look into his strategy. The Kai didn't do cheering. They stomped instead, driving their six limbs into the floor of their section in rhythmic approval.

Prysen had settled on a military republic with limited representation, citizen rights, and a focus on conquest. His nation quickly became a conquering juggernaut. Prysen didn't get involved in large-scale wars. He found a target he knew he could take and blitzed it, expanding his nation one small bite at a time. For the first half of the game, he was always at war, yet it never disrupted the lives of ordinary citizens. Unlike Bestata, he had invested in arts, sciences, and trade. His capital city was a shining jewel of civilization.

However, he also relied on slave labor, and once he exhausted the supply of the barbarian settlements in his immediate vicinity, that source of free workers dried up. Shifting to a paid work force proved costly and difficult. Inflation combined with labor shortages gave rise to corruption and tax avoidance. Cracks began to appear in the colossus' massive legs, and his two failed attempts to break through Nycati's monstrous fortifications only widened them. Still, his score was 62 points higher than Oond's.

The two women remaining on stage couldn't have looked any different. Amphie stood ramrod-straight, stone-faced, looking like a sword someone thrust into the floor. She kept touching the heavy silver necklace around her neck, stroking it as if it were a talisman. Lady Wexyn was smiling at Kosandion. He watched her, his face impassive. She gave him a little wink.

"At the top of the leaderboard, with an impressive score a full 107 points higher than her closest rival..." Gaston said.

The pause stretched.

And stretched.

And stretched...

"Lady Wexyn of the Temple of Desire!"

Amphie stumbled back half a step. In the Temple's section, Lady Wexyn's entourage pulled off their veils and waved them around, flashing half of the galaxy.

Lady Wexyn's scores filled the screens, her name glowing with golden light at the very top of the table. She reigned supreme. She had successfully transitioned to a monarchy with a democratically elected legislative body. She instituted meritocracy, allowing surfacing talents to rise, and guaranteed freedom of religion, organizing the representatives of various sects into a "spiritual council" so they could give her sage advice and squabble in person rather than through their followers. She redirected harmful tribalism by developing organized sports.

Her trade network was superb. She had instituted a policy that offered additional rewards for discoveries, so not only did her caravans bring back a variety of goods, but they also learned of new technologies and cultures and then delivered that knowledge back to their homeland to collect a hefty payout.

Despite staying away from large conflicts, she had a robust military. She had allowed one of the barbarian settlements to flourish into a 3-city civilization, and when she built new military units, she would send them to the border with that tri-city state, to repel their raids and carry out small invasions, always stopping short of conquering or debilitating the enemy. Once her military units had been seasoned in those wars, she sent them with the caravans as guards. Her people were prosperous, healthy, happy, and proud to belong to her nation.

"That girl is her mother's daughter," Caldenia murmured.

I looked at her.

"Her mother always planned long-term. She does as well. It is a common belief that one cannot build a foundation for a successful society in *Progress* without going through at least a brief period of slavery in the early stages of the game. When the civilization is in its infancy, the wars with small settlements provide a steady stream of captives, the level of technology and education is low, and large fortifications and a steady food supply are critical. Slavery is the most efficient answer."

"Slavery should never be the answer."

"Wexyn shares your view. She sidestepped it with her tiered citizenship system. It requires a very deep understanding of the game. Only one other high-profile player employed this strategy, and he could only make it work half of the time."

"Who was he?"

Caldenia pursed her lips. "Kosandion's father."

Oh. Her entire strategy was a tribute. As obsessed as the Dominion was with this game, they wouldn't miss it. Kosandion wouldn't miss it either.

I glanced at Kosandion. He was studying the screen, seemingly deeply immersed in it.

"Unlike some, she has talent." Caldenia stared at Amphie as if she were a worm. "A poor showing for the Dominion."

"And the last of the four is Amphie of Behoun!"

Amphie' s name appeared in the bottom row. She had the foundation for a successful state, but the war with Bestata had drained every bit of wealth from her coffers and demoralized her population. She had beaten Bestata by 24 points on the strength of her cultural achievements but lost to Oond by 7. She was staring at the screens now with a kind of strange slack expression.

"This is the non-interfering part, I'm guessing," Sean murmured through the earpiece.

My pulse sped up. *"Keep him alive, please."*

"Dina," Her Grace said, urgency vibrating in her voice. "Whatever is about to happen will either weaken Kosandion's position or make it uncontestable. If you resolve it for him, you will take away his victory. Promise me."

"What if he dies?"

"Then he's not fit to sit on that throne."

Gertrude Hunt and I were bound. Losing the inn would rip out my heart. But I would still have Sean. I loved him more than anything. Caldenia loved her nephew. For his safety, she had sacrificed everything but her life, and even that was barely kept and had been forever changed. Kosandion knew an assassin was after him. He must have made arrangements, because he had reached out to the Innkeeper Assembly in advance. Caldenia wouldn't risk his life unless she had confidence in his preparations.

It went against everything I was taught.

But Sean was with Kosandion. The small mountain supporting the throne was basically a triangle set on its side, with the slope facing the stage. The top of the triangle, where the throne was placed, was 20 feet above the stage. The bottom of the triangle, just like the bottom of the stage, was hidden in my fake clouds. Horizontally, 15 feet of clear space separated the stage from the slope. An attacker would have to clear these 15 feet, then run up the 30-foot-long slope, bypassing both Resven and Miralitt, and only then they would be within striking distance. That would give both Sean and Kosandion all the time in the world to prepare.

"Do this for me, and I will never forget it," Caldenia said. "I've spent years planning to secure him on his throne. Please don't let it fall apart now."

She said things like that a lot lately. "Fine. I will sit on my hands."

I hoped I wouldn't regret it.

Caldenia took my hand, squeezed, and let go.

Wow.

"I lost," Amphie said, her microphone-amplified voice echoing across the arena. "I lost to a *fish*."

That was uncalled for.

Prysen Ol was looking at Amphie. She turned her head slowly. Their stares connected.

The philosopher sprinted across the stage toward the small mountain, his eyes fixed on Kosandion on his throne.

In the observers' section six seats away from me, Tomato jumped to his feet and vomited a pearlescent orb the size of a basketball. The orb streaked toward the throne.

I clamped the green-bear-alien into a vise of Gertrude Hunt's roots. They couldn't blame me for securing him. He was an active danger to the observers.

Prysen Ol leaped. He didn't jump, he flew as if he had wings, shooting a full thirty feet up toward the Sovereign in a sharp diagonal line. A human being could not do this.

Sean activated a barrier around the Kai section.

Prysen reached the maximum height and streaked through the air toward Kosandion on a collision course with the orb. Was this levitation? What the hell was this? I could just snatch him right out of the air... Argh!

Prysen's right hand snapped out toward the orb. His fingers touched it, and the orb popped like a soap bubble, releasing a coiled whip. Before it could fall, Prysen snatched it out of the air and swung it. The whip whistled, spinning in a wide arc crackling with red lightning.

A whip-sword. Made not out of leather, rubber, or paracord, but of razor-sharp metallic segments connected by a glowing monofilament. Released, it was a 20-foot whip that could behead a human being in a single snap. Retracted, it became a 4-foot sword, the segments fitted together into a flexible blade.

Time slowed. Prysen was still in mid-air, defying the limits of human bodies and gravity and flying toward Kosandion in a slowly descending trajectory. The whip-sword sliced in a devastating strike. He was aiming at Kosandion's head.

The bladed segments whined as the whip completed its circle. Kosandion saw it coming but made no move to avoid it.

Lady Wexyn dashed to the edge of the stage, shot into the air like a bullet, and pulled a dagger from her cleavage. Prysen Ol never saw her coming. She caught him from behind, wrapping one arm around his neck like a lover, and drove the dagger between his shoulder blades.

Prysen jerked back, shock twisting his face. The end of the whip quivered, slicing a foot short of the Sovereign's nose. Kosandion observed it with mild interest, as if it were a random curiosity.

Lady Wexyn hurled Prysen Ol away from the mountain. He hurtled through the air, spun, twisting his body as he fell, and landed on the balls of his feet near the center of the stage. The knife was still embedded in his back. Bright red blood spread through his robes.

Lady Wexyn floated down and landed near the edge of the stage, her back to the throne mountain, blocking the way to Kosandion. It had to be a technologically assisted jump. Gravity didn't make exceptions.

Prysen Ol pulled a syringe out of his robes with his left hand and stabbed it into his thigh.

Lady Wexyn took a step toward him. There was nothing sweet or coquettish about her face now. She looked like Cyanide might have when she hunted her prey.

"Curse it! I'll do it myself!" Amphie snarled.

Her necklace melted, sliding under her gown. The liquid metal slithered out of her short sleeves, down her arms, coated her hands, and hardened into four-inch claws.

She dashed forward, ridiculously fast.

Sean and I simultaneously sealed the Behoun's section and sank the delegates into the floor up to their armpits.

Lady Wexyn glided sideways on an intercept course. Amphie raked at her with her new claws. Lady Wexyn caught Amphie's right wrist with her right hand, jerked her forward, moving with her opponent's momentum and pulling her arm straight, and twisted the arm elbow up. Amphie gasped. Lady Wexyn drove the heel of her left palm into Amphie's elbow.

The arm crunched with a dry pop. Amphie cried out.

Lady Wexyn let go of the ruined arm, spun behind Amphie, grabbed her other wrist with both hands, pulled her to the ground, as if Amphie weighed nothing, dropped to one knee, and broke Amphie's left arm over it. The entire fight was over in two breaths.

"Goddess preserve us," Karat whispered.

"Kosandion," Dagorkun said.

Karat nodded.

Oh. Lady Wexyn had echoed Kosandion's fight with Surkar. Same tactic: grab the wrist, pull the opponent forward, disable the arm. Except she didn't stop with one arm the way he had done.

Amphie laid on her back and howled in pain. The Behoun delegation screamed with her, a chorus to her suffering.

Oond froze in his habitat and slowly turned upside down, his fins limp.

"Oombole down!" Sean called out through the earpiece. *"It's okay, he just fainted."*

Lady Wexyn stepped over Amphie and stalked toward Prysen Ol. He bared his teeth in a grimace and snapped his whip-sword at her. The segmented blades pierced the air, ready to rend. Lady Wexyn sidestepped, and the whip sliced through the stage, scoring the stone.

Lady Wexyn pulled the golden comb out of her hair.

Prysen Ol swung again, sending the whip in a devastating horizontal curve.

Lady Wexyn didn't try to evade.

The whip-blade connected. The whip-sword should have cut her in half, but somehow, she was still standing, the whip fully extended between the two of them.

"The hair comb!" Dagorkun spat out in surprise.

She had caught the filament of the whip-sword between the teeth of her comb.

Prysen jerked the whip back. The filament snapped, spraying half of its segments onto the ground. Prysen Ol backed away and flicked his damaged whip. The remaining segments slid together, forming a blade.

Lady Wexyn crouched, elegant as if dancing, laid the comb down, and picked up a single segment.

Prysen Ol watched, focused on her every move.

She held the segment between her thumb and forefinger, clamping it across its blunt spine, showed it to Prysen Ol, straightened, and started forward again, unhurried, relentless, unscathed.

He walked toward her, light on his feet despite the knife in his back and the trail of his blood following him. They watched each other as they moved, each step, each minute shift in weight deliberate and calculated.

Sophie, the ruler of her planet and George's wife, once told me that she lived for the moment just before the clash, when both she and her opponent knew their lives hung in the balance. It was a world of possibilities, an infinite universe that shrunk to a single strike as soon as they moved. I finally understood what she meant.

Prysen Ol struck, a human blur too fast for the eye to follow. Lady Wexyn swept by him. They took a few steps past each other. She held his sword in her hand. Prysen Ol held nothing. A deep red line crossed his throat. His eyes turned glassy. He stumbled and collapsed.

Behind me in the second row of the observer section, the First Scholar let out a scream of pure anguish.

Lady Wexyn turned to the Sovereign. "Are you satisfied with the fulfillment of our contract, *Letero*?"

"Yes," Kosandion said.

Lady Wexyn smiled.

"And that's a wrap!" Gaston emerged onto the stage. **"Please join us tomorrow for the exciting conclusion to the greatest spousal selection in the galaxy!"**

He bowed.

Lady Wexyn sashayed toward her section. I dropped both Prysen Ol and Amphie through the floor right into the medward.

THE SCREEN IN FRONT OF ME SHOWED KLOOK, ONE OF THE FIRST Scholar's two disciples. They looked almost identical, but the tips of Klook's feathers had a slightly more pronounced pink tint.

"The First Scholar would like to inquire…"

"Would you like to see him?" I asked.

Klook disappeared, shoved out of the way, and the First Scholar replaced him on the screen, with his feathers in disarray and his eyes ringed by red, a sign of a koo-ko in acute distress. "I'm coming!"

I opened the door to his quarters and made a child-slide-style chute in the floor. A few seconds later, the First Scholar fell out of the medward's ceiling, spread his wings, and glided to a landing by me.

I turned. In front of me, two square cells sat side by side with six feet of space between them. The back wall of each cell was reinforced concrete with a space-hull-grade titanium overlay, while the other three sides were transparent plastisteel. The center of each cell housed a med unit. The left one held Amphie, the right Prysen Ol. Both patients were sedated.

I had sealed off the werewolf in her own quarters. She was mostly sleeping, as her body did its best to heal. Occasionally she would wake up long enough to eat, and then she fell asleep again. Sean had visited her. They spoke for about an hour, after which she slept for 14 hours straight.

The First Scholar peered at Prysen's relaxed face.

"He lives?" he asked in a hushed voice.

"Yes."

"How?"

"He's very lucky."

I once heard a story about a hockey player whose jugular was cut by a skate during the game. He should've bled out, but he survived against all odds. Prysen Ol should've bled out as well, but for the medical cocktail he'd stabbed into his leg. Besides a booster and a pain killer, it contained a wound-sealing coagulant. He was trying to stop the bleeding in his back. Coincidentally, it had patched his jugular enough to keep him alive until the med unit could take over.

"What happens to him now?" the First Scholar asked.

"That depends on his motives. If he carries a personal grudge against the Sovereign, there will be a punishment. If he was simply a hired killer, perhaps Kosandion will find some use for him."

The First Scholar's feathers stood erect. "I shall beg the Sovereign for leniency! Prysen Ol is an unrivaled talent. He cannot be thrown away."

Right. Funny how he ignored the whole "hired killer" part.

The First Scholar marched off, spun in a circle, looking around, and finally remembered I was still there. "Where is the exit?"

"Perhaps it might help to freshen up before you go to see the Sovereign?" I suggested gently.

The First Scholar slapped his head with his pseudohand, checking for his hat, realized it wasn't there, and nodded. "A most wise advice."

"I will return you to your quarters. Please let Tony know when you are ready to request an audience."

I gave the inn a push, and it carried the First Scholar back onto the slide and to his quarters. I sealed the ceiling behind him.

The two prisoners slept in their cells. When they woke up, there would be hell to pay.

But neither of them would die. The Assembly wouldn't be happy. I could just imagine the look on their faces. Still, up to now, we'd managed to keep all of our guests breathing. That had to count for something, right?

I reached through the inn, looking for Sean. He was still with Kosandion.

"Hey," I whispered.

"Hey."

"How is it going?"

"Busy. Behoun is trying to secede from the Dominion."

Just what Kosandion needed.

"I'm going to get some answers," I told him.

"Let me know how it goes."

———

I paused before the doorway to Lady Wexyn's quarters and tossed my voice inside.

"A word, Lady Wexyn?"

The doors swung open in front of me, pulled back by two veiled attendants. I strode in, with Beast trotting by my feet. Nothing had changed since my last visit. A clear stream still curved around a courtyard of brown stones, gently flowing into a wide pond. The yellow-leafed Fortune trees washed their long branches in the water. Even Lady Wexyn was in the exact same place, reclining on a chaise inside a wooden pavilion at the pond's edge.

I approached her.

"Please, sit," she invited.

I sat down in a cushioned chair. Beast jumped onto my lap and flopped.

Lady Wexyn gazed over the water, her expression serene.

"You have questions," she said.

"So many."

She nodded. "I'll do my best to answer as a thank you for your hospitality."

"Let's start with the simplest one. The flying?"

"Tuhl Gravity Disruptor. A tiny single-use gadget with an inaccurate name, since it doesn't really disrupt gravity, it simply creates a powerful lift for about 7 seconds. I had it attached to my right shoe."

"It doesn't sound safe." Using anything with "Tuhl" in its name meant taking your life in your hands. Tuhls made genius tech that killed them with depressing regularity.

"It isn't. It requires a lot of training and explodes about 25% of the time. Really, strapping anything that causes a subatomic reaction to your body is a terrible idea. I do not recommend it."

"It was very impressive," I told her.

"Thank you."

"Did Kosandion hire you?"

She nodded. "In a manner of speaking. He spoke to Clan Nuan, and Clan Nuan suggested I would be an excellent solution to his problems."

"So you're a bodyguard?"

"Not exactly." She looked over the water again. "When people think of desires, they usually think of love or lust, depending on how cynical they are. But there are many other desires. Wealth. Power. Freedom… Revenge."

She gave me a sweet smile. Suddenly she seemed wrapped in power. It suffused her, an unyielding merciless energy, contained yet ready to be weaponized at any moment.

Cold dashed down my spine.

"Some say that the need for revenge is the second strongest desire. Some say it's the most powerful one. I, like my mother before me, am a Priestess of Revenge. When the supplicants pray before my altar, they lay their grudges bare, and if their cause is worthy, I do what they cannot. Sometimes I am justice, but mostly I'm vengeance."

She had walked toward Prysen Ol like an unstoppable elemental force. She hadn't said a single word during that fight. She showed no emotion. It wasn't personal for her. Looking at her must've been like staring Death in the face.

The half-forgotten teachings of the Temple floated up from

my memory. The priests and priestesses of the Temple taught that unfulfilled desires created an imbalance in the universe. The deeper the desire, the greater the imbalance. Correcting that imbalance was their sacred mission.

"Harmony," I said.

She smiled. "Yes."

Amphie and Prysen Ol had conspired to assassinate Kosandion. His death would have thrown the Dominion into chaos. "Was today vengeance?"

"Today was one of the rare times when I stopped a future tragedy from happening. My contract with Kosandion put no limits on me. He didn't ask me to guard him. He simply asked me to enter the selection and to act if I judged my intervention was needed. If Amphie hadn't pulled the trigger, I would've continued to play my chosen role to the very end, taken my minor ask, and departed with no one the wiser."

"What's your minor ask?"

"A very generous donation to the Temple. I had to stay in character. A woman dripping in gold would ask for more wealth, of course."

"I thought you would ask for Clan Nuan to become the preferred partner of the Dominion."

She chuckled. "That is the major ask. A change like that would require reworking the Dominion's entire interstellar trade. It's all moot now. Don't worry. Clan Nuan knew it was a very long shot. They are satisfied."

The Temple would get their donation, Clan Nuan would drastically improve their trade with the Dominion even without the major ask, and Kosandion would look like a flawless ruler, who both anticipated threats and neutralized them. Declining the protection of the inn during the assassination was the ultimate power move. An overly poetic guest once described being inside of the inn as "being held in a god's palm," with your every need met in absolute safety. Even life's little accidents like tripping and hitting an elbow on the counter didn't happen inside the inn. Kosandion had showed to the Dominion that even in a god's palm, he would make his own contingency plans.

I looked at her. "That seems like a lot to leave to chance. Did he help you move up? What if you'd been eliminated in one of the earlier rounds?"

She laughed. It was a light, melodious laugh, warm and infectious. "Kosandion has his faults, but he would never insult me."

Even if he had manipulated public opinion in her favor, there was no way to fake the trials. She had done well in the debate, wowed in the talent portion, and then she effortlessly won the game. And when Prysen Ol's sword-whip hurtled at his face, Kosandion didn't even flinch. He had complete confidence in her skills.

"Kosandion and I are similar in a way," she said. "Both of us trained from birth to walk the path predestined for us. We are both good at what we do. He understands empires. I understand people. The biggest worry was that Amphie might have been eliminated too soon. There are limits to how much public opinion can be swayed in the face of abject failure."

"When did you begin to suspect her?"

"From the beginning. So did Kosandion. Behoun has grown prosperous over the last century. It is a kind of aimless prosperity without a clear direction. It breeds greed and laziness. They have systematically avoided all calls to contribute on the federal level. Of all the planets, they send the least troops, share the least resources, and exploit the most tax loopholes, and yet they scream for aid every time they have a minor disaster. They are content to be a part of the Dominion as long as nothing is asked of them, and all of their efforts are aimed at preserving the state of things just the way they are."

Not surprising. In the US, each state liked to think of itself as a small country. If the states were separated by thousands of light years, that kind of thinking would only become deeper.

An attendant appeared and deposited a tray with snacks and tea on the table.

"Thank you," Lady Wexyn murmured.

The attendant nodded and withdrew.

She poured two cups of tea and offered one to me. I sipped it. It was a delicate aromatic brew, with notes of peach and jasmine.

Lady Wexyn took a sip as well. "The previous Sovereign ignored Behoun because he had bigger worries. They mistook the lack of attention for weakness and grew more and more brazen. Kosandion is much harsher than his predecessor. His father was infected by his political opponents and arranged his own murder, his aunt threw away an empire and killed her own brother, and Kosandion had witnessed it all, knowing it was done for his sake. It hardened his heart."

Made sense.

"By the time Behoun realized the danger, the chance to cover up their blatant corruption had passed. When the selection was announced, they scrambled to find a suitable candidate and settled on Amphie. The plan was to wedge her into the spouse spot and use her influence to shield themselves."

"And to kill Kosandion if she failed?"

"Yes. They hired an assassin to act as her backup. They had to use an outsider so it wouldn't be traced to them, and Prysen Ol fit that bill perfectly. If Amphie was eliminated, Prysen Ol would attack the Sovereign. Nobody would connect it to Behoun. At the very least the attempted murder would disrupt the selection and create enough problems to buy them some time to regroup."

"Amphie went off script, then?" I asked. "The entire galaxy saw her give Prysen Ol that look."

Lady Wexyn nodded. "Hubris. She comes from a wealthy family, and she's been taught from an early age that she is special and that she deserves all the things she wants. Amphie is a narcissist, focused on herself to the exclusion of all else and pathologically addicted to attention, especially from men. Her biggest fear is being ridiculed. Losing to Oond pushed all the right buttons."

"She wanted to punish Kosandion for her failure?"

Lady Wexyn nodded. "She would've punished the whole world if she could. When a person like Amphie lashes out, there is no limit. If she could've disintegrated everyone in that arena with a flick of her fingers, all of us would be atomic dust right now."

"And Prysen?"

"The identity of the hidden assassin was a bit of a mystery. I had narrowed it down to three possibilities before the debate, but then he brought up the planetphage. It wasn't particularly relevant to the discussion. He'd slid it in there because he was enamored with the story of a creature that traveled from world to world, devouring all in its path and feeling sad for itself. He might as well have written 'Conflicted Assassin' on his forehead."

Put like that, it did seem obvious.

Lady Wexyn poured more tea. "I will say, the man committed fully. I had expected them to call it off once they realized what a pair of innkeepers are capable of, but he was given the signal and he made a good effort. If you are wondering, I doubt Kosandion will kill him. Why waste a perfectly good assassin?"

"You sound like Caldenia."

Lady Wexyn smiled into her cup.

"I've met him before, you know," she said.

"Prysen Ol?"

She shook her head. "Kosandion. When I was ten years old, my mother had business in the Dominion's capital, and she brought me with her to further my training. I saw him from afar during a state celebration, so that night I climbed onto his balcony to get a closer look. He saw me and tried to chase me. We had a lovely run across the balconies and rooftops. Kosandion is genetically engineered to be much faster and stronger than an average person, and he had gotten used to outrunning and outmuscling his guards. He gave it his all." She laughed. "He was so puzzled when he couldn't catch me. You should've seen his face."

I had seen the stone-faced Kosandion, the Sovereign Kosandion, the tired Kosandion, even the charming Kosandion, but never a puzzled Kosandion. I couldn't even picture it in my head.

"Eleven years later, he came to the Temple looking for my mother. Caldenia had petitioned her to avenge her brother's death."

"Did your mother judge her petition worthy?"

"She did." That hint of power simmered under her skin again. "Kosandion wanted details."

"Did she tell him?"

Lady Wexyn shook her head. "It wasn't his petition. If his aunt wanted him to know, she would've told him."

Her mother must've gone about it just like her daughter. Gathered information, assumed an identity, infiltrated the inner circle of those responsible, and finally brought it to a torturous and bloody end. The greater the grudge, the more severe was the punishment. Vengeance had to match the evil that spawned the need for it. It was the only way harmony would be restored.

"Kosandion spent three days at the Temple trying to convince her. We strolled through the Temple gardens together." She sounded almost wistful.

"You like him." It slipped out almost on its own.

"What's not to like?"

"He could still..." I let it trail off.

"He won't choose me. A consort can be beautiful, beloved, even worshipped, but they can never be capable of standing on their own. The greatest sin a consort can commit is to split the ruler's power base and become a threat. People like Kosandion do not marry people like me, Dina. They marry those who would make weak rivals, and I would be a very dangerous rival. The Sovereign in him understands that."

She was right but it felt so wrong.

I finished my tea. "So, what now?"

"Tomorrow all of us will meet again. I suppose the selection will be declared void, and a new selection will be announced to be held in the next 3 or so years with a fresh roster of candidates."

"What will you do? The galaxy now knows your face. Won't it make things difficult for you?"

She gave an elegant one-shouldered shrug. "I suppose I could change my face and my body. I'm too young to retire. But then again, perhaps I will disappear for a few years. Have an adventure while the wheels of the galaxy revolve slowly, grinding memories to dust. I don't know yet."

She must've known that this would be the outcome from the start, and yet she had done it anyway. Everything she had done from the moment she stepped into the inn until now was a love letter, written with the chiming of thin bracelets, the spin of a translucent veil, and the thrust of a razor-sharp dagger. It was exquisite. And now the message was complete. Tomorrow, she would sign it with a flourish, and they would go their separate ways. It was a farewell to Kosandion and to the girl who let him chase her across the Capital's balconies years ago.

I rose. Beast jumped off my lap. I bowed my head to her. She bowed back. I straightened my robe and walked out of her quarters the same way I came.

[27]

When we last left our intrepid heroes, Lady Wexyn turned out to be the Priestess of Revenge and revealed her history with Kosandion. But he will never marry her, because she is entirely too dangerous to have around. Oy, what a twist. Now the selection might be cancelled.

Will he get married, won't he get married? This is ruining our emotions! Enough with the suspense already! Get on with it!

"...Conduct unbecoming an innkeeper," Frank Copeland droned on. "That shitshow should've never happened."

I resisted the urge to take a page out of Sean's playbook and growl at the screen. The Innkeeper Assembly was perturbed by how Game Day had ended, so they'd decided to call me first thing in the morning, over Zoom of all things, and take me to task. To be fair, most of the condemnation was coming from Frank Copeland and Dawn Phillips. The two of them ran large-venue inns, Frank in California and Dawn in Alberta.

At least I wasn't dealing with the entire Assembly, only with the seven members of the North American branch council.

"You approved this shitshow beforehand," I pointed out.

"Quote: 'Make all reasonable efforts to accommodate the Sovereign's wishes.'"

"Reasonable!" Dawn said. "How are two dead guests reasonable?"

"For the last time," Brian Rodriguez recited, "Nobody died. Everyone is alive. Nobody sustained permanent injuries."

"And we're just supposed to believe that?" Frank demanded.

"Yes." I sank some steel into my voice. "I am an innkeeper. My word is sufficient."

"That remains to be seen," Frank said.

"How about my word?"

I felt cold magic bloom behind me. Out of the corner of my eye, I saw Tony's red ad-hal robe ripple as if touched by wind.

Frank clamped his mouth shut. That just annoyed me even more. I'd been an innkeeper for years now and apparently the only way my word counted was if I had an ad-hal to back me up.

"Help," Sean whispered in my ear. He was down in the oombole enclosure.

"Urgent?"

"Somewhat."

"I'll be right there."

"What I want to know is—" Dawn started.

"Enough. This is my inn. I determine what is reasonable here. I don't need you to hold my hand. I don't need you to tell me how you would have handled it. Mind your own business."

There was a moment of shocked silence.

Aiyo Iwata clapped. "Finally."

Manuel Ordóñez clapped as well and muttered something in Spanish under his breath. It sounded a lot like "estúpido."

"Finally, what?" Frank demanded.

"Finally, someone shut you two up," Aiyo said. "It is her inn. You are not her supervisor."

"We all know why we're having this meeting," Brian Rodriguez said. "The two of you were contacted by the Dominion with an offer to host this selection and you passed."

"What are you implying?" Dawn asked.

Brian leaned into his screen. "I am not implying, I'm saying it. This is sour grapes."

"You were offered a chance to do it, you declined, she did it, and she did it well." Magdalene Braswell crossed her arms on her chest. "You don't get to complain about it. She went a week with twenty Dushegubs in her inn and they all left alive."

"Oh, they can complain about it," Aiyo said, "but it doesn't mean the rest of us have to waste any more time listening to it."

"I have a legitimate point!" Frank pounded his fist onto his desk.

Magdalene snorted. "Bless your heart."

"Remind me, Frank," Tyrone Brightwell said. "Who made you king? I didn't vote for you."

"Ahahaha!" Aiyo cracked up. "I see what you did there!"

I looked at Tony, who had shifted back into his regular clothes. He nodded. We quietly switched places, and I hurried through the inn to the oomboles. I'd had it up to my ears with the Innkeeper Assembly and its branches.

We had modeled the oombole section after massive observation aquariums. The walls of their connected tanks were transparent, and the tanks themselves stretched fifty feet high. Walking between them was like strolling on the bottom of the sea.

The entire oombole delegation swam in a school inside the largest tank, the size of an Olympic swimming pool. I found Sean on the side by one of the smaller tanks connected to the larger one by a narrow channel. He was watching Oond. The spousal candidate was making tight counterclockwise circles.

Uh-oh.

I approached the transparent wall. Oond ignored me.

"How long has he been like this?" I murmured.

"Forty-five minutes," Sean answered. "He keeps circling, secreting stress pheromones, and urinating."

Everything about this was bad. The oomboles were not solitary. They didn't go off by themselves, and they didn't swim in small circles. They were foragers, which was why we had to make a giant tank for them. Oond was in acute distress. A guest in our inn was having a nervous breakdown. My parents would be aghast. I had shamed the family.

"Why is he swimming in his own piss?" Sean asked.

The oomboles were extremely fussy about their bathroom habits. We had had to redo their latrine area three times just to make sure it was aesthetically pleasing and private enough.

"It makes him feel safer. It's his equivalent of curling into a fetal ball. Have you gotten him to respond at all?"

"No."

I sealed off the small pool. "Let's try a lower temperature and soothing light."

Gertrude Hunt's massive temperature-regulating pumps came online, sending cool water into the tank. I dimmed the lights. The water plants inside the tank fluoresced gently.

"Let's wait," I said. "Have you had breakfast?"

"No."

I reached into the pocket of my robe, pulled out a cookie in a plastic bag, which I had stolen from the kitchen earlier, and passed it to him. He wolfed it down.

Oond kept swimming.

Humans carried an instinctual fear of the deep sea. Even if we knew that the body of water was perfectly safe and had no predators, swimming in dark water, where the bottom was too far to reach, awakened a primitive anxiety in most of us. The oomboles had an instinctual fear of terrestrial predators. At a certain point in their development, they were prey to massive reptiles and terrifying birds that dove into the water from great heights. Their tolerance for terrestrial violence was very small. It frightened them beyond all reason.

"Did you get a chance to talk to Miralitt?"

He nodded. "She liked the recording. She's onboard. I took it to Derryl. She's thinking about it."

"Will she go for it?"

"The offer is there if she wants it. She'll take it or she won't."

Oond was slowing down. The cold water was working.

"I've read the contract," Sean said.

Last night before going to bed, I had shown him the recording the inn made of my conversation with Lady Wexyn. She thought the selection would be voided, and I had been too wrapped up in her story to ask why. Sean decided to review our contract with the Dominion as soon as we got some sleep.

"She's right. They will likely void the selection. "

"Why?"

"The spouse can't be selected by default. There must be at least two candidates, so the Sovereign can choose one."

"I bet they put that provision in to keep them from killing each other. If only one of them is left standing, nobody gets to be the spouse."

Sean nodded. "If she withdraws tonight, that leaves only Oond. The selection is automatically canceled."

"Ugh."

"It gets worse."

I stared at him.

"If they void this selection, we're on the hook for hosting the next one."

"Galaxy, no. No. Absolutely not. Never again."

"We signed it."

"No." I realized it wasn't a rational response, but it was the only one I could come up with.

He hugged me.

We both agreed that in a perfect world Kosandion would

marry Lady Wexyn and have many hyper-intelligent, beautiful, and physically enhanced babies. Unfortunately, nothing indicated that such a match would be happening. Last night Orata started polling the Dominion's population regarding the best date for a new selection if the current one was canceled.

"I'm so tired," I whispered into his ear.

"I know, love. I know. I'm sorry I got us into this."

"You didn't get us into this. We held hands and jumped off this cliff together."

When we were talking and thinking about doing it a week ago, it hadn't seemed so...so...so big. So difficult. Galaxy, it had only been a week. How...

"It's like this bottomless hole and we keep throwing time, magic, and resources into it, and it just keeps getting bigger," I told him.

"I just want it to be done. I want this shit to be over with. I want everyone to fuck off out of our inn. They all need to go somewhere else, and we need to go get Wilmos."

I groaned and bumped my forehead against his shoulder. "And we don't even know what we'll find on the other side of the Karron portal."

We stood together for a few minutes. Sean stroked my hair.

"If they void the selection, they won't have another right away," I said. "It might take years to set one up again."

"Maybe he'll do us all a favor and marry the fish."

"I can't," Oond's mechanical voice said behind us.

We turned. He had stopped swimming and was hovering near the transparent wall.

"I can't do it. It's too dangerous. I'm not brave enough. I cannot go to the Dominion. I cannot stay there. I cannot be the spouse. Someone will kill me. Someone will kill my offspring. It will all end in tragedy and death. So much death."

"Well, there goes that idea," Sean said under his breath.

"I am so sorry. I am a failure. I have failed my people. I have come here for the minor ask. The survival of my people depends on it. If I withdraw, we leave with nothing. But I have no courage. I have no strength. I am miserable."

A slightly opaque cloud of water spread from him.

I hid a sigh. "I will speak to the Sovereign on your behalf."

Oond's fins fluttered weakly. "You will?"

"I will. You are our guest. Your wellbeing is important to us. I'm sure some solution can be found. Rest and try not to worry."

I took Sean's hand for moral support, before I lost it and peed myself too, and the two of us went back upstairs.

———

"I DON'T UNDERSTAND." MIRALITT FROWNED AT ME. "THE OOMBOLE does not want to be the spouse? Does he think we can't protect him?"

I sighed. Around me Kosandion's private balcony was a flurry of activity. Right after the Game Day assassination attempt, Kosandion had requested a private portal. Considering that a civil war in the Dominion was looming, refusing seemed unreasonable. The big portal was shut down most of the time anyway, so we completely closed it off, and opened a smaller one right on the balcony. It could only transport one person at time.

As soon as the portal was opened, Miralitt's guards came through and positioned themselves all around the balcony, ready to respond to any threats. Normally I might have taken that as an insult, but if I balked, Miralitt would've had an aneurism, and we needed a favor from her. This whole affair was a lesson in learning to compromise.

With the opening of the portal, the balcony transformed into the Sovereign's remote office. On one side, Orata sat surrounded by translucent screens, scanning their contents and issuing brisk commands to a small pack of her staffers. On the other side, His Holiness was in an identical position, with the screens and a throng of aides. He was pointing to the screens and delivering instructions in short confident bursts like a general in the middle of a battle. Kosandion sat at his table, closest to the rail and the water, reading and signing things, while Resven hovered nearby with a small army of staffers. Periodically he would single one out, and then the staffer would take off at top speed and vanish into the portal.

Tension vibrated in the air. The balcony sparked with it, as if the molecules that made it had somehow acquired a charge.

"A spouse hasn't been murdered for the last 70 years," Miralitt said. "It won't happen on my watch. I guarantee it with my life."

"It's not personal. It has to do with their evolutionary origin," I said. "Sapience evolves in many ways across a myriad of life forms, but the fastest and the most common category of sapient beings are either predatory omnivores or omnivorous predators that come from the middle of the food chain. For intelligence and problem-solving skills to develop, it helps if you are both a hunter and the hunted. Earth's humans are predatory omnivores. The vampires of the Holy Anocracy are omnivorous predators. The omnivorous quality is important because organized hunting, animal husbandry, and crop cultivation are essential progress milestones."

"The oomboles are also predatory omnivores," Miralitt said.

"Technically," Sean said.

"Their diet consists of plants and several species of crustaceans, all of which have evolved to be sedentary," I explained. "Their protective shells are attached to the ocean floor. They don't move."

"Why is that important?" Miralitt asked.

"Because they don't hunt," Sean said. "They are grazers. They don't chase and eat other fish, so they do not understand the predatory mindset. They only fear it."

I nodded. "They are closer to the bottom of the food chain than the middle, and they have a pathological fear of being eaten."

"What are you trying to say?" Miralitt asked.

"They are cowards," Sean said. "It's an evolutionary adaptation, and it will be almost impossible to overcome. Right now, Oond sees everything that isn't an oombole as a predator."

"This is consistent with their ask," Resven said.

I hadn't realized he was listening. "What are they asking?"

"Their planet is a single shallow ocean with occasional deep trenches," Resven said. "They've killed off the predators in the shallows. In the absence of predators, their population and that of other prey fish has exploded to unsustainable levels. Killing other fish who are not a direct threat to them is against their philosophical doctrines, so they are asking the Dominion to save them from themselves."

"How?" Miralitt asked.

"Targeted commercial fishing or the reintroduction of the predators," Resven said. "It is still being discussed."

"Oond is spiraling down," I said. "If you attempt to select him as a spouse, he will withdraw."

"What are the numbers from the pool about the new selection?" Kosandion asked without looking up.

"No change from two hours ago," Orata reported.

Kosandion gave a small gesture to Resven.

"May I have a few moments of your time?" Resven asked.

"Of course."

The three of us left the balcony for the privacy of a long hallway leading from it to the throne room.

"The Dominion is in crisis," Resven said, keeping his voice casual. "Our citizens are distressed by the progress of the selection process. They are dissatisfied and anxious, and they are rallying behind their Sovereign against Behoun. Over the past twenty-four hours, the number of premature labors has quadrupled. It is the best indicator of the population's overall stress level. Such a rise indicates that the Dominion has reached a boiling point."

"Are you going to void the selection?" I asked.

"I do not presume to speak for the Sovereign. Only he can make that decision."

Argh.

"I will say this, however," Resven said. "When the selection is declared void, all candidates who are still present receive their minor asks. Please do everything in your power to convince Oond to be present for the selection. If he withdraws now, his people will get nothing, and the Dominion will feel even more aggrieved."

"Can you guarantee that he won't become the spouse?" Sean asked.

"No. I also cannot guarantee that the First Sun won't explode in the next ten seconds. However, it would be equally unlikely." Resven smiled. "No matter what happens during the final ceremony, Gertrude Hunt has exceeded the Sovereign's expectations. You have the gratitude of the Dominion. All of us will be delighted to return. And of course, the Dominion will grant you all the benefits agreed upon in our contract."

They would cancel the current selection, make a new one, and they were counting on us to host it. Sean's face told me he thought the same thing.

Poor Lady Wexyn.

"It is imperative that Oond attends the final ceremony," Resven repeated.

"Very well," I said. "We will speak to Oond."

We had three hours until the final ceremony. Hopefully, it would be enough.

———

"I can't do it." Oond trembled in his fishbowl. "What if they kill me on the way?"

We'd been over it a hundred times. I'd tried everything: the soothing lights, the temperature setting, the right mix of plants, even a weak version of oombole-safe sedative. We'd gotten as far as the fishbowl, and that's where things stopped.

The ceremony was due to start in three minutes.

"What if I die...? Would they eat me? Would they cook my body?"

Sean stepped forward and pulled off his robe. "Look at me."

Oond obediently stared at him.

Sean's body blurred. An enormous alpha werewolf spilled out, seven feet tall and shaggy with dark fur. Golden eyes caught Oond in an unblinking predator stare. The oombole froze.

Please don't faint again. Please don't faint.

"Look at my teeth," Sean said, his voice a deep snarl. He bared his fangs.

Oond stared at him, unable to look away.

"Someone trying to hurt you will have to get through me. I will kill anyone who tries to harm you. Anyone."

Oond's fins shivered a tiny bit, then finally moved. "You will stay with me? You will guard me the whole time?"

"The whole time," Sean promised.

"I will go," Oond said. "Let's go fast."

I opened the door and the entrance to the throne room rushed at me. I didn't want to take any chances.

The throne room gleamed, awash in bright light. A swarm of Orata's cameras spun and twisted through the air, capturing the scene from all angles. The final ceremony was broadcast live, and the video feed was already going out. The huge screens that ran along the perimeter of the high ceiling showed the city centers on the various planets of the Dominion. Crowds choked the streets. Beings of all the Dominion's species stood, looking up, their faces tense.

Through the massive doorway, I could see the remaining delegates assembled in a semicircle, with a wide gap between the two center delegations leaving a direct path to the throne open. The

Kai were on the far right, then Behoun, both delegations sectioned off by force fields. On the other side to the far left, the oomboles waited in a cluster of fishbowls. The Temple was still MIA, but they were moving toward the throne room at top speed.

Both Prysen Ol and Amphie were in front of their respective delegations, restrained in the high-tech medical-assist frames, held upright but unable to move.

The observers had already taken their place in the gallery, on their feet this time, with Caldenia in the center like a crown jewel in a midnight-blue gown that shimmered with tiny lights, as if she had bottled a nebula and poured it over her dress. The gown's stiff high collar accentuated her neck, and large star sapphires of the deepest ultramarine shade decorated her carefully styled hair.

Kosandion was already on his throne, with Resven on one side and His Holiness on the other. Miralitt guarded the stairs as usual and Orata stood on the other side of the steps. All hands on deck.

Resven wore his usual robe. The Holy Ecclesiarch wore his white robes, but his overdress was gold. His cape was gold too, embroidered with silver accents. He stood firm, his shoulders straight, his gaze commanding. He held a long scepter in his hand, and he'd planted it into the floor at his feet as if it were a spear. The feinted frailty he had so carefully cultivated before was forgotten. The Dominion had started as a warrior civilization, and today the Ecclesiarch looked every inch a battle priest. But even with all his metallic finery, he couldn't outshine Kosandion.

The Sovereign wore black. His outfit fit him like a glove, its lines severe, more a military uniform than civilian attire. His cape, a carefully draped long expanse of black, edged with a silver geometric motif, was the only concession to the typical Dominion's garb he was willing to make. Kosandion was sending a message. He was ready to go to war.

Nothing about his clothes said groom. My last hope for the resolution died a sad death.

I entered the throne room. My long dark robe swept the floor as I walked. Behind me Oond's fishbowl slid along the polished floor. The delegates turned to look. Gasps whispered through the room. They had seen Sean.

We crossed the throne room. Oond's fishbowl slid to his designated place in front of his people. Sean stood next to him. I ascended the dais and took my place to the left of the Sovereign and slightly behind, between him and the Holy Ecclesiarch.

A soft melody floated into the room, led by a flute, a sad, archaic sound that reached into you and grabbed your soul. A female voice joined the flute, singing a wordless long note.

The air smelled of strange spice.

The melody turned vicious, no longer a beautiful song but a harsh, pained cry, filled with fury. A primal wail coming deep from an anguished heart. The hair on the back of my neck rose.

The Temple attendants entered the throne room. Burgundy dresses the color of old blood clasped their bodies, formed with lengths of diaphanous fabric, gathered and held in place by braided cords that crisscrossed over exposed midriffs and left muscular shoulders and arms bare. Their hair streamed down their backs, unbrushed. Some had painted bright red veins on their faces. Some had dark stripes across their eyes, others wore scaled veils covering only one side of their faces. They stalked into the room, a pack of insane wolves, flashing their teeth and ready to rip their target apart.

It was as if time had folded in on itself and spat out some ancient cult. The true face of the acolytes of Vengeance, mirrors of the souls consumed by their revenge, single-minded, half insane, bound yet unchained, and dreaming of blood and retribution.

The song howled, reaching a crescendo.

The acolytes parted, and Lady Wexyn appeared between them. She wore the same style gown, more elaborate but still ethereal. Snow white at her exposed shoulders, it turned a bright arterial red at the hem, as if she had walked through slaughter. A long, pleated cape rode on her shoulders, dragging five feet behind her on the floor. Bright red eyeliner bled across her eyelids. Her lips were black. A metal headdress crowned her hair, rising in an arc over her head, made with a multitude of long, razor sharp needles. When the supplicants came to the Temple and laid their hearts bare asking for retribution, this is who they saw if their request was accepted.

The Priestess of Revenge walked toward the throne.

Miralitt gripped her ceremonial sword. Oond shuddered in his fishbowl and Sean put his clawed hand onto the glass to steady him. The oomboles shrank from her as she came closer. The people of Behoun couldn't, because the force field restrained them, but they tried.

Kosandion watched her approach. He must've seen her before like this when he'd visited the Temple asking her to join the selection.

On the screens, the crowds of the Dominion roiled like a living sea.

Lady Wexyn took her place. Her acolytes formed up behind her, their eyes wild.

"Let us begin," Kosandion said.

The throne room went silent.

"People of Behoun," the Sovereign said. "I judge your candidate guilty of treason. She has acted with your consent. How will you atone for her crime?"

Amphie stared straight ahead as if she hadn't heard a word.

The leader of the delegation, an older woman, licked her lips. "We no longer recognize the authority of the Dominion."

The screens blasted outraged roars of the crowds. I muted them.

"So your Senate has already informed me."

"Even if you bring the entirety of the Dominion's military, we will stand firm against your tyrannical regime," the leader announced. "We will defend our liberty to the death!"

Kosandion remained unmoved. "I do not plan to invade Behoun. You have been sequestered, so I will let the Chancellor explain it to you."

Resven spoke, hammering each word in.

"As of twelve hours ago, all current and future import-export agreements between Behoun companies and the Dominion have been made void. All Dominion aid, including categorical and block grants, revenue sharing, and programs supplementing health care, public education, community development, job training, and environmental conservation, have been canceled. The planetary defenses installed by the Dominion have been mothballed. The in-system defense fleet is on its way to the Behoun jump gate, and upon reaching it, they will return to the Dominion. All Dominion citizens currently residing on Behoun are urged to return home. All Behoun citizens currently residing with the Dominion are to be expelled and must depart for Behoun within the next twelve hours, after which Behoun's access to all Dominion-controled planetary gates will be revoked."

Resven took a small pause to let it sink in and continued. "I believe that last item will be of particular interest to you, Senator Kolorea. You will be relieved to know that your youngest daughter's scholarship has been canceled, and she has been successfully deported to Behoun."

Kolorea gaped at him. "You can't do that! The Teplaym Robotics Institute..."

"Is a Dominion educational institution funded by the Dominion federal revenue," Resven said.

"What about the sports teams?" one of the delegates on Kolorea's right asked.

Another delegate spun to him. "Sports teams? What about the uranium imports?"

"I am giving Behoun exactly what it requested—no, what in its arrogance, it demanded," the Sovereign said. "Now, we will return to the matter at hand. How will you atone for your crime?"

"We have an urgent communication from Behoun, *Letero*," Orata announced.

The Sovereign nodded. The closest screen blinked, showing the interior of a large chamber with many rows of seats. The chamber was in chaos. Some seats were ripped, some stained and burned. A couple were still smoking. About fifty grim-faced beings, some sislaf, others from a variety of other species, sat in the section directly facing the camera, resolutely ignoring the damage.

A woman in a soot-stained formal robe appeared in front of the camera. "My name is Nelonia Eder. I am the new Speaker of the Behoun Senate."

"Where is the previous Speaker?" the Sovereign asked.

"He is indisposed and no longer able to perform his duties," Nelonia said.

Behind her, two sislafs in formal robes dragged a body across the floor, realized they were on camera, reversed course, and dragged it out of view.

"A rebel faction had temporarily taken control of the Behoun Senate and announced Behoun's secession from the Dominion," Nelonia said.

Kolorea choked on empty air.

"We regret this unfortunate occurrence. The insurrectionists have been suppressed, and we, as the lawfully elected government, condemn their actions. Behoun has never left the Dominion's loving embrace and has no desire to do so." She pounded her fist into her chest. "We pledge our loyalty to the Sovereign!"

The remaining senators rose as one and punched themselves. "Loyalty!"

Amphie's face was bloodless.

"The Dominion will take your actions into consideration," Kosandion said.

"Thank you, my Sovereign. May I address citizen Asturra?"

"You may," the Sovereign said.

"Amphie Asturra," Nelonia intoned. "You are hereby exiled from Behoun. Should you return, your head will be removed from your body and preserved in the Stronghold of Justice to be used as an example for future generations."

Nelonia bowed her head and stepped back.

The delegate who was worried about the uranium imports punched his chest. "I pledge my loyalty to the Sovereign!"

Kolorea jerked, as if shocked by a live wire.

"I pledge my loyalty!"

"...Loyalty..."

"...To the Sovereign!"

About half of the delegation pledged their loyalty. The rest remained silent.

"Very well," the Sovereign said. "The Behoun delegation will be detained and interviewed to ascertain their role in the assassination attempt. Their minor ask will not be granted. Citizen Amphie Asturra, for the crime of attempted murder of the Sovereign I sentence you to exile. You will be remanded to the custody of the Capital Guard, pending your recovery."

Miralitt's guards entered the throne room. It took about three minutes to corral the Behoun delegation and get them out of the inn.

"Candidate Prysen Ol," the Sovereign said. "I judge you guilty of attempted murder of the Sovereign. In light of your full cooperation, I sentence you to seven years of labor, so you can atone for your crimes, to be served under the authority of the Holy Ecclesiarch of the Dominion."

In the Observer Gallery, the First Scholar preened.

"I accept my punishment," Prysen Ol said.

"The People of Kai, you have failed in your due diligence and have brought an assassin as your candidate. Your minor ask cannot be granted; however, the Dominion acknowledges your efforts and is ready to continue our diplomatic relations."

The Kai leader spoke. "We regret this unfortunate happening.

We shall continue our efforts. May the Sovereign be healthy. May his mother be healthy. May his grandfather on his mother's side be healthy. May his grandmother..."

It took them a few minutes to run through all of Kosandion's extended relatives. Even Caldenia got a wish of health. Finally, they wished good health to his future spouse and children and departed.

"Now we must resolve the matter of the spouse," Kosandion said.

Oond shivered his fins weakly.

Lady Wexyn nodded slowly.

"There are those in the Dominion who call for this selection to be voided, so a new selection can occur," the Sovereign said. "They desire a new search so the perfect candidate to be my spouse can be found. Do the candidates wish to state their opinions on this matter?"

Oond's fins flashed. "No."

"No, *Letero*," Lady Wexyn said.

The acolytes bared their teeth and hissed.

"Very well." Kosandion rose, stone-faced. "I, *Letero Kolivion, Dystim Arbiento,* Sovereign of the Seven Star Dominion, He Who Is Immune to Fate, the Light of the Morning Sun, declare this selection to be over."

On the screens, the Dominion citizens stared, some horrified, some outraged. The sound was off, so only their images came through. The Dominion was in chaos. The throne room was silent and still like a tomb.

In this stillness, Lady Wexyn turned and walked back toward the door.

"Because the perfect candidate has been found," Kosandion said. "She is trying to walk away from me right now."

Lady Wexyn stopped.

Kosandion walked down the steps, off the dais, and crossed the floor to her. She turned, her face almost comically puzzled, completely at odds with her crown and the dress soaked in metaphorical blood.

Kosandion took her hand. His eyes were warm, and a smile stretched his lips.

"Have I finally managed to surprise you, my lady?"

She looked at his fingers holding her hand and then back at him.

"Think carefully, *Letero*," she told him. "Once it is done, it may be too late to regret it."

"No matter what the future will bring, this will be the one thing I will never regret. Will you marry me?" he asked.

She opened her mouth. Nothing came out.

He dipped his head to look at her face.

"Yes," Lady Wexyn said.

On the screens, the crowds of the Dominion exploded in cheers. I turned the sound back on and the happy roar flooded the room. Oond sagged in relief in his fishbowl. Caldenia beamed.

Kosandion hugged Lady Wexyn to him, his face glowing. She smiled back at him. They stood together, a perfect pair, completely focused on each other.

Orata was waving at me.

Oh. The finale! Almost forgot.

I tapped my broom. The floor, the walls and the ceiling of the throne room vanished into the darkness of the cosmos. A galaxy ignited in the black depths and blossomed into a myriad of stars. Radiant nebulae shone with brilliant color. The first planet of the Dominion, a jeweled orb in green and blue, rotated slowly in the distance, followed by other planets, the symbols of the interstellar nation's glory. In the middle of it all, Kosandion and Lady Wexyn stood, holding each other.

The First Sun of the Dominion rose across one of the hidden walls. Its light caught the couple, washing over them, setting them aglow.

Glittering stars and flower petals rained from the ceiling, swirling in a phantom wind.

Kosandion said something. His words were lost in the noise, but I was an innkeeper and I heard them anyway.

"I finally caught you."

"You silly fool," she whispered back.

———

KOSANDION AND I LEANED ON THE RAIL OF HIS BALCONY. IN FRONT of us, Kolinda's ocean shimmered with the light of early evening. A ghostly moon was slowly rising, a scrap of gossamer against the sky. Below us on the beach I had made, Caldenia and Lady Wexyn watched the water and spoke in hushed tones, too low to make out.

Both women had abandoned their elaborate dresses for more practical clothes. Caldenia wore a modest gown in her favorite sage, while Lady Wexyn left the crown of needles behind and switched to simple blue and white robes.

"Are you curious what they're talking about?" I asked Kosandion.

"If I said yes, would you allow me to spy on them?"

"No."

He smiled.

"Is this really what you want?" I asked.

"It's what I've wanted for a long time."

"You realize that you might have been manipulated?"

"I know I have. But the question is, to what end?" He looked at Lady Wexyn. "She doesn't want power. She doesn't want wealth or prestige. She just wants me. Nobody has ever gone to that much trouble just for me."

"What about the Dominion?"

Kosandion turned around and leaned his back against the rail. "You've asked me if public opinion could be swayed before. Since the beginning of the selection, before we even entered your inn, I had committed every resource at my disposal to doing just that. I wanted her to win. I knew that she would take advantage of every opportunity, and she has done it brilliantly. At first, they were amused by her. Some of them ridiculed her. Then they grudgingly acknowledged her skills. They began to like her, and with every appearance, she seduced them a little more until she had them in the palm of her hand. She had endeared herself to them and by the end they wanted her to win as much as I did. Last night I nearly brought my nation to the breaking point by implying the selection would be canceled. The public outcry in her favor drowned out the remaining critics. The Dominion loves her."

"You never meant to marry Nycati, then? But you told him he was your first choice."

"He was about to take his life into his hands. He was doubting everything, from his birthright to his own abilities. I merely steadied him on his feet."

"And Vercia?"

"I ended that relationship as soon as Wexyn agreed to enter the selection."

"So it was about her from the very beginning?"

He nodded.

"Why her?"

"I don't know. There is something about her. I can't describe it, but I feel it. My life is very regimented, and it always has been. My time is rationed like water in the desert. So much of it isn't mine. And she, she is chaos. She loves me for me, and I'm a deeply selfish man. I want all of that love. She is the one person who is just mine, outside of the rules and regulations. Nobody picked her for me, nobody picked me for her."

"You picked each other."

"Precisely. It is indescribably rare in my world. An outrageous luxury."

He looked at her over his shoulder.

"I have worked beyond all limits to crush most of my pressing problems during this selection. I've steadied the borders. The Hope Crushing Horde will busy itself with Surkar and his faction. The Holy Anocracy must sort out House Meer. The largest Gaheas kingdom is about to have a civil war, and the rest of their kingdoms will sit tight to watch it. The Murder Beaks, who were itching to invade, will target the Muterzen Fleet. I've dismantled the leadership of the Conservative Alliance and forced Behoun to make their choice. The domestic opposition to my rule is reeling and will take some time to formulate a new strategy. I've done all this to buy us a little respite. Some quiet time for me and her. It won't last, but we will enjoy every moment to the fullest before the Dominion births yet another catastrophe and hurls it into my lap."

"Life is stumbling from one catastrophe to another."

"Yes, and you have waited, for my sake, to resolve yours. Access to the portal is yours. You may use it as many times as you need. It is the least I can do."

"You're always welcome at our inn, *Letero*. Anytime you and Lady Wexyn need another small respite or wish to relax by an ocean filled with monsters, our doors are always open."

He glanced at his aunt. "Monsters indeed."

Caldenia turned around and gave him a sharp look.

"She couldn't have heard us, could she?" he muttered under his breath.

"Your aunt is a remarkable woman. She has been my guest for years, and I'm still not sure of her limits. Sadly, there are still contracts on her life."

The selection had reminded the galaxy that Caldenia existed. Some of the contracts had expired but now they were back.

"She will be our guest for a while longer."

"I think she enjoys it," Kosandion said. "It is a welcome rest after decades of pressure."

Lady Wexyn turned to Kosandion and waved.

"I am summoned," he said. "It's been a pleasure, Dina."

"I'm glad Gertrude Hunt could meet your needs."

He took off down the stairs.

Resven approached. Below, Kosandion put his arm around Lady Wexyn's shoulders, and she slid her arm around his waist.

"They make such a lovely couple," Resven smiled. "He couldn't do better."

I almost did a double take. "You were in on it?"

He nodded.

"Since the very beginning?"

He nodded again.

"Resven, you are an excellent actor."

"Innkeeper, I am whatever my *Letero* requires me to be. I wish you luck in your search for your friend. Take care, Karron is a brutal place. I can't imagine what sort of creature would make its lair there."

"My..." "Boyfriend" no longer seemed adequate, and we hadn't talked about getting married. "Lover" seemed too cheesy. "Sean will come with me."

"I'm glad to hear that. Your partner is impressive."

"Partner." Yes, that was good. "He is."

———

I walked away from Resven, passed through Kosandion's quarters into the hallway, and entered the throne room. It seemed cavernous now, empty and abandoned. Guests gave the inn life. They came from faraway places, bringing their magic and vitality with them, and they breathed it into the spaces they occupied. But eventually they left. The guests always did.

I passed the Ocean Dining Hall. Orro and his kitchen helpers were drinking whatever liquids got their various species intoxicated. They had done their job well, and now it was time for the kitchen staff to party. I slipped by the doorway, dampening the noise of my footsteps. I had seen kitchen staff parties before, and I needed to steer way clear of this one.

At the far end of the throne room, two people were talking. Miralitt and Derryl. The werewolf woman wore the uniform of a Capital Guard. So, she must have decided to take Miralitt's offer.

The Capital Guard didn't hire werewolves. The people of Auul made great mercenaries, but they resisted assimilation into other cultures. They were loyal to each other beyond all others, and that loyalty made them immune to the Dominion's collective empathy. Sooner or later, they abandoned their duty and returned to their werewolf settlements.

Derryl was different. She wanted to leave the memories of Auul behind, and she desperately needed a place to belong and a cause that had nothing to do with growing fur and being compared to other werewolves. The people of Auul had fought the war for their planet for decades, and their martial arts were unparalleled. Derryl had all the proper training, and she had excelled in it, because she had pushed herself harder than anyone to gain that expertise. Technically, Miralitt agreed to hire her as a favor for Sean, but all four of us knew that it was a huge win for Miralitt. Hopefully, it would be a big win for Derryl as well.

I walked by them. Derryl bowed her head to me. Miralitt nodded.

It was almost as good of a solution as what happened to Prysen Ol. The First Scholar had been so pleased with himself, he'd actually squawked while explaining it to me. Prysen Ol was brilliant and conflicted, ripe for some guidance and conversion to a higher purpose. The Holy Ecclesiarch knew exactly how to mold him, and by the time he was done, the Dominion would gain a rare talent. Apparently, the First Scholar hadn't gotten very far with his pleas to Kosandion, so he had gone to his favorite debate companion and announced that he had found his successor. I had my doubts, but stranger things had happened.

They even let Prysen Ol keep Tomato with him. The assassin

and the green bear had a blood brother pact. There was probably an interesting story behind it, but I didn't have time to listen to it.

I passed through the last hallway and walked into the arrival chamber. Sean and Tony stood in front of the portal. Sean wore an enviro-hazard combat suit. Dark gray, it covered him head to toe, leaving only his face bare. His favorite green knife was in a sheath on his waist. He'd strapped a gun to his back, and another to his right thigh.

"... Got this. Don't worry, nothing will happen to the inn," Tony was saying.

The two of them turned toward me.

"Are you sure about this?" Sean asked me.

"Very sure." I took off my robe.

I wore the same suit. My energy whip rested in its holder on my thigh. Sean had insisted that I bring a backup weapon. I held out my hand. My broom landed in it, flashed with blue, and turned into a spear.

The suits came with respirators and full-face plates which could be extended on a moment's notice, turning the suits fully airtight. Light and flexible, this gear was designed for planetary combat in hazardous environments.

"I would rather you stay," Sean said.

We had been over this. If whatever took Wilmos had targeted Sean, it could have sent his corrupted ad-hals after him any time he had left the inn. Of the two of us, he spent more time away from Gertrude Hunt. It didn't want him. It wanted me, and I had to figure out why.

Tony agreed to stay behind to see our guests off. Most of them had left anyway. The oomboles had taken off before the final ceremony was even over, relieved after Resven assured them that their minor ask would be granted.

Cookie departed right after the oomboles. He'd been giddy about winning the Dominion from Clan Sai. Unfortunately, Clan

Sai would retaliate, and soon, so Cookie and his entourage were needed back at the Merchant house to prepare their defense.

Dagorkun had left too, after thanking Sean and me for our hospitality. He had a lot of things to discuss with his parents. Gaston and Karat were still at the inn. Gaston had the stamina of a camel, but his body finally gave out and he went to bed and likely wouldn't get up until tomorrow. Orro's kitchen helpers would leave after the party, the First Scholar and his assistants were already gone, and Kosandion, Lady Wexyn, and Resven would depart in the next hour or so. Tony would handle that.

We had to rescue Wilmos. I looked at the portal. No reason to delay any further.

"Ready?" Sean asked.

I held out my hand. "Hold my hand?"

Sean reached out and took my hand in his. We walked into the portal together.

[28]

A door opens...

The final portal gate was a rounded arch of pale blue metal. In random places, the smooth metal shell had broken away, exposing the complex tangle of electronics underneath. A small symbol had been etched into the center of the arch at the highest point of the curve—a stylized explosion.

"Of course," Sean said.

It was a Tuhl portal. Because why not?

"What are the chances of us exploding, do you think?" I asked him.

"Zero if we don't enter."

Not entering wasn't an option. Wilmos was somewhere on the other side.

For some reason, I'd thought that the Dominion's capital would have a direct portal to Karron. It didn't. It had taken three portals and an hour-long flight via small military shuttle to reach this point atop a remote mountain range on Shurb, the Dominion's least populated planet. The Dominion provided the craft, the instructions, and the coordinates, but no pilot. Fortunately, we had our own.

Sean had landed the shuttle on a wide platform cut into the side of the mountain, on the ancient stones worn by weather and time to near glass smoothness. The gate sat in the center of it. At the southern end, a huge door led inside the mountain.

We stared at the gate some more. It seemed completely inert. No mechanism to activate it. Approaching it didn't do anything either.

"Is someone supposed to meet us?" I wondered.

"That was the plan. Miralitt's brief said, 'wait for the operator.'"

We waited. Despite the dorky name, Shurb was a pretty planet. It was fall, and the woods below the platform were awash with golds and reds. The air smelled fresh and crisp.

The giant door swung open with a loud clang and a throng of creatures emerged, followed by something very large and covered with an enormous tarp. The keepers of the gate stood about four feet tall on slender legs that ended in hooves. They wore quilted tunics over their slim humanoid bodies. Their heads were slightly goat-like with long narrow muzzles and very dark elongated eyes. Their ears were long and pointed and they poked through their manes of coarse hair.

"Oh no." Our luck couldn't possibly have gotten worse.

"What are they?" Sean asked.

"Barsas. Our translator implants won't work, and I'm very rusty."

"Wow, a language you're not fluent in." He cracked a smile.

"Nobody knows every language in the galaxy, and they almost never come to Earth."

"There is no need to get defensive."

The Barsas stopped in front of us. Their leader, an old white-haired male, stepped forward and raised his arms.

Here we go.

"Barsa! Barsa, barsa, barsa. Barsa." Each word was accompanied by arm-waving and finger-pointing.

"You've got to be kidding me," Sean said. "Is that all they say?"

"Yep. Hush, I'm trying to concentrate."

"Barsa. Barsa, barsa."

The leader nodded sagely.

"What did he say?" Sean asked keeping his voice low.

"'Welcome. Thank you for being eaten.'"

"That couldn't possibly be right."

"I know." I stepped forward and held my palms out, making small circles. "Barsa?"

"Barsa. Barsa-barsa, barsa."

"Oh. 'Prepare to be eaten.'"

"That's not better, Dina."

The Barsas pulled on the tarp, and it slid to the ground, revealing a huge, wheeled platform, large enough to contain three semi-trucks side by side. The platform supported a massive mollusk in a spiral shell, dripping wet and brightly colored with blues and greens. It looked a little like the nautilus of Earth's oceans, except it was a hundred times larger. Its tentacles were a bright electric pink and six feet long. A big round head that should have belonged to a snail protruded from the center of the tentacle fringe.

"Unexpected," Sean said.

"There might be an underground lake inside the mountain."

"Probably a sea. I smell salt water."

That didn't make it any less weird.

"Is that the thing that will eat us?" Sean asked.

I pointed at the mollusk and waved my arms. "Barsa, baaarsa, barsa?"

The Barsas stared at me for a moment and broke into high-pitched squeals, rocking back and forth and clutching their tummies.

"Apparently, I'm very funny."

"I got that," Sean said, his face communicating zero enthusiasm.

The leader finally managed to get his giggles under control. "Barsa, barsa barsa, barsa."

"'Prepare to be eaten by the portal.'"

"Oh good."

A low hum came from the mollusk. The stripes on its shell began to spiral, first slow, then faster and faster.

"Barsa. Barsa. Barsa." The leader waved his arms.

"Give us your arms."

Sean gave me a look. I held my arm out. Two Barsas ran up to us and slapped small hexagonal timers onto our forearms. The digital numbers flashed with red. 5,000 long moments. 83 minutes.

"Barsa! Barsa, barsa, barsa. Barsa-barsa!" The leader put his hands together as if holding an invisible apple and opened his fingers, raising his arms. "Boom!"

"Portal must spit us back before the time runs out or..."

"We go boom."

"Yep."

I tapped the sensor by my right ear. A respirator unfolded, adhering to my skin over my mouth and nose. An earpiece slipped into my right ear and a clear faceplate unfolded in segments over my face. A short hiss told me my suit was sealed.

"Good?" Sean asked in my ear.

"Yes."

The suits had about 6 hours of oxygen, so we wouldn't run out of air. However, they wouldn't stand up to Karron's environment. Nothing would. The Dominion assured us that the conditions beyond the portal were optimal, but we didn't want to take any chances.

Sean pulled his gun off his back. From the outside, the faceplate was opaque, a dark gray, smooth egg, and he looked like some faceless alien creature.

A burst of pink lightning shot out from the nautilus' tentacles and licked the portal. It powered up in a burst of sparks and projected a small holographic screen to the side. Unfamiliar symbols glowed on it.

"Pressure: 15.2 psi," Sean said. "Atmosphere: nitrogen-oxygen mix, O_2 at 21.3%, CO_2 is a bit high, but we should be fine. Humidity at 88%, 60^0 F."

"You read Tuhl?" I asked.

"Yes."

I should've known. If it had to do with weapons or transportation, Sean could understand it and fix it.

The second burst of lightning struck the portal. The Barsas raised their arms in unison.

"BARSA!"

We ran into the portal.

———

My feet landed on something solid. It looked remarkably like a wooden floor. A rotting wooden floor, with boards marked with dark stains and speckled with black mold. Weird gray warts that had to be lichen or fungi sprouted between clumps of toxic-looking yellow sponges.

I looked up. We stood in the entryway of a house. The walls were coated in lichen and mold. Thick blisters the size of my head protruded here and there, caught in a net of plant roots. The liquid inside them glowed with dull phlegmy light. Flesh-colored slime dripped from between the gaps in the crown molding.

Where the hell were we? It was like we had landed in a petri dish with a bacterial colony grown from a swab taken at a truck stop bathroom.

I glanced over my shoulder. Behind us, the portal was a perfectly round, vertical puddle of pale pink on the wall. The holographic readout in the top of my faceplate was green across the board. The atmosphere was safe to breathe and free of contaminants, despite all the bizarre growth.

Magic slid around me, dripping from the walls, creeping just inside the floor, a revolting miasma, like decomposing body fluids.

It didn't feel right.

The magic sensed me. The nearest stream curved, angling toward me. The entire wall around the portal was covered with it. It poured out like a foul waterfall. I took a few steps away from it.

The revolting magic bubbled up through the gap in the floorboards and touched me.

The world swam. Blood pounded in my ears. I couldn't catch my breath. I gasped, but there was no air. Black circles crowded at the edge of my vision.

My stomach jerked.

I slapped the side of my helmet. The faceplate and the respirator retracted in a flash, and I vomited onto the floor. A horrible stench bathed me, a cloying, sickening odor of decay, and mold, and rotting wood, like the inside of a grave. I planted my broom into the floor, clung to it, and retched.

The magic spiraled around me, clamping at my feet, trying to get at my soul. I reeled. I had to get out of here. This was wrong, so very wrong. I had to get away! I had to—

Sean caught me by my shoulders and pulled me to him. Gradually his voice penetrated the haze, calm and steady. "You're okay. I've got you. Breathe."

I sagged against him, shivering. The magic pooled at my feet, and more was coming, rushing toward me. It veered around Sean and went straight for me. Despair rose from it like a tsunami and dragged me under. Spasms rocked me, and I cried.

"Take your time. It will be okay."

This was so much worse than the corruption I had felt in the dead ad-hal. This was something deeper, more obscene, more horrifying, worse than anything I had ever experienced. Worse than the baby inn dying, worse than...

Sean clamped me tight. "Does it hurt?"

I tried to answer, but only sobs came out. I felt so sad. All I could do was grieve. I shook and shuddered, but the tears wouldn't stop.

Sean turned me and stepped toward the portal.

"No," I managed.

"You're going back."

"No—"

The wall to the right burst open. Two corrupted ad-hals rushed at us. Sean fired. The weapon whined, spitting a stream of supercharged plasma. It took the first ad-hal in the chest. The creature shrieked, throwing its clawed hands in front of it, trying to conjure a barrier.

I had to help. I forced myself upright and stabbed my broom into the floor. My magic swelled inside me.

A slimy, rotting tendril burst out of the wall behind me, caught my waist in its loop like a lasso, and dragged me back. My feet left the ground. I flew backwards, through the house. Sean spun toward me. I saw his face, bleached with alarm and shock, and then walls snapped closed between us one by one, as the tendril carried me through the rooms, right, left, right, ripped the broom out of my hands, and hurled me into darkness.

———

I TUCKED MY HEAD IN AS I FELL, ROLLED ACROSS THE FLOOR, AND came up to my feet. The practice sessions with Sean paid off. I'd have a few bruises, but nothing was broken.

I was in a small room. The lights came on, the same nasty blisters. A trail of smashed fungi and moss darkened the floor where I had fallen. My broom was nowhere to be seen.

I wiped the nasty smudge off my cheek with the back of my hand and turned. A doorway formed in the wall in front of me, a rectangle of blue-green light.

This was an inn. I was sure of it. The rotting corpse of one, but still an inn. Somehow it was here, inside the Dominion's mining facility, slowly decaying, decomposing into sludge.

Who would do this? This was monstrous.

Magic spilled from the walls. The floorboards sweated it out in large beads. It streamed to me. I understood now. I was an innkeeper, and this wretched abomination of an inn knew it. It was beyond healing, but it was reaching out just the same, like a dying dog, crawling to a human for one last pet on the head. Dragging itself, battered and broken, for just one more cuddle to ease the pain.

It hurt so much.

I wiped my tears. I would find whoever did this. I would rip them apart with my bare hands.

And I would have to find them. If this was an inn, someone was controlling it. They would never let me get to Sean. My best chance was to locate the innkeeper and kill them.

I took my whip out of its strap and walked through the doorway. A big domed room spread before me, lit by a blue cube caught in a network of robotic arms that formed a pillar between the floor and the ceiling. Ahead the rotting boards ended in a ragged semicircle, leaving a bare polymer floor. The rotting walls went up about one third of the way up, and then fell short, mirroring the boundary defined by the floor. The rest, the walls, the high rounded ceiling, was transparent material, and beyond it, olive nothingness spread.

The cube pulsed. A pearlescent wave passed through the glass-like dome. It took me a minute to put it all together. We were under Karron's ocean, and the base was running a short range forcefield generator to keep the planet at bay. Someone had brought an inn inside the mining facility, but it couldn't thrive here. It was poisoned, corrupted, and dying, so weak it couldn't even claim this room all the way.

High-tech instrument consoles lined the perimeter of the dome. The lights still blinked. If I was right, the cube was a zero-point energy generator siphoning power from a micro-scopic dimensional pocket. I had seen one before, powering an artificial wormhole. The Tuhls had no respect for the universe, but occasionally their gadgets worked. This was one of those rare times their tech was stable. No wonder Kosandion was sure the mining facility was operational. The cube would power it nearly indefinitely, running all support systems and keeping the force field bubble around the facility so Karron couldn't touch it.

And right now, the robotic arms were blocking my view.

I walked forward. The magic followed me, chasing after me, pooling in my footprints. I stepped off the boards onto the high-tech floor. The magic swelled behind me, unable to follow. More and more of it flooded in like a tide, desperate to keep touching. Every contact with it hurt like watching a loved one take their last breath.

"I'll be right back," I whispered.

The magic tide shivered, emanating so much distress I stumbled.

I walked across the floor to the far end of the dome, rounding the pillar.

To my left, in the open, Wilmos stood frozen in a column of light, caught in a stasis field.

He must've come to after they brought him in, because the werewolf inside the column was in the wetwork shape. Big, with a shaggy dark mane streaked with gray, Wilmos looked ready to leap, his arms raised, his mouth gaping, the sharp fangs daring an attack.

My pulse sped up.

I stood very still, listening and looking. Wilmos was bait.

The dome lay empty.

"Daughter of the Wanderer..." a male voice said behind me.

I turned slowly. A creature stood on the polymer floor. No, not a creature, a man. An innkeeper in a dark robe, tattered and torn, with his hood up, holding a white broom. The robe flowed, shifting color from tar black to mottled gray, and black again. Its frayed hem flared above the floor, moving, sliding, melting into nothing and regenerating.

The tendrils of the innkeeper's power slithered to me. It touched me. Ice washed over me in an electrifying wave. My skin crawled.

The robe wasn't fabric. It was the corruption, the source of the darkness inside Michael, my brother's best friend, and the ad-hal I had crushed out of existence at Baha-char. He was clothed in corruption. It was pouring out of his body. He and the robe were one.

And he knew my father.

"Your father is a problem." He had a terrible voice. It faded as he spoke, brushing against my skin like cold slime. "Your mother is a problem. Your brother is a problem. Now you are a problem."

"Is." He said "is." My parents were still alive.

Everything in me wanted to lash out at him. No innkeeper could see that putrid husk of the inn and not want to disintegrate the one responsible. He was an abomination. But I had to talk to him. If I didn't, we would never know why any of this had happened.

The man turned his head and looked at the olive ocean outside. I could just make out the narrow sliver of his jaw. It was an odd color, a kind of slightly purple tint, like a Caucasian body frozen in mid-livor mortis.

"There are two of us. You and me."

Okay, we established he could count.

"Did it hurt when the seed died?"

How did he know about the baby inn? Should I answer?

I took a shot. "Yes."

He nodded. "Does it still hurt?"

"Yes." It hurt me every time I thought about it. Most innkeepers never survived the death of the inn they were bonded to. Even though our bond had lasted mere minutes, witnessing that inn's death nearly ended me. I had been very lucky to survive it.

He nodded. "It hurt me too when I killed my inn. Every inn I kill hurts. The pain is never-ending."

What inns? How many?

"Why?"

He didn't answer.

"Why would you kill your inn? It trusted you. It loved you. Why would you betray it?"

He turned to me, and I saw the bottom half of his face. "Ask them."

Them who? "The other innkeepers?"

"Ask them about Sebastien North. Ask them what they've done. How I have suffered."

Oh.

"You have." His voice rolled through the dome, melting into a hiss. "They didn't tell you."

"What didn't they tell me?"

"Of all of us, you and I are the only ones who survived to know the pain. We carry it with us, always." He paused. "I will give you one chance. Take the werewolves and go. Leave your inn. Leave your planet. Don't look back, and I will come for you last."

"Why would I need to leave the planet?"

"Because I will devour it. Every inn, every innkeeper, every ad-hal. Every human."

410

There was an awful finality to the way he said it. He wasn't angry, or hurt, or conflicted. He simply stated a fact.

He wouldn't tell me anything more unless I found common ground. He sympathized with me because we had both endured the greatest tragedy an innkeeper could suffer. If what he said was true, he existed in a state of constant suffering. There had to be some shred of human emotion left in him. I had to find it and exploit it. I needed to know why he was doing this.

"Did you have a cat?"

He didn't answer.

"I found a cat, a big gray Maine Coon with green eyes. He has a collar with the initials SN on it."

"Belaud."

Oh wow. It was his cat.

"He yet lives? Is he well?"

"Yes. If I had my phone, I would show you. I took pictures of him. He walks through the inn as he pleases. It opens walls for him."

The man's voice was almost wistful. "That was always his way. I found him during a thunderstorm. He was so small, he fit in one of my hands. It was May 30th. I remember because the next day, Royal Governor Martin fled the Tryon Palace for New York, and my father had opened a treasured bottle of whiskey. That was my first sip of spirits."

Tryon Palace was in New Bern, North Carolina. My father had taken us there to visit. Martin was NC's last Royal Governor, and he'd fled in 1775. I knew this because dad remembered Martin and didn't like him. Holy crap. This man was my father's age.

"Why do you hate my father?"

"I don't. The Wanderer got in the way. He always gets in the way. Now you are in my way."

And we had come full circle.

"I know you are looking for my soul," the man said. "You will not find it."

"I want to understand why. What is it you want?"

"To kill us all."

"But to what end? Something terrible must have happened to you but murdering everyone won't make you feel better."

"It's not for me. I will feel nothing. The inns and innkeepers shouldn't be. I will purge their symbiosys from existence. It's not necessary for you to understand it. Accept it as inevitable and go."

"No."

A deep sigh echoed through the dome. He turned, his robe swirling. "Why do you persist in being difficult? Take my gift. Get out of my way, foolish child. Do not trample on my last act of kindness. There will be no more."

"You were an innkeeper once. You felt the bond with your inn. They rely on us. They trust us. Whatever faults innkeepers have, whatever crimes they committed against you, the inns are innocent. Does that not mean something to you?"

"Why should it? My inn was taken from me. My family, my face, they took everything, and I will leave them with nothing. I will kill every inn in the galaxy, so the innkeepers can never resurrect themselves again."

"But you still feel the pain. You still long for the bond." I pointed to the remains of the room at the other end of the dome. "You brought an inn here, and now it's dying. It's rotting and suffering. How can you stand this?"

He turned to fully face me. His bloodless lips stretched, and he smiled, showing sharp conical teeth.

"I brought it here for you."

What?

"Do you still not see? Look around you. Does it not look familiar? Does it not feel like home?"

I stared at the semicircle of the rotten floor, the slimy walls, the remnants of the decaying furniture... There was a couch on the left. Mildew had slicked its upholstery, but some of the original color remained, a happy summer sky blue with big yellow dandelions. My mother had upholstered that couch for me when I was seven years old. I had picked out the fabric. Our dog, an old boxer, had chewed on the front leg of it, and the bite marks were still there...

Oh my God.

I saw it now. The crooked lamp—Maud and I had knocked it over when she was chasing me around the house, and we could never get the lampshade to sit straight again. My old desk. The remnants of my rug.

This was my bedroom. This was my parents' inn. My home. He ruined my home. He was torturing our inn.

I stumbled away from him, toward the rotting floor and the magic that waited for me there. It washed over me, stabbing into my heart, and I felt the last weak pulses of Magnolia Green. The magic I had sensed, the one so desperately trying to touch me, was the lifeblood of the inn spilling from its dying core.

His voice chased me. "Do you understand now?"

I made my mouth move through the pain. "Yes."

I understood.

"This is a demonstration of my power."

"It's a demonstration of your fear." I called on my magic and poured my pain into it. I shaped and molded my power as only an innkeeper could. "You feared my parents. You tried to kill them and failed, so you defiled their inn in your impotent rage. You used its suffering to convince yourself that you won. And now you fear me. You have gone through all this trouble to give me a warning, because deep down you are afraid. You're right to be afraid."

He sighed. "So be it."

The man smashed his white broom into the floor. Corruption burst from him in twisted dark currents and bit into the walls, burrowing into the inn, forcing it to comply. The wooden floor moved like a churning sea, speeding toward me.

I sank all my magic into the floor under me. It burst through the currents and eddies of Magnolia Green's lifeblood, colliding with the corruption squirming through them. My power shot through the fading inn, rushing through its branches, its roots, all the way to its injured core.

Our magics collided. The bond reignited in a blinding burst of power. The patina of corruption that permeated the inn, sliding over its branches and smothering its roots, burned away in an instant, opening a clear bath between me and the core.

Magnolia Green was *mine*.

The corrupted innkeeper screamed. His polluted currents slammed into me, battering the inn, hammering at my defenses, each blow sending an agonizing jolt through us both.

I held my hand out, and my broom landed in it.

"It won't help you!" he snarled.

My power wound through the broom in a tight spiral, ready to be unleashed. My body buckled, struggling to channel all that power, and I had to force the words out.

"This inn cradled me as I took my first breath. No matter how hard you try, it will never be yours."

I planted the broom into the floor.

Magic tore out of me like a magic hurricane and smashed into the corrupted innkeeper.

The corruption flailed around me, burning and raging. It was pure hate. Hate and anger, a torrent of it streaming from him. There was so much of it, more than any being could contain, and I could not understand how it didn't tear him apart. Every lash of it frayed my soul. There was blood in my mouth. My chest hurt, every breath a conscious fight against the anvil sitting on my ribs.

I gripped him with my magic and squeezed.

We tore at each other, he with his corruption and I with my innkeeper magic. The dome quaked. I felt the rotting walls collapsing behind me. The substance of the inn disintegrated, as it sacrificed more and more of its power to feed my attack.

He'd drowned Magnolia Green in his corruption. It fed like a leech on the inn's magic for nobody knew how long. The inn had fought against it, trying to survive, trying to preserve some small part of itself. But now I had asked for its help.

Magnolia Green loved me from the moment I was born. It gave everything to me. All of its power. All of its magic. Every last drop.

Its branches withered. Its roots turned to dust. It kept nothing for itself.

Magnolia Green was killing itself to protect me.

I pushed against the current, trying to hold it back. The magic swept my resistance aside and poured out of me. The inn had made up its mind. It would defend me. I was powerless to stop it.

We were bound, the three of us, caught in a terrible circle of power—me channeling my innkeeper magic, him whipping currents of corruption that seared agony into me, and Magnolia Green, tied to us both, split in the moment of death between coercion and love, devoured by one and freely sacrificing itself for the other.

The horror of it was too much to take. I heard a sound and realized I was screaming, crying like a child from pain and grief. I would be the end of my parents' inn. Magnolia Green knew it and still it fed me. Its desperation coursed through me. It knew that its death throes would take me with it. I would not survive the death of the inn where I was born. Our bond was too strong.

We would die together here. But we had to kill him first, so no other inn would be violated and left to rot.

We pushed against him as one. The magic pouring out of me had color. It glowed like a blade of grass with sunlight shining through. I had merged with Magnolia Green.

The corrupted innkeeper howled, hammering at me with pulses of his fetid magic. I turned my magic into a pale green dome around me, trying to shield myself enough to stay conscious. Orange lightning sparked within the corrupted currents and smashed against my defenses. The explosion of pain nearly dropped me to my knees.

He flailed harder, whipping the lightning back and forth across my shield. The corruption bit at me, and its teeth were freezing like the space between stars. It was not human. It was a part of him now, but it wasn't born from him. He had found it and made it his own.

If only I could separate the corruption from him. If I could isolate it, I could crush it out of existence.

It was pouring out of the center of his chest, from behind his breastbone. He'd hidden it before, but he'd gone into a frenzy and forgot to guard himself.

I could either attack or defend. Not both. This would be it. Magnolia Green was at its very last limit. There was nothing left except its core and one last root, too weak to break through the floor and reach me.

I dropped the dome, shaping my magic into a needle-thin beam of brilliant green and stabbed at his chest with it.

The corruption slapped me and tore right into my soul.

There was no word for that kind of pain...

My magic struck him. He screamed and yanked his power back, whipping the corruption about him in a tight spiral, forming his own shield. My green beam bore at it but couldn't penetrate. I couldn't get through it.

There wasn't enough power. I didn't have enough.

I failed...

Sean burst through the wall, a huge, enraged beast, covered in slime and blood.

A single whip of fetid darkness snapped from the corrupted innkeeper's dome and lashed Sean, cutting a bloody gash in his shoulder.

He ignored it and cleared the distance between me and him in a single leap. He landed in a crouch, gripped my broom with one clawed hand, and drove the other into the floor. I felt his magic stream from his fingers into the floor. It was just like my own, the power of an innkeeper accumulated and nurtured over months of taking care of the inn.

The floor under our feet split. The last remaining root of Magnolia Green broke through and wound around us. Power punched me, nearly taking me off my feet.

I fed it all into my beam. The corrupted shield popped like a dirty soap bubble. The green beam struck the corrupted innkeeper in his chest, right into the source of his power. His robe tore. For fraction of a second I saw the smudge of the innkeeper's true face and his eyes brimming with fear.

He screamed and hurled something behind him. White lightning tore from the cube as something drained the zero-point energy generator's power in a flash. The fabric of space split, and through the ragged tear I saw trees the color of blood.

No! No, damn it, no!

He dove through the dimensional rift, the tatters of his robe spinning around him as he vanished. The tear snapped shut.

He got away. He escaped. Aaaaaa, he escaped!

The generator's cube turned dull. The pearlescent light dissolved into nothing. The dome around us creaked as Karron took the mining facility into its mouth and bit down.

My arms were red. My face felt wet, my neck, my body inside my suit... All of me was covered in blood. It had slipped out of my pores. It didn't matter. Magnolia Green was dying, and I would go with it. Every pulse of its core resonated through me, and they were so weak and slow. I would hold the inn to the very end, so it wouldn't perish alone. I owed it that.

The stasis light around Wilmos died, and the old werewolf collapsed onto the floor. The dome quaked, groaning.

Sean sprinted across the room, slung Wilmos over his shoulder, and hurried back to me.

The core of Magnolia Green had grown so dim. It wouldn't be long now.

"We have to go!" Sean snarled.

"It's okay," I told him. "Leave me."

He grabbed me. "Dina, you can't be here when it dies!"

Something crunched. Cracks formed on the dome. Karron's ocean was coming in.

Sean grabbed me by my waist and jerked me off my feet, away from my connection with the inn.

"I can't let it die alone! Leave me, Sean!"

"Never."

The last root of Magnolia Green snapped, caught the three of us, and dragged us through the dust, through the sterile hallways, through the hole in the ceiling... Behind us thunder pealed.

The portal loomed in front of us.

"No! I won't—"

The root clutching me split. A thin green sprout spiraled out of it, beautiful and free of corruption. It broke free, a little branch with a single leaf on it, and I caught it.

With the last pulse of its core, Magnolia Green hurled us into the portal.

———

I cradled the sprout to me, trying to shield it against Baha-char's sun. It was like a four-foot-long grape vine, but it was a brilliant shamrock green, as thick as my wrist at the base and narrowing down to a wispy tendril with three tiny leaves. Two more had sprouted in the time I carried it. It hugged me as I paced on the far side of the alley leading to Gertrude Hunt's door.

I had no idea how long it could survive. Every moment counted, but this was an incredibly dangerous idea. It was better to be safe than sorry.

The sprout glowed softly, brushing against my neck like a kitten eager for a stroke.

"Don't die," I whispered. "Please don't die."

An hour ago, Sean, Wilmos, and I fell out of the mining portal in front of the Barsas. I couldn't even talk at that point. Sean had loaded me and still unconscious Wilmos into the shuttle, stabbed me with every medical cocktail he could find in the shuttle's first aid kit, and then he flew at breakneck speed toward the planet's portal center.

Sometime during the flight, the last echoes of merging with Magnolia Green had faded, and my sanity returned. I remembered who I was. And then I cried, and Sean said soothing things, and I told him I was sorry for scaring him and wanting to die with the inn, and that I loved him.

After I was done crying, I realized that I was carrying what was left of Magnolia Green with me. It wasn't a seed. It was a branch without any root, almost like a cutting. If it were a normal plant, I would put it into a nutrient-rich solution and let the roots form, but inns didn't work that way.

Inns were multidimensional organisms that broke the rules of physics. Even at the seed stage, their primary root was already formed inside the seed's shell. When you planted an inn seed, the root anchored it to reality and physical space. Without it, even if the seed sprouted, it couldn't hold on to our world and died.

That was why as soon as an inn opened a new door, it would try to root through the space around it to claim some of it for its grounds. That was also why two inns couldn't coexist in proximity—it wasn't their branches, it was their roots that created a problem.

If I put that cutting into a solution and waited for it to grow, it would only wither. It had survived this long, because it was bonded with me, and I fed it what little magic I had left.

In gardening, there was one other method to preserve a cutting, and no innkeeper had ever tried it before, because nobody before me had been given a cutting by an inn. I had no idea what would happen if we tried it.

I told Sean about it during the flight. He smiled and told me he trusted me. At the very least, we had to try it. But it would have to be done very carefully. Bringing the cutting right into the heart of Gertrude Hunt through the portal was out of the question. We had no idea what would happen. We needed to introduce it to the inn outside of the grounds, on neutral, territory, and we would need to evacuate Gertrude Hunt's guests first, just to be safe.

Sean and I had retraced our steps all the way to the Dominion's capital, dragging the comatose Wilmos with us, and then we split up. Sean took the portal to Gertrude Hunt, while I took one of the Dominion's portals to Baha-char.

I made my way to the alley and waited.

A door opened in the empty air and Tony came out of it.

"Dina!"

I waved at him.

He sprinted to me. Behind him the door remained open. Beast burst through it and dashed to me as fast as her little legs could carry her. A moment later Sean appeared in the doorway.

Our gazes met. I looked for reassurance and found it. We were still on the same page about trying this.

"Let's do it," Sean called out.

"Are you two out of your minds?" Tony demanded, braking in front of me. "If you bring a seed into the inn, both inns will die!"

"It's not a seed. It's a cutting."

"What?"

"It's a cutting," I repeated. "There is no root."

Tony swore. "It's a fucking inn, not an African violet."

The cutting of Magnolia Green slid off my neck and gently stretched toward the inn.

"Did you evacuate everyone?"

"Orro is with Marais. Everyone else went through the portal to the Dominion," he said. "Karat, Gaston, and Wilmos are guarding Caldenia. She is...unhappy."

"She owes me. She can wait a few minutes under the heavy

420

guard." As soon as this was over and if everything went well, everyone could return to the inn. "Is Wilmos conscious?"

"Yes, and pissed off as hell."

We did save him. I should've been happy but right now it barely registered.

Sean waved me over. I started toward the door slowly.

"Two inns can't occupy the same space," Tony said. "Best case scenario, both die. Worst case, we collapse reality. If this happens, I can't contain it."

A long branch slipped from inside the door and waited, hovering.

"Dina, even if you bring it into the inn, you won't be able to get it to root," Tony said.

"I'm not trying to get it to root."

We were almost to the door. The branch of Gertrude Hunt shivered a few feet away. Sean patted it, reassuring it.

"I'm going to graft it."

Tony swore again.

The branch reached out to me. The sprout uncoiled itself from around my neck and stretched toward it. It was almost as if the two of them knew what they had to do.

I held my breath and reached out with my hand.

Gertrude Hunt brushed against my fingers.

Magic shot through me like an arrow from Gertrude Hunt, straight into the cutting, and back to the inn. The world vanished. A star-studded darkness blossomed in front of me with a glowing nebulous vortex unfurling at its center. An electric current of magic strummed through me, vibrating in every bone and tendon.

The darkness vanished, and I saw the branch of Gertrude Hunt slide across me back into the inn, with the sprout growing from it.

The branch slipped into the inn. A magic pulse rocked Gertrude Hunt.

Sean disappeared into the depth of inn.

I sprinted to the doorway and dove through it, Tony right behind me. The door slammed shut behind us.

The inn quaked and rumbled. The cutting was moving through it, a knot of magic sliding further away. We chased it, through the inn's many rooms, through the hallways and the walls, to the back, to the plain hallway where a nascent door waited.

Reality exploded open before our eyes. The wall in front of us disintegrated, fracturing into exuberant sunlight. A stretch of flat ground lay ahead, sheathed in soft green and blue grass. A hundred yards ahead the ground ended, and beyond it an ocean of air stretched, with a grassy plain at its bottom. Groups of white stone mesas thrust from it toward the sky, crowned with turquoise trees. We were on top of a plateau.

A root slid under our feet, burrowing deep into the soil. It sped toward the cliff. The ground erupted. Branches spiraled up, high, higher, and higher. Hunter green leaves burst open. White flowers as big as my head opened, showing a whirl of pink stamens topped with a bright yellow clump of carpels.

A colossal magnolia, taller than the tallest redwood, wider than the widest sequoia, spread its giant branches over the plateau. Connected to the inn, and yet separate from it, but vibrant and so much alive. It felt like Magnolia Green. It was more than a tree but less than an inn. It grew from a Gertrude Hunt root, and both were well. Relief washed over me. I slumped forward, and Sean caught me and grinned.

"We can never tell anyone about this," Tony said.

"Are you speaking as an ad-hal or a friend?" Sean asked him.

"Both. Nobody can know. The Assembly will... I don't even know what they will do, but we won't like it."

"Then they don't need to know," Sean said.

A beautiful bird cried out overhead and landed on the magnolia's mighty branches. I had never seen one like it.

"Where are we?" I wondered.

Tony was looking out past the tree, where twin moons rose, one larger and tinted with purple, and the other small and orange.

"This is…" he said.

"Daesyn," Sean finished for him. "Home planet of House Krahr."

The End

CAST OF CHARACTERS

SPOUSAL CANDIDATES

SHORT LIST

Amphie of the Dominion, girl next door, representing planet Behoun, Team Smiles.

Bestata of Holy Anocracy, vampire knight, representing House Meer.

Cyanide, space snow leopard, representing the Higgra.

Donkamins, visually disturbing, representing Children of the Silver Star.

Ellenda of Uma, same origin as the Sovereign's mother, representing planet Kyporo of the Dominion, Team Frowns.

Nycati, psionic and elf-like, representing the Gaheas

Oond, jazz fins, representing the oomboles.

Pivor, with easy smiles, representing the Murder Beaks

Prysen Ol, the philosopher, representing the six-limbed Kai.

Surkar of the Hope Crushing Horde, representing the Southern Tribe of the Gar.

Lady Wexyn, she of many precious accessories, representing the Temple of Desire.

Unessa, the blonde master of smothering, representing the Dushegubs.

Amphie

Full name: Amphie Asturra.

Amphie, who had a privileged upbringing, is **the** daughter of a prominent Senator from Behoun.. She is an enthusiastic young woman, typical of the majority race of the Dominion, the humanoid Sislaf. She has taupe skin, big gray eyes, and soft, dark gray hair, which she styles in an asymmetric wave. She gazes upon Kosandion with worshipful adoration and tries very hard to come across as practically perfect in every way.

Her planet, Behoun, is one of the Dominion's core 7 worlds. They are seeking to put her into a high position with hopes of future political benefits.

Bestata

Full name: Bestata, Lady Emindra, Stratego of House Meer, Daughter of Konrrat and Ulize.

A statuesque female vampire knight of House Meer, with platinum blonde hair and the even skin tone particular to vampires, Bestata is usually sneering at someone. She appears in the black syn-armor, customary to vampire knights, which she dresses up with cloaks and flower hair accessories, as a nod to Dominion fashion. Snarly to the point of rudeness, she is, however, an honorable and agile warrior.

She represents House Meer. House Meer and House Krahr, into which Dina's sister Maud is going to marry, have a tumultuous history. House Meer refused to honor their pledge to fight on Nexus, which forced House Krahr to return to that war ahead of schedule. When House Krahr, The Hope Crushing Horde and the Merchant Clan Nuan met at Gertrude Hunt in hopes of reaching a peace agreement, House Meer sent representatives to try to derail those negotiations. The three House Meer knights attacked Sean, who was wearing Turan Adin armor at the time, and he killed them in self-defense.

The refusal to fight on Nexus resulted in House Meer being excommunicated by the Hierophant of the Holy Anocracy for the sin of cowardice. While they are still part of the Holy Anocracy and are subjects to its laws and protections, this punishment barred members of House Meer from holding political and military appointments at the federal level until the excommunication is lifted. The cloud of shame has cast its shadow upon House Meer, and they must find a way to banish it if they are ever going to regain their honor.

Cyanide

Full name: Cyanide and then some growling.

Cyanide resembles a snow leopard, although she is larger and looks different enough to where not many people would mistake her for one. She is 3 feet tall at the shoulder and is covered with brilliant white fur splattered with flecks of gold and gray. She has big golden eyes and fluffy paws with very dexterous digits and long claws. Her gums and tongue are a vivid Prussian blue. She is a master weaver and is considered an artisan by her people.

The Higgra are an odd species. Their civilization didn't follow the established milestones. Instead, they seemed to have leaped over some key evolutionary advances, which caused some people to speculate that the Higgra didn't evolve but were biologically engineered by some mysterious galactic civilization lost to time.

The Higgra are very spiritual. They believe that their fate is predetermined, but that one should strive to earn that fate. Like a lot of felines, they tend to be mercurial in their social interactions, and they rarely explain their actions.

Donkamins

Full name: unknown.

Eight feet tall, thin, hairless, covered with pale pearlescent skin, the Donkamins set off alarms in most humanoid species. An innkeeper legend says that the first innkeeper who encountered them opened the door of his inn, saw the new visitors, and blurted out, "Don't come in!" which is how they got their innkeeper nickname.

They appear unmistakably humanoid, with four appendages that resemble arms and legs, 7 nail-free fingers and two rows of pink pseudo-nipples on their torso— however, they are not even mammalian. They have large eyes, nasal openings shielded by a trilobite shell, and wide lipless mouths studded with conical teeth. The ridges protruding from their chest slide and elongate, allowing their necks to stretch in an arc as far as eight feet long.

Donkamins call themselves Children of the Silver Star and very little is known about their civilizations. They are relative newcomers to the galactic power scene. At the moment, they are focused on playing catch-up and trying to further their scientific achievements.

Ellenda

Full name: Ellenda of Sahava Branch, Pride of her People.

Ellenda is an Uma, and she comes from a fierce and reclusive people, like Kosandion's mother. She is tall and muscled like a gymnast, and she moves with natural grace. Her skin is the deepest indigo, her eyes are black, and her glossy dark hair is braided into a complex crown arrangement. She is defiant, proud and mournful.

The Uma had been discovered a thousand years ago by Earth's time by one of the slimier galactic nations. The newcomers arrived bearing gifts and sweet promises, and it took almost twenty years before the Uma realized they were not being helped, they were being colonized. The invaders severely underestimated the Uma spirit. In less than a century, the Uma purged them from their planet and shut their doors to most galactic visitors. The lucky few who had been invited told a story of a beautiful world populated by fierce people.

The Uma treasure their freedom above all else and would rather end their lives than be forced to endure against their will.

Nycati

Full name: it's a secret.

Nycati is graceful, lithe, with long limbs, perfect amber skin, and a face that is androgynous in its delicate beauty. His hair is very long and deep purple. He has the bearing of a scholar and carries himself with an air of elegance, whether he dons scale mail or robes. Like all Gaheas, he wears a diadem that enhances his psionic potential.

The Gaheas are a complicated civilization. Their world is that of political intrigue and assassination and heartbreaking beauty. They are committed to the notion of achieving a personal completeness and place a lot of emphasis on arts and education.

The Gaheas are fragmented into several kingdoms, which exist either at war with each other or in a state of uneasy ceasefire. Normally this would make them easy prey to other aggressive civilizations, like the Hope Crushing Horde; however, the Gaheas are deadly psionics. They kill their opponents with their minds, and their destructive potential is devastating. A single Gaheas of a prominent bloodline can easily wipe out a battalion of invading otrokars.

Oond

Full Name: Oond, born in the ray of light shining through the green waters.

Oond is an oombole, a 4-foot-long aquatic species that resembles terrestrial fish. He is covered in orange scales and has spectacular fins that range from yellow, through orange, to red. When he activates his bioluminescence, he looks painted with fire. Oond is an Ookarish, a being of extraordinary beauty, who soothes the pain of other creatures through his dance.

Oomboles come in all colors of the rainbow. Their round heads with a slight overbite, big eyes and brightly colored snail-like antennae give them hilariously comical expressions. A fringe of tentacles sprouting from under their chin enables them to wield specialized tools.

Oomboles are peaceful creatures, concerned mainly with survival and safety. They rarely leave their oceans, but when they do, they travel in oversized fishbowls. Oomboles communicate with their fins, which their specialized habitats are able to translate into sounds for the rest of the galaxy.

Pivor

Full name: Wait for it.

Pivor is a remarkably handsome, stocky man with lemon yellow skin and brilliant green eyes. His wavy brown hair is side-swept in an artful curve. He smiles easily and often and enjoys being the center of attention.

Pivor represents the Murder Beaks. He was a last-minute addition to their delegation. Midway through selection preparations, the Murder Beaks discovered that their DNA is not compatible with the Sovereign's genetic profile, so they scrambled to find a suitable humanoid candidate.

Murder Beaks are avian, flightless, and armed with huge beaks and powerful clawed feet. Their species would've given Earth's prehistoric Terror Birds a run for their money. They have a strong prey drive and kill for sport. The Murder Beaks isn't a nickname, but a literal translation of what they call themselves. Their ferocity makes them terrifying opponents, but they lack subtlety, and sometimes the nuances of other species' behavior elude them.

Prysen Ol

Full name: Prysen Ol, the senior disciple of Great Fiend of Sa Monastery.

Prysen Ol is a lean, beautiful humanoid male with long, silky blue hair, golden skin, and pink-colored irises. He speaks all three languages of the Dominion flawlessly and is possessed of a dignified, quiet calm. He wears a pale blue robe cinched at the waist and a white circlet. Like all Sa Monastery disciples, he is versed in philosophy, history, and other civil and social sciences. He has a tendency to get lost in complex moral debates and spends too much time looking inward.

Prysen Ol represents the Kai, a six-limbed species from a high gravity world. The Kai thrive on ceremony and ritual and are very methodical, which makes negotiating with them rather difficult since they are also highly hypochondriac. They avoid leaving their planet for the fear of contamination and infection by foreign pathogens and their appearance at the selection is one of the very rare occasions when they travel outside of their star system.

The Kai DNA is incompatible with that of the Sovereign, so they sought the help of Sa Monastery, renowned for their scholars, to find a suitable candidate to represent their interests.

Surkar

Full name: Surkar, son of Grast and Ulde, Champion of Tribe of Gar.

Surkar is a remarkable example of the Hope Crushing Horde's warrior. He is tall and powerfully built, with stunning muscle definition and a body that communicates superior strength, speed, and reflexes. He would snap any adult human male in half like a twig. He moves like a large predator and is quite arrogant. Like most otrokars, his behavior is dictated by the rich traditions of the Horde, and as the champion of his people, he is under a lot of pressure to succeed at all costs.

The Tribe of Gar hails from the Southern Tribe faction of the Horde. Although much has been done to unify the various otrokar tribes, some internal rivalries still exist, and Surkar and his people have an agenda they prefer to keep hidden from Khan and Khanum of the Horde, who are both from the North.

Lady Wexyn

Full name: Lady Wexyn Dion-Dian.

Lady Wexyn is five foot even and voluptuous, with large full breasts, round butt, and a soft tummy. Naturally pale, she has a glowing tan, long dark brown hair, and big dark eyes. She favors diaphanous clothes in vivid colors and frequently wears several pounds worth of jewelry in the way of bracelets and very elaborate hair arrangements. Despite this, she moves with hypnotic, seductive grace. Some describe her as a "free spirit", but she gives answers of deceptive nuance and empathy.

The Temple of Desire is an enigmatic organization, one of the famed Temples located in the White Rose cluster within the Cassiopeia constellation. Within the Cluster, entire moons are devoted to the worship of universal aspects. The Temple of Kindness, the Temple of Rage, the Temple of Grief... The Temple of Desire explores desire, the urge to obtain something beyond your reach at any cost. Within its walls and gardens, the priests and supplicants ponder the exact nature of desire, whether it is inherently selfish, whether it is just, if it can ever be pure and selfless.

Unessa

Full name: Unessa of... *Creeeeeak hisss hisss creeeeak knock.*

Unessa is statuesque and very pale, with long golden hair in ringlets around her shoulders, and big violet eyes. Wears flowing gowns that show off her frame and assets, and she rolls her hips. Aggressive, straightforward and not prone to intellectual nuance, Unessa is cunning and physically very capable. She is strong, fast, and has no hesitation when it comes to resorting to violence.

Unessa is Dushegubs' response to "humanoids like sex." The Dushegubs are sapient trees, unable to feel most emotions or form emotional attachments. They are calculating, homicidal, moving trees that feed on animal life, so they view most other civilizations as potential prey. Their first option is murder, their second option is murder, and if that fails, they go straight to murder.

Dushegubs are banned from most places outside of their solar system due to their aggressive nature.

DOMINION

Kosandion ka ret Maggran, *Letero Kolivion* — Sovereign of the Seven Star Dominion, in search of a spouse. Caldenia's nephew.

Resven — Chancellor of the Dominion, who manages the entirety of the Capital palace and is the Sovereign's right-hand man for all affairs involving domicile and family.

Miralitt — Prefect, head of the Sovereign's personal security guard, Sislaf with vampire heritage.

Orata — Kosandion's head of PR, in charge of the broadcast of the spouse selection event and its ratings

Holy Ecclesiarch — religious leader of the Dominion.

Required to be present throughout the entire spouse selection process for its validity.

OBSERVERS

Karat, Lady Rendara – vampire knight of House Krahr, Maud's best friend.

Dagorkun – a strategist and a general of the Hope Crushing Horde, son of the Khan and Khanum.

Nuan Couki "Cookie" – the rising star of Merchant Clan Nuan, Nuan Cee's nephew, several times removed.

Caldenia – the lady needs no introduction.

Tomato – green-furred bear-like alien from one of the star nations neighboring the Dominion.

First Scholar Thek – the koo-ko philosopher who first came to the inn during the Treaty Stay.

CANDIDATE FUNNIES (COURTESY OF MOD R)

HERE BE SPOILIERS

These are the online extras, which the readers of the serial asked to be included in the published book. If you haven't followed the serial as it was posted, some of this might not make sense.

Name: **Ellenda from Team Frowns**
Harmony &: Progress
Debate Stance: Duty > happiness. Submitting to and successfully carrying out one's duty ensures the continued survival of society.
Date: Taking charge of her fate
Keywords: Defiant.

Name: **Pivor of the Murder Beaks**
Harmony &: Cooperation between species
Debate stance: Happiness > duty. The purpose of society is to create individual happiness.
Description: handsome stocky man, yellow skin. Permanent smile.

Keywords: Handsome and selfish.

Name: **Bestata of House Meer**
Harmony &: Battle Tradition
Debate stance: Her purpose in life is devotion to the honour and glory of her House, and the pursuit of personal excellence.
Talent: Obstacle course (with blindfold and otrokars, oh my!)
Date: Focused on the military ambitions of her House.
Keywords: Vampire Knight

Name: **Unessa Sybate of the Dushegubs**
Harmony &: Smothering the enemies
Debate stance: Me Unessa, you man. Sex make babies.
Talent: Smothering, forgetting her rebuttals at home
Date: Sex. Do you wish to discuss?
Keywords: Aggressive Dryad, #underlog

Name: **Prysen Ol of the Kai**
Harmony &: Teachings of ancient masters, logicians and philosophers
Debate stance: Well, we still don't know why he's here...but at least the First Scholar had fun!
Talent: Poetry, the writing and reciting of
Date: Bore fest
Keywords: Educated philosopher, Dignified wisdom

Name: **Nycati of the Gaheas**
Harmony &: Artistic Beauty
Debate stance: At most, he was ready to admit that time flows. Possibly. When paired with Prysen, they have a future in the caffeine selling industry.
Talent: Love song for a vampire
Date: A royal heart to heart
Keywords: Psionic Elf, metal head (in more ways than one)

Name: **Surkar of the otrokar**

Harmony &: No harmony. Only bloody harvest of enemies!

Debate stance: The best thing in life is crushing your enemies in victory, making them fear and submit.

Talent: Making a fool of himself

Date: forfeit

Keywords: Brash warrior

Name: **Oond of the oomboles**

Harmony &: Urinary awareness

Debate stance: The best thing in life is safety. Make yourself indispensable to others, for apart you struggle but together you prosper.

Talent: Soothing Dance

Date: One hour of fin dancing, playing to his strength (again)

Keywords: #Jazz fins, #TeamFish, #GoBeyOond, #BDHDarling

Name: **Cyanide of the Higgra**

Harmony &: Sound judgement

Debate stance: Que sera, sera. To earn one's fate, one must prove one is worthy of it.

Date: Attentions. All of them.

Talent: The (very long and very yowling) song of her people

Keywords: Kitty pretty.

Name: **Donkamin candidate (nameless)**

Harmony &: Scientific Exploration

Debate stance: We are the architects of our future. Fate is an empty concept.

Date: No touchy touchy.

Keywords: Creepy

Name: **Amphie from Team Smiles**

Harmony &: Unity

Debate stance: Love is a layered phenomenon that must be examined in a specific context. Its power is immense and its impact is lifelong.

Talent: Saccharine Singing

Date: Trying way too hard

Keywords: Practically perfect in every way, take-home-to-mother type

Name: **Lady Wexyn of the Temple of Desire**

Harmony &: No harmony. Would just love their offspring the best.

Debate stance: Love is what she feels for Kosandion, he is her favorite.

Talent: Dance like only Kosandion is watching

Date: Beach & Chill

Keywords: Agent of chaos, wild card

DINA'S APPLE CAKE RECIPE

<u>Dough</u>

    4 egg yolks
2/3 cup white sugar
1 stick of butter (1/2 cup)
1/3 cup of sour cream
1 1/2 cup flour
1 tsp baking powder
1 pinch of salt
1 Tbsp vanilla extract
Zest of 1 lemon

<u>Filling</u>

    3-4 large Granny Smith or other baking apples
1 tsp of cinnamon
1 pinch of flour
Meringue:
4 egg whites
2/3 cups white sugar

a mixer
springform pan

Preheat oven to 350 degrees. Grease a springform pan. I used 2 6-inch ones, because smaller cakes are easier to store, but 9 or 10 inch springform pan would work as well.

Separate egg yolks from egg whites. Refrigerate egg whites.

Grate zest from 1 lemon. Peel apples, slice them into 1/2 inch thick slices, add cinnamon and flour. Mix thoroughly. If the apples are on the sweeter side, add a bit of lemon juice. Set aside.

Cream 2/3 cups sugar with room temperature butter with a hand mixer. Add egg yolks one by one, mix thoroughly. Add sour cream, vanilla, and lemon zest. Mix.

In a separate bowl combine flour, baking powder, and salt. Mix. Add to the wet ingredients and pour into the springform pan. Layer the apples on top. Bake for 30 minutes.

After 30 minutes, removed the pan from the oven. Whip egg whites until stiff peaks form. Add sugar a little at a time and continue whipping until meringue forms and the entire 2/3 cups of sugar is gone.

Layer meringue on top of the apples. Bake for additional 20 minutes. Meringue should be blush and pretty. Remove from oven and let cool to room temperature. Gently run a knife along the edge of the pan just like Dina did, to cut meringue, otherwise when you release the pan, half of it will come off. Release the pan and lift straight up.

Enjoy with tea or your favorite beverage.

ALSO BY ILONA ANDREWS

Kate Daniels World

BLOOD HEIR

Kate Daniels Series

MAGIC BITES

MAGIC BLEEDS

MAGIC BURNS

MAGIC STRIKES

MAGIC MOURNS

MAGIC BLEEDS

MAGIC DREAMS

MAGIC SLAYS

GUNMETAL MAGIC

MAGIC GIFTS

MAGIC RISES

MAGIC BREAKS

MAGIC STEALS

MAGIC SHIFTS

MAGIC STARS

MAGIC BINDS

MAGIC TRIUMPHS

The Iron Covenant

IRON AND MAGIC

UNTITLED IRON AND MAGIC #2

ABOUT THE AUTHOR

Ilona Andrews is the pseudonym for a husband-and-wife writing team, Gordon and Ilona. They currently reside in Texas with their two children and numerous dogs and cats. The couple are the #1 *New York Times* and *USA Today* bestselling authors of the Kate Daniels and Kate Daniels World novels as well as The Edge and Hidden Legacy series. They also write the Innkeeper Chronicles series, which they post as a free weekly serial.

For a complete list of their books, fun extras, and Innkeeper installments, please visit their website at https://ilona-andrews. com/.

CPSIA information can be obtained
at www.ICGtesting.com
Printed in the USA
BVHW061054151222
654223BV00014B/657